William Keller
Seton Hall
June 11, 1969.

D0849758

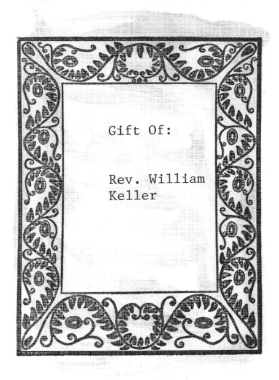

Gift Of:

Rev. William
Keller

MYSELF
MY SEPULCHRE

MYSELF
MY SEPULCHRE

Mary Teresa Ronalds

MACDONALD: LONDON

© MARY TERESA RONALDS, 1969

FIRST PUBLISHED IN GREAT BRITAIN IN 1969 BY
MACDONALD AND COMPANY (PUBLISHERS) LTD.
ST. GILES HOUSE, 49 POLAND STREET
LONDON, W.I

SBN 356 02470 9

MADE AND PRINTED IN GREAT BRITAIN BY
TONBRIDGE PRINTERS LTD, PEACH HALL WORKS
TONBRIDGE, KENT

"Myself my sepulchre, a moving grave;
Buried, yet not exempt,
By privilege of death and burial,
From worst of other evils, pains and wrongs."
Samson Agonistes, Milton

Author's Note

We live in an age fascinated by monsters. After all, it is only twenty-three years since one died in the bunker underneath Berlin. We tend to forget, however, that even monsters have a point of view and how terrible to find that it perhaps differs very little from our own. This is a novel putting such a point of view. It is not concerned so much with historical accuracy as with the thoughts and feelings of a rather unfortunate human being who was the victim of both his heredity and his environment and had not the strength of will to rise above his own weaknesses. Of such stuff are monsters made.

Contents

Prologue

So this is the end. It is not as I imagined, even in my worst depressions. I thought that I should at least perish with dignity in my own palace or, better still, in the Senate itself like esteemed Julius. But whatever dark force rules our fate decreed otherwise and so here I lie stretched on straw in a dirty courtyard with the stink of pigs in my nostrils and the blood seeping out from my split throat, I, Tiberius Claudius Nero, great-great grandson of divine Augustus and, until now, Nero, Emperor of all Rome.

The whole business has been dirty and vulgar. In fact, the fatal sweat I feel on my forehead is almost a relief like the sweat of a task honestly done. Only mine has not been honest, neither the task nor the carrying out of it. How can you control a spirited horse and not use whip or spur? My great-great grandfather managed it by feeding sugar at the same time and keeping a smile on his face but I looked sour and the horse knew it, even though I had sickened him with sugar. The gods have a fine sense of humour. Nothing on our miserable earth is more ironic than the good beginning which withers in anarchy and black despair. Have you seen a flower bloom bright in spring sunshine? Then breathe its scent quickly for soon the canker will start and beauty will shrivel in ugly waste.

I feel cold. I can see the ravenous stain eat up my robe even in the half darkness; sweat blisters my face. This body, grown fat and grotesque from ten years of lust and gluttony, pants to be free. The world is shaking. Is it the thunder of the gods at my passing; am I, after all, worth an impressive epitaph? I ask and someone says: "The storm, my lord. It continues."

Figures stir in the shadows. I no longer know them though I have a feeling I knew them once. Someone crouches whimpering in the corner. It puzzles me; the grief cannot be for me, no one will mourn my end. Voices buzz, in whispers, now louder, now whispers again. How long does it take? Has my vast body accumulated such blood that it takes this time to empty itself? A moment ago I was in pain; now there is nothing, only this weakness which is worse than any pain, a numbness beginning at my feet.

I could have sworn... The light is bad; my failing eyes multiply figures. We started out as four; now I see six, now seven. One is a woman, one a young boy. I try to ask again and a voice murmurs: "He says something; it's delirium." There is another woman and another, now an old man with a philosopher's beard. The place has filled with strangers. Even at this time I am tormented and mocked. Yet for a moment the shadows lift with a lightning flash and suddenly they are not strangers any more...

Book One

LUCIUS DOMITIUS AHENOBARBUS

"Our birth is but a sleep and a forgetting."
WORDSWORTH

Chapter One

A woman's cry. A sunlight flash and into it dipped a squalling new-born baby to ensure good luck. This was my beginning. My head touched the floor after the ancient fashion and I was here, I existed, a prince and citizen of Rome.

Look carefully at the woman in the bed. She leans back, satisfied, the black hair sticking to the sweat on her face; her breasts still heave with the struggle now ended. Even on the battlefield her beauty has remained. She smiles and looks at the squealing scrap of life which the midwife has transferred from sunlight to water. They have brought it heated in silver bowls and the steam fills the room. The baby yells; the woman smiles again as though recognising an understandable emotion. The doctors assure her the baby is healthy and put it into her arms but she holds it indifferently. Sleep grows heavy on her eyelids.

Beyond the window is a blue bay with villas stretching to the cliff edge. Red and gold light expands on the sea line and spreads outwards, catching tiny clouds and turning them to fire. It is dawn. That sunlight was the first of the day and the first of the baby's life. Because of this the light is considered propitious and the baby's immersion in it a defence against future disaster. At the door stands a priestess to keep away evil spirits; soon she will go to the temple and sacrifice to Juno, the light-bringer who presides over births, that she might protect the new life. The beautiful mother is oblivious. She sleeps, exhausted, and the baby is taken from her.

I was born feet first as if reluctant to put my head into this bitter world. It was thought unlucky. Later I was told for such a baby to live was unusual; more often than not the child suffocated or grew up imbecile. My unblemished survival convinced many that I was meant to fulfil some divine destiny. You would not have thought so at the time. They called me Lucius Domitius Ahenobarbus, the last being my paternal surname, and if you wonder how I acquired the name now dreaded by every civilised human being, that comes later.

My mother was Agrippina, daughter of Rome's beloved Germanicus, great-granddaughter of the Emperor Augustus and descended on her father's side from the unfortunate Mark Antony. My father was of the gens Domitia, a big red-haired brute of a man whose handsome looks had coarsened by the time he begot me in middle-age. My mother was twenty-five years younger than him. I sometimes think I was conceived in hate or even as the result of a nuptial rape, for my mother despised him and in my early years when the topic arose I was told my father was a bad man who had treated his poor wife disgracefully; I must never mention him nor even think of him. That was not difficult since I never even set eyes on him. He died when I was about three, presumably worn out by dropsy and debauchery, and I, the seed he had carelessly shed to root where it could, was left to flower or wither in isolation.

A little child does not bother particularly about the scandals of political life, nor even of his own family. My maternal uncle Caligula was Emperor when I was born but I knew nothing of his insane cruelty, nor did I know of my mother's fashionable life mixed up with court intrigue. These were not the faces important to me. Two which come to me from that blurred, uncertain time are female, gentle and watchful. That is all I remember, that and firm hands which supported me when the hard mosaic floor suddenly sprang up to meet my tender knees or forehead. Later I learned they were two nurses employed by my indifferent mother who was too busy at the imperial court to bother with me.

I was learning to walk. There were vast pillars either side of me, thicker than trees which rooted on the Palatine when Romulus was king. The floor spread to infinity, swirling with colour. When I put my hand down it felt icy cold. Something still and white stood on a pedestal, looking at me. I tried to talk, to put out my hand, but it never moved and I retreated as always in the face of something incomprehensible.

Beyond the pillars green leaves flourished and something bright and sparkling leapt high in the air. Here it was light. A golden glare beat on my eyes, warmth touched my limbs. Purple awnings were strung between each pillar to keep away the heat and they made a red glimmer on the pavement. I half crawled, half toddled towards the bright thing which still jumped above the leaves. I reached out joyfully to grasp it— then fell back, shocked, my hand dripping and my tunic soaked. Hands came from nowhere, a voice spoke sharply, and I was snatched back from the edge of the pool where I would have drowned.

When I was older and spoke of this people thought I was making it up, denying that memory could reach so far back. I could have been only two or younger. Yet I remember it in vivid detail as if a picture remains in my mind. Ever afterwards when I looked at water or heard it splashing from a fountain I felt uneasy and the memory crept slyly back. It seemed monstrous, this clear charming element which nearly took me away before I had properly begun.

After that there is a gap. Some great change must have occurred for I recall wandering into the courtyard, whimpering because I was hungry and no one would feed me. The place was in upheaval. A money chest lay open in one of the rooms with coins spilling from it and one of my nurses was weeping and saying: "Oh, the shame of it. What shall we do; where are we to go?" The other, more brisk, said: "Pull yourself together. She'll be here soon for the child and we must put a brave face on it."

"Poor little Lucius," continued the weeper. "What will happen to him? His father dying in Pyrgi and his mother sent away like this..." I crouched shivering behind a column, not understanding yet feeling their grief and fear as an animal will who howls at a funeral.

Slaves came into the vestibule carrying a litter. It was set

15

down, the curtains parted and out came a tall red-haired lady in a white linen robe and blue cloak clasped with silver; something red and gold twinkled in each ear. I pressed closer to the column. She looked stern and strange, this lady. Her mouth was set hard and she looked at my dear nurses as I had seen them look at beggars on our doorstep.

She said: "Where is the child?"

The next moment I was in her arms, shrinking from that strange face. Close up her earrings burned like stars; there were black lines drawn round her eyes and the strong scent on her flesh made my nose tickle. My hand rested on something hard; it was her clasp, carved with a tiny cupid. She smiled and said softly: "Well, well, little Lucius—oh, my dear, you are the image of my sweet brother. How did he beget something so lovely with that black-haired witch?"

She ruffled my hair and held my hand and all at once I felt safer. She was kind, after all. Yet her face spoke to me of something beyond this quiet house and the gentle voices of my nurses who looked only to my happiness.

Sudden darkness came. I was inside the litter, on her lap, her scent smothering that confined space. I began to cry. She was taking me away; it was all wrong. I lashed out with my arms and one of her earrings went flying. She said something angrily and smacked me; I cried even more, she smacked me harder. Then something sweet was pushed at my mouth. I remembered my sick hunger and chewed greedily; she was watching me closely her eyes black in the dim light.

"There, there," she said. "Poor little Lucius . . ."

My eyes were heavy. Unearthly sounds came muffled from beyond the litter. I didn't understand, I didn't know where we were. I only knew this little world bounded by curtains. It was dark and warm. I had a comfortable lap and breast, strange though they might be, and I was very, very tired.

Everything was different again. I remember a big comfortable house but I also remember that much of the time I was bitterly uncomfortable. There were no kind nurses to watch every step, to feed me when I cried for food and sing me to sleep when I

16

was tired. Instead there were two strangers, both men, with whom I seemed to spend most of my day and the red-haired lady whom I learned to call aunt. When I saw her she was kind and used to give me sweets but so often she went away and I was left alone or with the two slaves. I learned their inferiority through seeing how she spoke to them. To me adults were infinitely strange and wonderful. I did not see why she with her piled-up hair and swinging jewels was better than they. I did not attempt discrimination; for me they were all one, bigger, stronger, sometimes terrifying, to be obeyed and submitted to without question.

There was a wide courtyard with a fountain in the centre where water spouted from the breast of a nymph. The pillars were violet-spotted marble ringed with scarlet at top and bottom. The roof sloped and when it rained the water beat down it like liquid silver. A big dip in the middle of the hall trapped the rain till it was brimming full and I sometimes dipped my feet in when no one looked.

I loved this courtyard. When I could I wandered out there and sat on the pavement edge, watching the water and the naked girl and wondering why her body was so smooth and rounded when mine was flat and thin. I remember all this, too, and later people laughed but only because their own memories were not wide enough to store so much whereas mine was boundless. Sometimes I have cursed it because I cannot draw a curtain over mutilations in my mind.

There were good times and bad times. Sometimes I went hungry because they forgot to feed me and I scrabbled up grass or dirt in desperation. Often I slept on the hard floor of the dining-room because no one put me to bed. There were strange creatures on the walls there, a woman with snakes instead of hair and a horse with wings. At night when they had forgotten me these things seemed to breathe and whisper in the darkness and I would lie watching the window, praying for dawn. Once I cut my knee and no one noticed for three days by which time it began to look green and they called the doctor who hurt me even more to put it right. I remember his hard hands and the prick of a knife cutting out the poison, then my aunt saying: "Be careful. One day the child may mean something."

I did not understand my aunt. Sometimes she was nice, sometimes angry. She would hit me one moment and kiss me the next but always in her good moods she would say: "Dear Lucius—so like my brother." If she found me neglected she was angry and washed and fed me herself but she went away so often on strange errands and, you see, the slaves committed to my care had their own jobs, one being a dancer and the other a barber.

I have a vague memory of a man coming one day in a golden litter with purple curtains, carried by black men six feet tall. They gave an entertainment for him and the dancing slave came out in a short white tunic edged with gold and a painted mask representing a beautiful youth. Gold shone in his ears, on his wrists and his ankles and jingled as he moved. I watched entranced as he leapt to the clash of cymbals and swung gracefully with the song of the flute. He told some tale with his hands and feet, with all his body except his face. I understood only the movement and not the meaning; it made me forget the odd man in the place of honour. A brown-haired girl with a painted face fanned him with peacock feathers as he lounged on the couch and it was then he saw me behind a pillar (as usual) and called me over.

He had a long nose and small mean mouth and he stank of stale perfume. His hands shone with rings; they bit into my flesh as he pulled me nearer.

"So this is Agrippina's brat," he said. "He has her eyes, don't you think, Domitia? In fact, they are so like hers I should like to tear them out, the faithless bitch."

His pale eyes stared at me, long and hard; they seemed to eat up his face. All I could see were the black pupils, expanding and contracting as though they possessed their own life. I have never forgotten those eyes.

"By Hercules," he said, chuckling, "what a brute he'll make with that parentage. If the gods are good, Domitia, they won't even let him spit at the throne. He'd make me look like Cicero. What a thought! " He spluttered with laughter and wine ran

18

from the corner of his mouth. I drew back, trembling. "Never mind," he went on, sobering. "His accession is as likely as my reform so you can see the odds. Bring more wine!"

I scuttled behind the pillar again, shaking and disgusted. Tears began behind my eyes. Though I had not understood what he said I sensed the mockery, the ugly language of humiliation. I would never have known who he was had I not heard someone address him as Imperator and then I knew this was Uncle Caligula. It was the first and last time I ever saw him.

So dark alternated with light. The happy times came when I could watch the dancing slave practise his movements or go with the barber to his shop. Otherwise I wandered alone in the house or, even worse, was locked in a small room to keep me out of mischief. I can remember beating my hands on the walls of such a room till the finger-nails bled and crying till my voice was nearly gone. This rebellion always ended in defeat. I would lie down exhausted and fall asleep sucking my thumb. Then out I would come, there would be smiles and sweets and caresses as though imprisonment were nothing and all would be well till the next time.

Sometimes I saw my Cousin Messalina about the place, an insolent, pouting child with her mother's hair; she used to toss it over her white shoulders and imagine she looked seductive. She was fond of bangles and earrings like her mother only on her they looked gaudy, and black lines round her eyes made them pop like a frog's. As soon as her breasts began to grow she pushed them up to make them look bigger, tying a ribbon underneath and letting the dress part to show them off. I thought her ridiculous. She didn't care for me either and called me cry-baby Lucius. When she thought no one looked she pinched or prodded me and pretended ignorance when they wanted to know why I was crying. I hated her slyness. Though so young she was already married; the times I saw her were visits made frequently to satisfy her solicitous mother. Her husband came hardly at all. He was old, I knew that much, and disapproved of by my aunt.

I liked being with the servants best; my aunt still frightened

19

me. Sometimes I wandered into their quarters when they sang songs together and one would play some sweet-sounding instrument and my dancing slave would even mime to the tale whatever it was—a war or a love story or a divinely inspired revenge. I was little enough to creep in unnoticed and sit under a table or behind a chair but too little to understand. Some of the slaves did not speak Latin at all but barbaric-sounding tongues which puzzled me, nor did they all look the same. One was huge and blond, another dark with black hair on his body. A tiny brown-skinned girl with gold disks in her ears used to take me on her lap and sing in a sweet, rhythmic tongue which sent me to sleep. I did not understand that they came from other lands far away; I only realised that not all people are the same. Whatever god made us used many moulds to cast his creations.

The barber's shop. What could be more fun? What was more delightful than watching my slave and others like him use their skill to make silly old men look passably elegant? The sweep of the comb, the click of the iron scissors, the twist of the curling-iron heated on burning coals so that even the most stubborn hair responded—what was more enchanting? Often Marcus took me there out of kindness so that I should not be left alone in the house and I would sit on hard benches with the waiting clients, watching the victim in the centre, protected by a muslin wrap like a corpse in his shroud while the barber fussed round like the undertaker, trimming here, curling there, pouring on dye to enhance nature and spraying the curls with perfume. I have seen a dark-haired man go blond in a moment and a rich old man whose vanity outran his looks force the barber to spread out scanty hair and cover baldness. To me it was a comedy. After all, grown-ups were comedians only they never knew it. In these circumstances I could forget my healthy awe and begin to laugh.

Huge mirrors covered the walls of the shop. It was here for the first time that I saw my own reflection, staring back like a stranger. I was too small to reach by myself. Someone lifted me up and I sprang brazenly into view with a cloud of red-gold hair and wide blue eyes. The details I do not remember. I recall only the smallness of my face beside that of the man who had lifted me up.

One day something odd happened and finished my visits. I sat as usual on one of the benches having been banished from the centre of operations because of nearly splitting my hand open on the scissors. The shop was crammed. A good many people had not found seats and were standing together, chattering pointlessly as grown-ups will. The air was hot; perfume and smoke thickened the atmosphere and made me sneeze.

I was sitting beside this man. He smiled and asked me my name. His face was smooth and clean; he looked young. I told him. He said it was a nice name. Then he put his arm round me and swung me onto his lap, saying: "What a pretty child you are." I could feel the softness of his robe and a ring on his finger pressing hard into my back. He began to kiss me. The slaves at home often kissed me, so did my aunt; it did not seem strange. I liked this sudden affection, being used to cruel loneliness. His arms tightened; I tried to wriggle free but he would not let me. Suddenly the kisses were nasty, I felt suffocated. His hand was under my tunic and that was all wrong; I didn't understand; something dreadful was happening. I began to scream and he put his hand over my mouth but I bit him and screamed and screamed with all my strength.

The voices stopped, the crowd parted. He let go of me suddenly and I tumbled off his lap, grazing my knees on the rough floor. There was an arch of staring faces above me. My knees were hurting; I felt sick. I began to sob with terror. And there was Marcus, dearest Marcus, picking me up and soothing me while a group of people chased out into the street after the man. I clung to him and he stroked my hair and told me not to be afraid but there was a terrible anger in his eyes and also a kind of fear.

Shouting voices spilled between the columns. I sat shivering by the bright fountain with the graceful nymph who stared at me in a new way as though she saw some change.

"Are you mad," shrieked my aunt, "to take the child to such a place? Everyone knows what sort of person patronises

21

it. And how do you suppose I shall tell his mother, should we ever see her again, that her precious child has been debauched?"

"I doubt if that is so," replied Marcus calmly; the places of slave and master seemed reversed. "He screamed before then."

"And the blood?" demanded my aunt.

"He hurt his knees. If you will permit me to dress the cuts . . ."

"I'll permit you to do nothing," my aunt retorted. "Get back to your quarters and be thankful I haven't had you thrashed."

He turned obediently like an animal and I wondered at his meekness. Why did he not answer back? Now I felt guilty that he had suffered for me. It was not a substantial adult emotion, only a vague sensation which reminded me of hunger or sickness. I was very tired.

My aunt was leaning over me with furious eyes; her hair seemed a fire blazing around her head. She said: "What sort of little slut are you, Lucius Ahenobarbus? The gods protect us, has your mother impregnated you with her own monstrous appetites? Or is it a paternal inheritance? I should know the likelihood of that."

I was bewildered. Over her shoulder I could see silly Messalina gaping like a half-wit, enjoying my humiliation, and far behind the faint figure of her husband watching from the column. The fountain threw up its diamond darts which bruised my eyes. Suddenly only sleep seemed good.

"I'm tired, aunt," I began. "Let me go to bed . . ."

"The right place for you, my child," she said savagely, "as your mother spends most of her days there—or did until her brother flung her out. I'll give you bed!"

She dragged me up and out of the courtyard into the back somewhere, a place which smelled animal. Then I saw it was the stables. I used to play there sometimes when I was lonely and the horses offered companionship.

She flung open a door; the hot smell of animals in a closed space came out to meet us, then the darkness smothered me.

"Stay there till you learn better behaviour," she shouted; the door banged and I was alone.

I lay for a little while in total stillness. I felt all bruises, not only my body but something within as well. I understood nothing, only this bitter non-physical pain. I wanted to hit back but knew I had not the strength and here there was nothing to attack, not even a horse. She had condemned me to complete isolation.

Voices began again from the house; Marcus was arguing.

"But the child is innocent," he said. "Can you really imagine, my lady, that a child of four would deliberately——"

There was a sharp stinging sound. "That," said my aunt, "is for daring to question my authority. I say he is to be punished. He is of tainted stock; monsters abound on both sides of his family. I have every affection for him and that is why I want to crush this evil before it chokes him. Now get out before I whip you myself."

I pressed my face into the dirty straw and wept and wept till the hot tears soaked the neck of my tunic. My aunt was angry with me and I could not see why. The ways of adults were beyond me. I did not understand the man in the barber's shop; I did not understand my aunt. I only understood Marcus who had tried to protect me and suffered for it. Yet everything was somehow my fault.

I forget how long I lay there, choked with crying. My knees were stinging, pricked by the straw; my head ached and my nose was running. A storm had begun outside and the thunder broke like rocks overhead, shaking this frail, grubby shelter. I could hear the horse whinnying in terror. I, too, covered my ears and shuddered for my earliest memories of fear were connected with storms, that rampaging of the elements which seemed to hold divine destructiveness. Lightning flashed silver through the little window and over the top of the door. Then the rain came. It thudded on the roof and began to seep through at the weakest points, falling in long drops to the sodden straw. It seemed the leaking away of all my hope and trust.

In the hot darkness, staring at the slow drop, drop of water I felt again the exploring hands of the barber's shop and my belly shrank. I did not recognize this sickly stirring as the beginning of shame; I knew only its discomfort. I could not say why I blushed and wriggled at the memory. Everything was odd and twisted like one of my bad dreams when I leapt twenty feet or fell down a great precipice. I wanted someone to be kind and hold me in their arms; I wanted to bury my face between warm breasts and lose the sound of the storm. Instead I wept again and choked and pressed my burning face against the angry straw.

Agony dissolved in sleep. When I woke again it was dark and still raining but otherwise all was still. I could see the liquid spears drive down beyond the stable door; the sky spilled broken clouds. I listened and listened, in panic at the silence, not even a squeaking mouse to assure me I was not a single survivor in the land of the dead. Had they gone away and left me to starve for my wickedness? Then why had Jupiter not struck me with one of his silver thunderbolts as Marcus used to say he did? Or was something worse waiting? What stirred in that dreadful darkness, behind the bush gleaming with rain? I could hear footsteps tread the wet earth, coming nearer, then nearer and nearer again. An image flashed in my mind: the face staring like stone with twisting snakes instead of hair.

I began to whimper against the horrid straw. It was all wrong. I was innocent; that was the cruelty of it. Even a guilty man may gain nobility by meeting execution bravely. But all I could feel was resentment and confusion like the child who is smacked for the vase his brother broke. The footsteps were nearer; I fancied I saw the polished snakes, spitting and writhing, the tiny eyes deadly points of fire. Her breath was on my face; her claws reached out——

I squealed and ran sobbing to the door, beating my hands against it. Then suddenly, far away in some quiet room, some-one began to sing. The voice caught my heart and stilled its terror; I leaned against the door listening. It rose and fell in its sweetness, silver-clear through the rain and the night, telling me of gentleness, beauty, a warm breast and a soft pillow. The horror was gone. The snakes sank back and vanished; the courtyard was empty under the sky. Then even the rain stopped and stars twinkled out but the voice continued and sang me to sleep, there on the filthy stable floor.

In the morning they took me out. My aunt fussed; she washed me herself in her own bath, letting me go down the marble steps into the water while she held me up as I was too little for its depth. The water gushed in through silver pipes; above my head the ceiling arched in glorious colour. After the sticky misery of the night everything was cool and bright and comforting. She lifted me out and dried me, combed my hair, dressed my hurt knees and put on a clean tunic, all the time saying I was a good boy and I must not be naughty any more as she loved me so and hated to punish me. I could not see how I was good after last night's viciousness nor how imprisonment showed love. But I accepted her affection passively, grateful for kindness.

Then she sat with me in the courtyard and told me stories as a peace-offering, how the founder of my father's family met a pair of handsome twins in Rome one day, being none other than Castor and Pollux, the sons of Jove, who told him that the Battle of Lake Regillus had been won by the Romans. To prove their divinity they touched his beard which turned from black to bronze and ever since then my father's family have been red-haired. One day, she said, I should go and see the temple in the Forum dedicated to the divine twins. Later she fed me with her own hand, giving me grapes and wild cherries till I was full and could eat no more. I began to forget her unkindness. I clambered up near her smiling face and tapped her earrings so that they swung and threw out white fire; they were diamonds dangling from little gold scales.

Not long afterwards there was another change. I remember another confusion like the one which transferred me from my kind nurses to my aunt's house and because of this it frightened me. I had learned to measure the moods of my elders, so infinitely superior to me and yet so prone to sudden disaster. I knew when anything went wrong in this world of giants. The ground shook with their running here and there, the air rang with raised voices. Olympus was not impregnable.

I heard my aunt say: "When did it happen?"

"Midday," someone replied, a voice I did not know. "In the theatre after the games. He had no suspicion."

"Well, it was to be expected," my aunt observed, "considering the way he carried on. How are they taking it?"

"Wild rejoicing. The people are drinking wine in the streets and garlanding the gods on the Capitol. Mind you, at first they thought he had invented the tale himself to see what people really thought of him. Then, when they knew ... But it was an ugly death. They dashed out his baby's brains against a wall."

"And who is it now?" asked my aunt. "Have they named a successor?"

"Claudius, his uncle. He tottered out from behind a curtain while the soldiers were looting and fell on his knees in a panic, begging for mercy. Then they suddenly acclaimed him Emperor and off he went to the Guards' Camp. The Senate were doubtful but there it was. He had the army behind him. It started as a joke but now they can't find anyone else."

"Claudius!" said my aunt. "Claudius the idiot! Sweet Apollo, what has Rome come to? We exchange a maniac for a feeble-minded fool and expect to survive. Jove have mercy, Marcellus!" She clutched his arm and looked wild. "Then Messalina is empress and I'm the imperial mother-in-law. Oh, how heaven mocks us. Chained to that silly old fool, now first lady of Rome at sixteen; and I thought she made a bad match. But what an Emperor——"

"The mob only think of him as Germanicus' brother," said the other speaker quietly.

"If the gods had let him live," my aunt murmured. "A new Golden Age, only better. He would have surpassed Augustus." Then she saw me and her eyebrows rose. "Of course, I never thought ... Marcellus, this means the return of the she-wolf. She will demand the child as sure as the fates. And why? Because she has her eyes on the golden laurel wreath, that's why; she won't blush to ascend to power through a child."

She called me forward and lifted me up, caressing me and saying what a shame it was I should have to go away. She made me frightened and I began to whimper. Then her face hardened. "Only I shan't let you go without a fight, little Lucius. What sort of mother has she been to you? The good part of you is my doing, mine and my brother's."

*   *   *

She stood there, this tall, beautiful woman like some kind of goddess, her black hair braided and raised on pads above her forehead, the rest tumbling either side of her dazzling neck. I gaped at her. There were no glittering trinkets as with my aunt but she had no need of them. She stood in her flawless grace, proud as a spirited stallion, and I felt suddenly small and mean.

"Is this him?" she said.

"Yes," said my aunt. She sounded cold and angry. "I see he does not recognise you."

"Who would expect him to?" said the goddess. "Come here, Lucius."

I crept forward. She said: "Look at me." I glanced up carefully as though her eyes might bite me. What glorious pools of blue they were, darkened with powdered antimony and swept by her black lashes. Above them arched her blackened eyebrows, thick and strong. The thoughts beneath those eyebrows seemed incalculable.

She said: "I am your mother."

The word meant nothing. I knew my aunt and no one else; this woman was a stranger. She went on : "You are going to live with me now. You must call me mother and obey me in everything as you have obeyed your aunt."

"I find this insufferable," burst out my aunt. "You have no right to take him away. I virtually brought him up while you were tumbling in and out of bed and ignoring your responsibilities."

The black eyelashes flickered. Something had pierced Minerva's armour. But she said without emotion: "I observe your mistake, Domitia. I was existing in exile on the Pontian islands, poverty-stricken and incapable of supporting any responsibility. Now I'm making up for that. I'm taking back my responsibilities from you. Thank you for your trouble."

My aunt smouldered and reddened and opened her mouth for another protest but the goddess said sharply: "He is mine. No court of law will give you the right of ownership. Be content, Domitia, that you have influenced his early years and remember to praise yourself when he sits where my brother did."

That is all I remember. Then there was a new house, new slaves, a whole new life. Even in the middle of all my tears, the strong grief of separation and the coldness of a strange environment I realised that an important influence had taken me over. New doors opened; new possibilities waited in the shadows. I was now my mother's son.

Chapter Two

From here began the life which is now bleeding away on this rubbish heap. Outlines harden and become recognisable; faces have names, places locations. The dream world of childhood begins to crumble at the edges and the naked girl of the fountain and the woman with the snake hair no longer speak to me.

My mother's house was on the Aventine hill next to the Circus Maximus where they had the chariot races; it was an elegant villa. She was not poor, my mother. My father's estates ensured against that. We had about thirty slaves and used silver at table; we were, in fact, highly respectable. For some reason my mother was much admired, not merely for her beauty which even I could understand, but for her breeding. I never knew my grandfather; I hardly even heard of him till I came to my mother. Then suddenly he loomed into view, beloved, handsome, virtuous Germanicus, who won triumphs in Germany and was loved by all, then died at thirty-four in the strangest circumstances. He was Rome's hero. Unfortunately, dead men are impervious to praise but luckily my mother was living. She built capital on her father's investment. I saw a statue of him once near the Forum. It made me jump. It might have been me but for the military uniform; then I understood why my mother's visitors patted my head and looked approving.

The change from my aunt's house to my mother's marked a deeper change in my status. I was suddenly important. I could not see any reason for this though I guessed it was somehow due to my mother. No longer did I wander unattended or go hungry and sleepy due to forgetfulness; I lived by a rigid timetable. A slave woke me at dawn and dressed me, another slave washed me and brushed my hair, yet another took me to the triclinium where I breakfasted on bread, fruit and honey with my mother. Then began lessons. I had two Greek tutors called Anicetus and Beryllus who taught me letters and numbers by showing them written on a tablet and making me repeat them, hour after hour. I got so bored. The only pleasant part was hearing their soft-tongued Greek as against hard Latin. It had a rhythm which I liked. The lesson room was wide and bright, looking out onto the court where water bubbled from the mouth of a huge fish. A statue of Diana stood chaste and athletic between the bushes; she seemed to sympathise. I never learned till later that to have the virgin goddess in my mother's courtyard was a sort of bad joke.

It was letters before midday, numbers after. In the middle we stopped for cold meat and a glass of water, figs as well if I were lucky. Numbers were more fun. I learned to count on my fingers, then on a wooden frame where you pushed little beads along one by one and worked out the problem. They went click-clack in the stillness. I liked to see how fast I could make them go, rushing them along till they became streaks of colour and you could count nothing. But my mother caught me at it and threatened to whip the tutors for letting me be lazy.

In the hot weather I rested after dinner, then on went the labour till two hours before sundown when at last I was free and could play as I liked. The best time of the day was dinner at dusk. Sometimes I ate by myself in my room, sometimes with my mother in the triclinium. It was always good food then, pork or tuna fish with salad, followed by fruit and honey. She would never let me have wine though she drank it freely herself. She used to say it would make my head burn. If guests were present they smiled and approved a thoughtful mother. When she went out to dinner I ate alone; I didn't like that so much. The slave stood like stone and never talked and only the fountain's splash stopped my ears aching with silence. I had a terror of isolation. Then my mother began dining alone at home, that is to say, I was never allowed near the triclinium,

30

but I learned from Beryllus that she had a guest. When he told me he winked and his eyes danced with laughter but I couldn't see the joke. "Your mother is a modest woman" he said. I didn't understand that either but wheedled him till he read me some poetry, about the only cultural activity I enjoyed.

"This is your new father," my mother said.

I blinked and re-arranged my ideas. I thought you had only one father and when he was dead you went without, but here was my mother in her boundless generosity giving me another.

"Passienus, darling, this is my son," she said, turning to the man beside her. He was tall and courteous looking with kind eyes but his hair was flecked grey. I automatically assumed that fathers were always much older than mothers.

"Come here, Lucius, dear," she went on and when I went forward she kissed me and stroked my hair, such an unusual event that I felt shocked. I imagined mothers should never kiss their sons, not like aunts.

"He is like you," said the courteous gentleman, "but even more like his sadly mourned grandfather. I welcome him as a son."

And that was that. Suddenly our standard of living rose up. We employed more slaves, we began to use gold at table and we acquired a second home. This belonged to my new father and stood high on the Esquiline hill amongst cypresses and palm trees, its pillared front opening into a garden. The air was sweet there and city noises muffled but all the same I preferred my mother's villa because I could watch the chariot races from the balcony. We used to go backwards and forwards between the two but it was always the races I thought of.

My mother had many visitors. When we were at our home on the Esquiline she used to hold dinner parties in the evening and I liked to stand near the entrance and see the litters arrive. It seemed to me that my mother knew many people and that all were extremely gracious, affable, and intelligent. If she were in a good mood she would let me come into the triclinium where I would sit on the steps of her couch and say nothing.

31

It was always her decision, not my father's. He was submissive to her in this as in everything. He was always good to me and gave me sweets and I saw this was genuine whereas when she fed me at a dinner party like a solicitous mother it seemed part of a play performed for the guests' benefit.

The guests were elegant, witty and talkative. Not that I understood half of what they talked about but I liked to watch their changing faces which betrayed attitudes. They reclined on couches and sipped wine from my father's gold drinking cups and I thought how infinitely graceful they were. My mother was like a luxuriant flower; she drew a swarm of handsome bees.

"It's a scandal, of course," someone said. "A man of his age marrying such a child. And after three wives; I ask you, what an appetite."

"I wonder the tree has any sap left," observed another slyly.

"Even a skeleton would spring to life if offered Messalina," returned the first. "That's what makes it so disgusting."

I looked at my mother to see if she reacted to my cousin's name. She was staring at her cup as though a fly had crawled into it and her fingers tapped the embossed stem.

"No one begrudges him the enjoyment of beauty," remarked a man with a short greying beard. "We have the Ancients' example for that. It's the unsuitability of such a wife for his position which we object to."

"Exactly," replied the first speaker. "But surely, Seneca, we cannot expect him to exert great wisdom on this score or any other for that matter. Does one expect the family idiot to equal his brothers and sisters?"

Then they started laughing as though someone had made a joke, not that I could see what was funny. Their laughter had a cruel sound. And all the time my mother sat staring into her cup and frowning.

"We must remember the child had no upbringing to speak of," said the bearded man. "Her mother was a most negligent woman. Happily little Lucius, in contrast, has had the benefit of a good mother's attentions."

He smiled at me and bowed to my mother who smiled slightly

in return. Suddenly they were all looking at me; I felt their eyes and their admiration. I heard someone say: "He has Germanicus' looks. Did you ever see such eyes?"

I blushed and looked down, then they laughed. My mother gave me a plum and they went back to their talk.

I was about six or seven when I saw my first proper chariot race and that was illegally and at a distance. I was supposed to be studying but Anicetus was ill and Beryllus said he felt tired and told me to run off. There I stood on the balcony pressed tight against the ledge with the wide blue sky above me and the crammed Circus below. It was an enchanting place. That great oblong, rounded at one end, breathed and moved with its colossal burden, about 150,000 people all yelling and cheering loud enough to split the seats they sat on. The sound came to me muffled, drifting above the tree-tops; the thunder of wheels and hooves shook the summer leaves, the dust they stirred up seemed to rise even to this little place where I stood. I pressed closer to the ledge, leaning over as far as I dared so that I could see the bouncing chariots and flying horses, all mane and tail. The straining charioteers were bright dots of blue, green, red or white. I imagined the fierce joy of it, the crack of the whip, the reins beating in your hands, the wind tearing your hair; and always with you that roar of exaltation, the people's praise. It seemed the sport of the gods.

"Lucius!"

The voice punctured my ecstasy. I turned, startled, and there was my mother, standing stiff and angry behind me. Her mouth was set; her eyes fixed on me and drained out all my joy. I never knew such eyes as hers. They could eat you up and yet retain their marvellous beauty. As she looked at me I remembered her brother and the hand which pinched.

"Will you tell me how you come to be watching races," she said, "when you are supposed to be at lessons?"

You could not hear the anger, only sense it. Her voice was cold on my heart, still shaking with excitement.

"Beryllus was tired, mother." My voice quivered; I thought she would hit me. "He wanted to rest so I came out here."

"Rest!" Her eyebrows rose. "My child, there is no rest for

him nor for you. Those whom the gods have picked out cannot sleep."

I stared; I didn't see what the gods had to do with it. She pulled me into the room by my hair and my eyes filled with water but I bit my lip before I should cry out. She despised weakness. Beryllus was waking up, rubbing his eyes; I never saw such mortal terror in any man's face. I knew then that my own fear was healthy. But she only said in a still, icy voice: "Beryllus, your task is to educate this child, not to rest your miserable body. If you differ with me on that point you can argue it out with the lions."

He went on his knees, pleading for mercy and acknowledging his wretchedness. He tried to kiss her feet but she withdrew in distaste, telling him to get up and earn his bread. I felt tears in my throat. I remembered Marcus and the stinging slap. Why was it always me they suffered for? We went back to lessons. But that evening my father told me gently that I must work hard, otherwise how would I become a lawyer or a senator and bring credit to my family? My mother stood behind him, her face stern; her mouth flickered at the mention of senator as though he had said something out of place. Next morning Beryllus came to the lesson room with ugly red marks on his neck and arms.

Sometimes we went to visit great-uncle Claudius on Palatine Hill. It was from there that I first saw the Forum of Rome in all its marble glory, not that I fully realised why it was so important; I only saw its beauty, the wide square white in the noonday sun with pillared temples and public buildings on either side, the columned statues of heroes or politicians with base painted gold standing on proud marble flagstones where senators walked. It spoke to me of things I had never even thought of. This was another world outside lessons and boredom and games in a quiet court, a world run by strange, powerful people. It did not occur to me that I had already seen many of them in my mother's triclinium.

To reach great-uncle Claudius' house we followed the Via Sacra through the Forum and went up a road which climbed the hillside. Here was a palace beside which my father's villa seemed a peasant's hut. There were archways and pillars and porticos climbing on top of one another in bewildering profusion, stretching half the length of the hill it seemed to me, but then I was small and most impressed. I had realised, of course, that great-uncle was the Emperor but this place seemed fit for a god. Two praetorian guards stood at the gilded entrance with spears crossed. As we approached and my father announced himself the spears swung back with a sudden clang and I jumped, expecting to see Apollo himself appear in the doorway.

But great-uncle Claudius wasn't like that at all. We were ushered into a huge atrium, so big that your neck ached with looking at the ceiling which was plastered in stucco relief of flowers and grapes. The floor was paved in green and red mosaic which seemed to slip away into nothing it stretched so far. There was a painting of Venus and Adonis on one wall with a delicate landscape; the marble columns swirled gold at top and bottom. In the middle of this sat my great-uncle, as incongruous as a pig in a silken bed. He was perhaps fifty, not much older than my father, yet he might have been twenty years beyond him. His face had a withered look as if it had lived too long. There were great pouches under his eyes and chin and he was going bald which made his head look moth-eaten. Even his eyes were weak and faulty. And there, with her hair in a ridiculous roll and her dress so low that it almost fell off, was Messalina. She looked at me, then away again; perhaps I reminded her too much of a prosaic childhood. Her earrings were emerald and ruby and hung almost to her shoulders; her face was like an enamelled mask. As for the scent it would have knocked you down at twenty paces. Yet under all the fuss and paint I could see the child who gaped and giggled and thought it funny to scc her cousin locked in the stable.

"How are you, Agrippina?" said great-uncle mournfully. He sounded as if he had a cold. "And you, Passienus? I liked your speech the other day in defence of Quintus Tullius, not that he deserved it, the rogue, trying to avoid imperial taxes. Well, sit down, my dear, sit down; don't get dust all over your lovely robe. So this is little Lucius. Dear me, I haven't

seen you, young man, since your name-day—what a confession."
He drew me nearer and sniffed, saying: "You're like your
grandfather which isn't bad at all, not at all. If only . . . if only
you repeat his character how wonderful . . ."

He choked, patted my shoulder and turned away, overcome
by some memory. Messalina glared. And all of a sudden I
realised the absurdity of it. Horrid Messalina who thought
it the greatest joke to pinch and torment me and whom I hated
as my worst enemy was technically my great-aunt. She had
married great-uncle Claudius. I started laughing. My mother
grew angry and said: "Behave yourself! " but I couldn't stop.
Here was Messalina who thought herself so grand tied to this
shrunken, bumbling clown, the most powerful man in the
world. Then I sobered. I thought of the splendid Forum, the
gold and marble, the treasures taken from far places over the
sea, the praetorian guard and crossed spears—all leading to
this. A silly, pathetic old man besotted with his child bride.
Perhaps this occurred to me later when I was capable of filter-
ing my experience; I was, after all, still only a child. But when
I look back it is the ludicrousness I remember.

We went into the triclinium and slaves brought us shellfish,
chicken and sprouts followed by pears and pomegranates on
gold dishes. It was a family meal. Just before it began my
aunt came in; I hardly recognised her. Lines had aged her face
and her hair looked stiff and bright as though dyed. Her mouth
was very red. When my mother saw her she frowned and drew
up her head as though a slave had entered but Messalina said,
in a tinkling voice: "Oh Mama, look who's come to see us.
Hasn't he grown?" The sweetness was so false I wonder the
chicken didn't curl up. My aunt smiled with an effort and said:
"Yes, indeed. How are you, Lucius?"

I mumbled: "Very well, thank you." I felt conspicuous in
this great place with the gold and the frescoes and perfumed
Messalina sitting a few steps away.

After dinner a slave sang, accompanying himself on a cithara,
a bitter-sweet song of Apollo's love for Daphne and how she
was turned into a tree by the gods' grace to escape his advances.
I watched his hands, fascinated; they rippled over the strings

in per   the melting notes. My body
seemed   voice was high and pure like a
mounta   a dream. I could have sat till
I starv   the end when Apollo sank
down b   is lost love I felt tears prick
my eye   bored. Uncle Claudius was
half asl   interested in grapes on a
silver sa   t her cup as I had so often
seen her   ngry or preoccupied. Aunt
Domitia   Messalina smiled languidly at
no one in particular, jingling her bangles. I thought them all
barbaric.

When the slave had gone they roused except for great-uncle
Claudius who had to be poked by his dutiful wife. His eyes
were bleared and red; after the images called up by that exquisite music he seemed disgusting. I felt affronted as children
will when dreams are shattered.

"How is your son?" asked my father.

"Two years old and running like a young deer," replied my
great-uncle. He sounded enthusiastic. "A fine child, Passienus,
and he will make a fine Emperor. It's a great satisfaction to
see my dynasty secure thanks to my lovely flower." He leered
over Messalina and patted her hand; I was not watching with
particular attention but I saw her flinch. I could not visualise
her as a mother. She had seemed too brittle to reproduce her
own kind and not break.

My mother looked up and said: "I hope he is strong, uncle.
Young children have a dreadful habit of being carried away by
some absurd illness."

There was an awkward silence. Messalina's mouth drooped
as if someone had pulled strings and great-uncle Claudius
looked hurt; Aunt Domitia looked furious. Soon after that we
went home. I remember thinking how odd my family were and
wishing I could keep the slave with the cithara at home so that
he would sing whenever I wanted.

It was the hour before sunset when I was allowed to please
myself instead of my tutors. The sky was flooded pink and

primrose where the sun sank behind the Palatine and its light glowed on the empty seats of the Circus.

I wandered into the courtyard. My father was away, seeing one of his estates near Naples, and the house was quiet. Then I heard my mother laughing. Her room looked out between the columns of the peristyle, on to the cool garden. I passed under the sloping roof and peered through the door with childhood's curiosity; to me her laughter was uncommon.

I saw the marble floor paved in squares of blue and white and bordered with silver; the pillars at the doorway were shining grey. A bronze statue of Apollo stood near her dressing-table which was a mess of pots, alabaster jars and little silver boxes; I could not imagine what they were for. I did not connect them with her flawless face. In another corner was a shrine with a Lar, our domestic god, a little statue of a dancing youth with a bowl and horn of plenty. There were others in the peristyle. She scrupulously kept her religion if only for outward appearances. Above the bed was a painting of Perseus and Andromeda, the black sea monster rising up behind them. Just below its dripping teeth was the pillow and my mother's head.

I had never seen the man before. He was thick and dark, not at all like my father, and I stood bewildered, wondering if this were yet another father who had not been introduced. I heard him murmur her name and shivered; I had never heard it like this on a man's lips. She was laughing and running her hands through his hair. He said something and she replied: "Be careful; the child may hear." Then something began to happen which I didn't like and I slid away from the view, under the roofed peristyle; but I could hear their murmuring. My heart beat thickly. I remembered the barber's shop and the moving hands but it seemed wrong to connect that with my mother. When I looked back she was lying still and smiling, her hair wet where it lay on her forehead; I could see her breasts above the cover. I blushed to the tips of my toes. The bronze Apollo looked straight at me with blank eyes as though saying: you see what comes of prying. Behind me I heard the fountain tinkle and nothing else except their breathing.

38

I ran away across the court, my feet tripping on the paving stones. In my own room I sat and looked at the painted wall, innocuous cupids making flower wreaths, and tried to understand. The stiff figure of the mother I knew had dissolved and become a stranger, as remote as Andromeda on the wall. I had never seen her kiss even my father whom she was supposed to love. I felt resentful at the stranger's presence; he had shut me out. Why should he see this laughing, affectionate creature when I trembled at the sound of her footsteps?

The very next day my father came home. I could hear her talking to him in the atrium, eager and lively. It seemed strange to me that she had enough charm to pour out for both him and the stranger and yet the source of it was so deep that I never drank from it at all. She came into the lesson room while Anicetus heard my reading. It was a passage from Virgil, one of his pastoral scenes, and my tongue stumbled on the words; I could feel her eyes rake the top of my head. The transformation back again was complete even to the stiffness of her bearing and the set of her mouth.

When I had finished she said: "I want to talk to you, Lucius." Anicetus bowed and vanished and we were alone. She sat in one of the chairs with claws carved at its feet and rested her hands on the arms.

She said: "You are nearly nine now, Lucius. In five years time you will enter manhood according to Roman law which means you will be looked upon as a citizen in your own right. Therefore, I consider it is time you should be told about your future." She was cool and correct, knowing what she wanted. I looked at her hair, parted in graceful waves either side of her forehead, and wondered how it could ever have tumbled so delightfully on her bare shoulders. She went on: "First you must know of your own family and lineage, then you will see that your destiny is different from the common man's. Royal blood runs in your veins; always remember that."

Then she showed me a chart marked out on papyrus beginning with Caius Julius Caesar, father of the great Julius, and branching out into a bewildering network of descendants which made my eyes ache. At the very bottom ringed around in black ink was my own name. Carefully she traced the line for me while I knelt at her knee.

"Here," she said, "is the divine Augustus. This is his daughter Julia who was my grandmother. Here is your father, Domitius Ahenobarbus, grandson of Mark Antony by Octavia who was Augustus' sister. And here and here..." Her finger slid across, the chart and back again, "are your Uncle Caligula and great-uncle Claudius." She straightened and looked at me. "The Julian house traces its origins back to Aeneas, prince of Troy, who was the son of Venus which means, my son, that your ancestry is divine. I should hope you will live up to it."

I looked at her, round-eyed. It sounded grand to be descended from a god though I wondered how it was managed, this mixing of human and divine. To me the gods were only names.

"Do you see," she said, "how near you are to the throne?"

I stared, not quite taking it in. "But great-uncle already has a son," I objected.

"He is a frail child," she said. "Anything might happen. You must always keep in mind, Lucius, that this divinely appointed task might fall to you. Remember it when you study and offer prayers to the gods that you might be worthy when the time comes. One day..." She tapped Claudius' name on the chart "One day that throne will fall vacant."

After this we seemed to visit great-uncle Claudius much more which I enjoyed if only because it meant a release from lessons. There they sat, exchanging niceties while I played "nuts" with my cousins, where you shoot your nut across the floor and try to hit your opponent's nut out of the way. Octavia was now seven, a pale child who never said much. You would not think she was Messalina's daughter; if Messalina was like exotic silk she was very plain linen but no doubt serviceable. I suppose she took after her father. Now and again when she turned her brown head to the light and smiled you could see a flash of her mother but in a subdued and refined form. Britannicus was six. His father had named him after some squalid little island which he had conquered off the coast of Gaul but since it was full of savages I wonder he bothered. He was a dark-haired scrap of a boy who looked so like Messalina it quite

40

unnerved me. I expected him to toss his head and pinch me as she used to but he was very well-behaved and displayed good manners like a well-trained animal. Where he got them from I cannot imagine. Occasionally he grew officious and self-righteous, telling me I had cheated by not keeping the right distance or else I had misplaced his nut when he wasn't looking. Octavia never took sides. She sat leaning her quiet head on her hand and counting the squares in the floor mosaic. It made me want to hit her; I could not endure such submissiveness.

One day we were playing in a little hall next to the big triclinium where the adults talked when a man passed the doorway. He was thick and dark and moved with his nose in the air; I could see a large gold ring on his finger embossed with a seal. It was the man in my mother's bedroom.

I pushed Britannicus and said: "Look! Who is he?"

"Who? Oh, him. That's Pallas, my father's treasurer. He looks after all our money and Rome's as well."

"You wouldn't think he was so rich," Octavia said dreamily. "He's very mean. He spends lots on himself but he would never lend you any."

I sat back on my heels and watched him through the doorway as he talked to great-uncle. I could just see my mother's face to one side. She never moved; he might have been the poorest slave in the palace. They leaned together, the five of them, in some discussion. Then Messalina said: "I don't see why. Has he any right to it?"

My mother said coldly: "He is your husband's great nephew and a prince of the Imperial house. I am Augustus' great-granddaughter, remember." It was a dig at Messalina who only claimed direct descent from Mark Antony.

"I object," Messalina said. Her voice rose. "Claudius, darling, why don't you say something instead of sitting there like a stuffed dormouse? Tell her she can't do it."

She sounded petulant and childish. After all that paint and glitter, an imperial marriage and two children, she was still the same.

"Well, my dear," said my great-uncle, "if we are going to do it we may as well do it properly and if Lucius doesn't take

41

it then some silly little upstart whose father has a hold in the Senate will be pushed in. I agree with you, Agrippina, a very good idea."

There was a furious silence. Messalina turned scarlet and my mother smiled with infinite charm and stretched back against the couch.

"What are they talking about?" said Britannicus, leaning his chin on his hands.

"I don't know," I answered.

"I don't think my mother likes your mother," he went on. "Aren't grown-ups funny."

We discussed their oddities for a little while, then went back to the nuts.

Next day my mother said: "Lucius, in a few weeks you are going to do something very important." She was solemn. I looked at her with the submissiveness I had cultivated so carefully and said: "Yes, mother?"

"Your great-uncle," she went on, "has decided to revive the Secular Games traditionally instituted when Rome threw out her kings in the 245th year of her existence." She sounded like a passage from Livy. It began to grate on me but I knew better than to fidget. "You should know," she said, "that the main part of the festival is the Trojan game but in case you don't it was begun by Ascanius, son of Aeneas, and is a military parade composed of boys between six and twelve who emulate their elders in war. Your Cousin Britannicus will lead the first squadron; you will lead the second."

I said: "You mean we are going to have a battle?"

My heart sank; the idea of blood did not appeal to me.

"A mock battle," she said. "An exercise if you like. No one is hurt." She must have seen my anxiety; I could feel the touch of contempt. "You start practising right away," she said. "And no slackness or you will hear from me. This is the first time you will appear before the people and you are going to impress them. I want them to be proud of Germanicus' grandson."

Rehearsals were laborious; we did the same thing over and over again, under the sharp eye of a praetorian lieutenant. At first we practised at the Campus Martius, firing arrows at a mark, throwing the javelin, crossing swords, using a shield, learning how to sit on a horse without falling off. Britannicus took a tumble before I did but never made a sound. They picked him up, dusted him off, made sure no bones were broken and put him back on the horse again. They were tough men, hardened by rigorous training. When I looked at their proud faces, marked with years of victory, I saw why no emperor could reign without their support. I never forgot my tumble; I had the bruises for a month.

When we moved to the Circus I felt interested. Here was this marvellous place which till now I had only seen from a high balcony; there was the floor stirred by thundering hooves, there the seats which shook with cheers. I almost heard them as we led our troops through the east gate, under the great archway and into the arena which looped a full mile. Then someone yelled: "Keep your head up, Domitius, and your back straight! You're slumping like a woman."

Britannicus giggled and I said from the side of my mouth: "Don't laugh so soon. It will be you next." And sure enough he didn't keep a firm enough hold on the reins and the brute tried to throw him.

"Jove have pity," said the lieutenant. "Emperor's son or not you're the worst horseman I ever saw."

He was a good man but we made him impatient. I think he would have liked to beat us but not even a praetorian can do that to royal flesh. Poor Britannicus got more despairing looks and hard knocks than a girl at her first riding lesson. When we practised swordplay on horseback he not only dropped his sword but tangled it in the reins and terrified the horse; I was frightened he would decapitate me. Our respective squadrons, made up of boys from noble patrician and senatorial families laughed fit to split their sides although they were not always so efficient; but then we were the leaders.

There were two bronze posts in the middle of the arena joined by a wall on an embankment with statues of gods favourable to sport, and around this we rode our horses and rehearsed the battle. As I grew more practised I began to like it. Since it was a play with no blood or pain and we only acted the parts

43

of brave warriors I no longer shrank from it. I liked to pretend it was a real battle and that Britannicus and his troops were Gauls or dark Numidians while I, the adored Emperor, urged my men in the thick of it amid cries and blood and the clash of steel with the golden eagle riding high above our heads, unconquerable. Soon I felt like Julius Caesar himself.

When I went to bed the night before the Games my mother said: "Do you know what you have to do?" The lamplight caught the edges of her hair; her face in the deepening dusk looked far and inscrutable like Juno on the Capitol. I nodded. "Remember your heritage," she said. "Show your nobility before the gods and the people as befitting a great-great-grandson of Augustus. They will know you for what you are."

She went without even a kiss to reward all my hard work. I turned to the pillow but never slept till the early hours; I was too excited.

Chapter Three

The morning burned blue and gold over the Palatine. For hours before dawn the people had crowded the streets, making for the Circus. The buzz of their voices reached me where I lay in bed watching daylight come.

The slaves dressed me in a short cream tunic and a red cloak clasped with bronze and sapphire, girded on my sword, strapped on my quiver, bow and shield and placed the big plumed helmet on my head. It weighed heavy; the broad side pieces pressed on my ears and cheeks and muffled my hearing. Everything had been made to measure, of course. I was a miniature Trojan warrior from the scarlet plumes to the laced-up sandals worked with gold. It was easier to play the part now I had the costume.

In all my life I never saw such a procession. It began on the Capitol and trailed down the hill into the Forum where the buildings were strung with banners and flowers, dazzling in the sun, down through the shops in the Tuscan quarter where the keepers had left their wares and come to cheer, over Velabrum and the cattle market and finally through the high middle gate of the Circus.

At the head was great-uncle Claudius in his purple toga, riding a triumphal chariot. He wore a tunic embroidered with palms and carried an ivory sceptre with an eagle's head; over his own head a slave held a wreath of golden oak leaves spangled with gems. Yet with all this he had no dignity; I felt sorry for him. Messalina sat beside him encrusted with pearls and rubies and breathing perfume, her eyes flashing pure self-satisfaction. You could see the admiration rising up from all

45

sides. Octavia on the other side of her father looked drained and weak in comparison, her only ornament a pair of beryl earrings.

Britannicus and I rode behind them at the head of our troops; behind us came the statues of the gods, Juno and Minerva carried on litters, Apollo and Jupiter drawn on flower-massed carts with the priests beside them. Diana was with Apollo as she is his sister and shares his honour at these games. Horses drew Apollo but Jupiter followed a grey monster of an elephant, the first I had ever seen, a beast so big it dwarfs the best stallion and makes a man seem a fly. I could hear it trumpeting above the cheers. Behind them came the senators in white togas, then the musicians; altogether a procession fit to honour gods and terrify barbarians.

We entered the Circus to the sound of flutes and trumpets and the crowd rose cheering to its feet; I heard invocations to patron gods asking for luck. There would be big bets on these races. I watched the archway pass over my head and widen into the brilliant arena while the people roared and the flutes shrilled and the elephant's heavy feet beat the ground and I thought: This is an important time for me. But I felt no nervousness, only ecstatic excitement.

Great-uncle and family settled in the best seats, near the ground, with a fringed canopy above. Then I saw my mother and felt proud. She outshone Messalina like an upright lily against a gaudy rose nearing its end. Her hair was simple, drawn back to show off her magnificent features and she wore a plain white dress. Two great pink pearls hung from her ears; that was all. She sat looking calmly across the arena, acknowledging the cheers, and the crowd went wild. I heard someone say nearby: "That's the sort of wife he should have had," and another answered: "She'll drag him to ruin, that other one, sitting up there like a whore."

On the same level sat the Vestal virgins, their white robes bright in the sun; you could not tell what went on behind those delicate veils. I knew they were powerful because of the goddess Vesta whom they served but I was not quite certain how or why. In her simplicity my mother looked like one of them.

46

The races came first. I sat beside my mother to watch them and felt proud to see her admired. At the west gate were twelve doors with a rope barrier stretched between two marble Hermes; behind this stood the eight chariots, two of each colour. The horses chafed and stamped; their manes gleamed with pearls, their breastplates with coloured plaques and amulets to ward off bad luck. On their fine necks were a flexible collar and a ribbon dyed blue, green, red or white, whichever party they raced for. The drivers stood apparently relaxed but you could see the muscles taut in their bare arms. There they were, beloved of the mob, helmet on head, whip in hand, leggings swathed round calf and thigh, tunic matching their horse's ribbon; and by each man's side a dagger. This was for emergencies. The reins were bound to the driver's body and should he be dragged out only a knife could save him. The crowd were tense and still, waiting.

From a balcony above the entrance dropped a white hand-kerchief, the starting signal, down came the ropes and out charged the horses, nostrils flaring to the crowd's roar. I knew then why Neptune chooses to become a horse. They flew down that arena, god-like things, velvet skin shining with sun and speed, glorious hooves beating the dust into a storm, ears back, manes streaming, exulting in their strength and beauty. My body moved with the pulse of their running. I came out of myself; my hands were damp, my head an empty hollow filled with galloping.

The eight chariots tore in their wake, the drivers whipping, yelling, pleading, using angry words and love-names to keep their horses straight. But I knew the horse heard nothing; he was his own master. I fixed my eyes on a black beauty with glaring eyeballs whose driver wore green. He must have been the best as he was yoked outside on the left with the three others reined in to the right; it is the left-hand horse which must make the fatal turn round the embankment. His chariot was ahead, a streak of paint and wood in the dust. I could hear people yelling for him: "The greens, the greens!" while others shouted for the blues or whites. He had swept the corner like a hawk in flight and was now into the second lap. A slave on the

47

embankment took down one of the seven bronze eggs and dolphins which marked each circuit.

The dust rose higher; the horses went faster. He still held the lead, passing the third lap, now the fourth. His control was perfect. He neither went too near the turning post, risking collision with it, nor swung out too far with the danger of losing position or running into the chariot behind. The red chariot was gaining on him; a sudden spurt and it might pass. The crowd were delirious, shrieking, groaning, swearing; a forest of arms beat the air. I was muttering: "Come on, come on, oh please come on!" I felt it would be a personal defeat if he lost now. Then the green driver made a dangerous swerve and blocked the red's path, yet thundered on driving crooked. I gasped; it was a superb gesture but one I was sure which would cost him his life. The crowd yelled louder. Still he raced ahead, strung across the track like an acrobat, and the red driver was forced back.

Down came the fifth dolphin; he swung into the sixth lap. Then I stood up and shouted: "The greens! Come on the greens!" My mother caught my arm and said: "Sit down! Don't make an exhibition of yourself." I wriggled free and leaned almost off my seat in excitement. The dust stung my eyes; the wind they made caught my hair. I was in ecstasy. I invoked every god I knew and yelled again: "Greens, greens! Come on greens!"

He was approaching the seventh lap. People clutched each other and chewed their knuckles or threw handkerchiefs in the air. The place shuddered with noise; I thought any minute the top seats would tumble down. He drew near the bend and was about to turn, then the red chariot regained lost ground; my driver went wide to try and block him again, the black horse cannoned into the bronze post and the red chariot crashed with the green. There was a frightful rending of wood and convulsion of wheels. I saw my driver try to cut himself free but too late; the horses careered on in fright and down he went into the dust, all that skill and heroism crushed under their flying hooves. They lifted him out, tangled and bleeding; for a moment I saw his face. He had not died yet. The other driver lay under his own wheels. The crowd groaned and women wept and the white chariot rode to victory. I began to cry uncontrollably. The black horse had fallen in his mad rush and now lay whinnying, a leg broken. I knew they would kill him. A maimed race horse is no good to anyone. All that beauty ruined in a moment, all that strength and grace and pride.

My mother snapped: "Be quiet! Don't let them see you snivelling." Her voice cut my heart, soft with grief, but I knew her too well; I choked back the tears. But I think I hated her for not taking me in her arms as my aunt would have done and soothing away the pain.

Next came the Trojan Games. I could not have felt less like such exhibitionism but I feared my mother. As we formed up behind the east gate I wiped my face and repeated inwardly: Show your nobility before the gods and the people as befitting a great-great-grandson of Augustus. The trumpets were sounding; I drew myself up before my squadron. I was Germanicus' grandson; the blood of Caesars flowed in my veins. I must not flinch or weep because a king is more godlike than other men and to do so now would betray my breeding. But as we entered the hot arena I smelt the odour of close-packed bodies and saw his blood in the dust near the turning post.

The Games went well. We performed our exercises, shot our arrows, threw our javelins, crossed swords on horseback, and rode in formation around the arena. I could see Britannicus was uncertain. He had never really gained the knack of horsemanship; he jogged dangerously in the saddle and went white at one point when he felt his balance going. During the "battle" as I crossed swords with him I heard sudden cheering break out and realised with shock that it was for me.

"Hurrah for Germanicus' grandson!" someone yelled and I turned to see the people on their feet, waving and shouting. Later I realised it was my face; they saw their dead hero there. But also I had performed with skill (all that labour had borne fruit) whereas Britannicus, so much smaller and less able than me, seemed puny and ineffectual. I saw his face darken as I

49

acknowledged their praise; after all, he was their future emperor. They clapped him but feebly as if in pity.

I looked across to my family and saw my mother's satisfaction, not that it was obvious for she would not let emotion show; but I knew her. Messalina sat red and furious; poor great-uncle Claudius looked abysmally miserable. My father was clapping. I swung round to wave and met the crowd's roaring approval like sunlight on my face. I half closed my eyes and felt their love, their admiration. It warmed my body and filled me with an uplifted joy; I fancy I could have flown. Every sense of fear or loneliness or rejection vanished. I was theirs. As the trumpets burst and we rode from the ring I heard them call my name and I pledged that I would always love the people of Rome.

"You did very well," said my mother.

I took off the plumed helmet and laid it on the bed. I was dusty and tired and a lump hurt my throat; but my heart lifted at her restrained praise. I never knew her break into enthusiasm. Messalina used to shriek with joy and shower presents on everyone if something pleased her. Whatever my mother thought or felt was deep inside.

"Keep it up," she said. "When you appear in public you must be dignified. The people know you now and will expect much from you. Dignity and restraint are the marks of royalty."

I thought of Messalina, jewel-encrusted, and felt another flash of pride. My mother's imperial ancestry was obvious. She kissed my forehead before I settled for sleep and her mouth was cold; but it warmed me to know I had earned it.

Next day was stifling hot. By the fifth hour the house was an oven and I drowsed over my history. At midday I swallowed a glass of water, unable to eat anything, and tumbled on to my bed. I slept for a little while, the shutters closed to keep off the sun; even the covers on the mattress made me itch. A little bronze Pan grinned from the shadows and piped on his flute. I smiled and dozed and imagined I heard the dancing notes.

A face leaned over me. I thought it was Beryllus or my mother and turned away to sleep again, then someone grabbed me. I began to scream but a hand went over my mouth, other figures loomed behind; then I saw the knife. I closed my eyes, believing it my end. Then one of them shouted in terror; the knife clattered down and they flew for their lives through the door. I sat up trembling and there beside the bed reared a dark, shining snake, its wicked head thrusting at me with its split tongue. I yelled and yelled and they came running. Beryllus flung wide the shutters and my mother shook me, saying: "What is it?" I was shivering and crying; my tongue would not move. "What is it?" she repeated. She looked angry and shook me harder.

"Look," said Beryllus, and held out the knife.

"Men," I blurted out. "Horrible men. They tried to kill me but there was a snake and they ran away.'

They thought I was wandering and shrugged; then they found a sloughed snake skin under the bed, patterned in faded green and black.

"Gods preserve us," said Beryllus.

He looked quite white. My mother rose up, clutching the snake skin; I saw in her eyes the look of understanding and purpose which boded no good for someone. I leaned on the pillows, sniffing. They had forgotten me. Now I could begin to think I supposed the snake had crawled in from the grass outside to escape the heat though I did not remember it there when I came in. I thought of the stone face with snake hair, the darkness and the storm.

Later on my mother called me to her and said seriously: "Lucius, someone ordered those men to kill you."

I blinked; it made no sense. I was not yet old enough to have felt the touch of active hatred, and politics were far away, hidden behind the Palatine.

"Kill me? But why?"

"You were too successful yesterday." She was calm, meeting the facts squarely. "It's best for you to learn as quickly as possible, my child, that in your position success breeds hatred."

I thought of the cheers and Britannicus' sullen face, then I remembered Messalina's eyes.

"Someone saw you were dangerous," she said. "I'm not a

fool. A mother's jealousy is the most potent. But this is the important thing." She held out the snake skin and I flinched. It looked withered and ugly in her smooth hand. "It was no accident," she said, "that this saved your life. The gods are assiduous in protecting those they have marked for a divine destiny. Hercules strangled snakes in his cradle but for you a snake was a god-sent defender. Do you understand?"

I nodded, though my mind was spinning; I suppose I still felt the afternoon's shock. From her seriousness I somehow realised that the gods had been good to me because I was special; and, even more startling, that murder stirred in my own family. My mother had the snake skin set in gold and made into a bracelet for me with two rubies for eyes. She said I must wear it till I died as it was a god's gift and brought good luck. Despite her strength she was superstitious. I obeyed because she said so but the thing meant little. More impressive was my new realisation of an unthought of enemy. My cousin Messalina had tried to kill me.

Life went on the same. Gods or no gods, I still learnt my history and practised reading and numbers when I would rather have recited poetry or tried to play the lyre. Sometimes Anicetus let me declaim Virgil or Homer as though I were on a stage and I could picture smiling faces and applause like that of the Circus. I made the words roll and flung out gestures in accompaniment. I grew interested in painting and sculpture and examined every statue we had to see how it had been carved. It seemed wonderful that a second life should spring from marble or bronze; I thought a sculptor must be part divine. I used to see them meet on the Aventine at the temple of Minerva who was their patroness, and discuss business, who had been commissioned for what and whose prices were highest. Poets and actors came, too, those strange people whose arts so improved our lives. I envied their easy talk, their grace and their skill. When we visited great-uncle I stared at his wall paintings and tried to see how the paint had been applied, appreciating the exquisite curve of flesh and hair, the ripple of material; but my mother got annoyed and said it was bad manners.

Above all I had fallen in love with the races. My mother stamped on that by forbidding me to attend them; she saw it as a kind of wine, dangerous and intoxicating, and even when she went with my father I stayed behind. It made me furious. It seemed pointless, merely the operation of her supreme authority. Once when this happened I threw my little Pan in anger and it broke, then she made me go all day with no food. I never felt so scared as when I saw her staring at the pieces on the floor.

Lack of medicine made the illness worse. I spent half my time trying to find out who was on top, who had won and who had crashed, and which horses were running best; and the other half talking about it to anyone who would listen. My tutors had told me never to mention racing at lesson time; I knew it would go to my mother if I did. I now had my lessons with a few other children of my own age who came from good families but not patrician status. I suppose my mother thought I should mix if not with the plebs at least with children not royal; it looked better.

One day soon after the Secular Games I was telling them about the collision; Anicetus had left the room and I held forth in grand style, using my hands to express the movements. They gaped appreciatively.

'... and then he thundered round, caught the turning post and crashed with the red behind. You never saw such confusion. He was thrown right out and dragged along by the horses, just like this—"

I swept my hand round, then saw Anicetus standing in the doorway; my audience still stared. I was caught; to draw back now would prove my guilt. I thought of my mother and the whipping to come and a sudden idea burst on me, born of desperation. Without flinching I went on: "... and all round the walls of Troy they dragged him and that's how he died such a hero."

My audience looked blank. I turned smiling to Anicetus and said: "I was telling them about Hector, how Achilles' chariot dragged him round Troy just as Homer says."

He seemed convinced. The others heroically kept straight

faces and stifled their laughter when his back was turned. I had escaped a hiding but, more important, I had discovered my own ability. I could act.

I was now ten years and nine months. I worked hard; I obeyed my mother. I still wore the golden bracelet and considered myself protected. Sometimes when my father was away I saw Pallas around the house, usually in my mother's bedroom but sometimes in the atrium when they would talk and not kiss. Occasionally he came when my father was home which seemed odd. I saw him as my father's rival, yet my father greeted him as a friend and offered him wine while my mother sat graceful and composed. Adults were still strange to me. I wondered if they had some private arrangement. One day I heard them talking.

"Has he any idea?" asked my father.

"Not at all," Pallas replied. "It's quite pathetic. You would think he was blind or stupid when in most matters he is neither though people often think so. Where she is concerned he prefers to look crooked instead of straight."

"I wonder she has the courage," said my mother.

"It isn't a question of courage," observed Pallas. "She just never thinks; why should she? She sees her beauty in the glass and imagines it a charm to destroy all opposition. But it has grown worse lately like a disease when indulged."

"Poor Uncle Claudius," murmured my mother.

"One day he will find out," said my father wisely, "and then Jove have mercy on her."

One morning soon after that Pallas arrived, panting with urgent news. We had hardly got up.

"It's over," he said. "She's dead."

My father clicked his tongue and folded his hands, saying: "It was to be expected." My mother stood in only her stola, unpainted, her hair dishevelled from sleep; her mouth was parted. I imagined I saw triumph in her eyes but that seemed wrong.

"How did it happen?" she asked.

"A scandal broke; what else? Everyone knew about Silius, except for Claudius, until she perpetrated the most dreadful hoax and it exploded in her face. She told Claudius that an astrologer (one of the best) had foretold that her husband would die a violent death before the Ides of September. Claudius got in a panic—he believes the stars more than the oracle, you know—until she suggested he divorce her till the Ides were past; that way they could fox fate, they thought, as he would no longer be her husband. It was her husband doomed, you see, not the Emperor as such."

"What complexities," said my father.

"There is worse to come. Claudius agreed to this all right without another thought, then realised there must be a second marriage in between or he would not be able to 'remarry' her according to the law. So he picked on Silius as a temporary husband, on Messalina's advice, of course, and she agreed the whole thing would be merely formal, no nuptial rites or anything like that. He signed the divorce papers, poor deluded creature, and left for Ostia. When he got back he found the marriage had taken place accompanied by obscene Bacchic revels and his lovely Messalina was in bed with her Silius."

"Merciful Jupiter," said my father. "What a mentality. How could she do it?"

"There was talk of an assassination plot," Pallas went on. "I should think Silius was behind that. Messalina hadn't an ounce of political feeling in her. Well, now it's done. Claudius signed the death warrant with an option of suicide but she couldn't do it and a Praetorian colonel ran her through with his sword."

There was silence. I leaned on a cold pillar and accustomed myself to the idea of my cousin's non-existence. Poor silly Messalina. She had still been the child in my aunt's courtyard, painted and prattling, thinking all doors would open for her pretty face. I was too young to see it then but later I realised her to be the victim of her own sexuality. She had never imposed any control and her doting mother had never imposed it for her.

"How did my uncle take it?" asked my mother.

She was totally calm, no triumphant recriminations or unsuitable joy.

"He is numb with shock. The doctors had to give him a

sleeping draught. I wonder it didn't kill him. As much as anything there is his own humiliation, and then there are the children . . ."

"Poor darlings," said my mother quickly. "Can anything be done?"

"Not yet," said Pallas. "The wound must heal."

It did not take long. Three months later my great-uncle announced that he would marry again. His main aim apparently was to give his children a mother. There was no immediate candidate; I suppose it were merely to let all the available ones know. To me it appeared callous. Messalina had been dreadful but surely his grief had died very quickly, even for such a wife; now she was gone I felt almost sorry for her.

We visited the palace every other day, at least it seemed that often. My mother was concerned about her uncle; she fussed over his health, his state of mind and the state of his children. Britannicus was the worst affected. His eyes were red and bounded with shadows as though he had wept himself to exhaustion. I wondered how he could love such a mother. Now I appreciated my own; if I felt unable to love her deeply at least I could admire her noble qualities.

Octavia was indifferent, still a shadow of a child drifting bleakly from room to room. She seemed insulated from events; only her mouth looked harsher and her face thinner. They were affronted by my high spirits and talkativeness and refused to play with me as though I had insulted them. That made me cross. Their mother had deserved it, I pointed out; she had been bad, completely un-Roman, in fact. Why not forget her and cheer up? But they would not.

Left to myself I stayed more with my mother until I found she didn't want me. She liked to be alone with great-uncle Claudius in his private apartments and put me outside the door more than once like a naughty dog. One day I stood behind the curtain in rebellion and peered through the crack. The guard did nothing; after all, I was of royal blood.

Great-uncle lay on a rich couch with lion's feet on the legs and silver stars on the cushions. He looked peevish, saying: 'My head aches, Agrippina. Oh, what an ordeal I've been through. Do you know, sometimes I wake sweating in the night with a constriction on my heart. Fan my face, would you, dear; it's so cooling. How white your hands are. My poor Messalina's hands were white and her eyes so beautiful; what a tragic, cruel waste ..."

"Sh," said my mother and stroked his brow; her broad sleeve, patterned with gold, touched his face.

'How soft your hand is," said my great-uncle. "My dear, good, kind niece ..."

She bent and kissed him on the mouth. He put his hand on her arm; she sank beside him, her arms round his neck, and he held her tighter and tighter. I dropped the curtain as if it had burned me and scampered down the corridor. The guard never moved. When I reached one of the archways and open air I stopped. There were paintings over the door, huntsmen shooting deer; one of their arrows had hit me. The only clear thought in all my tumbled resentment was why I never experienced that side of her. She showed it to my father, to Pallas, now even to my great-uncle, but for me a veil concealed the shrine. The injustice of it hurt me. I was her only son; were uncles worth more kisses than sons? To my horror I felt tears coming. I plunged through the grass and lay on my stomach under a cypress, promising that I would never let her see them.

Shortly after that my father collapsed at table one evening and was carried unconscious to bed. There was a flurry; people running here and there, voices raised, bowls ringing together; I recognised the signs of invaded Olympus again. The doctor came but shrugged and said: "It is in the hands of the gods." My mother stayed by his bedside and I crept to the door of his room where he lay inert on pillows and mattress, covered in a red damask quilt. It was warm and dark; incense burned before the domestic shrine. I was aware of dreadful change, of things I knew dissolving into the unknown. When he died it was like a feather blowing into the wind; one breath and he was gone. The incense bowl flickered and I fancied the god moved. The doctor listened to his heart, then stood back and called his name as is the custom; when there was no reply my mother covered her face in her hands. The slaves were weeping. He had been a good master. Then the doctor said: "This is no place for the child. Take him out." The last I saw was my mother not moving, her shoulders straight even under grief. When I look back I am sure she was not crying.

It was a fine funeral. They bathed and washed him and dressed him in his toga and carried him in splendour on a pyre, preceded by flutists, horn players, and a chorus of dancers and dramatic mimers who wore masks representing his noble ancestors; and down he went to the Forum where his colleagues praised him from the rostra outside the Senate House. He had been a good orator, too. My mother wore grey and veiled her face and walked holding my hand. Ahead were the children of his previous marriage; that was the first time I knew my mother was his second wife. When I thought how he would no longer take me on his knee and give me sweets nor act as a cushion against my mother's anger I almost cried. He was the only father I ever knew.

Outside the city gates they burned the funeral pyre together with his weapons and clothes and books and threw incense on the flames. They cut off his little finger first and kept it to bury apart. I thought it barbarous. Better for him to go in cleansing fire than for any part of him to rot in the ground. The sky was blue; I looked up and saw my life till now disappear in a splutter of bright sparks. The urn containing his ashes was placed along the Via Appia; it carried an inscription, his name and achievements. We left offerings by it, food, wine, garlands, and silver plate to propitiate his spirit, and came home to the funeral banquet. I ate little. I felt cold and uneasy, believing everything must now be different and fearing what I did not know. I thought of him crossing the black river to the under-world; would he remember us or was he already a shadow without a mind, squeaking like a bat in those deep caverns? Then death seemed appalling to me, a divine insult. For the first time in my changeable life I feared the greatest change of all. I remember my mother laughing at the feast; it hurt me like her lack of kisses. Yet when people looked she was the bereaved wife again.

We went to the palace more and more. I began to feel that my cousins resented us, that we were an intrusion on their solitude. Britannicus was growing taller. He looked like his mother even more, only purified and calmer, Messalina scaled down and made bearable. He was beginning to ask questions. Why had his mother been killed, why did my mother spend so much time with his father? Would he one day be Emperor? Once I told him not to be so curious; it only led to trouble. He looked at me with wide dark eyes and said: "If you don't ask you will never learn. One day I will rule Rome and then I must always ask questions." For some reason it annoyed me. He was becoming distinctly aware of his position. Octavia was as silent as ever, yet stubborn; you could not make her talk or play even with bullying. She pleased herself.

And then something most strange happened. My mother married my great-uncle.

Book Two

TIBERIUS CLAUDIUS NERO

"The flower that smiles today
Tomorrow dies.
All that we wish to stay
Tempts and then flies."
SHELLEY

Chapter Four

I remember thinking it wrong. Her husband had been dead only three months yet here she was in the midst of an imperial wedding feast, laughing and drinking wine as though he had never existed.

It seemed wrong, too, for niece and uncle to marry. I did not understand the complex ins and outs of incest but I knew that relatives were tied by some special knot which marriage would sully. But she had got around that. The Senate obediently authorised it by special decree and suddenly one knot broke and another was tied; they were man and wife. Pallas had figured in that somehow. I used to wonder about this man, why he was important to my mother and why he persistently supported her. Sometimes I remembered his voice in the bedroom, only I preferred not to think about it.

She came to me the evening before, the last night spent in our Esquiline villa, and said: "Now listen to me, Lucius. Tomorrow we will leave this house and go to live in great-uncle Claudius' palace on the Palatine and from now on you must look upon him as your father. I expect you to behave as befitting a prince and member of the royal household."

I realised this was a lecture and listened politely. It always amazed me that she so carefully explained these things to me as though I were somehow important, yet never gave me the attention showed to Pallas or great-uncle Claudius. It was part of her plan that I should understand.

"Remember your heritage," she said. "Remember you have the protection of the gods."

I don't remember the wedding very well, only the feast. It

was held in the vast triclinium of the palace, often used for state banquets. The pillars were yellow marble from Numidia, the kind which has green veins, the arched ceiling coloured glass mosaic and the floor dark marble tiles. I could not count the guests. The place was crammed with tables from end to end, each with three couches and each couch with three places except for the place of honour shared by my mother and her new husband. I saw why he had married her. She was thirty-three and at the height of her beauty; her breasts were high and firm, her waist nipped in with the nuptial girdle; her skin was like milk. She had not painted herself as obviously as Messalina used to. Only her eyes stood out, wide and deep beneath those eyebrows. The orange of her cloak and veil suited her black hair and threw up its blue lights. Her tunic, with no hem as tradition demanded, was white silk embroidered with gold, and gold filigree earrings, each with a blood-red garnet, swung from her ears. I saw how my great-uncle looked at her. Despite his befuddled aspect and unlovely looks he had a passion for beauty; that was how Messalina tricked him. Because of his age I found it unpleasant. I thought of the nuptial chamber but knew only vaguely what must come to my mother.

We ate oysters, mushrooms, black and white chestnuts, fatted hen, thrush on asparagus, followed by boiled and roasted duck and pig's head with Picentine bread; we finished with every fruit you can think of. Wine was drunk, cooled in snow, and I was allowed one cup; it tasted sweet and made me a little dizzy. My mother was flushed and laughing with it, yet not beyond control; she exerted that inner restraint which Messalina had been incapable of. My great-uncle gobbled the mushrooms, his favourite delicacy, and dribbled with eagerness. His eyes bulged slightly; sweat dotted his forehead. I felt revolted again.

I was in my new bedroom by the time she had gone to his apartment with the usual noisy train, the flutes and spilling wine, the bawdy jokes which I didn't understand. I only imagined her in his arms and ached to think of all that beauty going to such a lover. My room was bigger than at home with a black and white floor mosaic and grapes carved over the door; the ceiling relief was stars and flowers. Otherwise it was plain; only the bed seemed fine and rich, fit for the Emperor's house. It was carved citrus wood with a purple wool cover and silver patterns on the quilt. I felt grand and elegant stretched across it. The stars looked out one by one from the sky and the sounds of revelry faded. I lay watching them; it was a warm night and the shutters were open. I thought: my mother is the Empress, and it seemed remote like a tale told in childhood. Of her I was proud but for myself I felt little. Violent changes defeat feeling; you withdraw and postpone experience until you adjust to the environment. This was the third big change in my life and the most spectacular. I could go no higher.

"Lucius," said my mother. "This is your new tutor."

He stood behind her, a lean man and grey-bearded. I thought him familiar.

"Seneca, this is your pupil," my mother said.

And then I knew. He had been one of my mother's guests at our Esquiline villa. I thought his beard strange. Everyone went clean-shaven now except for barbarians or very old men who thought it dignified their age; but he was only fifty, I would say. Yet he looked learned. His eyes were mild and brown but shadowed underneath as if with tiredness; his hair grew long and curled on his forehead.

'You are to obey him, Lucius," said my mother, "and work hard for him. No more slackness and everlasting chatter about the races. Seneca will teach you to be the son of an empress."

"What about Beryllus and Anicetus?" I asked.

"I have dismissed them. From now on your education must be sustained and efficient; they were suitable for basic learning but now that is past. Soon you will no longer be a child.'

"I," said Seneca, "will teach him how to think."

"Teach him how to speak," observed my mother. "Oratory is vital in his position. Curb your love of philosophy, Seneca, and give my son a voice which will sway hearts. Ideas are all very well but they don't make an emperor powerful."

"I am your servant," said my new tutor.

He bowed his head and looked amenable. She smiled at him and I saw admiration in his eyes; they seemed bound together in some alliance from which I was excluded. He conducted her to the door and I heard him say: "A handsome child. I see his grandfather there."

"Has it not occurred to you," said my mother, "that his great-great-grandfather is there as well? Think about it, Seneca."

His kissed her hand and came back glowing as if with wine; already I thought him a flatterer. But he seemed a man of depth. I imagined he would interest me more than Beryllus or Anicetus.

In one way lessons became more rigorous than ever; in another they relaxed. He kept his word to my mother and wrote speeches which I had to practise saying aloud. I would not have minded but they were so dull. You cannot fill with burning emotion such words as: "Gentlemen of the Senate, with reference to the recent claim of certain provincial cities to be exempt from taxation I would remind you that an empire cannot function on empty coffers." Mostly I did not understand and repeated it without thought like those brightly coloured birds brought back from Africa which echo your voice. But I had discovered a weakness in Seneca. If I put my arms round his neck and kissed him and said how nice and kind he was I could make him do almost anything. This way I persuaded him to let me recite Homer and Virgil and even some Sophocles instead of boring speeches on public drains and legislation. I wanted to do the long speeches from the Greek "Oedipus Rex" but he would not let me, saying it was not suitable for young eyes; not even kisses changed that.

He engaged two teachers to help him called Alexander and Chaeremon who were listless creatures and annoyed me. Every word they said came from him, only he said it better. They taught me the mundane things, history, reading (my pronunciation was not all it should be) and some geography, showing me a papyrus map of the Empire with the names of all the countries my great-uncle governed. For the first time I realised his power. There it stretched, this world enclosed with Roman strength, from little Britain on the one side to Asia on the other, from Africa to Macedonia, and Gaul to Syria, rivers and mountains and sparkling cities and people of every race, colour, and creed. And just down the corridor was the man who pulled the strings. I remembered him slobbering over the mushrooms and wondered what the gods were doing. The man who controlled all this should be Apollo-like, grave and noble and just, with dignity to hold men in awe. If any man can ever be as the gods it should be the Emperor.

Seneca taught me the more lofty subjects, oratory and literature and some philosophy. Despite what my mother said he could not divorce himself from it. He told me about someone called Plato, a wise Greek who specified how men should be ruled, but it seemed very complex and I asked him why I needed to know it. "Our fates are with the gods," he said. "One day you may rule over men." I thought that most unlikely but did not contradict. He and my mother were always throwing the operations of fate in my face and dwelling on "if" and "but" and "perhaps". In fact, they spoke so similarly sometimes you might have exchanged the speeches and not noticed the difference.

One day I told him: "I like your lessons better than the other two," and he smiled and looked satisfied as if he were a dog I had patted. When he said: "You must attend to their lessons as much as mine," it was unconvincing. He taught me the rules of versification, how you divide the lines into feet and place your syllables so that they fit; he was no amateur at it. He had a taste for writing his own verse, mostly in dramatic form and let me say some speeches from one he was in the process of writing on Hercules. I remember one began: "Turn back thy panting steeds, thou shining sun, And bid the night come forth." I thought it magnificent, every bit as good as Aeschylus. My judgment was unformed then. His admiration of the Greeks showed in everything he wrote; he included a chorus and left the best speeches for the messenger as Sophocles always did.

I found the poetic rules boring but when I tried writing my own verse it all came to life. Suddenly I saw myself as a great poet, another Virgil. One of my poems, "To Apollo" began: "Oh thou shining light of mortal men Look upon us do." I was very young. I tried painting as well, using tempera on wood panels, and producing messy landscapes and deformed-looking horses. Then my mother found out, said it was a waste of time, and forbade me to do it; to make sure she took away my materials. I wept over that though only when she had gone. The sweep of the brush in my hand and the swirl of colour relaxed and gladdened my mind; besides I saw no harm in it. I sometimes wondered how chariot races, painting, singing, and philosophy were all so wicked. I was beginning to see that anything I liked was automatically bad. I said nothing of my verses. I could scribble those in my room when I was supposed to be resting.

I found the palace colossal and bewildering. It was a conglomeration of buildings built by each emperor, the foundations being Augustus' house which was a modest place. Tiberius built the first real palace next to it and Caligula's was opposite on the northern end of the hillside. He, believe it or not, in his crazy conviction of personal divinity which I had already heard about, made the temples of Castor and Vesta into vestibules for it. You could still see the wooden bridge he built to give direct access to Jupiter's temple on the Capitoline; it made his conversations with the god easier. My great-uncle had added his residence between Caligula's and Tiberius' and mostly we lived there although the rest was at our disposal. I did not care for the Domus Tiberiana; it was square and ugly; little light reached the inner courtyards and there were no gardens. No wonder the old man preferred Capri. For me, who had begun life in my aunt's little villa, the whole place seemed capable of containing Olympus.

About six months after the marriage my mother took me out from a grammar lesson and began one of her lengthy explanations.

"Two very important things are going to happen soon," she said. "First you are going to be betrothed to your cousin and secondly great-uncle Claudius is going to adopt you as his son."

I stared. As usual she had thrown the lot in my face without any preliminary. "But Octavia is already betrothed," I began.

"He was convicted of a dreadful crime," replied my mother, "and killed himself. Your great-uncle, soon to be your father, can think of no one better than yourself to marry his daughter. It is an honour."

"Marry?" I said. "*Marry* Octavia?"

I thought of that pale face and listless eyes and a voice that hardly spoke. And then I thought of Britannicus as a brother-in-law.

"An honour, Lucius," she said sharply. "She is the Emperor's daughter."

"But why?" I said feebly.

Some question seemed called for. I should have known better.

"Because I say so," she retorted. "You owe complete obedience to me in this as in everything else. I have decided it. You accept."

So there I was, betrothed to my quiet cousin whom I hardly knew. I was not mature enough to yearn after raven hair and ample breasts but somehow I felt the merchandise was dull and that better buys were available. I knew her silences would irritate me. Of course, I did not know what marriage entailed and thought it meant we had to be friends and live together always. I flinched at such boredom.

The betrothal was fun because of the feast. First we both made vows in the presence of friends and relatives who stood around beaming stupidly except for my mother who remained austere. Seneca was one of the witnesses. I did not realise the legal aspect; I imagined it was only a kind of announcement. Octavia was passive; she never even looked at me. I gave her my betrothal presents, a necklace of gold and ivory, vessels of green rock crystal, and a golden Venus, then I put the gold band on her wedding finger to symbolise the contract. Her hand was clammy. I fumbled over the ring and thought every-one must be staring.

The next year I was received into the gens Claudia. My adoptive father looked miserable like a farmer who must kill his best cow for a disease but my mother stood at his shoulder; he did not hesitate over making the statement of paternity before the witnesses. Pallas made a speech, quoting Caesar who had adopted Augustus and Augustus who had adopted Tiberius, to show how respectable the whole thing was. Then Octavia had to be adopted into another gens otherwise, legally speaking, she would be engaged to her own brother. I thought how silly it all was. They gave me a new name, Tiberius Claudius Nero Drusus Germanicus, such a mouthful that the lawyer had to take a deep breath before pronouncing it. When it came to picking which name I should be known by my mother chose Nero because it meant courage.

Once this was done I noticed a change in Britannicus. He had been growing more serious since his mother's death and rarely appeared in public. He disliked my mother. I never saw her treat him badly but sometimes there were bruises on his arms. He had a lazy tutor who never taught him much and the slaves largely ignored him; even his father's affection had dwindled. I tried to be friends because he was my cousin and once we had been happy together but he was rough and cold. I said: "One day I will be your brother-in-law. We *have* to be friends." But he only looked over my head and said: "I choose my own friends." When I met him in the palace the very day after my adoption and said good morning he stood to attention like a Guard and said: "Hail Domitius!" At first I didn't realise. Then I saw him with that arrogant look and his mouth beginning to smile and anger took my tongue.

"How dare you!" I said. "You know very well I'm no longer a Domitius. I'm a Claudian, the same as you, you little pig."

He was gone before I could get the words out but the point was made. Claudius was my father but Britannicus did not recognise a brother.

I went straight to my new father and complained. He sat looking at me wearily, his mouth loose and his hands flopping as though nothing really mattered, not even that sprawling empire on the map. Messalina had aged him. He was a man you could not amuse any more.

"Why the fuss?" he said, yawning. "A perfectly natural mistake."

"It was deliberate," I insisted. "He hates me. He doesn't want me as a brother."

"You always were a little dramatic, *Nero*, my child," he said with emphasis.

I said: "I shall tell my mother."

He pulled himself up suddenly and became almost alert like an aged dog stirred by a rat. "Yes," he said, "tell your mother, my dear, tell her all you want. She knows where to stick the knives."

I retreated, a little confused. However, my mother dealt with the matter. Britannicus' tutor was removed and another, more submissive, was appointed. The first one had been Messalina's man. After that Britannicus was the soul of politeness but his eyes were his mother's, smouldering with something of her held back and controlled. He bothered me.

I was thirteen and coming to the odd and awkward time of adolescence. I became self-conscious in company and blushed if someone sneezed; I wondered about my looks and studied the mirror. Sometimes I could have soared above the clouds with joy in living and sometimes I wept into my pillow and considered jumping from the Palatine. My desire to write poetry grew overpowering. I scribbled sheet after sheet, then threw it out of the window in despair; I was no Virgil and never would be. I did not understand myself. When I woke from a pleasurable dream and knew my body was playing games with me I used to wonder why the gods made us so peculiar. At the bad times I wished they had never made us at all. I dreamed of greatness. When my mother scolded me I imagined sitting on a high throne and ordering her to be whipped. I longed for supremacy; the child in the dark stable crying for want of strength had come back again.

I got hold of a copy of Ovid's *Art of Love* and read it in secret, then Seneca found out and took it from me in indignation. When I asked what was wrong with it he said: "It's a

71

disgusting piece of work not fit for civilised eyes." When I said it was interesting he retorted: "You're too young to think of such things. What would your mother say?"

With extraordinary boldness I asked: "Are you frightened of my mother?" He flushed and coughed; I thought he would cuff me round the ear. Then he said: "Truth knows no fear." He could throw dust in your eyes with words. I persisted: "I don't see why I shouldn't read Ovid." I had reached the time of arguing but then it was easy with him; before my mother I was silent.

"Your great-great-grandfather Augustus banished Ovid on account of this work," he said impressively. "He considered it lascivious and dishonourable. If you have any wish to emulate your noble ancestor you will never look at it again."

I said: "I don't want to emulate great-great-grandfather. I want to be a poet.' '

"Tell your mother that," he returned and I heard a certain satisfaction like a child who tells on another.

"Why, wouldn't she like me to be a poet?' I asked.

"Your mother is a strange woman," he said. "I shouldn't like to pronounce on anything she may think or want."

For a moment I imagined I saw an ally; common ground opened between us. I put my arms round his neck and said: "Dear Seneca, please let me have the book." But he pushed me roughly away, saying: "You're too old now to behave like that." It was the last of *The Art of Love*.

This strange new time brought conflict with my mother but it also brought fights with Britannicus. The only person who never bothered me was my adoptive father. He was beyond argument or troublemaking; the last things left to him were food and drink and my mother in his bed. With these he built a barrier and retired behind it. I was coming to the age when you criticise your elders and feel superior but I could never do it with him. Once I fought badly with Britannicus. We played at archery in the palace grounds and he swore I jogged his arm when taking aim. I said: "I never did. You shot crooked."

"I felt you push me," he objected.

"I did not. It's my turn now. Give me the bow."

He held it out of reach and said self-righteously: "You cheated. It's wrong to cheat."

"You're a liar!" I shouted. "Give me the bow!"

He stepped backwards and I grabbed at it, he missed his footing and fell down, cutting his knee. He never even whimpered. I struggled for the bow but he held it tight, saying: "You're a brute, Lucius Domitius! You come into my home and try to push me out of the way—me, the heir to the throne."

I could hear the grievances flowing out with the blood from his knee.

"Don't try to be so grand," I said. "Your mother was a whore."

I had learned the word from Ovid and produced it with pride. His shock pleased me; but then he said deliberately: "Your mother is a bitch *and* a whore."

I think I tried to strangle him. Someone rushed up and parted us with an effort; he had tried to claw my eyes like a girl but I had bruised his throat and made his nose bleed. Still he did not cry. He had an endurance his mother never did.

Later my mother said: "If you behave like that again, Nero, I'll have you beaten." She called me Nero when she was angry, Lucius when she was pleased. "You must learn to be a gentleman and show people what you are. Only plebeians fight like dogs."

I wanted to say I had been defending her but I was too afraid. She might not understand. After that Britannicus and I were diffident together. I wanted to be friends again but he was sullen and proud, putting his nose in the air whenever I approached. It wounded me; after all, he was my cousin, legally my brother. I had never had a brother. But like his father he had erected a barrier which I was not meant to break.

One day I discovered I wanted to be a singer. A pantomime came in to entertain us during one of the feasts and I sat entranced. Apollo himself could not have held me more. He wore a long robe painted with stars and fringed on the sleeves

73

and he sang of Phaedra's guilty love for her step-son and how his horses carried him away to a god-sent death on the sea-shore when Neptune's bull wrecked the chariot. Normally one person sings and one mimes but this was a true cantica, music and mime combined, and as he sang he gave the actions; the horror of Theseus at the discovery of his wife's guilt, Phaedra's despair, and Hippolytus' confusion in death. Even in the song he showed emotion in his face which I would have thought impossible. He was accompanied by flutes and lyres and the notes fell on my ears sweet as spring rain. His actions had infinite grace and meaning; every toss of the head and move-ment of the hands signified some deep emotion. At the end when he was Theseus sinking to the ground in despair at losing his son the whole room was strung tight; one breath and every-one would weep. I sighed aloud like a lover or a dreamer awaking and he smiled at me as he stepped back to take the applause. Later I found out his name was Paris.

The day came when I was to receive the toga of manhood and become a citizen in my own right. It was a little premature. I would not be fourteen for another nine months but my mother wanted it and persuaded my father to authorise the process. He took me before the Senate himself and declared me a legal citizen. I remember the great Senate chamber paved with travertine and decorated with marble reliefs of our history, glory and blood, courage and beauty, all staring out on to the assembly as if to remind the members what they stood for. As I faced the rows and rows of senators in their tiered marble seats, upstanding men with good war records and minds fit to administer city government, I felt my heart go fast. This was the heart of things, the pulse of our power; here was Rome in her ideal, the best and the beautiful, and I was going to join it.

They cheered me and declared me to be princeps juventutis (prince of youth; only the emperor was princeps senatus) and consul elect with entry into office when I was nineteen. As a substitute I was to assume immediate proconsular powers out-side the city. I stood before them with my head up, Seneca behind me and my father to one side. I was aware of Seneca with a teacher's pride. As the Senate rose to acclaim me again

I heard someone say: "Alexander and Aristotle—a fine omen."

I came out into clear March sunshine and a light wind. The Forum was crammed; I had not thought I meant so much. My mother and father sat on thrones upon the Rostra which is the speakers' platform outside the Senate House, a purple canopy above their heads. The stage was ready; up went the curtains. I rode down the whole length of the Via Sacra, leading my troops, past the house of the Vestal Virgins, past the Temple to Castor and Pollux, on past the law courts and into the square before my parents. Behind me the sunlight made gleaming points on the armour and helmets and spears of my men; their plumes puffed scarlet; their horses trotted sleek and proud. These were the Praetorians, men whose courage made the struts of the Empire; and I rode at their head while the trumpets rang out, my tunic gold-spangled as though I wore fire. I came before the Rostra, saluted my parents and swept high the golden shield which the knights had presented for my coming-of-age. It blazed like a small sun. The applause rushed upon my ears; they clapped and cheered and called my name and my heart swelled with pride. I thought it might burst and I would die here in a moment of glory. But then I looked at my father and Britannicus behind him; it was coldness on the warmth of my joy. The Emperor seemed sunk in total apathy, unaware of my success. Britannicus stared sullen and icy, his hands white where they gripped the top of his father's throne.

That evening as the sun sank I came out on to the Palatine, the point near Apollo's Temple where you can look down and see the whole Forum below. The cypresses were black and still. Some flowering bush scented the air and the last bird-song began to fade as twilight came. To one side was the temple, built of lunar marble with Numidian columns, the great doors carved with ivory reliefs of the Gauls' defeat at Delphi. On the roof was Apollo himself riding a chariot. The sun, always brightest before it dies, caught his bronze hair and made it stream out molten. There was only him and me. I felt strange, drawn out of myself, and pulled tight like a lyre string ready to be played.

Below the rosy light shone on the Forum. There was the vast

75

temple of Castor and Pollux with marble columns and next to it the round, graceful Temple of Vesta. In front of that was the Temple to Caesar, surmounted with his statue, and then the square, the Rostra, the law courts on one side and the Basilica Aemelia on the other where the business men met. If I leaned round far enough I could see the great temple to Saturn with its wide steps and roof turning gold in the sunset. And there was the Senate, crowned with a triangular tympanum, the carved relief sharp in the sun's full glare. It did not shriek grandeur at you; beside rich men's houses on the Palatine it was a modest place. But as I looked my heart trembled and my ears filled with sounds, there in that quietness, the clatter of trumpets and voices raised in protest or peace, one man holding the storm while Hannibal's elephants bellowed at the gates of Rome; then a single voice breaking with regret: "Et tu Brute." There were tears in my eyes. The people in the square below were like tiny dolls, unconscious of me above their heads staring down as a god might. They looked defenceless; one rock from this hillside would crush them. I thought of our beginnings, the rough huts in a circle of stones, a people proud but brave looking always outwards to the horizon and never in upon themselves. To hold this heritage seemed the greatest gift the gods could give me. As I stood with my heart open and quivering and tears in my eyes I burned with love for this beautiful city and its people; I whispered: "Apollo, sun-king and father of oracles, hear my vow and hold me to it; that I will always love Rome and dedicate myself to the good of her people and give up my life for them if the gods ask."

The sun dropped behind the Senate House. The birds were silent; the air swam with dusk and the perfume of blossom. Only the god stood looking at me, his hair filled with darkness now the sun had gone. I stood in a dream. Then a lizard ran over my foot and woke me; I was cold. I ran back to the palace and my feet seemed to leave the ground as though I had Mercury's wings.

In the days that followed I was a centre of attention. The Senate authorised the four great religious colleges to accept me as a member and so I took an honorary place amongst the priests of the Roman state. My mother emphasised that this was exceptional. They struck coins with my head on, carved inscriptions on monuments and erected a couple of statues, one wearing a toga and one armour. The sculptors had been good to me. In one I looked like Germanicus, in the other I resembled Augustus. It did occur to me at this time that more fuss was made of me than the Imperial heir. He was ten now, bright and alert; he could catch me out more than once. His mother appeared in him more and more. You would have thought her attractiveness should charm the crowd but they appeared not to notice him. He did not appear in public as much as I did; I thought him silly, knowing the appeal of exposure. The mob like a man willing to show himself.

Seneca and my mother decided I must show myself as a lawyer.

"It will prove to the Senate what sort of mind you have," said my mother ."They have seen you lead troops but that isn't enough."

Enough for what? I wondered but said nothing. She had given the orders again. I asked: "What sort of speech must I make? I'm not very ..."

"Seneca will write the speech and you will learn it," she said.

It was a struggle. I never had liked learning by heart. The petition I was to defend came from the town of Bononia which had been gutted by fire and needed money. As I stood before the Senate assembly my mouth went dry; I wanted to run away. They were so eminent, so clever; and I was only a child. The opening words of the speech went clean out of my head and I should have been lost had Seneca not given me the cue. But it was a success. Their faces approved me. To these elderly men I must seem like a son or grand-son denying their fears for the young generation. I made my voice suit the words, sinking when I described the people's grief and ringing out when presenting the impassioned petition. At the end they clapped and made a grant of ten million sesterces to the city.

Next time it was Rhodes. The people had forfeited their independence by mishandling Roman citizens in their territory.

I pleaded for them in Greek. The words were soft, the rhythm gentle; I let it carry me like a wave. Seneca knew Greek as he knew Latin. In the end I won them over and the Senate restored Rhodes' independence. It opened their hearts to me; they loved and admired me, they wrote praises in verse and prose. At first I felt embarrassed, not being used to adulation. I had expected to meet failure and punishment everywhere. Then I remembered I had dedicated myself to Apollo who was Augustus' special protector, governer of Roman destiny and averter of pestilence. He knew my oath; the people acknowledge it unknowing. One of the poems written by Antiphilos of Byzantium, began: "Rhodes which was once the island of the Sun is now the island of Nero." I hoped Apollo was not insulted.

June brought Feriae Latinae, the old Latin festival of Jupiter celebrated on Mount Alba with libations of milk and sacrifice of a pure white heifer who had never known the yoke. Ancient tradition demanded that the head of the state remain on Alba till the festival ended; this meant my father needed a deputy for that time, a Praefectus Urbi. He chose me. I grew frightened, saying I was too young; I should make mistakes. I didn't understand an Emperor's duties. My mother took me on one side and said angrily: "Stop your nonsense! Am I to be ashamed of my only son? Your father has placed his trust and responsibility with you and you must take it. No man can shirk his duty." She made me ashamed. I hated my weakness then and longed and longed for her strength. Seneca was gentler, promising to help me. "And anyway," he said, "your mother will make most of the decisions. It's merely that a woman cannot be Praefectus Urbi."

All the same I had the imperial prerogative of being judge in open court in the Forum. My father had said only matters of secondary importance should come before it during his absence. In fact, most complex cases were argued. Leading barristers liked a big audience and this was the time for them; they wanted to watch me. I sat on the judge's bench in cold fright with a gold canopy over me and wearing the purple toga normally allotted to my father; every pair of eyes stabbed me like spurs on a horse. For the first time I had lost my own identity. I was no longer Lucius Domitius nor even Tiberius Claudius Nero; I was Praefectus Urbi, Judge supreme. Seneca stood at my side showing me the documents and explaining each case in an undertone, this one a slave who had run away, this a woman found in adultery. One which came forward was postponed. Seneca said to the lawyer concerned: "You can't expect a child of his age to pronounce on a case of incest. It must wait for his father." I think I should have run away without Seneca.

The lawyers bored me to tears. They talked according to the time allowed by the water clock but some asked for six or seven water clock allowances which meant one man harangued us for two and a half hours. I twisted and turned, I itched, I yawned; I started to fall asleep and had to be nudged by dear Seneca, ever-watchful. When I came to pronounce judgement for the first time I felt sick; the Forum square started to sway and retreat from me but the faces closed in, the eyes stared, the lawyers waited, the defendant pleaded mutely. Then Seneca whispered: "You are the judge."

"Gentlemen," I began, "in my position of Praefectus Urbi while my father sacrifices to Jupiter . . ." and suddenly the fear broke. It was like a play with me in the main part. I had only to remember my lines. I summed up calmly, I praised both lawyers, I showed mercy as Seneca said I must and released the poor devil whose master had beaten him till he fled. When I saw his face flooded with joy and gratitude I remembered my oath and knew I had not violated it. I loved him because he was one of my people, slave or not.

The cases of adultery I found more difficult. I started blushing at revelations from the bedroom and wished to be elsewhere; again it was only Seneca who pulled me through. "Judge in favour of the husband," he would whisper when we were faced with a painted, jewelled woman who denied having lovers but fluttered her eyelashes at me as though I were twenty instead of fourteen. I grew more practised in my rôle and the audience appreciated it. No one ever had such a good script. When my father returned and it ended I was almost sorry.

My mother's only comment was: "Good." I had learned not to expect extravagant praise from her, yet it hurt me. I tried hard for her sake and also, it is true, because I dared not disobey but she behaved as though I were a slave who had done her hair nicely. I saw her give more praise to her horse when it won races. Seneca was different. "Excellent! " he said. "You're a credit to me, Nero."

Poor Britannicus was fading into the shadows. He began to look white and ill and a rumour went round that he had fits. Where it came from I cannot think because it was not true; he was pining from neglect, not epilepsy. I felt sorry for him because I remembered myself in that position but you might as well have offered your hand to a starving lion as try to comfort him.

In November his father was kept to his bed with vomiting and my mother sent me before the Senate to announce that I would offer Games in the Circus at my own expense for his recovery. In fact, it was my mother's money. Legally I had none of my own. I did not even care about my father enough to spend money in the first place; he whined with illness and became a burden on my mother. But the Senate were delighted at such devotion; most of them were fathers. Later people said Britannicus had been negligent in not making a similar gesture. Soon after that my adoptive father announced to the Senate and the people that should anything happen to him I was capable of governing. It shocked me. Britannicus was his son, after all, even though I was older, and the thought of such a thing put me into a sweat. But somewhere in me there was pleasure at the flattery.

And then after all this when I was wearied and exalted, joyful and afraid, I had to face the event which I had pushed to the back of my mind three years ago. I married Octavia.

Chapter Five

The sun on my face woke me up. It was May and very warm and orange blossom was thick white on the Palatine. It was my wedding day.

I looked at my face in the mirror and saw its youth; I was fifteen and a half. She was two years younger. According to Roman law we were too young but dispensations are easy for imperial children. As with coming-of-age so with marriage. I studied myself. My hair was still gold with red in it but darker than in childhood; my eyes were wide like my mother's and just as blue. I had her eyebrows, too, but fair. My nose was small and straight, my mouth as you still see it in some of Augustus' busts. I knew my attractions. I had seen people look at me as they looked at my mother, men as well as women. I had not fully learned how to exploit my looks though I had begun to with Seneca almost unknowing. I took admiration as it came.

"Well," said my mother. "This is your wedding day."

I turned and saw her in the doorway. "A great day for any young man," she went on, almost talkative. "A time when you show honour and respect for womanhood."

I didn't quite see that. I wanted to tell her I was nervous but lacked the courage to confide in her. She told me again of the honour I was receiving and left the room; I suppose she wanted to make sure I stayed in the right state of mind.

We gathered together in the atrium of the palace which was decorated with flowers and vine leaves. Octavia stood by her father, eyes cast down, in the hemless tunic secured by the wool girdle with the double knot and over it the orange marriage cloak. Her sandals were orange, so was her veil which covered the upper part of her face and was crowned in a wreath of myrtle and orange blossom. Her hair was protected by six pads of artificial hair separated by narrow bands such as the Vestal Virgins wear and round her neck was a metal collar. It made her stoop slightly; she was too thin for it. I do not remember my mother with all this, certainly not the collar; perhaps it is different for virgins. I was reminded of a dog which you tie up for being a nuisance.

Her father was gloomy. His hair was whitening fast and he sagged as though it were too much of an effort to stand up. Britannicus stood straight and cold. I thought he looked sick. My mother took everyone's eyes as usual in a brilliant silk palla of rose colour, her ears, neck and arms clasped with sapphires and pearls. But some of the looks were for me.

The sacrifice was done before Jupiter Optimus Maximus on the Capitol. For an imperial wedding it looks better and people expect to see the nuptial pair. The procession was long and embarrassing. The flutes and cymbols deafened me and this time the cheers seemed a mockery; my heart was not in it. Poor Octavia; she was just my quiet, unobtrusive cousin and I felt nothing else for her. The whole thing was a blind act of obedience to my mother.

Incense burned before Jupiter's altar. Tied upon it was a struggling ewe, her white neck stretched for the knife. Behind was Jupiter himself, all gold and ivory and reaching to the ceiling. The priest stood ready. We assembled and I stood beside her near the sacrifice, my hands damp, thinking of my own sacrifice. The knife flashed down, the blood spurted and the animal went limp. I swallowed hard; I hated blood. Some of it spattered Octavia's robe and I saw her flinch. The incense swam before my eyes but I knew I must not be ill, not now. The blood was running away down the runnels leading from the altar; heaven's propitiation was done. The priest split the animal's stomach, examined the entrails and pronounced the signs favourable. My hopes fell; I had thought some omen might prevent it. We exchanged our mutual vows before our family and friends, before the representatives of the Senate and the knights and the people. Then congratulations burst out on all sides: Feliciter! May you have happiness. Feliciter! They shook my hand and kissed Octavia and she put back her veil. Even painted her face was pale and undemonstrative. She smiled shyly at me, then looked quickly away. I remembered my mother at her wedding feast, brilliant and laughing under the orange veil.

The wedding feast was in the same huge triclinium where I had seen my mother share the place of honour with Claudius. Now I shared it with Octavia. The guests wore rose wreaths and the floor was scattered with rose petals. We ate dormice rolled in honey, sea-urchins, loins of does, game pie and fricassee of fish; also a rare delicacy, the tongues of flamingos, pink birds found in Egypt and Africa. The fifth course was sow's udder and roast hare with tunny fish sauce, then in came the main dish, a peacock on a great gold plate, surrounded with dates and black and white olives. The slaves poured out Falernian wine, the very best, and kept flies from the food with peacock feather fans which shimmered and burned like rainbows. I drank as much as I dared with my mother there; I thought of the night to come. Each course was divided by an entertainment; first came acrobats, then clowns, then a singer who sang a bawdy song which I only partly understood and finally a Spanish girl who danced to castanets, tossing her long black hair and wriggling her hips. She leant all over me and her perfume nearly choked me.

The night wore on. They were laughing louder and drinking more and becoming progressively ruder in their jokes. Some were directed at me, a few at Octavia. I don't think she understood. My adoptive father lay red-faced and thoroughly happy on his couch; a slave came with a silver basin of scented water for his hands but he waved him away; his eating was not done yet. My mother sat straight and sober. She seemed the only sane person in the place. Britannicus was not there at all; I envied him. I felt hemmed in and helpless, partly angry at their dirty minds, partly frightened at what must come when this hideous feast was over.

My father stood up, raised a goblet and said: "My friends, I suggest we propose a toast to my son and his bride and then let them get on with what they've been wanting all evening."

Loud laughter. Octavia never moved. I tried to forgive him. He was an unhappy man and drink was one precious escape. They drank a toast, demanded I answer it, then swept us off to the bridal apartment, a noisy, bad-mannered and cruel procession led by flute players and five torch-bearers. Three boys accompanied Octavia, one carrying the nuptial torch made of tight-twisted hawthorn twigs; the other two held her by the hands. When we reached the bedroom they stopped their filthy singing and said I must lift her over the threshold which dangled white curtains and green leaves. It was traditional; I swung her into my arms and felt how light she was as though she might break. The bridesmaids followed. I offered her fire and water as custom yet again demanded, then the third bridesmaid led her to the bed. She lay down. I could see the drunk, laughing faces at the door and felt a terrible anger; I would cheerfully have broken their heads.

"Go on, Nero," someone yelled. "Undo the wrapping and see what you've got."

She blushed and turned her head. I stared and stared and clenched my fists.

"Undo the nuptial girdle, Lucius," said my mother calmly. "It is customary."

Even in my fury I noticed she was pleased with me. I began to untie the knot; it was double and resisted. I grew hot, feeling her waist under my fingers and hearing the laughter at the door. At last it gave way. They cheered, broke a couple of wine goblets and trooped off. The curtains were drawn; the tramping feet and voices dwindled down the corridor. We were alone in dark stillness with a tiny flickering torch nearing its end in the wall bracket. She lay looking at the ceiling.

"Octavia?" I said.

She looked at me and said: "Why are they so dreadful?"

"Custom," I replied.

There was silence again. Her face was like thin ivory in the dusk but ivory not carved by a master's hand. We were so

84

young. Her breasts were hardly grown and her hair still had its childish softness. I thought of *The Art of Love* and all the stories and jokes I had heard, whispered as though they were impious. The torch fluttered down and down, reddening her hair and showing up the blood spots on her dress. I knew enough to realise that soon it should be stained with more blood but not from an ewe's neck. I felt the pressing sense of a duty.

I said: "Octavia?" again and she looked up. I bent and kissed her. Her mouth fastened on mine and her arms dragged round my neck; she held me tight. Pictures rushed through my mind, the barber's shop and a man's face, my mother in bed with Pallas; I could feel Octavia's child breasts against me and, horrified, realised her desire. I broke free, panting like a swimmer and slid to the other side of the bed.

She sat up. Her hair was coming down. 'What is it?" she said. She moved nearer. "Nero, darling, tell me. Oh Nero, how I love you. Please, Nero . . ."

She pressed against me, touching my face. I shuddered and shrank back against the wall. It was all a dreadful trick; the pale face and chaste mouth, the childishness. She was old beyond her years. All this time she had nursed a fire behind her passiveness and now it was breaking free. She tried to kiss me again and her mouth was horribly warm; the touch of her revolted me. I pushed her away and said: "Don't come near me! If you come near me again I'll kill you."

She sat back in the darkness, looking. The torch had burnt out.

"What *is* the matter with you?" she said. "Don't you like me?" Her voice had grown cold.

I said: "I don't want to make love to you. I can't."

I was still shaking. She said: "If you don't like women there is something the matter with you. I've heard about it."

She spoke with a kind of worldly knowledge. I felt bewildered. It was like a play when the masks come off and reality clashes with myth. She was Messalina's daughter, after all. I wanted to laugh for all my pity, my fear that the dirty jokes would hurt her. And yet she was to be pitied. She had been crippled with Messalina's disability without Messalina's looks. Or was it merely an isolated passion for me? At the moment it made no difference. I grew cruel through fear.

"I do like women," I retorted. "But not you."

Her shoulders crumpled. She still wore the metal collar and it looked grotesque in this light as though her head were parted from her body. She began to cry.

"Oh, how could you," she said, "when I love you so. I can't help not being pretty . . ."

It was her father's self-pity emerging.

I said awkwardly: "I'm sorry."

Then she drew up her head, saying: "I'm the Emperor's daughter. I don't expect this sort of treatment." That was Britannicus. "And I'm your wife. Have you no respect for my honour?"

I thought of my mother that morning and the injustice of it struck me. She had compromised the pair of us. It was easy to blame my poor father but unrealistic; I was beginning to see that every move he made had originated with her.

"I didn't ask to marry you," I retorted.

"But I know why you did," she said.

Her eyes were like stone; the cloak had slipped from her and she was beginning to shiver. I waited for more of her extraordinary revelations, not knowing any longer what I should expect.

"You want to be the next emperor," she said. "If you are my husband it makes it easier."

I stared. I remembered my father's recent edict, the Senate speeches the judicial activities, and then I said: "Don't be silly. I don't want to be emperor. I'm going to be a singer."

She laughed; in the darkness it was unpleasant. "Ask your mother about that," she said.

Something crept in my mind, stirring the hairs on my neck. I recalled her nagging and pushing, the emphasis on my ancestry and insistence on lessons, good behaviour, dignity. There was an echo in the shadows, repeating itself. ". . . this divinely appointed task might fall to you."

"No," I said. "No; I'm going to be a singer or a poet."

86

"You're not a very good liar," she said. "Why has poor Britannicus been pushed on one side? He hates you; I don't blame him."

At last it was appearing, the fruit of my rejection. She was sitting on the other side of the nuptial bed in her tousled finery with the orange blossom on her head like a mockery, walled up behind her frustration, her inexplicable desire. Pity gnawed at my heart; I knew how it felt to be unwanted.

"One day," she whispered, "your mother will get what she wants and then I shall be empress but only in name. The gods plague us. Either that or they don't exist at all."

I went cold at such impiety. And yet she was right. The prayers had gone unanswered.

I said: "I'm tired."

I lay down on the far side, away from her, with no covers; it was too warm. The wine had begun to pull down my eyelids. She settled, too, her face turned from me. I could hear her catching her breath with tears. As I began to drift into sleep I thought: "Feliciter," and nearly laughed. The gods have placed a thin line between laughter and tears.

My mother never asked me if the marriage was consummated. Whether she assumed it had been or was merely satisfied at the external bond I do not know. The contract was sealed; legally Octavia and I were united.

She had her own room next to mine with a connecting door; it was always shut. I thought at first they must find out. Soon when months passed and there was no child they would ask questions. But it was only the prick of my guilt, showing me my own fears. In public I played the affectionate husband and even kissed her damp cheek if necessary though it strained my acting powers. She never complained nor did she tell anyone as I feared she would. It was her humiliation as well. Besides, she felt herself a true patrician whose nobility remains apparent even with a breaking heart. Her calm acceptance and blatant bravery made me ashamed; then I felt angry. I was aware now that she knew much more than you would ever think but her mouth was closed again; what she felt or thought

87

was concealed. And my usually astute mother never said anything.

But one day when I was reading Cicero's *De Re Publica* aloud and my mind was wandering Seneca said: "You're not happy with Octavia, are you, Nero?"

I suppose I looked startled. He laughed and said: "I have eyes, my boy, and a brain. I knew the very next day that the virgin knot was not broken."

Like a child caught in the larder I began to make excuses.

"I couldn't help it, Seneca, believe me. I just couldn't touch her ... though she wanted me to. It was dreadful—Seneca, is there something wrong with me?"

He smiled wisely, a man so knowledgeable on human nature that I felt awkward to sit there.

"No, my prince, there is nothing wrong with you," he said. "You were pushed into the marriage by your admirable mother and love is not made that way. Women seem to think men can feel physical desire for any one of them without preliminary as though we were animals. Poor Octavia. So she loved you, after all."

"Oh, yes," I said, pleased at his reassurance. He was on my side. "She wept over it. But I couldn't—Seneca, are you going to tell my mother?"

He laughed. "Nero, such terror! You looked like a man in the arena. No, I will not tell her because I suspect she already knows; she is no fool. But what goes on in your bedroom is of no consequence; only the outward form matters."

"Matters for what?" I asked.

"Appearances," he said and changed the subject.

I went back to Cicero with a clearer mind but not entirely at ease. Whatever support Seneca gave me could not wipe out the look of her face that night.

She sat beside me on official occasions, a dutiful wife. Her hair was neat, her face only touched with paint; sometimes she wore earrings, nothing else. Unlike Messalina everything was inward. I looked at her sometimes and wondered how such a fire could contain itself. I expected to hear that she had lovers but there was never a whisper of scandal; I thought then that her passion was only for me, after all. Or was it her arrogant sense of duty? She knew the value of that; in public everyone praised her Roman virtues, her womanly dignity.

To escape the sense of guilt I surrounded myself with friends, young noblemen of my own age who asked for nothing except to be cheerful and uninhibited and have enough wine to last for an evening. Not that the evenings were long. My mother said late nights and too much drink were unhealthy and broke up parties before eleven just when we were into the swing of it. It was humiliating to be a self-assured young man at dinner and a child once my mother came in. I am sure they laughed behind their hands over it. You might have thought this would have given me the courage to answer back but one look at her eyes stopped me. Sometimes I went to my room early in the day and wrote poetry; it was often an ointment on open wounds. I would pour out grief or fear or anger into poems on lost love, treason, war, and revenge. I could murder a hundred people in verse, even my mother.

My best friend was Marcus Salvius Otho, a young man of good senatorial family; he was five years older than me, straight and handsome with thick dark hair which he wore curled on his forehead. I enjoyed his company. He was elegant and witty and told a joke better than anyone I knew; but even his tongue fell silent before my mother. She was, after all, the empress and could have him thrown out when she chose. I told him she controlled every moment of my life and he said his father had used a whip on him for small matters like staying out late. We agreed on the depravity of our elders. But even to him I never mentioned Octavia and my mock marriage. I knew he had plenty of girls and would take a dancing girl to bed five minutes after meeting but I would not copy him. A dog does not go twice to the master who beat him.

Sometimes there were events to take my mind from trouble such as when my father opened his new waterway between the Fucine Lake and the River Liri. It was the first time I saw staged fights. We sat in the place of honour by the lakeside, my father in royal purple, my mother in cloth of gold; she

89

looked all light and fire. Octavia was silent as usual in maidenly white. I did not miss her preference for white; it was a studied prod at me.

There was a sea-battle first; two fleets of twenty-five war vessels with three banks of oars met head-on in the middle of the lake, manned by 1,900 criminals under professional direction. At first when the water swirled blood I felt sick but then excitement got me; it was like the races again. I was in it heart and soul, moving with each thrust of a sword or clang of a shield and groaning when a favourite tumbled in or died on the deck; only the excitement of the races had been wholesome. This was disturbing as though some dark part of me were revealing itself. My heart beat hard with the flow of blood, the cries and thuds and crashes; I forget my name and where I was. When I saw a man stare stupidly at his amputated hand I laughed aloud.

When it was over and we sat down for the great banquet on the lake's shores with senators, knights, and guards officers my own self returned and I couldn't eat. Neither did anyone else. Before we began, the waterway was opened and something went badly wrong; I only remember a roaring sound, then a wall of green water topped with white rushing up the channel from the open sluice gates. We were directly in its path. My father lost his head and had to be dragged up the hill, my mother lifted her gold skirt and ran; I followed, taking Octavia's hand as a good husband should. She didn't need my help; she was faster than me. About twenty people were drowned. All the banqueting tables with gold plate, food, garlands, and precious rock crystal were swept away into the lake. The crowds thought it a divine vengeance and groaned or prayed. I stood trembling, a far memory struggling up in my mind; a bright fountain and a pool and my hand stretched towards it; I had nearly drowned once before. The lake was calm again and beautiful, but littered with the wasted banquet. My mother suddenly lost her temper, I suppose with fright, and screamed at Narcissus, one of my father's trusted advisers whom she had never liked, accusing him of appropriating imperial funds put aside for construction and of concealing the fact that the channel was not dug deep enough just to save his own name. I had never seen her like this before. Her face was red, her mouth wider than you would think possible and those eyes I feared so much blazed like Vulcan's fires bursting from a mountain, all the worse because it has been long hidden. I knew then that my policy of silence was wise. Everyone backed away and looked embarrassed except for her victim who yelled back; my father parted them. I think she realised her dignity was gone and marched off, head high, to the waiting litter.

My father, too, had made a fool of himself earlier on when the gladiators had marched out to fight with their usual greeting: "Hail Caesar, those about to die salute you," and he, no doubt soured with some digestive upset, replied: "Or not as the case may be." They in return took it as a free pardon and refused to fight. My father saw his embarrassing position and went stumbling down to the water's edge, purple-faced and shouting, threatening to have the Guards slaughter them. Twice he fell over and the crowd roared. My mother stiffened and looked furious. Now as I saw her sweep to the litter and my father pull his tangled cloak around him in utter defeat I thought how absurd they both were; yet to them was given power. The gods must be laughing above our heads. But I knew I could not oppose my mother; that was the irony of it. Those same gods had killed all spark of opposition by revealing the depths of her nature.

I still visited my aunt Domitia who went back to her old villa after Messalina died. She was always pleased to see me, saying: "Goodness, Lucius, how you've grown," and giving me some present, wine or a gold bangle, even money. Occasionally she said: "How is your mother?" in a joyless voice as though mentioning a plague. When I said: "Very well," or "Just the same as usual," she would smile and put her head to one side, saying: "Lucius darling, I know what you mean. Has she nagged you very much?" We were like conspirators. Her house was a haven to me simply because it did not contain my mother. I knew they disliked each other. Perhaps it was some throwback to Messalina or even further than that, to my own child-hood when my aunt saw my mother as thieving me from her. When I looked back to those times I saw only the good. Compared with now, the freedom my aunt had given me seemed a life fit for gods.

My father's affection for my mother seemed to be dwindling; he no longer held her hand and stroked her cheek at banquets or looked besotted when she was dressed up. One day when he was drunk at supper he said: "It is my destiny to have to endure the faithlessness of my wives and punish them after-wards," and everyone looked shocked; I did not see what he meant.

Soon after that my mother called me from my studies one morning and took me into her private apartments. The door was curtained in heavy material to muffle voices. There were nymphs on the wall in one of those woodland scenes which painters turn out so easily; it looked sentimental. I remember thinking that my mother had little artistic taste.

"Now listen, Lucius," she said. "This is a serious matter." She looked drawn and solemn and I felt uneasy. "Your aunt," she went on, "has committed a crime against the state." She saw my face and continued: "I know this may seem incredible but she has always been a vicious, foolish woman with too much ambition; your father was very like her as I know to my cost."

"What has she done?" I asked, disbelieving.

"Incited revolutionary feelings amongst the slaves on her estates," she answered, "no doubt with a view to overthrowing the established government and placing herself at the head of some traitorous regime. The last thing we want is a slave re-volt, it would be Spartacus all over again. Imagine the danger when wild beasts run riot."

I said: "It's nothing to do with me."

I felt hurt and disillusioned; but I still did not really believe it.

"Oh, but it is," she said. "You liked visiting your aunt, didn't you?"

"Yes, I suppose so."

"Why?"

"She was kind to me. She gave me presents."

"And why should she give you presents?"

"I'm her nephew," I said, beginning to stammer.

"Presents are given for favours," she said. I stared, not seeing. "Did your aunt ever kiss you?" she asked.

"Yes, of course. As a greeting when I arrived and left; she is my aunt—"

"I suggest," said my mother, "that she has been more than your aunt."

Cold prickled on my neck. Her words moved in my mind and began to take on a dreadful shape.

"Tomorrow," said my mother, "you will come as a witness before a special council called by your father to give judgement on your aunt. You will tell this council that she tried to debauch you."

The nymphs dissolved on the opposite wall. Only my mother's face was clear, white and terrible; it was the face of a stranger.

"No," I said. My voice came out like a drunken man's. "It isn't true. I won't say it. How could you . . ."

"Listen, Nero! " She took me by the shoulders and her fingers hurt. "Your aunt is an evil woman. She has seemed good and kind to you because that is the side you always see." I shook my head, trembling; she grew angry. "You silly child, how little you know. Do you think it so terrible for her to seduce her nephew? Not for a woman who slept with her own brother! "

The nymphs sank in darkness. When they emerged again she was saying: "I took your father from her. Not that I wanted him but my great-uncle Tiberius thrust him on me. Your aunt never forgave me."

I looked at her blindly; I suppose I thought she was lying. But she looked at me straight and said with sudden sweetness: "Lucius darling, it's true. Oh, I know what a shock it is but I had to tell you. She has to be stopped for Rome's good and your father's; you must see that. If you give this evidence it will help convict her. You have the council's good-will and

93

indignation at such a crime against you will decide them if they are uncertain."

"No," I said thickly. I resisted automatically like a man withdrawing from a nettle. I was in shock; otherwise I should never have dared. "I won't; I can't. She was good to me ..."

"You will, Nero." Her eyes flared. "Do you dare to disobey me? Come along, let me hear."

An escape route opened, a place to take a stand. A man in war always knows the point where he can run or hold firm. I was no hero.

"No," I said, looking away from those eyes. "I'll do it."

My father sat in purple on the throne of judgement; with him were ten leading senators, Pallas, Narcissus, and a man named Burrus who held sole command of the Praetorian Guard. He was a stiff grey man with only one arm, the result of some war wound, I suppose. We were in the council chamber of the palace; a domed ceiling arched above me set with Arabian porphyry and a glass mosaic of Jupiter as judge. The floor was plain and austere, so were the walls. Only the soffits of the archways were bright, set with ivory.

My mother sat with Seneca to one side. She looked confident; how well she knew me. My aunt stood pale and stiff before my father's throne with guards either side; she did not seem a woman guilty of treason. I thought of what my mother said; surely such a monstrosity must show in the face, or could you act virtue as I had acted love for Octavia?

I was the last witness. They were gentle, knowing my status and my age.

"Nero," my father said. "When you used to visit your aunt did anything unusual happen?"

I looked at Jupiter, the lawgiver, and thought: Forgive me. My mother had told me what to say. I had every word ready like an actor. I said: "She used to kiss me and say I was beautiful and she told me that one day I would be free of my parents' authority; she said my mother was wicked."

My voice came and went in my ears; it seemed to lose itself in the great dome. I was blushing but they thought it modesty.

94

I could see my aunt's face, blank and shocked; I might have been Pluto risen from the ground to drag her off.

"Anything more?" said my father.

"Yes." My hands were cold. The faces in the tribunal danced and blurred. "She used to caress me and say any woman would be pleased to have me as a lover. And then she tried to . . ."

I broke off. The faces were alert. My aunt looked as if she would faint.

"Yes?" said my father.

A dozen images invaded my mind; her hands holding me up in a pool or feeding me cherries, her warm lap, her earrings; and then I thought of the stable and the storm.

"She tried to make me . . ." My voice failed again and I took refuge in emotion. "Oh, don't make me tell you, please; I can't. I don't want to remember . . ."

There were tears in my eyes; I could still see her face with that dragged look of a person fatally wounded. The senators were of ancient noble families, severely moral. Her doom was written in their faces.

"You may leave the chamber, Nero," said my father.

I walked out slowly like a man trying to be brave though impaled on a spear. My mother sat with the most genuine look of righteous anger I have ever seen but Seneca seemed sympathetic. I wondered if he would despise me.

They ordered her to commit suicide. It was the noble prerogative; at least she could go with dignity and quickly, not stretched on a torturer's rack. I wept myself nearly sick that night. I was the child in the stable again, craving comfort, but no comfort came. Octavia was shut in her own room, my mother had avoided me, and now there was no good aunt with a warm embrace. I believed the gods must be playing with me as a child plays with flies. And then I remembered Octavia: "Either that or they don't exist at all."

To make matters worse Britannicus had grown even more sour. He said to me one day: "Have you been measured yet for your purple toga?" When I looked questioning he went on: "My father may look ill but he is strong. What are you going to do about it?"

He was trying to draw me, looking for a release of aggression. He maddened me with his superior attitude, an aristocratic awareness as though he were emperor and I a barbarian.

"What do you mean?" I asked.

"You know," he said. "Or your mother does."

These oblique references to my mother infuriated me simply because they were disturbing.

"What do I care," I said, "what you think? No one notices you, anyway. The people have even forgotten who you are."

It was cruel. I should have preferred kindness but when a horse refuses sugar you give him the spur. He was so stubborn. He walked away then, still arrogant; I do believe that he would have walked to his death like that. He was not Messalina's son even if he looked like her.

His father had grown openly more affectionate with him. He now had him sit by his couch at banquets and kissed him, saying how he loved him being his only son. My mother was furious. It was a direct insult to me, legally his other son. He and my mother used to quarrel now and grow nasty with each other in public but my mother was stronger; he would end by mumbling and calling for wine. I think sometimes he even wept. Then I felt sorry for him, knowing how her tongue could sting you.

October came with the first drifting leaves of brown and gold on the Palatine. On the eleventh we celebrated Meditrinalia, the tasting of the new wine sacred to Jupiter. It was full and rich and red with a flavour to make you think of grapes ripening in a southern vineyard, the taste of summer; yet when I looked into my cup I thought of blood. That same evening my father called me to his library where he sat behind an ebony desk normally covered in state documents. There was a bust of Socrates at one corner. Such a summons was so unusual that I remember it clearly. I was nearly seventeen.

"Well, Nero?" he said.

It seemed a question. He looked very old; his cheeks were sinking in and his eyes could not see beyond me. But he looked at peace like a man who knows his fate.

"There have been signs," he said. He spoke so low I hardly

heard. "Three days ago a comet like the one before Caesar died and it still burns in the western sky so the portent is not fulfilled. A pig born with claws like a hawk, a phoenix reported in Egypt and last night my father's tomb struck by lightning." He looked at me, his eyes reddened and closed up. I thought he was wandering as the very old do; then I remembered with a shock that he was only sixty-four. "The gods tell us," he went on, "when our time is played out. Your mother knows, too. Nero, my child, you don't know what . . ." He seemed about to reveal something, then stopped and wandered again. "I never have seen what I should. My mother laughed at me, you know because I stammered and limped and couldn't express what I wanted. Claudius the idiot." He laughed feebly and wiped his eyes, I said: "Sir?" feeling hot and uncomfortable. "I suppose," he said, "I've had a good life. Two of my wives were very beautiful but one such a deceiver; and when I trusted her so. I never even imagined . . . And now your mother. Nero! " He looked up, startling me. "Nero, don't fight with Britannicus. Live in peace with him even if you find him difficult. He is my only son. I don't want to lose—I wanted to send him away but he would not go. And now I . . ." He roused and became suddenly lucid. "You can't fight yourself, Nero, or the gods or what is written for you in the oracle. Only sometimes I have thought all this is nothing and it is only yourself you must fight; if you conquer that you have conquered the gods."

I said: "I'm sorry sir."

This outpouring seemed to demand an apology. He looked at me with great weariness. "It is not for you to be sorry," he said. "I used to be sorry for myself but now I'm not even that."

Then he said no more and I stood till I realised he was in a dream and no longer wanted me.

At supper next evening he looked quieter and enjoyed his food. My mother sat beside him in white edged with silver and a large silver drop in each ear. Her hair was curled up in the style Messalina liked. I looked at her and she smiled as though reassuring me of something, then away again. Her eyes were never still; she seemed waiting for something. Seneca leaned over and said: "Nero, how do you feel?"

"Well," I answered. "Why?"

"You looked pale," he replied.

He seemed nervous; his fingers twisted round his cup and when he nibbled a date his hand trembled. Pallas sat near my mother; I thought my father could not miss how he looked at her but he continued to eat unaware. Britannicus sat at the foot of his couch refusing food. Beside me was Octavia in a linen palla, picking daintily at olives.

An Egyptian slave entered with a great dish of mushrooms. I suppose they had been ordered for my father. At first he took no notice but my mother ate one and offered them to him. I noticed he chose the largest; they had always been his favourite. He swallowed it in one gulp. I was just thinking how appalling his manners were when he suddenly fell sideways, his eyes clouding over; his face was yellow. My mother screamed. It cut through the chatter and clink of plates like a trumpet. I gasped and spilled my wine; then felt Seneca's hand on my shoulder, calming me but also holding me to my seat.

She was down on her knees beside him, saying: "Oh Claudius, my darling, what is it?" then there was a rush of people blocking out the sight. I heard Pallas say: "Keep your head, Agrippina. He's only drunk."

"Look at his colour," she retorted; her voice was breaking. "For Apollo's sake someone fetch the doctor."

Someone else said: "Quiet! You'll start a panic. It's only drink I tell you."

I was surprised at my mother, normally so self-possessed. The next moment I saw him carried out from the crowd by four slaves, his head lolling and the tongue protruding slightly. My hand turned cold, still holding the wine cup. I began: "Seneca—" but he tapped my shoulder, saying: "Ssh, this is no time for questions." Octavia's mouth was open; I had sense enough to think she looked very foolish. My mother followed, pale and staring; then they were gone and after a moment's silence everyone broke into talk. Pallas stood up and said: "There is no cause for alarm. The Emperor has drunk a little too much, that's all. The Empress requests that you continue your meal."

I wanted no more food. I could see Britannicus on the other side of the room, white-faced. He looked at me as though I were a snake who had bitten him.

I said to Seneca: "I'm tired. Please excuse me."

I looked at Octavia but she shook her head. She would never retire at the same time as me.

A slave came with me carrying a torch. It sent bright ripples up the dark corridor, lighting the walls in brief flashes; I thought the painted faces moved. I could hear a muffled din somewhere in the palace, hurrying feet and voices raised. The air breathed uneasiness.

I could not sleep. My room seemed hot and the ceiling pressed down on me, heavy with its stars and flowers; the dark shutters closed me in. My breath came faster. A dog started howling and the sound crawled on my flesh. I could still see his face with the tongue showing; I had seen him drunk before and did not remember this. His voice echoed again and again in the darkness. "... There have been signs ... the gods tell us when our time is played out." I drifted into a half sleep and thought he stood by my bed telling me not to worry because he was quite well. I distinctly remember the fierce sense of relief.

Then light flooded my eyes. I sat up blinking, still in my dream, and there was my mother all silver against the torch held by a Guard. Behind her was Seneca and next to him Burrus, the Praetorian prefect, who stepped forward and snapped to attention. He looked straight at me, raised his right hand in the imperial salute and said: "Hail Caesar!"

Book Three

CAESAR
---

*"Why, man, he doth bestride the narrow world
Like a colossus."*
JULIUS CAESAR

Chapter Six

At first I thought it was a joke. In the torchlight their faces were like masks and the whole thing seemed a comedy where they salute the clown or the country idiot and the audience roars. But no one was laughing.

I looked to my mother. Her face was white as her dress, the eyes dark caverns; her earrings tossed out brightness against the flame.

"Your father is dead, Lucius," she said. "He died without opening his eyes again. You are his heir; in a few hours you will be proclaimed Emperor."

"But Britannicus..." I began stupidly.

They looked at each other. Then Seneca said: "Britannicus is a child. You have superiority in age and in the people's affections. At a time like this when the state is in danger of anarchy a strong leader is needed to preserve continuity."

The walls of my room were fading and moving outwards; the floor spread like the sea and I fancied it roared in my ears. When I looked my mother and Seneca were small and far, tiny as the people I had seen from the Palatine. I thought they were leaving me and cried out in panic: "Mother!"

She said: "I'm here, Lucius. Don't be afraid."

My hands were cold. She took them in hers and said: "My poor child, such a shock. But you will be all right. What the gods decide comes to fruition."

My head was spinning and sweating. The distant walls began to lurch, the floor heaved. Voices buzzed like bees.

"It's shock," someone said. "Fetch wine. No, a doctor."

"We mustn't cause a panic. If they think the child is sick, too, we'll have a riot on our hands."

Something hard was shoved at my mouth, then sweet liquid burned my throat; I couldn't swallow properly and some dribbled out.

"Ssh, my sweet, my darling," said a stranger's voice. "I'm here, I won't leave you."

A hand stroked my forehead. The roaring faded; my eyes began to clear and I saw the stranger was my mother.

It was the first time she had shown me physical affection since marrying Passienus. Her face was near me, still painted for the feast. Dazed, I looked into her eyes but saw no tears and no marks of weeping on her clear skin. I remember thinking her brave.

Seneca stood there, making a speech. "My child," he said, "remember what I taught you, that rulers are no greater than their virtues and that the gods look kindly on power tempered with mercy. Where should we be but for their clemency? Remember your great responsibility..."

"All right," said my mother impatiently. "Leave that till later. He needs rest."

I looked at them, those three with a Guard behind whose expression never changed (Praetorians bear everything with a Stoic countenance) all standing so solemn, so weighted with their heavy news. Then I looked beyond them to the Palatine, the Forum below, and Rome spread in darkness with her sleeping million, and beyond that to Italy pointing into a blue sea, and Spain and Gaul and Germany, then beyond again to Britain, Asia, Africa, lands stretching to the earth's limits with every race Jupiter made; white, black, brown, and golden, savage and civilised, intellectual Greeks and primitive Britons, fanatic Jews and fatalistic Negroes, cities, temples, rivers, and mountains throwing back all languages you can think of and every god imaginable. And it was all mine. Then I looked inwardly at myself, sixteen and silly, sitting up in bed with rumpled hair and a sweating face; and I started laughing. I laughed and laughed till my heart ached and I lost my breath and my mother said: "Nero, stop it! "

"Shock," murmured Seneca again.

I lay quiet, staring. My mother said: "Fetch Xenophon.

He'll give him a sleeping draught. Nero, listen..." She sat on my bed. I noticed she was calling me Nero; I did not realise till later that this was my imperial name. Besides, Lucius was for softness; now she was going to be tough with me. "You can sleep now," she said. "But be ready to wake and come for official ceremonies at any moment. We do not know yet what will happen but at some stage you must speak to the Senate and the Guards and see the people. Seneca, what hour is it?"

"Third past midnight," he answered.

"Perhaps by dawn," she said, musing. "We must see."

She was intent, completely in command. Some part of me was demanding grief for her dead husband; she never even sighed.

I said: "I want to see my father."

She raised her eyebrows. "A corpse? It will upset you, my dear. Lie down and sleep."

"No, please let me see him. For the last time."

I felt unaccountable regret as though I had loved him deeply instead of thinking him a silly old fool.

"Tomorrow," she said. "You need sleep."

"No, mother, please. Now." Suddenly it was immensely important. "Let me see him now."

Perhaps it was a desire to convince myself of reality. When I saw him dead I would know my own place. Yet there were tears coming in my eyes; sympathies bloom like flowers given a storm to nourish them.

"I'll ask the doctor," she said.

You might have thought it a victory except that she was indulging me like a crying child. The doctor appeared, a spare man grey with tiredness.

"May the child see the body?" she asked.

I noticed my juvenile status; presumably she wanted to make sure the sight would not upset me. He looked surprised but nodded.

When my feet touched the floor I nearly stumbled; they would not hold me up. I dragged a cloak round my shoulders and followed them down the corridor. The dizziness came and went with walking but I said nothing. In all my confusion that remained clear; I must see him.

105

He was lying on a great bed of citrus wood like mine but with carved ivory legs. They had smothered him in a quilt of red wool hanging gold tassels but it was not long enough and his feet stuck out ridiculously like something forgotten and left to lie. There was no incense burning before the shrine; I thought it odd. I came nearer, barefoot on the cold tiles of dark Lucullan marble. An oil lamp stood beside the bed. Its twisted wick hung downwards and made his face brilliant in the darkness, underlining the fact of death. His skin was stretched and colourless except for where it collapsed into hollows under his eyes and cheekbones; they had closed his eyes, shutting out the horror of an empty stare.

I had seen men die bravely in staged battle and I had seen Passienus breathe out a noble and distinguished life with more ease than falling asleep; but this was something else. I thought of him yesterday, seeing nothing but oblivion yet welcoming it, recalling pitifully an early life of inferiority and humiliation, then the throne and a wife who stabbed him through while pretending love. The death of such a man seemed sordid, the final kick of fate. I would have wished him happy in the last days but knew there had been nothing, only my nagging mother and a sense of doom. He had trusted too easily, wishing to believe people better than they were while they laughed behind his back. Power had not twisted him. He had let it lie too loosely in his hands, only wanting to build some comfort and security on its foundations. When I imagined his childhood, deprived and unhappy as mine had often been, I felt we had missed an opportunity. He and I had been very close, after all.

I knelt by the bed and felt tears in my throat. The others stood awkward. While I knelt someone came in and said breathlessly to Burrus: "Sir, the cohort has mounted guard over the palace entrances as you ordered and the military tribunes are on their way for instructions. Madam!" He turned to my mother. "The imperial treasurer asked me to tell you that the Senate is already in session and likely to remain so till dawn."

I heard all this vaguely as in a dream. My father's face assured me it was not. I had asked for reality and been given it. Kneeling by this corpse in a chilling room with night pressing on the shutters and an empty throne waiting to be occupied I remembered my dream of supremacy and knew it had come true. But I learned too late that dreams are bearable; reality is often not.

My eyes opened with the first birdsong. I felt dull and heavy and thought I had drunk too much last night; I recalled only the banquet and something wrong at the end. Then the night flooded back. I lay watching the bright crack of light between the shutters. Now there was no night to shield harshness, no sense of a dream from which you will quickly wake. I faced truth in daylight.

I thought of many things; being hungry and miserable and alone because no one cared about me, the barber's shop and the dark stable, my mother's face when she was angry; and then the bright fountain which I had reached for, at last within my grasp. But I still had fears of getting wet. I thought of Britannicus and Octavia and wondered how I could face them, one with his inheritance taken and the other coming into a title which she saw empty. Then I thought of Otho and my fashionable friends and wondered how my attitude must now be with them. In the moment when my father crumpled at the table a whole world had shifted out of focus. Trying to see straight hurt my eyes.

I was kept in the palace till midday. I wanted to visit the Temple of Apollo to renew my private vow and ask for strength but there were guards at all the doors and no one came in or out without permission from the empress, not even the new emperor. My mother sent orders that I must stay in my bedroom. I asked the messenger if the people knew my father was dead but he looked blank; everyone seemed bewildered. Slaves came with food and even a singer to entertain me but I could not enjoy either. Then Octavia appeared.

She looked sick. Her eyes were washed out with weeping and she moved slowly like a person shocked. When I looked at her face, ugly with grief, I felt sharp pity. It was her constant tragedy that she only received from me what any beggar would.

I said: "I'm sorry, Octavia."

"For what?" Her voice cracked. "For your new glory?"

"For your father's death." Her coldness made me angry, rubbing where I felt sorry for the death she thought I welcomed.

"Your father," she contradicted. "I belong to another gens, remember."

"Then why are you weeping?" I asked, hitting back.

She turned away, defeated. I reached for her hand, saying: "Octavia, don't be angry, I really am sorry..." but she moved sharply away. Since my wedding night I had never touched her except in public; now she didn't want it, fearing, I suppose, to eat and begin the appetite afresh.

I said: "You are empress now. Does that mean nothing to you?"

"You know why it never will," she said, her back to me and her voice muffled.

It started off the guilt again, pinching at me like a tight belt. Mixed with my nervousness and last night's shock it was too much.

"All right!" I said. "Have it your way. I wanted to be friends..."

"Friends!" She faced me suddenly blazing. It was Messalina except for the looks and I stepped back. "Is that all you can offer? Don't you think I'm pleased to be your wife and know that everyone whispers behind their hands and wonders why I've not had a child? Or do you think I'm content with clothes and jewels and a hundred maids and a mockery of a status?"

The passive acceptance had broken at last; I suppose her father's death had defeated all restraint. I saw danger in her face.

I said: "If you have nothing better to say get out."

She went, sweeping her dress along the floor and holding her nose in the air as Britannicus always did. I saw she would brawl no further; it was undignified. She would resort to cruel little prods like Britannicus, unobtrusive but effective and feeding a sense of injustice. When she left the room it was my defeat, not hers.

It rained all morning. The clouds were black over the Palatine and if I leaned from my window I could just see the

108

rain beat on the top of buildings in the Forum, showing between dark, wet trees. I had nothing to do. I watched the water drum into puddles and wondered what they were up to. It did not occur to me that they were waiting for the weather; rain is a bad omen.

Just before midday my mother came in. She looked dressed up as if for something important, in a gold-edged palla of blue silk clasped with a silver fibula and gold flowers in her ears.

"Are you ready?" she said. "The time has come for the Guards and the Senate to acclaim you as emperor." She saw my anxiety and went on: "Don't worry, it's a mere formality. Everything is arranged. The important thing is to be dignified, yet pleasant; the soldiers will not like an austere attitude and the senators will criticise flippancy. You must follow a middle road. Keep your head up, smile, and speak distinctly. Here—" She gave me a papyrus roll. "Seneca has written these speeches for you. The first is to be recited at the Guards camp, the second at the Senate House. You must memorise them on the way to the camp; it is two miles and will take an hour or so in the litter."

"I wanted to ride a horse," I said meekly.

"In this rain?" She looked patronizing. "Dear child, what sort of sight will you look, soaked through and spattered with mud?"

I saw her point but disliked the form of address. Imperial accession had not changed her attitude; I was still a child. She had everything entirely under control like an expert charioteer manoeuvring awkward corners. You would have thought it nothing, watching her. She spoke as if arranging a dinner party instead of putting the empire into new hands.

She said: "Nero, my son, this is a time to remember. You have come into the inheritance of your ancestors; to you the gods have given sole power, trusting you with it. Don't stand shaking like a slave."

I smiled uneasily. I could not see if her kindness was genuine or whether she was trying to avoid the disaster of a nervous emperor. Kindness from her seemed wrong. When she spoke of inheritance I remembered Britannicus, alone and neglected somewhere in this palace while his adoptive brother rose to power. It bothered me. I felt as a thief must, attacked by guilt when rifling the silver.

It was still raining as the palace gates swung open. The dark tips of the poplar trees streamed wetness and the road which sloped down the hillside to the Forum sank in mist. The air smelt of autumn and decay. I had to lift my toga to avoid wet leaves straggled near the gate. As I emerged a great cheer broke out and I looked round, startled; there were two troops of Praetorians, their plumes bedraggled, standing to attention at the gate with their arms raised in salute. Someone yelled "Long live the Emperor Nero! " and the sound echoed between the treetops like a wind.

"Hail Caesar! Long live Caesar! " I stood bewildered till my mother pushed me forward. Seneca patted my shoulder and said: "Look cheerful, my boy." I smiled acknowledgment and returned the salute and they cheered again; I heard a war-hardened veteran say: "A fine looking lad. Reminds me of Germanicus." But as I climbed into the waiting litter I heard an underground mutter in the ranks: "What about Britannicus?" Then the thick curtains swung together blotting out rain, soldiers and all; I was left alone to learn my speeches.

The journey was uncomfortable. We bumped along, the curtains blowing about with the wind and the litter swaying as the bearers slid on wet cobbles. I began to feel ill with nervousness and jogging. I wondered what on earth they would do if I was sick. I tried to tell from sounds outside if the city was in a turmoil but I heard only rain and the normal clatter of a working day. Then there was the click of military boots, a smart: "Sir! " and the curtains went back to show the Praetorian barracks, long buildings dismal in the rain and totally devoid of grace or beauty. This was the army, utilitarian to the last degree.

As I got out the rain stopped. They thought it a fine omen and cheered themselves hoarse while I climbed on to the platform set up on the parade ground. It had gathered puddles but was better than nothing. Behind me stood my mother, Seneca, Burrus and Pallas. I knew the importance of Burrus

110

and Seneca but could not see the point of Pallas being there; I had forgotten that military devotion is encouraged by gold. He had grown thicker since the day I had first seen him with my mother and his face showed the acuteness which measures money. You could tell by his look that he still saw my mother as his.

I looked down at the arrayed plumes, blood-red in the grey air, and beneath them the faces of men who had backed the accession of four emperors and knew what their support was worth. I reckoned there were about twelve thousand, not counting officers and tribunes. They waited, standing firm and arrogant with swords slung by their sides, swords which held the empire's boundaries and mine, too. I might captivate every senator in Rome yet be powerless without the approval of these men. I felt afraid.

My mother said: "Gentlemen, I present my son to you," and pushed me forward. I came to the edge of the platform and began: "Men, I should like to thank you for your support and assure you of my trust in you . . ." My breath came out warm and my voice shook; but as I went on it became calm. "Every emperor trusts his Guards; where should we be without you? You are bodyguards and defenders as well as protectors of imperial territory. I salute your courage, your loyalty to Rome . . ." There was rather more of this along the same lines; Seneca knew the right approach. I ended: ". . . and so I confirm the payment of 15,000 sesterces a head for the ranks and 30,000 a head for the officers as granted by my lamented father Claudius. Thank you."

There was a wild burst of cheering and further cries of: "Long live the Emperor! Hail Caesar!" As I looked at their approving faces and the drawn swords gleaming in salute I felt a strange exaltation which brought tears to my eyes. Large-scale admiration is weakening. By the time I reached the litter I was shaking with emotion.

We were meant to visit the Senate House next but I began to feel faint and my mother said I should eat first. She did not want the embarrassment of a new emperor collapsing before the Senate assembly. My stomach was still sick with nerves. A

111

slave served me chicken and vegetables with fruit and wine mixed with honey but I could only eat half; even the wine brought nausea. I wanted to sleep.

This time I was taken in a litter with the curtains drawn back so that the people could see. My mother did not come; women are not allowed to attend Senate assemblies. We went along the Clivus Victoriae which runs the length of the hill crest where the pillared fronts of rich men's houses face the Forum, then down the road which leads out near the Temple of Saturn. Its marble beamed in the sun which had emerged as if to greet me. The Forum square was bursting with people. They sprawled over the steps of the temples and spilled out from the law courts and the Basilica; I even saw someone perched on the round roof of Vesta's temple. I looked straight ahead, not wishing to meet their stare. There was no cheering from them only a low deep muttering like the sea before a storm.

As they carried me past the Rostra trumpets broke silver-clear on the waiting air and there was the portico of the Senate House and the façade crowned with its shining tympanum; beyond the pillars the great bronze doors swung slowly open. I could see the embossed design, stars and leaves, and as they faded from sight and the dark hall unfolded behind I felt as if I were being swallowed up. Since last night everything had become vast. Walls were further from me, floors wider, roofs higher, trees leapt to touch the clouds and roads stretched forever; only people were tiny, crawling like the flies which I could see on the huge bronze door. They must have been crushed when the door swung against the wall.

Inside the Senate I dismounted and faced five hundred senators who were on their feet, cheering and clapping; it was almost a full assembly I stared at the ground, embarrassed, but at last I had to take the floor and look at them straight. The speech I must say blurred on my tongue. Seneca stood up and said: "Gentlemen of the Senate, I present to you Tiberius Claudius Nero whom you are asked to accept as Emperor, remembering his noble lineage and the virtues of his great-great grandfather Augustus ..."

112

While he talked I watched their faces. They already approved me from my previous speeches but a boy trying out his oratorial powers is very different from a boy claiming the Purple. I thought they would laugh in my face. Seneca's voice dragged on and my heart sank down and down as I visualised my own absurdity.

"... and so I present to you Tiberius Claudius Nero Drusus Germanicus."

More clapping; Seneca hissed: "Go on," and I rose bewildered from my seat. The pretentious speech I was supposed to say sank back in my throat; all I could think of was my youth, my immaturity, my complete lack of political knowledge apart from what I had learned parrot-fashion from Cicero or Plato. I began: "Gentlemen of the Senate, I am very young. I beg you to excuse my inexperience and foolishness..." and suddenly they were cheering again, this time really meaning it. I saw now that previously it had been forced. "If you accept me as emperor," I went on, choosing the words carefully, "please be patient with me; I know little except that Rome's greatness must be sustained and Roman virtues upheld by whoever sits on the throne, that the gods support a merciful monarch—" (That was Seneca.) "—and that whatever I do must be for Rome's good, not mine." I was confident now, the words coming easily. I knew my part in the play but this time I had written it, not Seneca. I ended: "If you place the laurel wreath on my head I swear before Jove that I will rule as my great-great-grandfather did, with peace and justice and in honour before the gods."

This time there were no restraints. I sat down, dazed by the noise. Then a leading senator, benevolent and grey-haired, stood up and said: "I know I speak for all my colleagues when I say that this House will instantly pass a decree to authorise your accession and that we admire your youthful spirit of honesty and integrity." There were murmurs of "Hear, hear," and someone said: "Look at him; it could be Augustus again." "May the gods bless your reign," said the leading senator. "Hail Caesar!" The chamber echoed as they all rose, crying: "Hail Caesar!" and I looked at the rows of raised hands in a

113

single salute, thinking that the gods had honoured me beyond my merits.

Another senator stood up and said: "I suggest that, despite his youth, we bestow on our new Emperor the title of Father of the Country as it was held by his esteemed and greatly mourned father."

I stared in amazement. It seemed they were flying higher and higher; any moment they would suggest divine honours. I did not know whether to refuse and perhaps offend them or accept and seem arrogant, then Seneca poked me and said softly: "Refuse; it's too much." I thanked them politely and said I was honoured but that my youth bade me turn their offer down. This pleased them more than any acceptance; they saw a modesty which would not allow the insane excesses of Caligula or the injustice of Tiberius.

From here I went to the Rostra and faced my people. The sun glinted on its decorations, the beaks of ships captured at Antium, and I looked out to the massed faces, Rome personified in her people and seeking a new captain for the ship. I thought of my vow and of the god's quiet face. They were mine to guide, to feed, clothe and teach, to protect from war and famine and give my life for if need be. I looked and in the square I saw my responsibility.

I cried: "People of Rome, the Senate has just authorised my accession but I want you to know that I will not take up the laurel wreath if you do not support me. I can only say that I will serve you faithfully and show you justice, honour, peace, as my great-great-grandfather did, that no slave will be too mean to escape my attention and no crime too great to avoid my pardon. Your good will be my good. To you I say this and from the gods I ask guidance; our noble countryman Cicero said Rome owed her greatness to her honour of the gods and I can do no better than echo him."

I stopped, breathing quickly, and a mighty roar struck my face like a blow; it was the crowd cheering and shouting. I thought their hearts would burst. I heard the repeated cry: "Hail Caesar!" to which I was now used but here in the political heart of the city from the people I would rule it had a greater power. The Guards and the Senate had been a formality. This was genuine emotion, a realistic contact between ruler and ruled. All Rome was here, patrician men and women in fine clothes, artisans and shopkeepers with their calling in their face, professional men, doctors and lawyers; there were slaves and freedmen, beggars and millionaires, painted prostitutes and graceful actors. And there were children, laughing and chattering like monkeys or watching wide-eyed and solemn. My people, held in my hand as the gods held me, the great pyramid of which I was the top. I seemed lifted beyond myself, raised up till my head touched heaven; I was colossal, bigger than the huge statue of Jupiter on the Capitol who reaches the Temple roof; and the faces below dwindled to dots while their cheers beat upwards like a surf up a cliffside. The weeping child in the stable had come into his own.

When I got into the litter my head rang and my eyes saw far and clear and bright. I still trembled with a god-like ecstasy. Seneca said sourly: "What happened to my speech?" I said: "I forgot it." He annoyed me, breaking into my vision. I remember nothing more till we reached the palace again and there was my mother at the gates, waiting. Immediately I shrank; I was a child again. I went to her and kissed her hand, a dutiful son, and she said: "I'm very pleased with you, Lucius." I flushed at her praise. She said: "I could see you down on the Rostra. Your hair was like fire; it pleased them. They see Augustus and Germanicus again."

Uneasiness moved like a shape on the horizon; two men so great and I must try and be like them.

An officer of the Guard presented himself with a salute and said: "Sire, may I know the password for tonight."

This fooled me; then I looked at my mother, tall and beautiful in the coming dusk, and I thought of how she had supported me today. Without her I should have hidden in the Palatine woods. Besides, I knew what would please her.

"The password," I said, "is The Best of Mothers."

I was weary beyond the cure of sleep. As I entered the palace the guard saluted and said: "Hail Caesar," and suddenly it was as if everything had been a dream and now I was awake. I was emperor. There was no one above me except the gods, no hand except mine to control this huge ship. All day some shield had stood between me and reality. Now it was gone and I felt unbearably weak. I said: "I'm afraid." The corridor was blue with twilight and the whisper magnified along the arches. "Of what?" said my mother.

"Power," I replied.

"A foolish attitude," she said sharply. "Power is only a burden on the weak man. I will not let you be weak, Nero."

I had forgotten she despised fear. But for her it was easy; she never visualised dreadful possibilities, a moment's slip or an insoluble problem. To her all problems were disposable.

Suddenly Otho appeared; he had obviously been waiting for me. In the shadow he looked different, more serious and distant. He saluted me, then said: "Sire..." and went down on his knees. It shocked me like a rebuff. I said: "No, for heaven's sake, Otho, get up." I called him Otho because he thought Marcus a dull name. "I'm no different."

"You are the emperor," said my mother.

She sounded cold. She had never liked Otho but then I don't believe she liked any of my friends; they could all sap her influence.

"I'm tired, mother," I said. "I'm going to the bath and then to bed."

She saw I wanted to be alone but did not object. Her part was done, anyway. When she had gone Otho said: "How do you feel?"

"Tired," I said and laughed. "That was true for once." I had often protested tiredness when my mother was demanding. "It was like a dream," I went on, "that began last night while I was asleep and never finished. Now I'm awake and it's hard."

"Hard?" He looked puzzled. "My dear Nero, you have what men would kill their own mothers for and you say it's *hard*? Why, it's all a marvellous game. You can do what you like now and no one to say no."

"I'm responsible to the people," I objected, "and to the gods. It's not easy."

"Responsible?" He laughed. "By Hercules, look at Caligula. He did what he pleased and that was that. Who stopped him?"

"There is my mother," I said.

"Oh yes, your mother." He looked serious. "Nero, how in heaven did you land yourself with such a woman?"

I started laughing and he slapped my shoulder, saying: "There you are! It's all a joke. Nothing in this whole stupid world is as serious as you would think. By heaven, Nero . . ." He had the expression he adopted for telling funny stories. "I shall have to mind myself now. No more dirty jokes or dancing girls. You can have my head off if you feel like it. Do you think I can reform at my time of life?"

"Your neck, dear Otho," I said with a mock bow, "is too tough for a Praetorian sword to slice through so consider yourself safe. And if you dare to reform I'll have you banished."

He roared with laughter, flung his arm round my neck and said I should be the best emperor since divine Augustus. Then I went for my bath. He worked on me like wine, dissolving a sense of dread or heavy responsibility; he was too easy-going to see anything serious. We should all go mad without people like him.

The bath was cold; I had sweated, so I could not endure heat. The bath itself was edged in bright blue and purple marble from Africa and Phrygia and water gushed from the gaping mouths of silver satyrs at two corners. The floor carried a mosaic of Neptune whipping his seahorses. When I floated and looked to one side I could just see his flowing beard and fierce eye; he seemed to disapprove of me. The slave scraped me down with curved bone and waited while I swam from one side to the other. It was a wide bath and gave you exercise. All the day's tension flowed into the water and I relaxed; odd that the water which drowns can also restore. The slave rubbed me down with a curved bone and waited while I swam from one I imagined he was more careful than usual. At one point he accidently dug me with his nails and looked terrified but I said: "Why are you frightened? It was an accident." His relief made me smile.

I slept till ten o'clock next morning, a disgraceful excess, but

117

no one woke me. I learned later that Xenophon had said I would need it. They were all easy with me, pitying my youth, except for my mother who said an emperor worked for his living. Within a day she had me learning Seneca's funeral elegy for my father.

Imperial funerals are long and boring. I only endured it patiently because it was his honour, little enough return for a life of such disillusion. He lay in state in the great atrium of the palace, dressed in his purple toga and golden laurel wreath. The undertakers had done their work well; he looked sleeping apart from the yellowishness of his skin. All the self-pity and misery had gone, leaving his face smoothed out and peaceful. I looked at him and said quietly: "Mother, what did he die of?"

"His heart failed," she said. "Don't talk now."

His funeral pyre was four-tiered, covered with gold-braided carpets of scarlet and purple and paintings of his life and achievements between each tier except for the lowest which carried a relief of his British campaigns. The scent on him filled the atrium. The mourners filed past and laid their gifts on the pyre, flowers, heaped incense in alabaster jars, and silver cups and statues but not gold which cannot be buried by law, even for an emperor. I gave him a garnet ring which I prized. A real sacrifice would have been my snake bracelet but my mother would never have allowed it. Britannicus and Octavia were pale but even in grief they clung to their dignity; it was the last thing left.

Passienus' funeral procession was nothing compared to this. Before the pyre had left the palace the lictors leading us had reached the Forum. I could not count the actors who wore his ancestors' masks. They included Aeneas, founder of the Julians, Romulus and the Sabine nobles, all the old Latin kings of Alba and Clausus who founded the Claudii. It was my family lineage come to life and made me proud. Because of his age they had trumpets, not flutes, which blasted my ears and suggested a race more than a funeral. The whole senate were present and the consuls as well as the priests of the four religious colleges followed by the Pontifex Maximus, Rome's high priest. The statues of the gods were crowned with mourning cypress. Behind everything rumbled the pyre on its cart, drawn by white horses and lurching so with its own weight that I thought it would tumble. The Senate had voted him divine honours so it was fitting that he should leave us like a god. In the Forum square the crowds stood silent, waiting for the elegy. As I mounted the Rostra I saw my mother weeping and wondered why grief had taken so long to reach the surface.

Seneca's speech was pure flattery from beginning to end. I spoke on my father's ancient lineage, the consulships and triumphs of his ancestors, his historical knowledge and literary achievements. I thought it only right. People had seen him as a fool, not knowing how his mind had struggled to be thoughtful and learned against such odds. Seneca's aim had not been that; I knew he had never liked Claudius. But I tried to make the praises sound genuine by the emotion in my voice. The crowd listened politely. Then I mentioned his "wisdom and foresight" and realised Seneca had gone too far; my audience started tittering. I heard someone say: "Then why didn't he see what was coming to him, poor old fool?" I felt enraged. Seneca looked satisfied like a man fed on peacock; I could have struck him. When I saw Britannicus' eyes I knew he thought the mockery was mine.

They burned him in an open part near the Forum. He went up with a brilliant flare and fountain of sparks which turned the buildings red, the flames leaping high as columns. My mother began sobbing openly and the crowd looked sympathetic. To them she was still Germanicus' daughter, noble and handsome, a part of the hero they had lost. Octavia wept quietly behind her veil but Britannicus never moved. I did not know whether it was coldness or stoicism, as Seneca advocated, bearing pain and pleasure with an equal mind. I fancy it was his wretched arrogance. You lose aristocratic dignity with outward emotion. Even I who never loved him as a son should felt tears prick my eyes. It was not only his death but my final isolation, the transference of power which puts a man apart from all others. As I watched the flames surge upwards I knew that it was done. He had gone and now there was only me.

119

Chapter Seven

"A monarch," said Seneca, "has more need of virtuous living than other mortals because he is the gods' vicar on earth."

"Vicar?" I said.

"Substitute, my child," he said in a patronising voice. "You exercise supreme power in place of the gods who are in Olympus and cannot rule us in person."

"But sometimes they have come to earth," I said. "Or is that just a tale?"

He looked shocked. "Are you asking if the gods are myth, Nero?"

"I've sometimes wondered," I said. "Can we prove they exist? Tell me something that proves they do?"

It was curiosity more than genuine disbelief but he saw it as rebellion. He had a remarkable capacity for being shocked, either that or it was a performance for my benefit. I did not always trust him.

"Tradition insists they do," he said. "And Jupiter Fulgur sends us thunderbolts to remind us of his existence. Why do you think places struck by lightning are sacred?"

"They come from the sky," I insisted. "That's all we know. It might not be Jupiter at all."

I had cornered him. He said briskly: "Nonsense, Nero. If you don't mind we will abandon the subject." He was not quite honest that way. When questions defeated him he withdrew like an inefficient general.

"Just tell me one thing," I said. "If a god came to earth what would he look like?"

"A man," he said, "if he chose to take that form. Only

120

something would tell us he was not an ordinary man. If he were a swan or a bull identification might be more difficult."

I did not tell him that I found this hard to accept. When you are little it excites your imagination to think of Jupiter as a bull or a shower of gold, seeking the mortal woman he fancies; at sixteen a mind used to solid realities begins to find cracks in the whole thing.

I said: "When I think of the gods they are far away and their features are hard to recognise. Sometimes I have felt them near me and sometimes nothing at all, only a void."

"We all experience this," he answered. "It is a feature of the human condition that when we are happy or in good fortune the gods seem at our shoulder but when we suffer illness or poverty or loss of a loved one they might be a million paces away." He was quiet for a moment, fingering his beard, then he said: "When I was exiled to Corsica by your late father I felt the gods had deserted me. It is a brave mind which thinks they still watch over us in such circumstances."

There was silence again. He was beginning to reveal himself, a process he found painful because, I think, there were discrepancies between his outward manner and philosophy and inward emotions. Stoicism is easy to talk about but hard to practise.

"Seneca, did I do well yesterday?" I asked suddenly.

"Why, yes," he said, his face lightening. "The Senate felt themselves back in the time of Augustus. A speech which outlines a policy of continuous co-operation with the Senate and promises to keep the imperial household separate from the state insofar as justice is concerned would naturally please the Conscript Fathers who have seen too much private tyranny; promising to restore the Senate's ancient functions was a masterstroke, if I may praise my own work. It is the greatest compliment that they should have decided to engrave the speech on a silver tablet and read it every time a consul assumes office. It shows that they see your policy as a true basis for government."

I said: "It was good of them. I'm so young. It would have been absurd to erect gold and silver statues of me as they wanted or to make the year start in December and upset the whole calendar just because it's my birthday. When I'm fifty and have proved myself they can do that."

"Modesty becomes you, Nero," said my tutor, smiling. "You possess a rare distinction, almost unknown in rulers, and that is innocence. It will take you far. The people love you for that and because they know it is genuine, not a pose. The mask of goodness slips quickly to show true character."

I looked at him and said: "Do you think I will make a good emperor?"

"Only the gods know that," he replied, avoiding the issue again. "But one thing is sure. You have an excellent start."

A few days after my father's funeral I asked to see Britannicus. He came in reluctantly like a dog expecting to be whipped, his eyes showing what he really thought even as he saluted me. He was thirteen now and more like Messalina than ever. It was strange to see such aristocratic pride and dignity imposed on her features, she who never had any dignity at all.

I said: "Britannicus, I never expressed my sympathy for your father's death. Will you accept it now?"

"My father?" he said.

I could see he was going to follow Octavia. "*Your* father," I repeated. "I was only an adopted son."

"Is that why you found it hard to show grief at his funeral?" he said coldly.

I felt exasperated. Anything you said he would twist back to fit his own sense of resentment.

"I grieved as much as you," I retorted. "Though I never saw you weep."

"In public it's undignified," he said. "I am a Roman."

"What do you think I am?" I shouted, losing patience. "A barbarian from that flea-bitten island you're named after?"

He said nothing. Insults struck him harmlessly simply because he would never react. I had no way of breaking him down.

"Britannicus, listen," I said, almost pleading. "Your father asked me to be friends with you; it was the last thing he said to me the night before he died. Can't you honour that wish and forget how we quarrelled?"

"I don't believe you," he said.

I looked at him blankly. This was entirely unexpected; I had never imagined he thought me a liar.

"My father would never ask such a thing," he went on loftily. "He knew you for what you were and wanted to send me away to protect me from you. Whose idea was it? Your mother's, I suppose. She's clever enough to see that the true heir to the throne will not stay in obscurity very long; friends will rally to his cause. I have supporters, you know." He was almost obnoxiously confident. "Did you think you could stop it by binding me to you in friendship? I'm not blind, Lucius Ahenobarbus."

I did not think long enough to see that this was months of miserable resentment exacting its fee, nor did I remember myself in a similarly inferior position. I stood up and said: "Get out!" For a moment he stood his ground and I yelled: "Are you going or do I call the guard?" He bowed with the most insulting manner and left; from the way he carried himself it might have been Octavia. I wondered how such a graceless slut as Messalina could produce such blatantly snobbish offspring.

That was the last time I tried friendship. I avoided Britannicus as far as possible and gave orders that Octavia should live apart in a specially provided part of the palace; no longer was the room next to mine occupied. She never came to meals with me and only accompanied me at official functions for appearances' sake. It was like losing a weight from my back no longer to see that pale, suffering face reproaching me with injustice and unfulfilled desire. I also ordered that Britannicus should never visit her. They frightened me; I did not want them fanning mutual hatred which might lead to some sort of conspiracy. My mother never mentioned it. I knew then that my marriage had been purely utilitarian, intended to facilitate my accession. Had there been any other way out I should have taken it. I disliked feuds.

Imperial duties were not so crushing as I had imagined. I was only required to attend to state matters for one or two hours a day when I had to sign documents including criminal sentences. This was Burrus' task. He always pushed them at me in a terrifying pile, expecting me to sign automatically but I made it a rule to read each one. I feared some injustice otherwise. Sometimes I refused my signature on the grounds that the sentence was too severe, for example death for a slave who had run from a cruel master or a flogging for a starving child who had stolen. Burrus used to raise his eyes to heaven and look resigned. He was a military man through to the bone, raised in the idea of toughness for the criminal and no mercy; all was black and white with nothing in between. I tried to explain that someone starving or beaten every day was not responsible for their actions. "If I were starving," I said, "I should steal and so should I flee if I were treated cruelly. You would, too, Burrus, if it happened that way." He looked severe and said a Praetorian never fled.

"Seneca, didn't you say that clemency enhances a ruler?" I demanded.

"Of course, my prince." He looked pleased like a trainer finally seeing the horse run right. "In an emperor who possesses unlimited power yet chooses to be restrained in punishment it is the brightest virtue, shining like a star to illuminate other mortals." He was becoming pedantic, always a result of his enthusiasm. I should have known better than to start him off. "Some say," he continued, "that mercy is a prop for villains but that is narrow-minded. Medicine only functions amongst sick men yet is admired by the healthy; so should just men respect clemency."

It might have been a lecture. "Yes," I said hastily. "Yes, I know. That's why I won't have a child flogged."

Burrus retired defeated. But a few days later he brought me the death sentence for two bandits who had been terrorising travellers in the hill district outside Rome; they had killed as well as stolen. It was the first death sentence I had been asked to sign. I looked at it with my stylus poised and thought how one rush of ink would thrust them into oblivion. I said: "How will they die?"

"The arena probably," Burrus said.

I imagined it, the hot air and the dust, the cruel implacability of the crowd; a moment to realise what was coming and then the starving lions or the fight to the death where only luck plays judge. I remembered the naval battle at Lake Fucine. I put down the pen and said: "I can't do it."

He looked alarmed. "Come now, sire, it's necessary. They are dangerous men."

"Why must it be the arena; why not a quick beheading?"

"Sire, the arena must be manned. How do the games function otherwise; and what happens to an emperor who provides no games for his people?"

"I know that," I said.

Cut off popular entertainment and I would offer my own neck for the sword. It was like an unfair bargain; their heads for mine. I said, thinking: "If the people were not so poverty-stricken they would not bother so much about free entertainment. Burrus, I wish I could give them all enough money to live on."

"An impossible task, sire," he said. "Now, if you please, the order for execution . . ."

I saw he was immovable. Men like that do not possess sensitivity. I picked up the pen and said bitterly: "I wish I had never learned to write."

He took it away, signed and sealed, and for the next week I dreamed of their deaths. The thought of blood sickened me; I wondered sometimes how I could have watched the Fucine battle and thought it fun. At these times we are not ourselves. After that I grew used to signing death warrants and soon I could even see it as a mere piece of paper and nothing more. Familiarity hardens you.

Once this was done my day was more or less free except for when I granted audiences, received ambassadors or acted as supreme judge which I disliked, not having a legal mind; besides, it took me from my singing and poetry. A week after my accession I heard that Terpnus, the most famous living citharoedus and singer, was in Rome. He had been known to keep an audience entranced for four hours at a time. Some people said he was Apollo come to life; others, less extreme,

125

maintained Apollo had filled him with his own genius so that we should know what heaven is like.

I sent for him and he came dressed in his long blue robe which sparkled gold stars twined with leaves. I sat at one end of the atrium between the columns of honey-coloured alabaster and he stood at the other, lost in shadow.

I said: "Sing."

As he raised his hands to the cithara the flowing sleeves fell back to show his thin wrists, delicate as porcelain. He plucked the strings with his hands, not with the little wand which is normally used for accompanying singers; it proved his skill. The cithara is so hard to play that to concentrate on that as well as singing is complex indeed. He wore a beard like an ancient bard but trimmed to a point, not tangled like Seneca's. His eyes were brown and mournful; they only took life when he sang.

I have never heard such a voice before or since. It filled that great atrium, rising to the domed ceiling and echoing from wall to wall as though existing of itself instead of coming from his mouth. It made me think of wind and sky and drumming rain, water rushing from beaten rock and moonlight silver on a swelling sea. Fascinated, I left my seat and moved nearer, leaning on the cool columns. Then I ceased to hear only the music and began to absorb the words; it was Homer's elegy on the death of Hector, a piece not normally sung because it is more recitative but he made of it a song for the gods. I could see Achilles and Hector face each other and battle till Hector fell bright in his own blood, then the humiliation: his body dragged in the dust round the walls of Troy. The mourning dirge brought tears to my eyes. I watched him raise himself on his toes, carried with the music, and thought how fine a thing it must be to possess that genius. Emperor or not I was dissatisfied.

The song ceased; the last notes dissolved in echoing space. I clapped loudly, the sound clattering in that great hall, and he bowed, then stood waiting, a perfect gentleman. I said: "Thank you; the gods have blessed you with a great gift. You will be returning tomorrow."

126

He came not only the next day but the day after and the day after that, singing of Priam lamenting, Orestes raging, even Oedipus in horror at his incest, the piece Seneca had wished to keep from me. At the end of a week I asked him to help me.

"I should like to sing," I said. "In fact, I have already tried but my voice cracks and my fingers stumble on the strings. Can you advise me?"

He smiled and looked wise, knowing youthful ambition. "Sire, it is hard," he said. "In the beginning it is dull and exhausting for you must train your voice with constant exercise, trying to reach the highest notes without strain. I have known singers burst blood-vessels through straining too violently. Your throat must be healthy, your diet plain and moderate; excess food or drink finishes a voice. If you are enthusiastic you could sleep with a slab of lead on your chest for this strengthens the diaphragm. But perhaps for one so young . . ."

"Oh no," I said eagerly. "I don't mind."

"As for the cithara," he went on, "if you know the rudiments it is merely a question of laborious practice. And with your singing remember that your own emotions, properly utilised, will fill the song with meaning; you must *be* Priam mourning Troy, Orestes pursued by the Furies."

"For me it's hard," I said. "I'm young; I know nothing of these things."

He patted my shoulder kindly as if I were a pupil instead of emperor. "I know," he said. "But persevere, my child."

I went on a diet immediately. It was difficult to sit at table and see peacock and roast duck go by while I must feed on lettuce and cheese or honey, good for the throat; but he had hardened my purpose. I even adopted the slab of lead though it tended to interfere with my breathing and I could only keep it for half a night. I gargled, I avoided draughts; at one stage I took to emetics when I imagined I had eaten too much but then Xenophon said constant vomiting strained the chest and throat so I gave up. Soon I grew pale and thin and people

127

noticed; Otho kept asking if I was ill. Then my mother interfered.

"This nonsense must stop, Nero," she said. "Do you know what you look like?"

I shook my head, a defence more than the truth. She picked up a polished bronze hand-mirror from her dressing-table and thrust it into my hand. A face jumped at me, white and pinched with dark hollows round cheeks and eyes.

She said: "What will the people think if they see you like that, a Caesar who looks as if he might collapse at any moment?" I said nothing. She rushed on: "When you made your accession speech they saw you as Augustus and Germanicus combined because of your looks, your strength. Now you are like a strayed waif. They will either not recognise you at all or think you are near the underworld. You silly, silly child! Do you want to lose the empire?"

She looked really angry. I said in a strangled voice: "Seneca doesn't mind." It was an appeal to an authority apart from hers.

"Seneca!" She groaned and raised her hands. "Of course, Seneca doesn't mind. He sits in a philosophic dream all day and wouldn't notice if you burned the Capitol. Apart from which he fancies himself as holding the reins of government and the more concerned you are with your dieting and your singing the less you'll interfere."

I looked at her, beginning to feel hatred. She was cutting away at my one ambition, my frail hopes of attaining creative fulfilment; she did not see my dreams, my cherished desire to express myself in some form apart from politics or scholarship. All she saw was the clumsy shape of power, dwindling because of my thinness.

"You will stop, Nero," she said. Her voice was dangerous. "Sing all day if you like providing I don't have to listen but for Jove's sake *eat* like a human being and throw away that wretched slab of lead. And if I see you with another emetic I'll throw Xenophon to the lions."

She did not know what she was doing to me. Her contempt cut me; it seemed she could see no good in me, not even my

128

striving to perfect an art. I was still a silly child. I stood looking stupidly and she said: "Stop gaping. You would do better
to copy your great-great-grandfather and look intelligent."

I stopped my diet. I also abandoned the lead slab but instead of throwing it away I hid it in an alcove near the servants'
quarters. She watched me carefully at meals and to annoy her
I would eat from each plate but only a tiny bit; she could not
force me. I had vowed I would not talk to her ever again but
it became awkward at official occasions and when she addressed
me directly. Silence would have provoked a slap round the face.
Instead I adopted a cold attitude which I thought effective but
she ignored it. Oh, how clever she was, how damnably clever.
She had her foot on my neck and sheer terror prevented me from
wriggling out, *me*, imperial Caesar, lord of the world.

She was now thirty-eight but her beauty had not diminished;
maturity had deepened her looks. She was like a peach ripened
in the sun. She had a facial massage daily and bathed in milk
to keep her skin white which Otho and I made jokes about in
private; it was some retaliation. Her maids painted her with
the care of artists decorating a temple though not always; sometimes I heard a girl scream and next day you would see the
bruises or nail marks. She would not tolerate slackness in
anything.

She was sharply aware of her position. Strictly speaking she
was the dowager empress but everyone knew "The Empress"
referred to her and not Octavia. She had claimed the right of
sitting next to me at all official receptions and then she was
arrogant enough to demand that she attend Senate assemblies.
Of course, they refused. Any other woman would have admitted
defeat but not my mother. She told me I must summon the
Senate to the palace which I did in order to avoid trouble;
the senators assembled in the palace library surrounded by
busts of Plato, Socrates, and Cicero and there we held the
debates. I knew perfectly well my mother was in the next room,
only separated from us by a curtained doorway and listening
to every word.

This mania of hers led to embarrassing situations. On one
occasion Armenian ambassadors had come to ask my help in

a threatening war with Parthia and I was to receive them in solemn audience. The time came and my mother had not appeared; I was afraid to begin. I looked at Seneca and he said: "Your mother does not know this audience is to be held now. Start without her." I raised my eyebrows and he went on: "Do you want a foreign power to think us under the thumb of a woman?"

I restrained a smile, seated myself on the throne in the reception hall and ordered the ambassadors to be admitted. In they came, most deferential, bearing gifts of gold, jewels, and ornaments in exquisite ivory including a miniature palace studded with rubies. Their leader bowed and said: "Most gracious emperor, master of the world, we beg that you hear our petition for help against the Parthians who even now are preparing to destroy us. By ourselves we are weak but if—" then I looked up and saw my mother at the door.

She came forward, blazing, the hem of her scarlet palla rushing along the floor and her jewels winking angrily. I turned cold; the ambassadors looked round, mildly puzzled. I felt trapped. In a moment she would reach me, then all Jupiter's fury would break from the skies. Suddenly Seneca touched my shoulder and whispered: "Go forward and stop her; kiss her, hug her, do what you like but stop her."

I slid from my seat, rushed past the astonished ambassadors and met her full-tilt, flung my arms round her and kissed her effusively, saying: "Dearest mother, how nice of you to come." I think I half suffocated her. By the time she had breath to say anything Seneca was on his feet, announcing that I had not seen my mother for some time and would the embassy mind very much deferring the audience to another day? He emphasised family ties and mutual affection while I swallowed my laughter but the ambassadors were much impressed and withdrew graciously. This incident tied me closer to Seneca. I saw him now as an ally whom I could trust, a barrier against my mother's wrath like Passienus in my childhood.

At banquets I sat on the steps of her couch as I did when small; nothing had really changed, only the outward title of Caesar and the fact that she did not feed me before guests.

Otherwise our positions were the same, she in command, I obeying. The golden laurel wreath did not make me capable of defying her. One look from her eyes and I trembled like the poorest slave, shrinking inwardly as though before a whip. The one part of me where she had no power was in my poetic impulses. This was private creation, not a performance like singing. I could scribble for hours in my own apartments with no one any the wiser; at the same time I read Homer, Sappho, Ennius, and Virgil and tried to see how they had constructed their poems, what images they used, and how they made their ideas fit poetic rhythms. My favourite piece was Virgil's description of the sack of Troy from the *Aeneid*; it filled my mind with fire. I sometimes thought I would give my throne to write like that. Homer, of course, was fashionable amongst the scholars because he was Greek and to be capable of reading Greek was a social distinction. My favourite passage of his was from The *Odyssey* where the Sirens try to entice Odysseus and his ship to doom on the rocks. The more I read the more I realised how deficient I was. My rough copies were forests of alterations and crossings-out.

Strangely enough my mother did not forbid private dinner parties. She must have known I would become awkward if controlled to that extent. When she looked questioning I assured her we were very well-behaved and that the dancing girls left afterwards unmolested which was perfectly true; I did not answer for the time they were with us. Not that I ever touched them; I left that to Otho and company. He asked me sometimes if I fancied any of them and shrugged when I said I would rather not. He cannot have thought it was faithfulness to Octavia, knowing her enforced seclusion. It embarrassed me to see them with the girls so rather than have them think me foolish I looked the other way or pretended to be asleep.

One evening we got more drunk than usual. We were in one of the smaller tricliniums, a pretty room inlaid with snow-white Phoenician marble and painted with cupids in a vineyard. It was nearly midnight. The wine had been good, imported from Greece; the dancers had been pretty, the clowns amusing, and I was tired. The tables were scattered with half empty plates, the cores of fruit, and crushed garlands which gave off a sick-sweet smell; a girl's earring lay on the floor in a pool of wine. Some of my companions had fallen asleep already but I preferred the comfort of my bed. I yawned and said: "Goodnight, Otho," and got up to go but the wine had dulled me; I stumbled. He supported my arm and started laughing, saying: "You're drunk, Caesar. Shall I tell your mother?" I tried to hit him but missed and sat down again; this time he couldn't stop laughing.

"Come on," he said. "I'll support you to your room."

He called a slave with an oil lamp to precede us and we tottered up the corridor with linked arms, singing a bawdy song newly going the rounds. When we reached my bedroom I fell on the bed, hitting my shins on the carved leg. I swore and he laughed again and leaned helplessly against the wall.

"Your face..." he said. "It's like an apple; if you turn any redder you'll catch fire."

I looked up and there he was, just as bad himself, with his dinner garland slipping over one ear.

"And you..." I said, catching my breath with wine and laughter, "*you* look like a second-rate Bacchus who lost his Ariadne."

He came forward in mock disapproval, saying: "If your mother saw you now she would go up in smoke with rage. She's a se—severe *mora*list, your mother; why, she would whip your backside for this, Nero."

I swung out again with the flat of my hand but he caught both my wrists and held them tight; I could not move. His face was very near me, flushed and smiling. I saw how handsome he was even in drink. He had stopped laughing and my own laughter died; the room was still. His wreath had fallen off. I knew something had changed but I did not see what he meant to do. He moved suddenly, I fell back on the bed and he kicked over the lamp which rolled, spilling out its oil. We were in darkness.

I could see him lying still on the pillow, sweat spotting his forehead. The heavy beating of my heart slowed. There were

132

images in my mind, clear as poetic metaphors; the hand under my tunic in the barber's shop, my mother and Pallas, Octavia bedraggled in her wedding finery.

I said: "Otho?"

He reached out to touch me but I moved away and lay on my face.

"What is it?" he said, sitting up. "Are you ill?"

I said: "No." My voice was muffled.

"Then what is it?"

I looked at him and said: "What do you think?"

"Sweet Venus," he said. "Anyone would think I had tried to murder you." I did not answer. He leaned on one elbow and went on: "Why are you so odd? It's nothing, Nero; it's a game, that's all, like the dancing girls. Like eating and sleeping but over very much quicker."

"Is everything a game to you?" I said.

He looked taken aback. "My dear, what is this? Serious thinking? I thought Seneca had beaten that out of you."

Despite myself I laughed. It reassured him and he said, smiling: "You see; it's not a tragedy, after all." He ruffled my hair and said softly: "It wouldn't have happened without your face; it's the best thing your mother gave you."

I lay still, feeling strange and heavy, the cover twined round my legs; then I started trembling. He said: "I'll tell the slave to bring wine."

"No; I couldn't drink any more." My sight was blurred. "I should be ill. My mouth is sour."

"Water, then," he said and went to the door. I tried to stop him, thinking of slaves' gossip, but it was too late. My mind was not clear but I had an unreasonable sense of being different. He had touched something deep in me, hidden as an underground spring will be till it bursts into light. But when it comes does it ever stop flowing?

He touched my wrist and I jumped; he would never touch me again without this feeling of a fire. The slave coughed at the door; he took the water from him and poured me a cup; it shone blue in the rock crystal. I drank and drank, then slept with my head on his shoulder.

In the morning when he had gone I looked at my face in a mirror. There was a mark on my mouth where he had bitten me. I was afraid somehow of facing others, especially my mother; I thought her eyes would seek it out.

"Seneca," I said, "do I look any different?"

He looked at me, puzzled, and said: "No, my prince, I don't think so. You are perhaps a little fuller in the face since your mother stopped your diet but . . "

"I don't mean that," I said.

Strange that guilt should loosen your tongue. Wisdom would have been to say nothing but I had an urgent desire to confide in someone, to share experience. When I look back it seems odd that I chose Seneca, the severe Stoic. Somehow, I suppose, I knew that his morality was skin deep.

"I think," I said with an effort, "that I've lost my virtue."

I waited for anger or horror; instead I could see in his face avowed principles fighting with inward attitudes and a desire to please. I was still the Emperor.

"At your age," he said, "that isn't strange." The flatterer had won over the philosopher. "Who is the girl?"

"It wasn't a girl," I said.

"Ah." He stroked his beard and looked contemplative. "I think I know who. His father beat him for it when he was younger."

"Then it's wrong," I said, alarmed. "Have I done something dreadful?"

He coughed, took a few paces, then said: "No, not exactly. The Ancients give us a good example on that score; Plato considered such love admirable. On the other hand over-indulgence leads to general corruption and weakens a society's structure . . . like incest in Egypt who was once powerful and now is one of your provinces." He looked at my horrified face and laughed, saying: "My boy, youthful experiment is no crime." I saw he was back to tactful reassurance. "What moral senator or brave general can swear he never once engaged in such activities? Why even myself—" I gaped and he went on

134

hastily: "Many years ago when I was young like you. All the young are headstrong. Also, in your situation with a wife who does not please you some—shall we say—distraction is needed. No one would blame you. You even have a respectable tradition behind you; Julius Caesar was only a little older than you when he first entered into such a relationship with the King of Bithynia and some say that Augustus himself paid that price to Caesar for the latter's adoption of him."

I gaped again. One always thinks noble ancestors are perfect. I said: "Will you tell my mother?"

"You know I never tell your mother anything," he retorted. "Pretence of ignorance is the best defence."

"Would she be angry?" I asked.

"No doubt. Women see it as an insult. In her case she would object simply because her influence would be threatened. She nagged your father because he took a fancy to a pretty serving boy, saying he had dishonoured her womanhood and would make her the laughing stock of Rome. Women are so self-centred."

I said: "My father?"

There seemed no end to family revelation. He laughed again and patted my shoulder, saying: "Go away and forget it, Nero. Humanity is not so scrupulous as you think. A little wine or a little pleasure, what is the difference? Accept it equably and you will accept as easily trouble or deprivation when it comes."

I thought the argument rather forced but said nothing. He had not scolded me or moralised, yet I felt unsteady like a man poised over a chasm. He had not pushed me on to one side or the other.

My relationship with Otho grew closer, of course. He had bound himself to me in this mysterious way and I could not loosen the knot. One cup can start an appetite for wine. Sometimes he slept in my room and I thought the slaves must know and spread it about but if there was gossip it stayed from my ears. In the morning I would see his tumbled hair on the pillow like an indictment. But he was my friend, the best I had, and without him depression or anxiety or conflict with my mother

135

might have driven me to my knees. He was always there to turn the tide the other way.

Only a few weeks after my accession I became aware that Seneca and my mother were at odds over something. In public they were cold with each other, speaking like neighbours who have quarrelled but will not lose dignity before others; in private they shouted. Once I heard my mother call him a blind fool with his head in clouds of philosophy, unaware of political necessity. The air in the palace was all sparks; I thought one might start a fire. It made me uneasy. Otho said: "Leave them to it. What does it matter to us?" but then it was not his mother and tutor. Nor was he emperor. I longed for peace and quiet in which to sing and write poetry; some say art flourishes in a storm but for me the noise drowned inspiration.

When Seneca and Burrus asked to see me in private I knew affairs had reached a head. They looked set and serious; Seneca was pale and fidgeting, biting his nails. For a man professing Stoicism he seemed remarkably agitated.

"Nero," he said, "this is a grave matter—*very* grave. I hardly know how to put it to you."

A philosopher lost for words? Something cold touched my heart like the beginning of sickness. He began to pace, a sign of strain, his hands clasped behind his back. Burrus stood rigid, a soldier no matter what.

"When you came to the throne," said my tutor, "I visualised a new Augustan age, a Golden Age—a young emperor with no grudges or manias to poison his rule, a mind that I might mould into goodness, even greatness. Forgive my self-esteem but..." He shrugged. "All philosophers know that their ideas must rot unless they can be applied practically; that is why we seek to advise rulers—Aristotle with Alexander, Plato with Dionysos of Syracuse. I with you, humble as I am."

"I know that," I said, bewildered. "I'm grateful."

"But your mother," he said bluntly, "has destroyed where I sought to heal."

I stared; he turned away from me, distressed, saying: "Oh my poor child, how can I tell you? Innocence is so precious and so fragile; it withers at a touch."

136

I grew frightened. "Seneca, what is it? What has my mother done?"

He looked at me straight, gathering his courage for the final leap.

"She is a murderess," he said.

I started laughing. "Oh Seneca, such melodrama. Leave your dramatic metaphors. What has she really done?"

"Murdered," he repeated. "Murdered till her hands are deep in blood. Certain prominent men have died because she thinks them dangerous; Julius Silanus, pro-consul of Asia, because his brother was Octavia's first fiancé and he himself is descended from Augustus, therefore a possible claimant to the throne; Narcissus, your father's adviser whom she always hated and who knew her for what she was. She forced him to commit suicide, then burned certain letters he had from Claudius which were dangerous for her. The knight Julius Densus is awaiting trial because he showed attachment to Britannicus—the line is endless. And there are more waiting for the executioner."

I said: "It's malicious scandal." My voice sounded far away. "Why should people be dangerous to her, the empress?"

He looked at me pityingly as a doctor might, about to amputate.

"Poor Nero," he said. "You don't understand. Your mother murdered your father so that you could become emperor."

Chapter Eight

His face came and went in front of me, blurring white. Burrus stepped forward with his hand out as if to hold me up but I knocked him away.

"It's a malicious scandal," I repeated. My voice was wild and high, yet far, far away as though coming from a mountain peak. "It's scandal, lies. It's not true; it's not true!"

"It is true," Seneca said. His voice was hard. I could no longer be protected. "Think back, Nero," he said. "Think back. When your father died do you remember the mushroom he ate, the mushroom your mother offered him? It was full of poison."

"But she ate them, too," I said faintly.

"Not that one. The rest were harmless."

"But she was so upset; she went white when he fell ..."

"Your mother," he said heavily, "is a good actress. And stress will turn a face pale. Oh, it was a time of stress all right; she was in the process of forcibly transferring the empire from his hands to yours."

I said: "No."

"She had planned it for years," he went on, lost now in the rush of truth. "When Messalina died she saw her chance; it was a question of letting Claudius remain alive as long as he was useful, till he had made you his son and allowed you to adopt adult privileges. A few days before he died he had decided to send your mother away and declare Britannicus his heir, then she knew she must act."

"He knew the signs," I said. "Why did he do nothing?"

"Perhaps the signs convinced him he must die; I don't know. He was a tired man and death is easy for the weary and

138

disillusioned. She had overcome him always in life and she did at the end."

I said: "All for me?"

My head throbbed and my breath came wrong. I was still blurting out questions, looking for the loophole.

"For herself," he corrected. "Vicarious power, if you like. She knew her hold on you and intended to use it for pulling the reins of government. Women are never rulers, no, but they are wives and mothers."

This time my balance had gone. They dragged a chair forward and pushed me into it and Seneca sent a slave for wine. I could feel nothing; my stomach was cold and heavy as though I would vomit. I gripped the sides of the chair and stared at a decorated soffit over the door till I could pick out each feather in the cupid's wing.

"Burrus and I are not blameless," Seneca said. "We knew what she meant to do and even allied ourselves with her. Burrus influenced the Guard, I the Senate, encouraging them to think of you in terms of the next emperor, emphasising your merits, your youth . . . Jove, when I think of it!" He struck his forehead. "We thought we were preparing the way for a purified state; instead we have unleashed a female Caligula on mankind."

"Then the cheers . . ." I said brokenly. "The enthusiasm for me—it wasn't real."

"Oh yes, it was. When they saw you they needed no encouragement; you were a new Augustus to them, charming, youthful, and above all, innocent—no plots, hatreds, feuds. And how innocent you were, my child, how cruelly innocent."

I put my head in my hands. A hundred things burst out behind the pressure of my fingers; her white hand, so delicate, tracing my line of descent from Augustus, her voice running on nobility, honour, dignity, and the gods, when within she burned murder; her stricken face as Claudius died and then the eyes near me in the torchlight, tearless. Voices shouted in my head. *Tell your mother. She knows where to stick the knives,* and: *You will want to be the next emperor . . . one day your mother will get what she wants,* then Otho's drunken laughter: *Your mother is a se—severe moralist.*

139

I wanted to cry but could not. I remembered my father's tired face the night before he died; how she must have nagged and pushed and brow-beaten to get what she wanted, at least when her body failed to do it for her and I knew it had towards the end. And Pallas, too; plots need financing, so does loyalty in some quarters. Then it had begun that long ago when I first saw her with him in the Aventine villa.

The wine came. I drank it in sips, my hands shaking. Seneca said quietly: "I have been a fool. I was weak because I hated Claudius after he had exiled me—oh no, it's not easy even for a Stoic to live in drab exile amongst uneducated Corsicans who have never heard of Socrates. I suppose I wanted a good life again, wine and warmth and talk, but I persuaded myself I was building a new golden age, the perfect society with my protégé as figurehead. She said Claudius was old and foolish; his weakness had left Rome to drift like a rudderless boat. But can you kill for that? She was so merciless; he began to come round in the bedroom as though the poison had not worked and she made Xenophon put a feather smeared in poison down his throat."

I said: "Stop it! I don't want to hear any more."

I thought of the execution order I had not wanted to sign; how many had she signed simply by willing it? Only the gods can take life unless in war or under legal jurisdiction or when a man chooses his own death. This was the horror of it; a blatant arrogation of divine right, lives exchanged for power. I had seen her face when people bowed before her. I nearly laughed to think how I had seen her as incarnate of all virtue and nobility, a pillar of morality; my strong, beautiful mother whom I could admire even though I feared her.

I said: "No wonder she asked Xenophon if it was all right for me to see the body; I might have seen the poison in his face. Seneca, when I think of it—"

"It's better not to," he returned. "The gods torment a thinker. She was no fool; she knows poisons as a cook knows spices and picked one which would not discolour him. Imperial funerals are blatantly public."

Suddenly Burrus, silent all this time, stepped forward and

said: "Sire, I want you to know that though I abhor your mother's present behaviour I cannot turn against her entirely. She has been generous to me and always showed me consideration. Surely you see, sire, that as I owe my present position to her..."

"Yes," I said. "So do I. Seneca, what am I to do?"

"Nothing," he said, "unless you feel capable of charging her with it and facing the consequences."

"Sweet gods, no." I thought of her eyes and the deaths which had been conceived behind them. "Seneca, I'm trapped. She knows how I fear her even apart from the fact that she is a prop to the throne; if I knock her down I will fall. I sit here by *her* courtesy."

He said calmly: "Strictly speaking that is not true." He was back to analysis again, an intellectual even in crisis. "The populace are not in general aware that your father was murdered; they admire your mother, they love you. Gossip, even if true, rarely extends beyond the palace premises. Besides, a mere handful knew of the plot and most of their mouths are shut with loyalty. In other words, my prince, you are totally safe; nothing need change. Except—"

He had come to the exception, always the sting in the tail of a philosophic argument. I waited patiently; he was my only support.

"You cannot bring back the dead," he continued, "but you can save those already marked for the axe. Julius Densus and Senator Carrinas Celer are awaiting trial which, I need not tell you, will be a farce, and Plautus Lateranus has been expelled from the Senate merely for being one of Messalina's lovers. I've no doubt his head will roll before long."

"That's simple," I said, glad for a chance to make some reparation. "She will push the decrees arraigning them for trial in front of me, expecting me to sign without question. I will refuse. And Plautus shall have his seat restored to him. Oh Seneca, if I could raise the dead—"

"You would be divine," he interrupted briskly. "A hopeless wish, my prince. Be content with these excellent expressions of your mercy and commend your reign to the gods."

It was a grey November day with drizzle softening the air but I still went out on to the Palatine to the Temple of Apollo where I had made my vow. His statue shivered in the chill. This time I went into the temple, my head covered with my toga, and up the great inner sanctuary under an arched roof supported upon rows of Corinthian columns in Numidian marble which dripped stone leaves and flowers at the top. My great-great-grandfather had been generous to his patron god. I came up to the huge statue at the end, Apollo as thinker with his hand extended as if in friendship and his hair curled like a boy's; incense burned before him on a tripod. Someone had laid a garland at his feet and a gold wine chalice, some rich man's gift.

I stood before him with my palms upturned in the attitude of prayer, the incense filling my nostrils. The place was empty, even had anyone seen me I doubt if they would have known me for the Emperor with my hair covered like any humble suppliant. I thought of what she had done and of how Apollo goes in chase of murderers. It frightened me to stand before his pure all-seeing eyes, marked with innocent blood, for though I had been ignorant I had indulged in the results like a bandit who loots after killing. She had dragged me along with her. I had no will; I could not break free. Dear gods, how had she looked upon me; a mask of power which she could wear? While I was in the womb had she prayed to Juno, Lightbringer, that she might bear an emperor? I suppose had I been a girl she would have gone on until she had borne a male who would satisfy her power lust. No wonder I had no brothers or sisters. One child was enough and she had ways of preventing more.

My eyes smarted tears. The god's face grew blurred and distant. I thought: I never was a son to her, only an ambition, a dream of supremacy. No wonder I got no kisses; emperors have no need of them. She saved them for those who opened a path to the throne. I thought of Octavia and Britannicus whom I had wronged, of my adoptive father dying for a female whim, and of myself planted firmly at the top of the pyramid, its base littered with corpses; then I looked at the god and no longer saw hope or friendship. His marble eyes were blank. I tried to renew my vow, to say I should rule with honour despite my cruel accession, but the words died in my mouth. I thought: what kind of god mocks our good intentions? The echoing temple was cold; the space above his great, handsome head was a void, and the incense burned to nothingness.

She put the papers in front of me and said: "Your signature, please, Lucius. They are decrees of arraignment for trial."

She stood back waiting, so confident, my lovely mother with every hair in place, perfumed, painted, and elegant. She could have modelled for Venus.

My hands were damp; I shuffled the papers apart, took out the two relating to Carrinas and Densus and said: "I won't sign these."

Her eyes widened, nothing more. "Why not?" she said.

"The offences are negligible," I said, adopting my legal voice. "There is only circumstantial evidence against Carrinas, hardly that, in fact. The slaves *thought* they heard him express regret for my father's death and say bad times would come as a result; that isn't enough for a conviction of treason. Julius Densus merely expressed a private opinion, admiration for Britannicus. And another thing, mother—" I looked at her squarely though my heart went too fast. "Plautus Lateranus must resume his seat in the Senate. You can't expel a man simply because he made a fool of himself with Messalina."

"Why is this, Nero?" she said, looking cold. "Why do you doubt my judgement?"

"I don't doubt you," I replied, side-stepping conflict like Seneca. "I merely think our overworked lawyers don't need to bother with this sort of thing. Mother, they aren't crimes."

She said: "You are very foolish, Nero. These men are a danger to you; what may seem slight is often an indication of serious matters."

"I still won't sign them."

"No?"

She had caught me with her eyes and held me, unwilling. "No, mother," I said. "No." Her eyes were vast, deep, and unpredictable; I thought they might drag me down like Scylla's whirlpool in the Sicilian Straits but I stood my ground.

"Very well." She looked away; I had won. "You have the final authority."

She left me and the air was clear as though a storm had passed. I looked at the tumbled documents, and realised for the first time that her power had a limit.

In the days that followed I felt unbearably lonely. Knowledge is a sickness; an ignorant man may sleep quiet even in the midst of horrors. But when I wished Seneca had never told me I remembered that to walk blind may end in a trap. For distraction I turned to parties, singing, and poetry, and for affection to Otho, but here I found difficulties. Mostly he was good to me but at times he would go off with a girl and devote all his attention to her as if to make me jealous. The results were what he wanted; quite simply I could not do without him. He always came back apologetic; did I really think he had abandoned me? What, when I could have him burned or crucified? I'm a coward, dear Nero, he would say; and there we were, back in comradeship, the wine, the warm bedroom; it was all a marvellous game. Yet when he tormented me with a girl I wept into my pillow.

In one of his daring moods he suggested we go to the Circus in secret. My mother had not changed her ban on attending except on official occasions when my presence was needed. When I looked doubtful he said the fun was all in the risk; we should go in disguise, wrapped in cloaks, with a wig to cover my easily recognisable hair. It meant slipping out without anyone seeing and back again the same way. "Think of the horses," he said. "The thunder of hooves and wheels, the greens in the lead, no, the blues; it's neck and neck..." He convinced me. I got my barber to acquire a black wig from one of the best shops in Rome (can you imagine that old men are so vain as to cover their baldness in that way?) and off we went.

It amused me to mix unnoticed with my people, to share their talk and laughter, to listen to the bets being laid and the fights begin when supporters of different factions clashed.

Everyone came from near-starving beggars to noble patricians; the Games were free. I was shocked by some of the poor from the high slums which tower in Roman backstreets; children tottering on brittle-thin legs, open sores on arms and face, dirt and lice in hair which had never known water or a brush. These were the truly destitute who had not the energy to walk to the Baths and no money to pay for conveyance. Their smell made me feel ill. Yet they were mine, committed to me at the moment of accession as if the gods had pushed them aside, saying: They are yours; we are not interested. When I mentioned it to Otho he shrugged and said: "It's always been like that." Once I was home, under the same roof as my mother with the distraction of the races gone I began to think on these things; my heavy responsibility and shared guilt, the total isolation which I could only break for a short while at parties or in the Circus or at night with Otho. Awareness of poverty preyed on my mind. I suppose I had been foolish enough to think everyone lived like me, off gold plate. A slight shift in the stars and I might have been born in a backstreet slum while one of those starved children came to the throne. I wondered then if our fates were written irrevocably at the moment of birth; was I fixed to a pre-determined pattern or could I move out of it by will? Such thinking upset me. I already believed a god must have groaned when I was born. But then I met Acte.

I heard her screaming one day, a strange way to be introduced. You often hear slaves crying out in the palace especially from my mother's apartments but there I did not dare interfere; this came from my wife's bedroom. I knew Octavia's underhand cruelty. By the time I got there the screaming had become muffled sobbing. I tore back the curtain at the doorway and stood looking and there was the girl on the floor, her shoulders mottled with dark slashes; the whip hung from Octavia's hand. The room looked a wreck. The floor was a mess of spilled powder and paint, yet even in chaos the place was Octavia to the last inch, self-consciously feminine but subdued; it was not Messalina's boudoir.

I said: "What is this?"

"Get out!" said Octavia. "How dare you burst into my bedroom?"

"Madam," I said politely, "I have every right to go where I please in this palace but especially into my wife's bedroom. What has the girl done?"

"She's a lazy, disobedient slut," Octavia said. "What is it, Nero? Have you developed a pricking conscience?"

I saw isolation had not improved her. There was a thin, mean look in her face like a starved cat's; too late I realised what I had done to her. Then the girl moaned and my brief compassion died.

"Whatever she did," I said through set teeth, "this was not necessary, Octavia. Does such behaviour befit an empress?"

"Empress?" she said. *"Empress!* Who is empress in this stinking place. Not me; perhaps your mother or some whore you've dragged in to share your bed, but not me. Or would you prefer to confer the honour on Marcus Otho?"

I slapped her across the face and she fell against the bed. The maids were in a shivering huddle; I could see every word of this going round the palace next day and perhaps into the city. But I was Caesar; had Seneca not recommended mercy?

I touched the girl's shoulder and said gently: "Come along, get up. She won't hurt you any more."

She lifted her head and the fair hair tumbled back. I don't know what I thought when I looked at her; even tear-stained and marked with nails it was a face to make your blood run quick. The eyes were brown, unusual with light hair, and stared like a trapped fawn's. Her dress was torn and showed one breast. I blushed and covered myself by helping her up and saying to Octavia: "I'm taking her away. She can go to my mother or someone else here who is prepared to treat her well. And if you don't mend your manners, Octavia, you can do without maids altogether."

I thought that a fine threat. The girls looked admiring; odd how women like domination. The last I saw of Octavia was a face which reminded me horribly of Messalina, but a plain Messalina with brains. I suddenly realised that hatred supported by intelligence is deadly.

146

I took the girl to my room and sent for wine and a new dress; until it came I stared at her face like a gentleman. It was small and shaped delicate like one of those ivory miniatures so popular in Augustus' reign. She shivered and looked awed. In my rush of pity and kindness I had forgotten my status. Poor child, I had dragged her into the imperial bedroom without so much as a word of reassurance.

"It's all right," I said. "Don't look so scared. I shan't hurt you."

She smiled vaguely and rubbed away the tears; she seemed tiny, sitting in the middle of my great bed and sipping wine.

I said: "Why did my wife beat you?"

"The brush slipped when I was painting her eyelids," she said, "and it went into her eye. It was an accident, I never meant . . ."

"Of course, you didn't," I said. "Does she beat you often?"

"At her bad times she does but we try not to cry out because it makes her worse. Today she hurt me too much; I couldn't help—"

She flinched and I saw the bruises had darkened. I felt as if I had inflicted them, knowing that the "bad times" were frustrated desire for me. First Marcus, then Beryllus, then Claudius, now this child; all suffering for my sake and one losing his life that I might rise to greatness. Was it my destiny to stand aside and watch the blows strike others?

She said quietly: "What are you thinking about?"

"My life," I said, and I must have sounded bitter; she looked startled.

"A good life," she said. "You have always had everything, yes? Good food and clothes and a beautiful mother and now the throne—the gods have smiled on you."

"Do you think good living is everything?" I asked. "Or even a crown? And my mother! You don't know about my mother."

She looked bewildered. "My lord?"

She was like a child in her innocence, all idealism. Heaven was a silk dress, gold plate, and perfumed baths; and freedom. I had forgotten her slavery.

147

"Tell me," I said. "What sort of woman do you think my mother is?"

"Noble," she said. "Noble and dignified and brave; truly Germanicus' daughter. And so beautiful. Oh, to have her beauty—"

I looked at her, so fair and slight and pretty, and thought how different she was from my strong, black-haired mother. Then I said: "You are beautiful."

She flushed and looked down, pleating her dress between her fingers.

"No, my lord," she said. "I'm not."

Her fingers were shaking and I saw how her mind ran. "No," I said. "No, my poor little girl, I don't mean that. It's a compliment. Good heavens, even an emperor must state facts sometimes." Then she smiled. I said: "There you are, I'm quite human, you see, not a god like Augustus or Caesar. What did you expect? Incense and a clap of thunder?" I had adopted Otho's manner, trying to ease her. It worked. She actually laughed and I said: "Now tell me, what is your name, how old are you?"

"My name is Acte," she said. "I'm sixteen. When I was thirteen I was sold into slavery because my parents had died and there was nothing for me. I didn't mind when they took me to the slave market. We were poor anyway; I never knew my father, and my mother . . ." She looked at me, then away. "My mother worked in a brothel; she was killed in a drunken brawl."

It shocked me. Like a man who looks only on the outside I had imagined her unworldly and childish; her face did not show the marks of brutality.

"Where are you from?" I asked.

Her Latin had a rhythmic, lilting quality. I could not place the accent.

"Corinth," she said. "But I was born in Antioch."

Of course; fancy not recognising a Greek, I, who had Greek tutors. She must have bewitched me.

"With that hair you look Hellene," I remarked.

"My mother was Hellene but half my blood is Syrian."

148

"Then you are Hellene in your hair and Syrian in your eyes," I said, laughing.

"Yes," she said. "I am a mixture all ways. My father may have been part Jewish. My mother said he spoke of the Promised Land and the Messiah but he did not practise the old religion."

"Jews!" I said. "Oh Acte. Jerusalem is more nuisance than the rest of the Empire put together. You have troublesome blood."

"Only a little drop," she protested. "I'm really very good."

She could take a joke. It pleased me to see her become lively and lose the hunted expression Octavia had given her. But then she flinched again. I sent for Xenophon and he rubbed her back with ointment and prescribed hot baths for the next few days. I told her to make use of mine. She objected, saying I was too good; she would be a burden on me. Besides I was emperor. "I am a slave," she said. "We are a different race from yours." I said: "Nonsense," and added that as emperor I had the right to order her to take a bath. That brought out her sense of humour. She retreated, laughing, carrying all the perfumes and towels I had ordered for her; when she came back, scented and shining, maids were waiting to comb out her magnificent hair and paint her charming face. I had said: "Not too much paint. Paint is for hiding blemishes." I remembered my mother's technique. And after all this I invited her to dinner.

I suppose I knew what had happened to me but I was hiding it under a flurry of activities, planning a new surprise for her when the last one was gone. We ate alone. I sent word to my mother that I felt ill and wheedled Xenophon into spinning a tale about a chill on the stomach so while the court dined in noise and fuss in the great triclinium I reclined beside her in the little place where I normally held my select dinner parties. I don't remember what we ate or drank; I hardly remember what I said. They had curled up her hair on top and let it hang like polished gold either side of her neck. Her eyes stared at me in wonder, shaded with fine saffron till they seemed to eat her face; her mouth reminded me of a rose. She wore the most

149

fashionable dress, low-cut to show the line of her breasts. The designer had no thought for my peace of mind.

I remember she was graceful, talkative, and entertaining, thanking me for my gifts, the gold bangle and necklace of gold grapes and roses she wore, and laughing when I fed her real grapes from a fluted silver bowl. Near midnight she looked at me sleepily and said: "Where am I to sleep tonight?" In any other woman it would have been an invitation but she had the straightforwardness of innocence like a child who sees nothing wrong.

"There is the room next to mine," I said, "which should be for my wife. It's empty."

She went scarlet. I said quickly: "I'm sorry. I mean it's not being used and you can have it, nothing more."

She protested again, saying she could not possibly; she was a slave. I said firmly: "You have given me more happiness in one evening than Octavia has in two years. It's yours by right."

We went giggling up the corridor on tiptoe, wishing to avoid everyone; she hid her eyes from the torchlight, saying she liked the dark. When we got there she looked quietly into the room and stood staring.

"Was it your mother's once?" she asked.

I slept now in the imperial apartments which had been my father's and thought nothing of it till Seneca's revelation; since then I had not slept for bad dreams. I said: "Yes; why?"

"It frightens me to think of sleeping where she did."

She had become thoughtful; I saw she had sensitivity which must not be bruised. "There are no ghosts there," I said. "It's my room which is haunted."

"Truly?" She looked at me, scared.

"Only for me," I said. "You can sleep with no worries."

"Oh yes," she said. "Yes. You have been so good to me. This has been the happiest day of my life."

I could not sleep. She had entered my blood as no other girl had ever done. My mother had made me cautious of women; I thought them strange, dominating, dangerously unpredictable. She was none of these things, only gentle and sweet; a pretty child who had known unhappiness and cruelty yet was not embittered. Knowledge of her childhood loneliness drew me to her more. She would understand. I lay awake for hours in the deadly silence of that room with only dark shadows and memories for company. Once my adoptive father had lain here and got up to enter that curtained doorway and stand by the bed where my mother lay. The image made me hot. I threw aside the covers and went to the curtain; looking through I could just see her bright hair spread on the pillow and one arm flung out.

I slipped through on tiptoe, meaning only to stand and drink in her face as she slept, hoping it would quieten me. But she was not asleep. She smiled at me like a child waking to see its parent. For a moment I imagined my mother there with her bare breasts as when I saw her with Pallas but then it faded; the hair was fair, not black, the eyes brown. There were no ghosts here.

I said: "Acte?"

"I knew you would come," she said. "I couldn't sleep."

The lamp was still burning; she had taken my talk of ghosts seriously. It shone on the cover patterned with silver birds and threw up little pools of darkness on the legs of her bed, gryphon carved in ivory. Venus stretched on the wall with flowers and cupids, amorous in the dusk. I said: "Is the bed not comfortable?" My voice cracked as always with nerves.

"Oh yes." She stretched and kicked out her legs. "It's the best bed I ever slept in. But then it belongs to an empress."

"Yes," I said. "Yes; oh Acte—"

I was down on my knees by that shining hair and her arms were round my neck and she was shaking so that the bed trembled, her breath coming with little sighs. She said: "I couldn't bear to think—You are Caesar, all-powerful, and I am nothing, but when you took me away from her and you were so kind . . . and your hair is like fire and your eyes like the sky . . ." I stopped her with kisses and she pressed tight against me; beneath the coverlet were her tender breasts. I remembered Octavia and Otho and my mother and, far back, the man in the barber's shop but they were faint and unimportant. Soon they were not there at all. She said softly, her mouth muffled

151

in my shoulder: "I like the dark." I pinched the wick on the lamp.

She lay curled against me, her hair soft and tumbled. In stillness her face showed a blinding loveliness and complete contentment like a full-fed child. It had been a night of learning for us both. Despite her prostitute mother and early slavery she was a virgin; when she cried out I had felt shocked, fearing to hurt her, but she said it was nothing; she loved me too much. I felt pleased to think no one else had possessed her; she was all mine.

Her eyes opened and she smiled. "I dreamt of you," she said. I laughed and twined a curl of her hair round my finger. She looked at me, puzzled, and said: "Are you really the emperor? I cannot believe the emperor loves me."

"I love you more than my life," I said, and kissed her to prove it.

"In one day?" she said.

She was showing her questioning streak, something I had not yet seen. Her innocent looks did not conceal gullibility.

"In one day," I said. "In one hour."

"But," she said, "you have a wife and all the girls you want."

Why are women so devious? She was assiduously going the back ways, not asking me straight out.

"No," I said. "I have no wife. Octavia is still a virgin. And I never fancied any other girl until now."

I did not mention Otho; women don't like these things. She smiled and looked satisfied, leaning her head on my shoulder. I fancy she was thinking the same as me, that I was all hers.

Everything changed. I lived for her, for every moment by her side, for the scent of her hair and breasts, for kisses and caresses and her body at night. Sometimes the night was not enough and we made love in the day. When I had lessons with Seneca or sat in judgement, attended the Senate or received ambassadors, it was her face I saw, a block between me and the empire. The empire was nothing, a toy on a string. She was reality, my heart, blood and bones. I wrote poems to her. One which she liked was in Ovid's style, called "The Goddess". Part of it ran:

When sweet flowers bloom in springtime vale
Then comes Flora, blossom adorned, to entrance all human eyes,
Yet thou, my sweet, beside her stand with hair of gold and midnight eyes,

And she thou dost eclipse
As Apollo must his pale sister moon.

Perhaps it was not Virgil but it satisfied my urgent desire to express a delirious love. I even tried painting her portrait. It seemed that if I tied my art to her it must be more pure, more exalted. I could climb to heaven holding her hair, my face between her breasts.

It was not merely physical. We talked and laughed together as good friends will, we joked, we shared ideas. I would tell her of a boring Senate assembly where a venerable senator tripped down the steps while trying to be dignified and she would imitate my mother being charming at a banquet. It was so exact I used to laugh myself breathless. We did absurd things like running out in the rain and plunging together into the ornamental pool my father had built in the palace gardens. The centre piece was a marble nymph with a snake twined round her whose mouth spouted water. She would laugh and try to catch the spray in her hands; in the water she looked like a new Venus coming to birth. Afterwards we would lie under a tree and make love, oblivious of cold or discomfort or the dangers of being seen. Till now I never believed in the madness of Bacchanalian love.

Yet she was intelligent. I could talk to her of my art, of my hopes and fears and dreams, of my love of Rome. She understood. We shared unhappy memories of childhood, then forgot them in present joy. She was patient and tactful; she always listened, not like my mother who was too busy to bother. Her

153

interests were all-embracing which meant I could discuss any-thing with her, even the weak spots in Seneca's Stoicism. She could quote Plato better than I by the time I had finished. I had her freed, of course, although Augustus had ruled thirty to be the minimum age for manumission. These things can be arranged. Besides, custom had almost nullified the law; any sort of reason was good enough for liberty and I counted her love as one of the best.

When I spoke to Otho about it he slapped my back and said: "Well done. I knew you would find one who would please you. Why did you take so long?"

I said austerely: "I'm not an animal. I have to fall in love first."

"Why, so do I," he said. "Almost every night, in fact. No, my sweet Nero, that's an exaggeration; every other week, let's say. Only I fall out of love as quickly."

"What about me?" I asked.

"Oh, I never fall out of love with you. How could I?"

I was not sure if he meant it. You could never tell his true mind. "But Otho," I said, "I—"

"Oh, sweet Apollo, no; I shan't intrude," he said. "Don't worry; I'm a perfect gentleman. I shall be there when you want me."

This sounded serious. But I remembered his periods of faithlessness, not stimulated by true love as mine was, only a passing fancy or a strange desire to hurt me.

I said: "You are a true friend, Otho, and you always will be."

This pleased him. It had occurred to me that an appetite for one food remains even when you acquire an appetite for another.

"So," said Seneca, "you have a mistress."

I said: "Yes. Does it matter?"

"Why no, not in itself; it is perfectly natural. I was expecting it."

"Good," I said. "Because whatever you said it would make no difference."

He raised his eyebrows; I had never sounded so stubborn before.

"There is one thing," he said. There always was an exception with Seneca. "Appearances are important. It must not be generally known that you have abandoned Octavia in favour of a mistress. These things cause scandal. If you will permit me to say so, sire, you have been a little..." He coughed. "A little indiscreet."

"Have I?" I looked at him dreamily, seeing her face. "I don't remember."

"People in this palace have eyes and ears," he said. "I think it would be better if we arranged a little deception."

"Dear Seneca, always worrying about 'appearances'." I smiled fondly at him. "Let the world collapse so long as we have appearances. Isn't it rather dishonest?"

"Not when the empire is at stake," he said briskly. "Plato and Socrates placed the good of the state before all. Healthy state, healthy individual."

"I should have said it was the other way round," I remarked.

"Nero, please attend." He was the schoolteacher now. "Listen, I have a wealthy friend who is willing to pretend he is this child's lover which means you can visit her at his house, a much more politic arrangement. It will then seem that your presents come from him. I am glad by the way that you have chosen a little nobody to fall in love with; an aristocrat might have made trouble."

"Nobody?" I said. "How dare you! She is a goddess."

"Of course," he replied, humouring me. "Now, what about this plan? Do you agree?"

"Will he be very realistic in his pretence of lover?" I asked suspiciously.

"My dear child," he said. "He is seventy-five."

At first it worked. The house became a shelter, a paradise. We loved, talked, laughed, ate, and even slept under its roof; there I brought her my presents, jewels, expensive perfumes in clear alabaster, gold ornaments (including a fillet for her hair which I had ordered to be made specially) pallas and stolas of

155

silk, fine linen, cotton, some in Tyrian purple and gold-embroidered, the most expensive kind available.

Then one day I found her crying. I felt it like a wound and it made me stupid, not capable of comforting her; I could only say: "Oh my darling, what is it?"

She said, shivering: "I think I'm pregnant."

I stared blankly. In all my ecstasy of love this had never occurred to me. I said: "Can you be sure?"

"No; it's only one month's flow of blood. But I have felt sick and cold and besides—oh Nero, I'm miserable staying in this house. I want to be with you in the palace all the time; I want to be near you."

I said thoughtfully: "It's now December, six weeks since we first made love. It could be so. Oh Acte, my sweet..."

I took her in my arms and stroked her hair, saying the love names she wanted to hear. "It will be a son," I said, "and I shall love him as I love you."

"But what shall we do?" she whispered.

"What I decided a long time ago," I said. "I shall marry you."

Chapter Nine

"Marry! " said my mother. *"Marry!"*

She flared like a forest fire, her eyes staring as if they would jump from her head. I had begun bravely. Now I felt my stomach turn sick but I went on, thinking of Acte: "Yes, mother, marry. I love her and she is going to bear my child. I don't love Octavia and she hates me. It's like one of Seneca's logical propositions, quite simple when you see the basis."

"How dare you," she said, "how *dare* you talk to me like that? I'm not an idiot. It's Seneca who has encouraged you in this with his nonsense of secret meetings and presents behind locked doors. Now tell me, Nero, since you are so well-versed in logical thinking what do you think will happen if you divorce your virtuous well-loved aristocrat of a wife and replace her with a Syrian slave bitch? Do you think the Senate will approve, or the army, or the people who expect a monarch to be dignified? Do you imagine that they will want to be under the sway of a Caesar who is under the thumb of a slut?"

She paused to draw breath and I said quickly: "It makes no difference what they think. I'm going to marry her. And don't call her names, mother; it's undignified."

I did not know how but I was answering her back. It was like a play, the words coming as if I had learnt them, whereas before there had been a blank, only filled by her dreadful eyes.

She said: "You are not going to marry her, Nero. If necessary I will deport her."

It was like running up against iron. She had grown calmer but more deadly; it meant she was in command again. I took a desperate plunge.

"Then I'll go with her, mother. I mean it. We'll go to Rhodes; yes—" Suddenly the vision caught me. "They love me there and we shall be alone and happy, together for ever and ever. I never wanted to be Emperor, anyway; you forced it on me."

"What do you mean?" She was watchful like a dog on the scent. "You can't dispose of a throne just like that, my dear."

"I can abdicate," I said.

Her mouth opened. "No, Lucius," she said. "Let's be reasonable."

I had got her; for the first time in my harried life she was in the corner and I on the outside. It unnerved me. I said. "Mother . . ."

"Perhaps I was too harsh," she said. "I know what it means to be young and in love. But please be careful, I beg of you . . ." My mother begging! I went hot with embarrassment; it was all wrong. I had prepared for a fight. "Think," she said, "think, Lucius, of your position and your responsibility. The people love you now; one false move and they will hate you or laugh at you. Octavia is deeply loved and admired. To send her away will topple your throne; my child I'm only thinking of you . . ."

Her face was gentle and solicitous, her voice all mild persuasion. I thought: You're a liar, but then I looked at her eyes. They were soft as a summer day. I melted. After all, she was right; I had been foolish not to see that Octavia's dismissal would sour my name.

I said: "Thank you, mother; I'm glad you see it my way," and retired gracefully before she should change. What had frightened her? I knew her by now; she never made a move without good reason and she had each one planned like battle strategy. I had forced her into brief retreat. Dear gods, what a shock I must have given her, her obedient, frightened little son turning hero on the battlefield. But then I thought: a general used to victory finds defeat bitter. What happens now?

Nothing happened. She was strangely quiet, charming, affable, and sweet to me in both public and private. "Dear Lucius, have you tried this ostrich egg with spices?" "Of course, you may write poetry, Lucius dear, and I don't mind you singing at all." "And how is dear Acte? Tell her to ask Xenophon about morning sickness." It was frightening. When she offered us her own apartments to use instead of the house of Seneca's friend, I nearly swallowed my tongue in shock. I could only say idiotically: "Are you sure?"

"Of course, my dear." She smiled with extraordinary sweetness; it caught my heart. "I want only your happiness, Lucius. A mother should indulge her child." Later she said: "You know dear, if you ever feel the need for extra money everything I have is at your disposal. What is mine is yours."

I said thank you, blushing; she was embarrassing me. My skin had grown hard from continual lack of care or affection and now she was breaking it open bit by bit with pinpricks of kindness. And still I could not read the general's mind.

"Don't trust her," Otho warned. "Nero, if ever I saw a magnificent performance that is it; she knows her lines, she knows her actions. She even gets the facial expressions right."

"Do you think so?" I said.

"Why my dear, of course. Nero! " He looked solemn which frightened me. "You don't believe her, do you?"

"I don't know. I should like to believe her."

"She is a cruel woman," he said slowly. He was serious for once. "But clever. A stupid villain is no villain. She is pleasing herself not you, and the question is, why? Good heavens, you've frightened her at last." He patted my shoulder in congratulation. "I knew you would, I have great faith in you. First the girl, now your mother. You're growing up."

I said: "She never liked you; my mother, I mean. Perhaps that influences you."

"Of course, she doesn't like me. I was the first influence to counteract hers. She knew what was going on but couldn't stop it any more than she can stop you now with Acte. I tell you, Nero, she's dangerous, horribly dangerous. And a dangerous woman is like a snake; she hides and when you least expect it she bites."

I said, laughing: "Otho, I misjudged you. You're full of wisdom, after all."

159

He said: "I know women. They're carnivores, Nero. Why do you think men turn to each other?" He looked at me, then away, saying: "No, all right; it wouldn't be tactful. I know."

"I couldn't bear to hurt her," I said.

I had told her why we could not marry. She stared at me with wide, trusting eyes and said: "It doesn't matter. You love me just as much and a contract will make no difference. I only wanted to be here with you and now I am."

I took her in my arms and stroked her face, saying: "But I wanted to give you half my throne, to show the Empire you are mine."

"No." She rubbed her face against my hand like a young animal. "Don't talk of thrones, my darling. You have made me free but I'm still of slave blood; it would not be right."

"Little barbarian," I said, smiling.

She reached on tiptoe and kissed me. I said: "Because of you I defied my mother for the first time in my life. She couldn't frighten me. When she shouted I saw your face and thought of us together in the big bed at night and it was like a storm striking a wall. You made a barrier for me. Acte . . ."

"Yes?"

She looked up, enchanting between the golden streams of hair.

"If you ever stop loving me I shall die."

On the fifteenth of December I was seventeen. My mother gave me a gold medallion with my head on it and the words Claudius Tiberius Nero Imperator, Spes Romae surrounded by twined leaves and tiny rubies. I wore it on a chain. She kissed me when she gave it to me and it shocked me like a slap. The thick skin was all open now.

Two days later Saturnalia began. It is a magical festival, for all work stops and Rome goes mad; the air glitters excitement. Once it had been to celebrate the end of autumn sowing but now the reason was out of sight; people were concerned only with enjoyment. It began soberly in religious mood with the sacrifice of a suckling pig before the altar of Saturn's temple in the Forum; then out came Saturn himself to enjoy the fun.

His statue was set up outside the temple, the traditional woollen bands round his feet untied and discarded. It signified total freedom.

For three days all slaves were free citizens and could do as they pleased. The streets shivered to their singing, the night air blazed with torches and wax candles and swam with the scent of wine and evergreen garlands. Looking down from outside Domus Tiberiana the Forum burned light and movement; torch sparks drifted up to catch the stars, the great columns rippled in the glare and Caesar's statue stood luminous on its divine height. The dancing faces swept by and the seasonal greeting rose up on all sides: "Io Saturnalia." I saw a man seize a girl and pull her to the ground. It was a time of madness with all rules gone.

For me it was release, a brief reprieve from worry. On the evening of the seventeenth we all gathered in the big triclinium and dice was rolled to see who should be the mock king of the festivities. Everything was upside-down. For three days authority was centred in a Lord of Misrule, not the Senate nor even the Emperor. Then by some irony the lot fell to me. They set an ivy garland on my head and a mock sceptre in my hand and the feasting began. I don't think I slept the whole time. We gave each other presents, slender silver spoons, wax tapers, pointed jars of dried damsons and silly things like clay dolls, pickled fishes, sausages, beans, and nuts. But I gave my mother a silver dancing Venus, Otho a red cloak, gold-patterned, and Acte a rare piece of Etruscan jewellery, a necklace triple-tiered with gold chains and tiny droplets which cost me a million sesterces. I sent Octavia some earrings but next day they were returned.

I forget the feasts. They were too extreme, a blaze of colour, noise and pleasure which the mind feeds on and abandons; but, also, the pleasures were strictly sensual. Some of the time Acte did not attend and I seem to recall a couple of pretty slave girls who were indulging their brief freedom. I was drunk at the time; besides, Saturnalia stirs the blood. We ate our traditional suckling pig, drank our Falernian wine, broke some precious rock crystal in fun, held a mock fight in which Otho

F   161

emerged with a bruised eye and finally, in exhaustion, settled down for some entertainment.

Even this is different at Saturnalia. The Lord of Misrule is supposed to ask each guest to perform as singer, dancer, or whatever they please. First I chose one of the obliging slave girls who danced and raised the temperature of the room, then I picked Otho who sang a rude song and was cheered. Next I called Britannicus. He had attended the feast with reluctance, I imagine, being so dignified and grudging of pleasure but an imperial invitation is not refused. I had not seen him since Seneca told me how I had deprived him. It was a morbid fascination. They say criminals like to see their victim after the crime.

I said: "Will you sing for us, Britannicus?"

He came forward obediently but if eyes can kill I should have been a corpse. The feast had run off him like water on crystal; one small drink and a little food, that was all; not a girl, a joke, or a smile. For a moment the wine fumes cleared and I felt sharp pity, speared by guilt. An emperor's son and he stood like a slave.

His voice was good which annoyed me though the music of lyre and flute was soothing. Then I heard the words. It was the tirade of Thyestes from Ennius' tragedy.

It is my luck rather than my birth which is at fault.
Know that I possessed the throne. See now
From what good fortune, from what power, from what wealth
My fate has cast me down.

I could not believe it but his face, satisfied and unafraid, convinced me of truth. Had I been foolish enough to think he lived peaceably with no sense of loss? I knew his intelligence, his grasp of realities. I was the blind one. And he had courage, too, for it was not only me; the accusation had been made before all my friends. I looked round expecting to see anger or indignation; instead there was a great calm and their faces, pink with wine, showed sympathetic warmth. He still smiled; his dark eyes challenged me. The quietness prickled on my face and the girl's hand in mine grew damp.

162

"Thank you," I said with an effort. "An excellent performance."

And then they applauded him.

I believe I hated him after that. He was already a probe for my guilt and a reminder of rejection; perhaps I should have forgiven him had he become my friend as I wanted. He would not even allow me to ease my own conscience. It was clever of him; he knew how to weaken me.

I turned back to Acte for comfort. In sudden remorse I told her about the girls at Saturnalia and she shook her head, bursting with laughter; "Oh Nero darling, do you think I didn't know?" It astounded me; was there no end to female subtleties? "Every man does it now and again," she said, "but it means nothing. It hasn't altered your love for me."

I said: "Can't we have any illusions?" then she laughed even more and fastened her arms round my waist, saying I should never try to better a woman. I carried her to bed for revenge but she wanted that, too; I was helpless.

A few days later I got Pallas to open the palace treasury so that I could choose her a gift from the family jewels. I picked a set which had belonged to Augustus' wife Livia, necklace, earrings, bracelet and fibula in gold acanthus work set with amethyst and blue lapis lazuli. Then I thought of my mother. She had been very good to me recently and I felt an obligation. There was a heavy bracelet of pearl and turquoise with earrings to match; I laid them aside. Pallas watched me superciliously. He had already objected to opening the treasury, saying it was a nuisance as if I were a servant wanting to clean it. The man infuriated me.

Next day I ordered a Tyrian purple palla embroidered with gold and tiny pearls in the form of lilies and sent it to my mother with the jewels. I actually felt a good son; I imagined her pleasure. When the slave came back, white and shaking, saying she was in a fury I thought he lied or had illusions. I asked for details.

"She said, my lord . . ." He caught his breath and plunged on. ". . . she said it was an insult. It was not a question of giving her a present but of depriving her of all the rest and

163

that ... that you had given her merely a portion of the inheritance you owe her, anyway."

I suppose I could have struck him and relieved my feelings but the poor devil was already terrified. His face told me how she had been. I sent him away and sat down, feeling childhood tears sting my eyes. Then anger came to dry them up.

"If I were you," Otho said, "I should get rid of Pallas."

I said: "Yes, I know. He is her main support. If I'm going to weaken her ..."

"You *must* weaken her. Nero, for heavens' sake look at the situation. You send her a gift in all good faith and she throws it back in your face, saying it's hers, anyway. What sort of attitude does that prove?"

"Resentment?" I said.

"Resentment nothing! It's awareness of power. She knows what she has done for you and expects total control in return. You must disarm her before she thinks to attack." He paused. "I suppose you know he is her lover."

"Still?" I said.

He relaxed. "So you do know. Yes, still. The best songs are on it though you've never heard them."

"My noble mother," I said bitterly and laughed. "I must have been about six when I first saw him make love to her. Optima matrum, Otho, optima matrum. Anyone who gave that password should have died for treason."

I summoned Pallas and told him his services were no longer required. It gave me great pleasure to see his shocked, indignant look as of a man complacent in his strength suddenly being thrown. But like my mother he could put a good face on it. He bowed and said: "As you wish sire. I merely ask that I should not have to give any account of my handling of public funds." He might as well have said he had embezzled the lot but I made no objection; I was too pleased to get rid of him.

He left the palace like a departing ambassador, head high, followed by a platoon of clients and friends who looked as though an elephant had kicked them; at the very end was a drawn cart full of gold, silver, and jewellery. Someone told me

164

later they were all the presents he had given my mother and taken back again in pique. I watched from a window, laughing.

"Just look at him, Otho," I said. "He might be on his way to abdicate before the gods like a consul. Did you ever see such an arrogant fool?"

The palace gates swung apart and he passed through and was gone. I remembered the kisses I had envied him for. When I needed affection most he had stood between me and the only possible source of it.

Next morning my mother asked to see me. I went obediently, the slave at the door announced me and in I went to be almost blown out again by her rage. She was shaking with it.

"And who," she said, "*who* do you think you are, dismissing the imperial treasurer without a word to anyone?"

I said calmly: "I am the Emperor."

"And I'm your mother," she said, almost yelling. Her control was already gone; I remembered Lake Fucine and Narcissus. "Gods have mercy on me, what sort of child have I engendered? Do you know what you owe to him? Without his influence I would never have got near your father; your bitch of an aunt made sure of that. Nor would the Guards have accepted you as emperor without the payment he made."

"I know that," I said. "And I know what you gave him to get it."

She took a step and slapped my face. My eyes filled with water and I almost fell but I said nothing, clinging to my calmness as a protection while she grew hotter and hotter.

"Brat!" she said. "Stinking brat!" Her teeth showed like an animal's. "But then what do I expect? You're a monster, Nero, you come from a family of them. Yes, I slept with Pallas but that isn't the worst, my dear, oh no. Do you want to know what sort of blood you have?"

I said: "No," and my stomach went cold.

"When I was twelve," she went on, "I was raped by your uncle Caligula who had already treated his two other sisters the same way and I shared his bed intermittently until he exiled me for being involved in a plot against him which was hardly surprising. He was insane; he thought he was God, not one of

165

our gods, you understand, but the great god who was supposed to be born in Syria within this century."

I looked at her blankly, remembering something Acte had said about a promised saviour who would die young but gain world domination afterwards. She had got it from legend repeated third-hand in Antioch.

I said: "I don't want to hear any more," and turned to go but she caught my arm and held it tight. "You will hear," she said. "You will hear everything. Your father," she went on, "was the worst pig who ever breathed even counting your uncle. He was capable when aroused of running down a child with his horse and gouging out someone's eye in a fight. He treated me like a whore and divided his time between me, your aunt, and any girl or boy he fancied. And don't think, my sweet, that your great-great-grandfather was pure and idealistic. He slept with Caesar to gain his adoption and afterwards sold his body to the Governor-general of Spain for gold."

I said faintly: "Seneca told me that."

"Oh yes, Seneca. And what about your brilliant philosophic tutor, Nero dear? For a Stoic he quickly accepted the offer of my bed."

I said: "You're lying."

"Oh no, all this is true. I lie only to suit myself and at the moment I want you to face reality. That was a bribe to get him as your tutor; it looked good, a potential emperor taught by the greatest thinker of our time. Oh, and he does think, too, especially about his position and what people think of him and the wine or woman he wants. Claudius exiled him as an accomplice with my sister in a plot to oust Messalina. He didn't care two pins about Messalina but his association with Julia was enough, naturally so; he was her lover."

My head was spinning. I thought of his talk of a Golden Age, peace, justice and honour under my rule. "... that is why we seek to advise rulers ... Alexander and Aristotle ..." I wanted to weep.

I said: "I hate you."

"I've no doubt you do, my child. Oh yes, you are mine; don't think there is an escape that way—Domitius made sure

166

of it. So far as I know you were conceived when he was drunk."
She had grown breathless with talk and anger; her breasts
heaved. She let go of me but I was too stunned to move.
"You were my key to open the door into power," she said,
calmer now. "I've known what it is to be a woman in
this city. You are an animal, whipped, trodden on, unimportant.
I saw my mother beaten by a centurion until she lost an
eye; that was Tiberius. Then he had her starved to death and
my father, the only good man I've ever known—" She paused
and I imagined there were tears in her eyes. "Everyone knew
it was murder. The people loved him so much it frightened
Tiberius. And Caligula, making me walk to Rome carrying my
lover's ashes in a jar—poor Lepidus. He thought he and I
would rule together. The gods must hate women. When my
great-uncle married me to that—that male Gorgon I vowed I
would fight for a position where such a thing could never
happen again. Here that means political power and not just in
the Senate; I wanted the throne. Of course, a woman cannot
be Princeps but I had you. We are not weak, Nero." Her eyes
held me as they always had, fixed to the place and to her
words. "Men use physical strength like animals; that was
Caligula's way. Believe me, until he laid hands on me I thought
all men were kind, good, and magnificent—gods on earth. Now
I know them as vain, empty fools, tools to be used as I think
fit; oh such fools! One day you will all rot like meat in the
sun and women will run this world as it should be."

I looked at her, horrified, feeling her contempt on my flesh.
I said: "You killed Passienus as well as Claudius."

"No." She laughed. "He saved me the trouble. But had he
lived longer I should have helped him on his way."

I turned from her, sickened, meaning to run away and hide
but she caught my arm again and said softly: "Nero darling,
I'm sorry: I was angry. Can't we be friends?" Her face was
near me, pleading. This sudden change confused me as when
the wind drops and leaves you weak.

"See it my way," she said. "Cruelty breeds the urge for
power; you want to be as the gods who can't be hurt. Your
father left me all bruises sometimes and Caligula—no." She

looked away. "I won't tell you any more. But you see why I fought for your accession—for you and me, shared power. The bond between mother and son is the strongest. So please, my darling, recall Pallas and everything will be as it was..."

She moved nearer as if to kiss me and I tugged free in horror, saying: "No, I won't. No! No! I'm glad I sent him away. Why did you spoil everything when I wanted to be a good ruler, to make Rome even greater? I hate you."

She withdrew. The wind turned round again but this time it was icy cold. "Very well," she said. "I've finished with you, you ungrateful monster. Britannicus is no longer a child; he is of age to inherit what is his. I took it from him but I can give it back; I have the army's support. The mob will hear how you poisoned your father to get the throne and see me, the daughter of Germanicus, on one side with you, a usurper supported by a cripple and a philosophic fool on the other. I know how they will choose."

I said: "You wouldn't *dare*."

She smiled and turned her back on me. I stood for a moment thinking wildly, of shaking her, beating her, threatening to kill her; then my will fell inwards. I ran.

I went to my room. I lay on the bed and thought and thought till my head ached. I pressed my eyes to stop the tears but they were not coming; I was beyond physical emotion. Red stars burst behind my fingers. They seemed the colour of blood.

I knew she could kill me. She was so deep in her power mania that the destruction of her only child meant nothing. Was it her cruel life? I tried to think of her at twelve, a pretty child full of ideals assaulted by that pale-eyed man I saw in my aunt's house; I remembered his grasping hand. The image was sharp and brought pity. Then I thought of Passienus living his life with an illusion, of Pallas, of Seneca, of my adoptive father, of the innocent people she had doomed since my accession. I thought of her disdain for me; I was one of the "tools", meat soon to rot in the sun.

I said: be calm, Nero. Think; what can she do? Suppose it comes to an open clash? She may be Germanicus' daughter but I have the cripple; the Praetorians will listen to Burrus. But if she says I poisoned Claudius ... Will they believe her? They love me but then they see her noble. Remember Acte. Perhaps there are supporters of Britannicus amongst the people ... Julius Densus ... perhaps others. And Britannicus. He is intelligent, attractive; will they remember he was the imperial heir? What about Britannicus?

"Kill him," Otho said.

"I had thought of that," I said. "It seems the only way. And yet—oh Otho, I can't *bear* the thought of killing—not even him. Dear Apollo, is there nothing else?"

"I would say not," he returned shrewdly. "If he lives your mother will definitely carry out her threat."

I said: "I don't mind giving up the throne. I'll be an artist instead; it's all I really want."

"Oh dear." He looked sympathetic. "Listen, Nero, it won't work like that. You either remain emperor or you die; there is no half way on this road. She won't depose you. She will kill you."

"She is my mother," I said. "Otho, she is my *mother*."

"But you know, all the same, that what I say is true."

"Yes. Yes, I know. Oh Otho, why was I born?"

He grew comforting, put his arm round my shoulder and said not to worry. For a moment I clung to him. He had a strength Acte did not possess for she looked to me as the stronger. Then he said: "Do you remember Julius Pollio, the military tribune? He brought in Locusta a week ago on a poisoning charge, the woman who prepared all your mother's poisons; didn't you know? Oh, she's an expert. Well look, Julius is a friend of mine and I can get him to make her prepare a good poison. He's perfectly trustworthy. So is the woman; anyway, her life is at stake. It will be all right, Nero, it will be all right ..."

A terrible thing happened when I went to see Britannicus. My nerves were run rough like an over-used sword and the thought of his contempt frightened me, yet I faced him all the same. It was my last hope; his friendship.

He laughed in my face. "Do you think," he said, "that I will protect you from your mother or accept friendship from the usurper of my throne? Let your mother give it to me. When she has I'll throw her to the lions."

I had heard right. After all his dignity and good manners he was tainted like the rest. And he had Messalina's blood. I forgot the neglect he had suffered, the bitter loneliness. Your own sickness blinds you to that of others.

I said: "Please Britannicus, listen to me. My mother is evil; I know that now. You and I together can fight her..."

"Do you think I'm such a fool," he said coldly, "as to believe your lies? You love your mother; you used to cry because she wouldn't kiss you. You're a liar, Domitius, a filthy, cowardly liar!"

I caught him by the throat. We went down struggling like children and rolled till we banged against the wooden table leg. It was a small room and sparse; we had the space. He was nearly choking, his dark eyes staring, the hair tumbled back from his face. All my hatred and sense of inadequacy at his rejection rushed to my hands; I was stronger. I could crush him. And then there was something else. He began to scream but I put my hand over his mouth as the man long ago had tried to with me.

Afterwards he lay shivering. I got up, appalled, thinking I must have lost my mind. But these moments come, perhaps given by the gods, when we lose whatever makes us men; then I thought: are the gods there to give anything? I touched him tentatively, saying: "Britannicus?"

"You brute," he said. "You..." and began to cry, trembling all over as if with fever. Dust had made a long mark on his white face. Now I felt tenderness for him as you might for a woman but nothing could be done. I began: "If you dare tell anyone..." then stopped, knowing he was like Octavia; pride would stop him talking.

Otho and I had fallen back to mere friendship since I met Acte; perhaps that was it. He had begun an appetite in me which was exacting its demands. And now Acte was sometimes sick and out of gentleness I would not touch her, then the appetite grew stronger. Three or four times I went back to Britannicus, drawn by Messalina's eyes and mouth. He was quiet and submissive, afraid perhaps or beginning to acquire the appetite himself; he was nearly fourteen. He taught me that sexuality reduces everyone to a level, prince, senator, or beggar, empress or prostitute; all pretences are stripped away. There is no princely arrogance or superior dignity in the face of this divine force. I think then I saw it as a weapon.

Locusta prepared a poison. Britannicus' tutor who was my man undertook to give it to him at midday at the lesson break; I waited, ill with nerves, feeling that I had sold myself to my mother's ideals. I thought: she did it. Why shouldn't I? She has forced it on me, anyway. But it made no difference. Then in came the tutor and said the poison had failed. Far from killing him instantaneously it had brought on a violent attack of diarrhoea after which he recovered.

I had the woman brought to me. She stood there, so absurdly insignificant with her loose brown hair and dark face which made me think of a barbarian, the only thing between me and death. And she had failed. Any more delays and it might be my end; soon my mother would hear. In anger and panic I flew at her and hit her face with all my strength; her head snapped to one side.

"Fool!" I shouted. "Incompetent fool! You made efficient poisons for my mother, why not for me?"

They all gaped and looked foolish; Otho touched my arm and said quietly: "Nero..." I shook him off. "If the next one doesn't work *at once*," I said, "I'll have you burned."

"It will, my lord," she said.

I did not trust her. A room was fitted for experiments in my private apartments with a bronze urn for mixing and a small oven in which she heated water over the flame. She brought her own ingredients, rows of bottles and boxes full of herbs and the essence of deadly berries and mushrooms. She began work, mixing and heating, mixing again and adding water. I watched all the time. After half an hour she produced a thick dark liquid which I had forced down the throat of a young kid. We waited. It lived for five hours. She looked at me with her

171

sly, begging eyes and said: "My lord, it was too weak. It needs re-cooking." I gave her another chance though my stomach burned nervousness.

She reheated it four times, adding more ingredients; then we tried it on a young pig. It died at once, squealing.

"What hour is it?" I asked Otho.

"Near dinner," he said. "If I were you—"

"I know," I said, "but how do we get it down him? A slave tastes everything first."

That had already struck me as ominous; he suspected danger.

"The poison is too quick," Otho said. "The slave will die before Britannicus can taste it."

We thought about it and all the time my fear grew worse. Any moment I expected armed men to burst in, demanding my life.

"I know," Otho said. "It's quite simple. Give him the drink but make it too hot; the slave will taste it, no doubt scalding his tongue, but pronouncing it harmless after which Britannicus will want it cooled. One of our slaves removes it, adds the poison with the water and there you are."

"Will it work?" I said doubtfully. I had no trust in anything.

"We can try," he replied.

Dinner was in the large triclinium which cherished too many memories for me. I sat at the family table, my couch being the place of honour and facing the side left empty for service; my mother sat beside me. She would not relinquish that privilege. She wore the jewels and the palla I had given her, telling anyone who cared to listen that they were presents from her dear son. Her hypocrisy sickened me. But perhaps I was as bad. When Britannicus was announced and entered I rose and kissed his forehead, meaning it; like a fool I had allowed myself to become attached. The hypocrisy lay in my intentions.

He sat to my right in the third most important place; Otho had the second. Two of his friends his own age sat either side of him on the couch and regarded me bitterly; they must have shared his feelings. Octavia sat on the other side of me, stiff and drawn in plain white with no ornament. The room was nearly full.

The slaves passed to and fro, serving food and pouring wine; I kept my eye on mine, the one who would bring the fatal drink. Britannicus was eating well and so far asked for no wine. I ate nothing; my hands trembled and I thought she must see. But she only leaned back smiling at the glances of admiration which reached her from all over the room. She made the other women look insipid. I picked at some mackerel in sauce, spiced with oil and pepper, and waited.

At last he asked for a cup of wine, heated. I knew that in the winter months he felt the cold and preferred hot drinks. It came on a silver tray in a cup engraved with hunters; it seemed appropriate. The slave seated at his feet sipped the liquid. Nothing happened. Britannicus took it and began to drink, then winced; I felt my stomach tighten.

"It's hot," said my adoptive brother. "Add some cold water."

Out it went; when the slave came back I wondered stupidly and too late if the poison would discolour the drink. But he liked deep red wine from Campania; it might not show. As he raised the cup to his lips I realised that I didn't want him to die; his eyes were soft, his pretty face flushed with warmth. I was destroying beauty, I who loved it and thought only art and beauty made life bearable. He might have lived for me to love him; but I looked at the woman beside me and knew there was no other way.

He took a gulp, then to my horror passed it to his friend; I would have innocent blood on my hands. But there was not time. Britannicus went white, clutched his throat, gasping, and down he tumbled, the last of the Claudians, before the faces of his family and the household gods who stood enshrined on the table. He dragged his cushions with him and spilled all the wine. I saw him roll, then grasp with his hands as if he would hold on to life and his eyes looked at me, startled and reproachful; then they fixed.

There was silence. I saw my mother's face, unbelieving, staring at me with something near terror; she knew. Octavia never moved. Somehow she had learned to mask all feelings with marble. The guests were stunned; then someone said: "What is it, oh gods, what is it?" and a babble arose with

173

people leaving their couches and gaping. My heart was leaping like a shot deer. I dropped my cup and fell on my knees beside him, crying hysterically and saying his name over and over till someone dragged me up to leave room for Xenophon. The child who shared his cup had thrown it away but a few drops had touched his lips; he was the colour of a corpse and vomiting. Xenophon looked at the body, felt pulse and heart and examined its mouth, depressing the tongue with a spatula. I was shaking violently but Otho's hand lay strong and steady on my shoulder. Xenophon brushed his hands on his tunic and looked up, straight at me; still on his knees he said: "He is dead. Epilepsy."

We buried him that night. Otho had made arrangements for the funeral before dinner and a bonfire lay ready in the Campus Martius. We had to be quick; that fool Locusta had done something wrong and the corpse was beginning to turn white. By midnight all was ready and my dear cousin was carried across the Forum in violent rain which whipped at the cover on his body and soaked our clothes. I had wept myself silly. Otho said I should not go to the funeral pyre; it would look suspicious. I said I didn't care. I wanted to mourn for lost beauty, for a world gone wrong.

The rain struck the pillars of the temples and made them gleam in the torchlight. The air beat darts of fire just where we walked with torches high but soon they went out and there was only darkness. I looked at his face, swelling and turning colour, and remembered games of nuts in the palace, the three of us unaware of what life we had come into; our rehearsals for the Trojan Game, his laughter, his dark wondering eyes of the past few days when I had come to him, seeking. What had changed it? It seemed endless, chain after chain of cruelty binding us all, I killing because of my mother, she wanting power because of Caligula and he soured for some reason far back, and back and back again, a chain winding to the start of time with no end.

We passed by the arch of Octavia, built by Augustus in honour of his sister, and along past the Circus Flaminius and the Theatre of Pompey until we reached the bonfire near the river bank. The Tiber was in full flood, rushing thick and grey, shot through with rain. But the bonfire beat the weather. Its flames leapt up as if they would part the clouds and I watched him go in a glory of light which suggested life had been good. Otho looked at me, his face wet in the darkness, saying: "Why did you weep?" He knew me too well to think it an act. "For him?"

"For us all," I said.

Chapter Ten

Next morning I told Seneca and Burrus what I had done and why. Burrus was impassive, a man used to imperial intrigue, but Seneca's face showed anxiety; he said: "Nero, I should hope that you will not make a habit of this."

I said sharply: "Habits are formed from necessity. Do you deny me the right to defend myself?"

"No." He looked away. "I am aware that you had no choice. It's the judgement of the gods for your accession. Sweet Jove, may they forgive your mother's parents for producing such a creature."

His piety annoyed me. "You didn't think that once," I said. "Not when she offered you herself."

He went red which did not suit his beard. Burrus raised his eyebrows but remained blank, military to the last.

"I should prefer you not to dig up my foolish past," said my tutor grandly. "What I did once in the heat of wine and brief physical attraction is of no consequence in the present situation."

"Then there was her sister," I went on, heedless, wanting to strip the façade. Why should he protect himself behind rhetoric when my soul must be bare? "That was your downfall, wasn't it? Do Stoics seek pleasure so energetically? I thought that was Epicureanism."

He began to stammer and get mixed up like a child caught cheating in class, then he rallied and said: "How dare you intrude, anyway? It's none of your business."

I had struck at his pride. Anything else he could have stood but not a gibe at his philosophical convictions.

I said: "It's my mother."

He became flustered again, remembering, I suppose, who I was, that I had just committed murder and might be capable of turning on him.

"Nero, my dear child," he said in a wheedling tone, "these things are done and forgotten, foolish though they may have been. The present is more important. What you did was unavoidable and no one blames you. Burrus and I are at your complete disposal to do as you wish."

The flatterer had returned home. I smiled, knowing my strength, and said the people and Senate must somehow be told of Britannicus' death; Seneca agreed to prepare a speech, then he said: "There is the small matter, my prince, of the deceased's inheritance. How is to to be administered?"

I looked at them, so calm and correct, covering the whole nasty business with a layer of legality as though he had died in his bed. They were the hypocrites. I had done the murder but I saw my action clearly, undisguised; I knew myself.

I said: "Do what you like with it; I don't care. Keep half yourself and put the rest in the treasury. Now leave me alone."

Seneca gave a very good speech to the Senate. Claudius' dear son had died of epilepsy to which he had long been subject and the haste of the funeral ceremonies had been due to grief; one does not wish to linger over premature deaths. He begged their pity for me, lost in grief and now bearing sole responsibility, "the one descendant of a family born to the supreme rank."

For days afterwards I dreamt of him, waking in the night with a sudden cry and telling Acte he had stood by my bed, deathly white and weeping, his great dark eyes beseeching me to lay his ghost. She said it was a dream. Behind her Syrian eyes there was a Hellene rationalism which discounted magic and superstition. Sometimes at night I was tempted to pour out my guilt against her breasts as though her innocence might drown it; but that was selfish. I should merely hurt her. In February when Parentalia, the feast for the dead, was celebrated I took gold and silver ornaments, expensive wine in rock crystal and wreaths of violets and roses which had been cultivated under glass and were costly, and laid them beneath his funerary urn in the Mausoleum of Augustus. I even attended Lupercalia, the purification ceremony at the cave beneath the Palatine where the she-wolf suckled Romulus and Remus, a dog and goats being sacrificed and sacred cakes offered, made by the Vestal Virgins. When the blood was marked on the foreheads of two noble youths which signified the purifying element of the sacrifice I tried to imagine that I was clean but it did not work. Guilt does not wash away. At the Caristia family feast where family affection is supposed to link with devotion to the gods I made a speech, saying we must remember our dead and honour them, especially those who had left us recently in sorrowful circumstances. The words stuck in my throat. I saw how my mother looked.

A few days after his death I had received the usual summons. This time she was all ice and dignity, an affronted mother.

"You killed him," she said.

"Yes." I looked straight at her, murderer to murderess. "And you know why."

She moved impatiently, flinging out her hands. "You fool. You poor silly little fool. Do you think you can frighten me that way?" I recalled her face as he fell and knew she was bluffing. "All you have done is endanger your own position."

"If I hadn't done it," I said, "you would have killed me instead." She opened her mouth for denial and I hurried on: "I'm not your son. I'm just a creature you produced by accident who was suddenly useful, a key to a door." I threw her own words back at her with satisfaction. She had done an irrevocable thing, revealing herself to me, and she knew it. "I'm not a child any more, mother. You can't shout and bully as you used to because it won't frighten me. I can fight back now. You gave me supreme power as though it were a toy and if necessary I'll use it to show you I've grown out of toys."

"You little pig," she said softly. She was not Seneca, quickly making a compromise and assuming the mask of flattery. "Sweet Venus, you are your father all over again. Unless, of course ..." She smiled and I knew something abominable was coming "Perhaps I miscalculated dates. You may be a left-over from Caligula."

At first I stared, not seeing. Then her meaning took life in my brain and I came forward in sick fury, prepared to strangle her.

"You bitch!" I said. "You filthy—"

She swung her arm back and caught my mouth, so hard it began to bleed. I leaned against the wall, watching her blindly as she laughed, a light tinkling sound, and said sweetly: "Who is to say? I forget how long before your birth I had been in his bed."

I was shaking; I thought: if the gods exist they are monsters. She was standing by the window so that the light fell on her hair; it shone like dark silk.

"Think what you have come from," she said. "A union cursed by every god in heaven. And what an inheritance! Oh my dear, what will you become?"

"You're lying," I said. I clenched my hands to keep them from her.

"Perhaps." She smiled again. "But how do you know? Nero, my child, you can't defeat me. Stop trying. I grew you like a willow which cannot be torn from its roots; if it is it withers."

I turned then and ran. As I fled I heard her shout: "You can't get rid of your blood. It will be with you when I have crossed the Styx."

I went into a corner to think things out. Now the first shock was over I felt sure she was lying; according to my aunt, Domitius had made a formal statement of paternity and he was not the sort of man who would lie to suit others. But suppose Caligula had forced him in order to avoid a scandal? Who was to say? Both were dead. My mother held the reins and she was tugging them with all her strength. I thought: dear gods, who am I? Where have I come from? I searched the mirror, looking for signs of the long nose and small mouth but all I saw were the Augustan features. Then I looked at my eyes and remembered his, pale and fixed like a snake's. Mine were deep blue, Julian eyes. My reflection gave no certainty at all.

That night I said to Otho: "Who do I look like?"

He laughed, thinking it a joke, and said: "Your mother. You can hit me but it's true."

"Anyone else?"

"Well, yes, your grandfather from what I've seen of his busts and your mouth is Augustus'."

I said: "What about Caligula?"

He put down his wine, looked at me sharply and said: "What has your mother been saying?"

I told him. He banged the table in anger and said: "She's a vicious liar! Oh Nero, can't you see what she's doing? Any weapon is good enough for a soldier with his back to the wall."

I said: "If it were true I should kill myself."

He said: "Nonsense," told me to forget it and made me drink some wine while the dancing girls came on.

When I told my old aunt Domitia who was my father's last surviving sister she patted my cheek and said: "Dear boy, such ugly nonsense. You have the Ahenobarbus hair and square shoulders; no one could mistake them. Domitius told me you were his sure as the sun shines. Whatever she says Caligula broke off relations at the marriage and never touched her again till after you were born."

She calmed my mind a little. I made myself believe that my delightful mother was following a policy of terror, finding all the hidden wounds and opening them up. Her subtlety frightened me. When a man faces you in daylight, sword drawn, the fight is easy but if he creeps in the shadows unseen where do you look, how do you protect yourself? I thought: it's war now, Nero. Look brave. If you flinch she will claw your face like a tiger. I began by expressing open admiration for Uncle Caligula. What a fine man, so courageous, caring for no one but himself, spending his money as he pleased, taking any woman to bed as it suited him, even his own sister, having affairs with actors and letting the world know. That, I said, is the way to be; and looked at my mother. I had bewildered her. She had hoped to drive me mad with thinking on my parentage, instead here I was praising it.

"My son never knew his dear uncle," she said pleasantly to the other guests. "He jumps to conclusions, I'm afraid."

180

"Oh no, mother dear," I returned just as pleasantly. "You have told me so much about him that I am quite capable of making a judgement."

At this the guests tittered and looked knowing; Romans can recite imperial scandal by heart. It made her furious. Later I realised I had compromised myself by praising the most hated man since Hannibal but Otho said everyone knew my tongue was in my cheek; in fact, they knew perfectly well how things were between myself and my mother.

I had her watched. You would be surprised how these spies wriggle into the most strange places; he told me she was in the process of sleeping with each of the Praetorian officers I had allowed her to keep on as private guard. I said: "*All* of them?"

"In turn, my lord," he replied. "I think you should take note, my lord, of the fact that she alternates her kisses with talk of a military coup."

I had the guard removed. She turned tearful and pleading, saying she could not go unprotected in her position; did I want her assassinated? Like a gullible idiot I let her keep a corps of Germanic mercenaries, blonde giants with iron muscles and a reputation for fanatical devotion. Soon after my faithful spy reported that she was filling them up with patriotic talk of a new empire where every race ruled itself independently. I removed the mercenaries. Then I went to see her, flanked by a couple of sturdy Guards, and said politely: "Mother, I must ask you to leave the imperial residence."

I might have shot her full of arrows; she had not expected this.

"I am your mother," she said in a strangled voice.

"I know you are. You have never let me forget it." I was strong now, my Guards either side, Caesar in my own right. Her face reflected my superiority. "I must still ask you to leave. I feel we shall get on better if we do not live under the same roof."

She went with enormous dignity like her lover before her, no tears, no begging. She knew the impossibility of playing on my sympathies and preferred to go gracefully. The game was over.

I watched her litter bounce towards the palace gates followed by six carts piled high with all her gold, silver, jewels, and chests packed full of dresses. Her jewels alone filled one cart. Her retinue went, also, two hundred slaves or more, dragged along in their mistress' disgrace.

"Well," said Otho, "she's gone."

"You don't know her," I returned. "This isn't the end. She will have to be watched even more closely now she is away from here. The only advantage is that she can't kill me so easily."

I felt the bitterness of it. An emperor expects to face intrigues against him but he must be the only man who fears death from the woman who gave him life. As the guard saluted and the bronze gates clanged shut after her my eyes pricked tears absurdly; they seemed to shut on my heart. I suppose all along I had wanted her love as any son would and knew I had killed my last chance of it. The weakness brought anger. I banged my hand against the window arch and said: "I'm glad she's gone; I'm glad."

"Well, of course you are," said Otho reasonably. "Freedom at last, Nero. I should celebrate with an all-night feast if I were you."

In fact, I went to bed early. He could see no further than my apparent victory and was surprised. He had always disliked her; she was the one woman who could frighten him. But Acte with her usual acuteness said: "Are you sorry she's gone?"

I said: "Don't be silly. She's a wicked woman."

She smiled as though pretending to believe while knowing different. No other woman could read my heart as she did except for one who would do it no longer.

She retired to the house of her ancestress Antonia on the Esquiline amongst wealthy villas and neat, green gardens; the ground was part of the imperial estates. I went to see her at decent intervals for the sake of etiquette, accompanied by hand-picked Praetorians who stood outside the room while I talked to her. Occasionally I had one stand by my side. If I ate or drank with her one of them tasted it first. I took no chances. But she was always very correct, asking solicitously after my health and my activities and pretending concern for Acte whom I knew she hated. Acte had been the beginning of my defiance.

Sometimes we argued and the Guard would enter the room and wait. Her only method of attack was verbal. I saw it as no more than an outlet for her, she who had been the most powerful woman in Rome brought down to the shame of retired domesticity. Only I did not believe in her resignation to it. She was still watched but her behaviour seemed impeccable. It worried me. I brooded on it to such an extent that I began dreaming of assassination; my appetite dwindled, my sleep suffered and I grew irritable like a nervy old woman. The irony of it that even her quietness could torment me.

One evening Otho said: "You need cheering up. It's ridiculous to sit around biting your nails like a criminal. Listen, this will take your mind off it."

Quite simply he suggested a taste of the night life in Rome. We had all drunk a lot and everyone else was merry but I had become depressed. I thought of Acte and knew she would be asleep, wearied by the growing burden in her womb. Otho said I must put on my black wig and a slave's tunic because it wouldn't do for the emperor to be seen entering brothels. I said: "I'm not going to a brothel," and he said that was the best part of the night life.

Rome at night is blacker than the underworld. There are no lights, no doors ajar; all houses are shuttered and bolted except for those open on business. The narrow, twining streets shudder with traffic, wheeled carts and wagons which the divine Julius' edict forbade to move in the daytime. I realised how congested my city was, with people by day, vehicles by night; as we trailed out into the dark, laughing and shouting like young fools from a party, with one solitary torch bearer, I said to Otho: "These streets are too narrow. It's appalling." He groaned, saying: "Nero, for Jove's sake stop worrying. You don't have to walk in them so why worry?"

"My people do," I said.

He ignored me and started singing a bawdy song which the others took up as a chorus.

I forget exactly where we went. My senses were blurring with wine which Otho kept feeding me out of a large wine-skin he had brought along. We passed over Velabrum and along near the Aventine somewhere. I could smell the river near at hand and hear its heavy splashing. The black bulk of tenement houses reared high on either side, five or six storeys with scores of narrow windows; here lived the poor. The cool night air carried their smell. The streets were so thin that the buildings seemed to move, ready to fall on you, and, looking up, I thought the flat roofs swayed. The pavement ran with slops, thrown from the top windows; I dare not think what we were walking in.

After a time we staggered into a small, dingy place full of horrid cubicles divided by curtain partitions; I could hear girls shrieking with laughter. The paintings on the wall were obscene and the language more so. Something feminine and stinking of perfume caught hold of me and dragged me behind a curtain. Things were confusing for a while, then I became aware of fingers stroking my face and neck.

"Apollo," murmured a voice. "Hercules..."

The fingers twined in my hair; too late I remembered. A girl screamed and I made for the door, clutching my faithless wig.

We ran like thieves. "Idiot!" Otho said.

"It was your idea," I objected.

"Well..." He accepted fate. "It doesn't matter. She'll boast for a while of having made love to the emperor but no one will believe her."

We swung on our way, laughing and singing; I began to cheer up. Wine and activity brings forgetfulness. Otho said we should go to the Circus where the best prostitutes were, so off we went, stopping on the way for someone to be sick in the river; it ran dark as the Styx. Near the curve of the Circus a wagon lumbered across our path with a load of swaying marble from the quarries, drawn by sweating horses. "By Apollo, it's going to fall!" I said, looking up, then Otho dragged me back;

184

another moment and I would have been under the wheels.

"Dear heaven," he said, "a fine task I should have had explaining how a wagon ran over the emperor."

I apologised, bowing grandly, and nearly fell over. After that we got into some sort of fight. I seem to remember a tavern or brothel or something under one of the great stone archways of the Circus, a hideously painted woman and then someone trying to hit me with a bottle.

"Run!" Otho yelled. I did my best but got caught in someone's muscular arms. I kicked out hard and heard a stifled yell, then suddenly the whole place was full of flying bodies and women's screams with glass splintering and wine spilling everywhere. I saw Otho flailing a wooden bench and a couple of other friends scrimmaging on the floor. Then my wig came off again.

It was like a play when the god appears. The man with his fist drawn back, ready to hit me, stood frozen as though struck by a thunderbolt. Everyone else backed away, staring. "Gods preserve us," a woman moaned. "It's the arena for all of us now." I stood amongst the wreckage with my vivid hair all tangled and one eye swelling, the apex of the pyramid who had somehow fallen to the base.

"I'm very sorry," I said. "It was a mistake. Please don't look so worried."

They murmured and shuffled, a few falling on their knees. I picked up my wig. As we left the place a senator came along with his wife and several torchbearers, no doubt homeward bound from a respectable supper. He looked at us with distaste and said: "Young fools. What is our youth coming to?" then saw me; his jaw dropped. "I beg your pardon, sire. I—"

"A misunderstanding," I said, nodding towards the chaos. "And I fancy, sir, that youth is going home to bed," at which my companions cheered and a voice said: "Silly old fool." He drew himself up in anger and marched off, retinue and all.

I tumbled into bed aching all over but thoroughly happy. My brain swam with wine and tiredness; there was no room for sharp memories or sinister dreams, no sleeplessness in which to run things over and over in my mind. Next morning I sent

185

for Xenophon and he put some ointment on my eye. The bruise went almost at once.

A few evenings after we went again, and again after that, and then several evenings running. Each time we got into fights, usually in brothels, and ended by smashing all the furniture; if I was lucky my wig stayed on but if not the proceedings ended abruptly. The thing was I could not do it till I had got drunk which I did deliberately, wanting to lose myself. Roaming the streets I was nobody, not Imperator, not Nero, not Agrippina's son; I lost my own identity and this brought peace.

One night we came up against the senator Julius Montanus going home with his wife and retinue. Seeing us he looked disdainful and said to his lady: "Come along, my dear. Take no notice." She did not adopt his advice. I saw her look at me with that slight smile and flutter of the eyelashes which women are so skilful in producing; she was young and he nearing middle-age. I will admit I was drunk. All the same I felt like kicking Montanus where it would hurt, in the seat of his respectability.

I said: "Senator, your wife fancies me," and grabbed her; though my senses were confused I don't remember her resisting. The next moment something hard hit the side of my head. I broke away and there was Montanus, red with fury and fists squared for a fight. The lady retreated squealing, her dress slipping from one shoulder. He hit me again; I went down and he struck me a third time as I tried to get up. That was enough. We fled, gasping. Round the corner I leaned against a wall and tenderly felt my face; it seemed in pieces. Otho was breathless with laughing. "That," he said, "will teach you to leave respectable ladies alone."

"Well," I replied, "it was a fair fight. I can't complain."

Next day I received a letter from him, apologising profusely. He had not known who I was. Of course, he would never have dreamed of—Naturally it was only youthful high spirits on our part; he apologised for his quick temper and sincerely hoped I had not been too much hurt. In fact, I had been forced to stay indoors for a few days rather than show my bruised face.

"What!" I said, joking. "He knows he hit *me* and he's still alive?"

A few days later I heard he had killed himself. Someone had repeated my words without the humour and he took it as sentence of execution. I told Otho that was the end of night expeditions; I could not allow innocent people to die for them. He persuaded me out of it, of course, and said we should take Praetorians with us who could intervene when things got dangerous.

I said: "One word from me and a man dies even though I never meant it?"

"Of course," he replied. "You are emperor."

During my free hours in the day I played with tiny ivory chariots and horses, moving them round a table and imagining it a race. I could execute complex movements, a rush here to overtake, a dangerous turn round the embankment, and see myself as the charioteer. I had each chariot marked with a piece of coloured ribbon and usually I made the green win. Ever since that first childhood race the greens had been my favourite, the killed charioteer my hero. I also wrote poetry. I composed a couple of poems about my mother which burned hatred but oddly enough each one came back to her beauty as though this single overriding fact blotted out all else. I played my lyre and tried to improve my voice, singing ridiculously difficult pieces such as the climactic speeches of Orestes and Oedipus. You might have thought I would have avoided them since they both dealt with mothers but I saw them as a challenge; besides, in my present state of mind I made Orestes convincing.

At my dinner parties I often had Paris to perform for us, the pantomime I had first seen soon after my mother married Claudius. He was a fine artist. I enjoyed not only his performances but also his company; he had a certain wit and an easy-going grace often found in actors which relaxed my nerves. At court you mistrust everyone except for a few. He I did not have to worry over; he was wedded to art, not politics. Sometimes he performed canticas and sometimes merely gave the actions while the text was sung by a chorus with an accompaniment of flutes or lyres or both; occasionally I asked for cymbals as well. Then the sound would fill the triclinium, clashing and shrilling in my blood till I felt as though I might take wing.

One evening at the beginning of March he came in late as he was going to entertain us last with a performance of Ariadne on Naxos. It was about eleven; I had drunk well and felt happy. Then I saw his face; the painted linen mask was shoved to his eyebrows with only the full red mouth showing ludicrously above them. I said: "What is it?"

He moved forward, pale-faced, and my fears came leaping. The tragedy was not acted.

"Sire," he said, "I have been asked by your aunt Domitia and a certain Junia Silana to inform you that your mother is planning an assassination with the object of securing the throne for her lover Aulus Plautus who, being a descendant of Augustus like yourself, has a considerable claim."

So much for actors. He might have been a lawyer reciting a will. My guests were silent, all ears; I looked to Otho and saw his raised eyebrows as if to say: it's what we expected. I thought of her, alone in that house and planning my death while turning a face of sweetness to me; the wronged mother showing her wound to the world. I threw my wine goblet across the floor. It rolled with a wet trail and banged against the leg of someone's couch.

I said: "I'll kill her. I've had enough. I'll kill them both."

"My prince . . ." Seneca began.

"Plots!" I went on furiously. "Nothing but plots! I finish one and there's another just like the hydra's heads. It's no good cutting them off one by one; plunge a sword into the body and be done with it. Oh dear gods, Seneca, I hate her so."

"Sire," said Burrus, "permit me to—"

I turned on him. "And *you!*" I said. "What sort of Praetorian prefect are you? We have distinct proof from one of your own officers that certain members of the Guard promised to support my mother. Now, following the rules of logical thinking which my learned tutor advocates, either you knew what was going on and said nothing which means you are a traitor or else you did not know which means you are incompetent. Either way I'm tired of you. I have dictated an order dismissing you."

He bowed his head submissively; for a moment he looked very old, the cloak falling in where his arm should have been, and I felt cruel. But he was inefficient. I could not afford mistakes.

"Nero," said my tutor, "do not lose your head over this."

"I nearly have," I retorted sourly. "Seneca, go away. You're getting on my nerves."

"My prince, may I say something?"

He stood calmly, playing the Stoic for all he was worth. I could see his Socratic look; it always appeared when he intended to smother me with wisdom.

"Very well," I said. "Be quick."

"First," he said, "you cannot expect Burrus to know the thoughts of every man under his command; he is not an oracle. Furthermore you will be foolish to dismiss a man who has always served you well and will give support in any crisis. He has the Guards under his thumb; if you appoint a weaker man no one would answer for the consequences. As for your mother—" He paused. I thought: go on, excuse her. She warmed your bed for you. "We do not know," he went on, "if this accusation is well-founded. Your mother is widely hated. You would do the gravest possible harm by summarily murdering her with no trial; it gives an impression of—shall we say—callousness?"

"What do you expect with my parentage?" I returned.

"Nero, listen to me." I was back in the schoolroom. "You began your reign with a policy of mercy and the people loved you for it. Since then you have taken up certain amusements which are harmless enough if not carried to extremes but you must be careful; your love of actors, for example, and for night wandering." He was making it an excuse for a lecture. I knew his pretended disdain for such frivolous occupations. He would have liked to keep my nose in *The Republic* all day. "Therefore," he said, "a false move now might endanger your reputation considerably. My advice is to have a specially

189

appointed commission visit her at dawn and make an official enquiry."

He was right, of course; that was the infuriating part.

"All right," I said ungraciously. "I agree."

"And Burrus?"

"You can nullify the order for his dismissal. Now leave me alone."

I hardly slept all night. A double guard was posted at my bedroom door and I kept a dagger under my pillow just in case. Seneca and Burrus had headed the commission, the latter promising to execute my mother on the spot if she were convicted. As dawn came up, grey and damp over the Palatine, I woke and sat waiting, a cloak round my shoulders. I thought of her dead and turned colder. It was a bad day to die.

They came in respectfully; their faces told me nothing. Then Seneca said: "My prince, your mother swears innocence and begs an interview."

I said sharply: "What did you expect?"

"There is insufficient proof," he continued, undisturbed. "She said Silana and Domitia hated her and did not know how a mother feels; mothers do not change sons as whores change lovers—her exact words, my prince. She swore the whole thing was a fabrication."

I nearly laughed. She was so unbearably clever. I might know her to be lying but Rome would not; her death would lie heavy on my back.

I said: "Very well, I'll see her. And bring the boy as well."

He came first. They put him in an ante-room leading from the main atrium; I told the guards to leave us. He was about twenty with soft brown hair and an unformed face, pleasant and harmless. When he saw me he stood straight as if facing lions, adopting an heroic pose copied from gladiators I should think.

I said: "Are you guilty of the charges?"

"Yes." His head went higher; the lion had snarled. "I will not deny my beliefs." I looked questioning; he rushed on, suddenly passionate: "You have betrayed Rome and treated your own mother despicably. Your wife is humiliated by an upstart slave, you frolic with actors and wreck the city by night. I hold it my glory to free the empire of you."

It was my mother pouring out. Yet all the same he had a silly sort of courage, upheld by adolescent ideals of bravery, purity, and honour. At twenty he still had them. I was three years younger and hardened like a cynic.

"Was my mother your mistress?" I asked.

He blushed like a girl. "I love her deeply," he said. "Such grace and beauty, such virtue. She did not like to tell me how harshly she had been treated but I saw it and despite it all she only cared for Rome. We would have established a new rule, peace and justice. With such an adviser I could not have gone wrong."

I started laughing; it is an experience to meet yourself in the flush of idealistic faith. He stood quiet, hardening his face, thinking me a brute no doubt. I said: "She is old enough to be your mother."

"Do you think I care?" He was reckless. "There is no lovelier or more gracious woman in Rome."

Suddenly I hated him. He was a fool sweetened by lies and I should have pitied him; instead I wanted to kill him.

"You will die for your stupidity," I said. "And when the sword runs you through remember this—my mother is Medusa incarnate, even to the eyes. She has already turned your brain to stone."

He looked outraged, then stared above my head as if I were beneath notice. It made no difference. He would die with his illusion intact. I called the guard; he came in, sword out, knowing his task. I saw the boy's mouth flinch. Death is all very well in heroic dreams; close at hand it becomes ugly. I nodded, the sword flashed, and he sank down, blood coming from his mouth. In the end he kept his courage, acting his self-appointed rôle to the last.

I looked round and saw my mother standing at the door. Her lover was an unimportant heap in the corner but she remained impassive. She said: "What have you done, Nero?" as if I were a misbehaving child.

"Can't you see?" I said. "Come and kiss my successor." She

191

looked blank. "Mother," I said, raising my voice, "for heaven's sake stop playing the innocent. He told me everything."

She moved into the room, a slave drew the curtain and we were alone except for the deaf witness on the floor.

"And what are you going to do about it?" she said.

"Kill you," I said.

The words seemed to disappear down my throat.

"Very well," she said. "I am ready."

Her eyes struck me through. I went to the door and laid my damp hand on the curtain; I could not draw it back. Freedom waited on the other side and I was incapable of calling it. She smiled.

"Remember," she said. "Germanicus' daughter. Killed by her own son? What have the gods done, giving us such a ruler? Oh, but then they say he poisoned his father and killed her to protect himself. They do, don't they?"

"All right," I said with an effort. "You win. I knew you would somehow. Now get out."

She kissed my hand and said she would be a good, quiet mother, living in retirement and enjoying her son's success. Either it concealed further plans or else I had frightened her. I saw the value of the sword.

Seneca patted me on the back and praised me, saying the principle was the important thing; I had shown mercy. I said what about my neck? He demurred over this and avoided the issue till I could have hit him. Principles! Shall we die for them, these things we cannot see which float in the air of a philosopher's mind? I said: "Suppose I was wicked like Uncle Caligula and someone wanted to kill me for *his* principles?"

"That would depend on the extent of your wickedness and the validity of his principles," he said.

"Then who starts the principles in the first place?" I asked. "The gods? Or do we make our own? You never hear of Jupiter discussing a principle."

He told me I was arguing for argument's sake which was unscholarly and led nowhere.

Otho said I was a fool not to get rid of her when I could. I gave my reasons; he looked doubtful. "A bluff," he said.

"You should have faced it out." I did not tell him that I had been incapable of even calling the guard.

A couple of weeks later a sordid looking little man named Paetus who had been involved in dubious transactions with the treasury demanded audience with me and promptly denounced a plot which he said was instigated by Pallas. There were the usual boring details, corruption in the Guard, an obscure claimant backed by money and a vague plan for assassination. Seneca organised another tribunal. By this time I felt tempted to crucify everyone in sight; I yelled at Burrus, told Seneca he was an old idiot and retired, exhausted, to Acte's private apartments with a triple guard, leaving them to it.

My mother was not involved. Neither was Pallas apparently. It ended by Paetus being exiled for vicious lies and embezzlement and Pallas' name left clear. It had all been a figment of Paetus' nasty mind.

"Do you expect me to believe that?" I told Seneca.

"Sire," he said, looking wise, "sometimes it is best not to ask too many questions. Your life is safe and an offender has been punished. That is enough."

"What about the truth?" I said.

He replied: "To all intents and purposes that *is* the truth."

Soon after he presented me with a treatise, "On Clemency", where he praised my mercy and elaborated at some length on the virtues of a merciful monarch, emphasising Augustus' mildness and stating grandly that: "The ideal to which a prince might best mould himself is to deal with his subjects as he would wish the gods to deal with him." I found it ironic. If I treated my people as the gods treated me I should outdo Caligula.

Book Four

OEDIPUS

"O Light! May I never look on you again,
Revealed as I am, sinful in my begetting."
OEDIPUS REX

Chapter Eleven

Three years passed in peace and quiet. I ruled my empire as best I could, remembering the value of justice, strength, and generosity, and carefully showing myself at Games and Festivals to prove my good-will. Burrus was my intermediary with the army and Seneca my spokesman at the Senate. There were no more plots.

In the tenth month of my reign Acte gave birth to a son. It was July and burning hot, the time when I preferred to be at the sea. Not a breath of air cooled the room where she lay; slaves bathed her face with iced water and fanned her with peacock feathers while I stood beside her, saying: "You will be all right; you *must* be all right," as though imperial wishes moved the gods. She said: "I'm not frightened," then flinched in pain but never cried out. She was more of a Stoic than Seneca.

He was born at early evening, a squalling red scrap of a baby. At first he seemed hopelessly ugly but when I looked closer I saw the Julian eyes. She gave him to me with complete pride. She had always felt her slavery and the fact that she could give me nothing material of her own as I gave her jewels and clothes; this was her one gift and the very best.

I called him Germanicus after my grandfather. Of course, the whole thing had to be kept quiet. She bore him in secrecy and from that day no one knew of his existence apart from those nearest to me. It would not have done for the people to know that my mistress had become a mother while my wife remained sterile. I had not dared face Octavia since I met Acte. My abominable imagination pictured her agony of mind, the biting sense of rejection which I had known myself and therefore pitied. In fits of guilt I sent her presents which were always returned and singers to entertain her who were promptly dismissed. As for Acte she insisted on looking after the baby herself, so rooms were set apart especially for her. I visited her every day and watched the baby grow, showing my hair and eyes and her nose. When I look back these times seem the happiest; I could even imagine I was an ordinary husband and father living in quiet contentment with politics a faint dream beyond the window.

Outside her apartments the illusion vanished. There were petitions to be judged, legal cases to be decided, law-making and taxes to be considered with the Senate. I found my position as supreme judge a great responsibility. One word decided the fate of the litigants who looked to me as god on earth, infallible; the thought of injustice horrified me. In order to avoid making mistakes I never gave an immediate answer but asked my advisers to put down their opinions in writing, then considered them in the quiet of my room and came to a decision. Public speeches allowed too much emotionalism; actors work by the same principle. I suppose my scrupulousness arose from my childhood memories where thoughtlessness and disinterest had covered me in bruises, mind and body. I did not want any of my subjects to be like the child in the stable. I also insisted that each side should set forth the details of the case methodically, point by point, and not brush it off in one speech covering the whole affair. This annoyed the lawyers because it lengthened the process and made it more complex but I merely fixed them with my eye and said: "Gentlemen, we are here to see justice done whether it takes three hours or three weeks."

I also had a wonderful idea of abolishing public taxes. It made me furious to think of the tax collectors amassing vast fortunes at the expense of my suffering people. What better gift could an emperor make. Seneca said: "Don't be absurd. The empire can't function without money."

"It could function without the private wealth of the publicans," I said. "The people aren't supporting Rome; they

198

are feeding the tax collectors with peacock and wine."

He said that could not be proved; if I attempted to deprive the publicans I should empty the imperial coffers.

"Stop all taxes," he said, "and where are you? Poverty-stricken, my prince. It has always been the people's burden to pay for state responsibilities; they make up the state therefore they pay state expenses."

"They form the state," I said slowly, "yet the state is more important than them. It's illogical, Seneca." I looked at him. "For a Stoic you're very knowledgeable on finance."

"I should be a poor adviser," he retorted, "if I were not. We believe, my prince, that each man is born to serve the common good. That involves money."

"And individual freedom?"

"Must be sacrificed if needs be. The cult of the individual can lead to selfishness. Your generosity is commendable, Nero, but too extreme; you would do well to forget it."

I did not, of course. I fought it out with the Senate, recalling the brothers Gracchus who had first made wheat available to destitute Romans by placing cost of transport on the state. It was my duty, I argued, as Princeps Senatus and Imperator to remove crushing misery from my people. They objected, polite but firm. The empire would collapse without taxes; the people must bear their burden and be thankful for protection in return. They sounded like so many Senecas. I could not fight; when the emperor clashes with the Senate on a point like this everyone knows who wins. Money speaks louder than justice or pity. They allowed a brief edict which stated that all laws regulating taxes must be made public and that the praetor in Rome and governors in the provinces should hear complaints against the publicans. My grand dream died with a whimper. Still, the people were aware of what I had tried to do and showed their gratitude whenever I appeared. It gave me some sense of achievement. As a gesture of defiance I transferred forty million sesterces from my private treasury to the public funds which made the senators look tight-fisted. Again, it eased my conscience.

On top of all this there was the war in Parthia to be con-

sidered. Armenia had always been coveted by its strong neigh-
bour and as she was Rome's vassal we were bound to send
help once trouble started. Burrus advised that I send Corbulo,
the best general we had, to command Roman troops there. It
looked like being one of those long colonial wars which drag
on with no decisive victory on either side; I tried to forget it.
I was not like great-great grandpa; war bored me stiff. It
is ugly, cruel, often absurd, and a wholesale destroyer of everything beautiful from women to cities. I diligently read the
various dispatches and tried to look serious when Burrus held
forth on what should be done. He wrote the orders; I merely
signed them.

Naturally I needed relaxation. During the day I found it in
the form of driving a chariot, the fulfilment of a dream first
conceived on the Aventine balcony. I had an enclosure made in
the Vatican valley which lay on the other side of the Tiber and
was good ground for racing, flat but not too soft. Seneca was
critical.

"I consider it a mistake," he said pompously, "for the
emperor to show himself publicly in such a fashion. It attacks
dignity."

"Why?" I demanded. "It's a fine sport."

"For plebs, my prince, not Caesars. Charioteers have a reputation for lax behaviour, selfishness, and a hardened skin,
all caused no doubt by excessive adulation. If the people see
you in a chariot they will automatically attribute those
characteristics to you."

I said: "Rubbish! Really, Seneca, your arguments are weak.
Anyone would think I was going to have a public orgy."

He flushed angrily but said nothing. I was beyond his control
now and he knew it; it made him more fussy. Anything I
attempted independently, whether political or personal, he
disapproved of simply because he had not advised it.

My chariot was painted with golden nymphs and dark satyrs
and had Medusa's snake head embossed on the wheel hubs. I
had only two horses being a beginner, one a chestnut Hirpine,
the very best breed, and the other a white stallion bred in
Thessaly. They went as if winged. Like a fool I spurred them

on, craving the ecstatic speed I had dreamed of, a galloping wind and the ground spinning from under me like something living. My rein holder had two handles shaped as snakes which dug my hands; ahead were the streaming manes and ears laid back. I felt like a god.

Then we came to the turn. I realised I could not do it, not at this speed, and yelled at the patient charioteer who was supposed to be training me: "For Jove's sake what shall I do?"

"Tighten the reins! " he shouted. "Pull back so they feel the tug."

He might as well have told me to stop the wind. I dragged with all my strength but only succeeded in nearly losing my balance. I could hardly see for dust and speed; as we neared the turn I caught sight of his face, a white streak of terror. I was his responsibility; an emperor's blood lies heavy on anyone's hands.

"Cut yourself free! " he yelled. "And jump! "

I somehow got the knife from my belt and slashed at the reins; it seemed to take a century. The leather was tough and would not yield, then I felt the real panic-terror of a man seeing death at the next corner. I thought: Jove have mercy, and the reins snapped, I pitched backwards and tumbled out of the chariot all in a rush; as I went down I thought: what will Seneca say? The next moment I was in the dust. Hands turned me over and a frantic voice said: "Sire, are you—" I smiled weakly, said: "I'm perfectly all right," and fainted—

He was giving me wine when I came round. An interested audience stood behind, one of whom had fetched the wine from a nearby shop. The horses, believe it or not, had rounded the turn safely and were now cropping grass at a nearby bank, the chariot at rest behind them. Had I stayed in I should have been healthier than I was now.

"Are you hurt, sire?" said my trainer anxiously.

I said: "I can stand up," did so, and collapsed again; one ankle had gone. They sent for a litter and I went home bruised but happy; any pain was a small price for such utter joy. Even the danger seemed a pleasure. Xenophon said my ankle was sprained and forbade me to walk for the next few days; I also had bruises all down one side which hurt to lie on and a graze on my face. Seneca said: "My prince, I warned you ..."

"Not of this, you didn't," I retorted. "Don't try and take advantage. There is all the more reason now for me to go on and improve myself."

At the end of a month I could drive a two-horse team reasonably well. My trainer begged and pleaded with me not to go fast but I persistently did; he said pathetically: "Sire, have you no nerves?"

"Only where people are concerned," I said. "Not horses."

I learned how to handle the reins and use the whip, how to increase and decrease speed and round a bend without ending in a tangle. When I moved up to a four horse team I felt like Caesar conquering Gaul.

One day I noticed some children trying to climb the wall and watch me so I said they could come into the enclosure. Next day there were adults, too. A week later I thundered round the track to the cheers of several hundred people.

"It's disgraceful," I heard Seneca say to someone. "Why he can't see the indignity of it I cannot think." Then he saw me and assumed an admiring attitude, saying: "I hear your chariot racing is improving, Nero."

I had known he was two-faced but not to this extent. I said: "You're the worst liar I ever met, Seneca."

He looked pained and said: "Sire, forgive me, I don't see your point. I have it on the best authority that your riding *is* improving."

"And what about the indignity of it?"

He raised his eyebrows. "A debatable point, my prince. You already have my opinions on it."

I said no more. Perhaps he could not control me but he could still turn my head with words.

All this time my mother remained strangely quiet. I even went through periods of forgetting she existed until the next formal visit when her eyes would remind me of a permanent threat. I saw her once every month. She was always sweet and talkative, offering me wine in her best manner and chattering on inoffensive things like any domesticated matron. I kept cool and aloof while remaining polite. I did not tell her of Acte's baby nor would I have mentioned the chariot racing but she did first, praising my progress. To start with I had my food and drink tasted but then gave it up as nothing happened; she no longer seemed a woman prepared to kill. Little by little I reduced my accompanying guard as it seemed absurd to have polite conversation with one's mother while armed soldiers stood at the doorway. Eventually I took only one and I'll swear he went to sleep. The whole business was strange and brittle as though we acted a play or walked on ice which might collapse into the reality of water. I still felt she was planning something. The quietness frightened me because it gave no indication of danger, no more than summer air which brings a storm.

In looks she had not changed. She was forty-three now and lovelier than ever; her beauty was the kind which matures like wine not the Messalina loveliness which is gone after thirty. Her body was slender and her breasts firm, her hair still thick darkness. I felt sure that somewhere in that chaste villa there was a lover. So long as he was no one of political importance who could be corrupted I did not worry; it would keep her mind off intrigue. "I expect you'll find the whole Praetorian Corps in her bedroom," Otho had said. I contradicted him almost angrily and he grew wary, saying: "You're ready to fall into another trap, Nero; be careful." I called him a trouble-maker.

That December I was twenty-one. Acte was just twenty, a graceful fair creature who no longer looked a child; my son was toddling. Saturnalia came with its usual blaze of light and feasting, presents given and received before the Lord of Misrule. It is a feast for the family. On the last day of it my mother invited me to midday dinner. I went in good-will because of the season, taking no guard; it would be a household feast with all attending.

But when I entered the room I saw only her. She sat on the couch in a blue silk stola tied with ribbons under the breasts, covered in a palla all silver and glittering as if polished. Apollo knows what it must have cost; I had forgotten her vast personal fortune. Her necklace and earrings were opal set in gold and a bracelet of rubies twined three times round her wrist in the shape of a snake. It made me think of my own which I still wore. Her shoes were pearl covered and her hair was loose like a maiden's but curled high on top and held with a gold comb from which fell strands of pearls either side. When I looked to her face I was four years old again and seeing her for the first time; a goddess, appalling and beautiful.

I blinked, thinking I must be drunk without wine. She said: "Sit down Lucius. How are you?"

"Well," I said. "And you, mother?"

"I'm never ill." She was the calm hostess.

"Where is everyone else?" I asked. "It's quiet for Saturnalia."

"Oh no." She looked at me, wide-eyed like a young girl. "This is only for you and me, Lucius dear. A family meal."

I thought it odd. She was strangely careful and attentive and very beautiful; it seemed a device to divert suspicion. I sat and looked at the wine which the slave had brought and my mind ran on poison.

I gave her my present, a gold-embroidered dress of hyacinth shade, a most expensive colour. Hers was a cup of pale pink rock crystal from Egypt set with chased gold at the rim; I was not expecting it. I must have looked startled. I thought: does she want something? Beautiful clothes, an expensive present— and no slaves. I suddenly realised this. They brought our food and wine and set it down on the cedar-wood table between us but they did not serve us. She poured the wine herself.

I said: "Mother, can't a slave do that?"

"We don't want slaves," she said. "Not at a family meal." She leaned forward with the cup and smiled into my face. "Here, Lucius darling . . ."

I turned cold; there was no guard outside, no antidote near at hand, only her face and the shining goblet. I cursed my stupidity. As I summoned courage to refuse it she tipped it at my mouth as you would with a child and some went down; I pushed her away and said: "Mother!"

She was laughing. "Silly boy," she said. "Did you think it was poisoned?" I stared. "You still don't trust me," she said.

204

"My dear child, credit me with more intelligence than that. The emperor goes to dinner with his mother and mysteriously collapses; think how it would look."

I said nothing, only gulped the wine. An hour later, full up with stuffed dormice and roast pig, I was still alive but distinctly happier. The room looked delightful. Painted columns, twined with flowers, glowed on the wall amongst grape vines and maidens treading wine; statues of Corinthian bronze stood in all the corners. In the middle of the table stood the dancing Venus I had given her. The place felt warm with wine and well-being. I smiled and said: "Thank you, mother; that was a lovely meal."

"Dear Lucius," she said. "Have some more wine."

I must have accepted her offer. The maidens on the wall began to dance around and the flowered columns leaned sideways; Venus winked from amongst the empty plates. My mother leaned back on her cushions, with her cup aloft, flushed and smiling, her breasts pushed up by the ribbon; she might have been Venus herself. In a muddled way I was reminded of Messalina.

She said: "Come and sit beside me, Lucius darling."

I got up, clutching my cup, tripped against the table and subsided on the couch, giggling.

"Mother," I said, "I must *apologise* for thinking the wine was—"

She laughed and the sound seemed to fly to the ceiling and echo there. "My dear, it doesn't matter. You have my sense of self-preservation." She lifted my chin with one finger and said: "You have my face, too, or rather my father's with a little of Augustus—Augustus was so beautiful when young."

Her face was close, huge; the room dwindled behind. I could see each of her blackened eyelashes and the black dot expanding in the centre of the eye. I thought: Uncle Caligula. I was in a dream. The eyes were deep blue, her mouth was parted; her earrings flashed green and pink. Those eyes had so terrified me once; now I was slowly drowning in them, down, down, and down, losing myself. She kissed my mouth.

"Mother . . ." I said sleepily.

Images stirred and struggled out in my mind; a warm lap, warm breasts, a voice singing somewhere as I wept into straw. I was small and afraid and the arms were warm. The voice was murmuring my name and being kind. I clung tight and pressed my face against the soft breasts and soon I would sleep, very soon, and the storm would be shut away; the dark woman with the snake hair could not catch me here.

Stars burst in my eyes. I was trembling. Something pressed against me and I began to suffocate. It was all wrong but I could not escape; the hands of the barber's shop held me fast and I could not cry out, there was no one to hear, no Marcus to drag me away from danger. I groaned in the darkness and struggled, then suddenly I was free. I tumbled to the floor and hurt my knees.

My eyes were clear. I could see the couch support of grained wood, ending in a horse's head, every detail distinct. It was not a barber's shop. The floor was marble; a cup lay near me in a pool of wine. I looked up, shaking, and there she was, lying calmly on the couch and tying the ribbons under her breasts.

I knew then what it meant to look Medusa in the face. The blood fled from me, sinking back thick and soured to the heart which gave it life. I tried to move but I was stone; my teeth were chattering.

I said: "What have you done?"

She laughed. "Lucius darling, get up from the floor. You look pale. Have some wine."

I said: "What have you *done*?"

My voice was harsh, breaking on itself. She looked at me, suddenly shrewd; then it was gone. She smiled as I had seen her smile at Pallas, at Claudius, at every man she wanted to attract.

"Don't you remember?" she said.

I began to think I was dreaming, that it was all a dreadful lie she was thrusting at me like the tale over my paternity. Then I saw her silk stola where it was bunched in her hand.

Someone began screaming. The room filled with scurrying feet, hands seized me; a voice said, gasping: "No—leave him. It's a fit. Like his cousin; he can't help it." Hands relaxed.

The darkness was rolling back in terrible waves. I saw the ceiling swirl with its painted relief and dissolve; something sweet filled my throat.

"There," said my mother. "There, there, my poor child."

She leaned over me with the wine cup. Faces peered behind, strange faces.

"Shall I fetch a doctor, madam?" someone said.

"No; it will pass." She was stroking my face. I could see mottled bruising round her throat as though someone had attacked her. "It's all right, Lucius, you know me, don't you? You know who I am."

I said: "You are my mother."

They helped me outside and into the litter. I heard someone say: "Epilepsy like divine Julius. But it took him a strange way."

I said: "It wasn't—" but couldn't go on. She was settling me in the litter, pulling my cloak round me; I could see marks on her shoulders, not bruises.

I half slept in the jolting litter. It was the wine. But the food lay sick and heavy on my stomach; as soon as I stepped out at the palace gates I vomited.

Xenophon came hurrying, brisk and professional. "What it it, Sire?" he said. "Have you any pain?"

I said faintly: "A pain you won't be able to cure."

He frowned, a doctor and rational to the last. They got me to my room; he felt my pulse, my heart beat, examined my mouth, then he said: "There are teeth marks on your neck."

I turned my head on the pillow and looked at him; he was puzzled, biting his thumbnail. "Xenophon," I said, "do you know the story of Oedipus Rex?"

He stiffened. "I am a Greek," he said.

I said slowly: "When you find teeth marks you look for the lioness. I have just had dinner with my mother, Xenophon." He hardly moved; it was all in his face. I went on: "If you have any pity give me something that will be quick and painless."

He was still stiff but his mouth trembled. "It is not a doctor's task to kill," he said.

207

I began to cry. A brazier burned at one end of the room; he warmed something over it, then handed me a drinking horn full of a thick, white liquid. I began to sip it, then looked at him, asking. He shook his head. He said: "It will make you sleep, no more." I drank some and said: "You won't tell—"

"A doctor respects professional secrecy," he answered.

I said, wandering a little: "You know my mother. When my father was dying—"

"Yes," he said. "I know your mother."

A little later I asked: "What hour is it?"

"Near sunset."

"All that time," I said. "All that time . . ."

When I could see again it was daylight. Acte leaned over me, saying. "Oh Nero, I was so worried; you looked as if you were dying. Are you better?"

"Yes," I said.

She smiled and said: "Praise the gods," then leaned over and kissed me; for the first time I pushed her away. Her startled look cut me like a knife. I said: "I'm still tired, Acte. I'm sorry . . ."

She retreated awkwardly. "Then I'd better go away . . ." Her face showed pain; stoicism ended where I was concerned.

At first I pretended it was a dream. The potion had made me heavy and stupid; yesterday seemed a year back. Then little things came showing themselves; the silver Venus, her mouth near mine, a pool of wine and the horse head carved on the couch support. In horror I remembered the touch of her, her hands and mouth, the perfume swelling up from her breasts; beyond that was something unspeakable. I tried to close a door in my memory but could not. Truth forces a way quicker than a battering ram.

I nearly went mad with thinking. I retraced every moment, trying to find a loophole but all roads led back to the same point; the clothes, the food, the beautiful persuasive face; perhaps she had put something in the wine. No slaves or guests, and yet – if she wanted to destroy me she would need witnesses. Only the two of us, a tight-knit, intimate situation; my flesh shrank. *Lucius darling, come and sit beside me . . .* Her hand under my chin; *You have my face, too* ... Her eyes, her tumbled hair, her breasts—

I went blindly to the door. The guard there saluted me and stood stiff, his chin in the air.

I said: "Do I look any different?"

"Sir!" He clicked his heels, then looked at me from the corner of his eye. "No, sir, not that I can see." He was confused; soldiers aren't trained for this sort of thing.

"Tell me," I went on, "do you think crime shows in the face?"

"Not in my experience, no, sir." I had made him uneasy.

I said: "Thank you," and went back to the room. He had reassured me; if I acted well enough and tried to forget it no harm would come, not externally, anyway. I wondered what she meant to do. If she spread the tale they would kill her as well; was she monstrous enough to want it for its own sake? *The bond between mother and son is the strongest.* My hands were damp; my head felt bursting. I leaned on the cool wall and thought: Apollo, seeker out of criminals, know that what I have done I did unknowing in a darkness of mind, not meaning ... Then I thought of Oedipus. Ignorance made no difference.

I did not sleep that night. I tossed, sweating and murmuring, sometimes crying out her name like a child, but not "mother"; the barriers were going up already. Her face peered from every part of the room, dancing and laughing; the eyes were no longer cruel, the hair tumbled on her white shoulders as I had seen it so long ago, twined round Pallas' fingers. When I reached out she vanished.

"Nero, what is it?" It was Acte, her face a golden blur in the lamplight. "Are you ill?"

"No, it's nothing." I was resorting to absurdities. She must see the truth in my face.

"You're sweating," she said, putting her hand on my forehead. "Oh Nero, it's fever. Let me fetch Xenophon."

My blood was running in confusion and her touch went through me like fire. "No!" I pushed her away violently. "Leave me alone; let me sleep. Don't come near me."

209

I heard her footsteps drag to the door. In my mental sickness I did not even think of her pain; no one could help, not Otho, not Acte, not Seneca, not Apollo himself. I saw now why she had done it.

The next morning I went to see her. The slave announced me and I stepped in trembling, my mind a chaos. She sat on the couch, quite calm, her head leaning on her hand; as she moved the gold drops on her earrings shivered in a cluster of sparks.

"Why, Lucius," she said, "this is unexpected."

I knew she was lying; she had been waiting for me. Her face was painted as if for a feast and I could smell her perfume from the door. For the first time I saw her as other men always had.

I said: "Mother..."

She held out her hand; I took it. She said: "You are pale; you haven't slept," as if I were six years old again. "My poor darling..."

I fell on my knees and buried my head in her lap.

The bedroom ceiling was a mosaic of blue and red bordered with gold. It seemed very far away. She thrust a wine cup at my mouth, saying: "Drink this. It will make you feel better." When I looked I saw her dress inexpertly pulled together and showing her breasts; the hair was a dark tangle on her shoulders. It was not my mother. My mother was severe and elegant with not a hair wrong, a woman who never smiled or pretended she might love you.

I said vaguely: "You won't leave me?"

"No, my sweet, I won't leave you."

When I got home I was sick again.

The litter waited in the street, its purple curtains sweeping the ground; they trailed an edge of silver. The slaves stood idle and gossiping. The black-haired woman beside me said: "Take us anywhere you like but don't stop until I tell you." Their eyebrows went up.

"Yes, madam," said one civilly and drew the curtains back. Inside, resting on a thick wood support, was a bed with a cushion. I helped her in; she smiled. The slaves took up the litter on its poles, two back and two front; we moved off. I remembered the dark warmth of another litter long ago and someone feeding me sweets to stop me crying.

I got out at the gates of the palace. She was lying drowsy and contented like one of those sleek cats our men brought back from Egypt. Her eyes moved over my face. I pulled the curtains together roughly and went into the palace, ignoring the military salutes.

"Nero, where have you been?" It was Otho standing at one of the archways, his face dappled in shadow. "I never seem to see you these days."

I tugged up my toga and said: "I've been—out."

"In a high wind by the look of you," he said. "And whose hand ruffled your hair this time?"

I rushed past him and went running down the passage; I heard him call but he did not follow. I went straight to the bath, pulled off my clothes and plunged in; the water was warmed now for winter. I called the slave and said: "Bring cold water and pour it over me." He looked surprised but obeyed. It burst from the painted jar and struck me like a blow; then I woke up.

I swam and swam and cleaned myself as though the crime were in my skin and could be washed out; I found love-bites on my shoulder. I could not think any more. When I tried her voice hurried in my ears, whispering my name, and her eyes ate me up while I shivered, blind and stupid as the rat who waits for the snake.

I imagined I had always been like this. A child had returned, the child who watched her with Pallas and Passienus and Claudius; was that why I had sent Pallas away? And had I really removed her military lovers for fear of a plot? Perhaps the first move in the triclinium had not been hers; how could I be sure? Wine loosens inhibitions and lets out the true self. *You love your mother; you used to cry because she wouldn't kiss you.* The mosaic floor was cold; I scrambled out, trembling, and yelled for the slave. He came and wrapped me round with the towel. I thought he might see the marks but he said nothing;

slaves are trained to silence. As I left the bath I vowed to stop the fire before it burned someone.

For two days I did not see her; neither did I eat or sleep. On the third day I went back.

Days drifted. I lived from moment to moment as a child will waiting for some present or a treat. She was always there, in the bedroom or triclinium of her own house, in the stifled litter, and finally at the palace. After three years she returned. I did not think what people would say; I was beyond thinking. It did not matter. It was a dream; nothing has sense in a dream.

I went through dispatches, embassies, petitions, senate-assemblies and the law courts like a bad actor, uttering inanities. Till I was with her I merely existed. Other people were shadows; when they spoke I brushed them aside as you will a fly.

"Do you really think," Seneca said, "that it is wise to have her here?"

I said: "She's my mother. Why shouldn't I?"

Otho said: "You're mad. Next thing you know there will be poison in your wine."

Acte said nothing. Like Octavia before her she was being pushed aside. I had forgotten she existed. There was only one reality; I used to play with her long black hair as it lay on the pillow and fall asleep against her breasts. I gave her presents, I sat at her feet during banquets, I breathed her perfume; my world had become tiny. I said: "You must never stop loving me; say you never will." She laughed and wound her hand in my hair.

It was a small dinner, just the two of us. She wore virgin white which showed her skin and hair dark; she gleamed sapphires and pearls and square earrings with a tiny man engraved on the centre piece. I did not believe this world could hold anything lovelier.

The meal was done; we were warm with wine. Her face was near, smooth as cream with only tiny wrinkles beginning at the eyes and faint creases on the forehead. When she laughed she was like a young girl. "My sweet Lucius..." she said; her fingers traced my cheek. I began to sink in her eyes, away from this room with its littered tables, away from Rome and Seneca and Otho and Acte, away from myself. I was not emperor; I had no name. And she had no name either, only rich hair and gentle breasts and vast, wonderful eyes. She was a woman I desired.

Then I looked over her head and saw Seneca at the door. He was my tutor; I knew him as I knew myself. But as I looked it was no one, only a face stretched and gaping with horror like the tragic masks actors wear.

The next moment he was gone. I pushed her away and slid from the couch; she said: "What is it?" I said: "I can't stay with you—it's Seneca..." My hands were cold, the wine already turning sour in my stomach.

I went to my room. Something uncomfortable pricked and stirred in my mind; I remembered lying in straw with the sound of a storm, and I felt suddenly dizzy. I sat down.

Someone said: "Nero?" I looked up and there stood Acte with her hair flung about and a wild, empty look in her eyes; she was panting.

"I went to the triclinium," she began. "Seneca said..." She struggled with the words.

"Yes?" I said.

"Oh no, Nero." She fell on her knees beside me. "It's not true; he was lying. No, I mustn't say that; he is a philosopher and a good man. Then he was mistaken. Tell me he was mistaken, Nero, tell me he made a mistake."

I said coldly: "You've been running. Why?"

"He told me to be quick. He said: stop them before..."

"You can tell Seneca," I said slowly and carefully, "that he's too late. He's late by several weeks."

She got up and backed to the wall. She looked as when I had first found her, bruised and quivering in Octavia's room; but the whiplash had been nothing. I saw that in her eyes.

"Why?" she said. *"Why?"*

I said: "Is it so dreadful?"

I was holding up the barriers with all my strength but the

213

flood waters were swelling; soon they would break. She shook her head.

"Oh my poor Nero, what has she done to you?"

I said: "It was my fault."

"No!" I had forgotten her astuteness. "*She* started it; she *made* you ... Oh Nero, don't you see, she wants her power back."

"I don't know what she wants," I said. "I don't care."

"Nero!" She was beside me again, her hand on my arm. "Oh Nero, for the sake of every god that lives, see reason. See what you've done. Sweet Jove, how has she bewitched you? Nero, she is your *mother*."

She was half shaking me. Noises came and went in my ears like a sea-surge. Her face was pale, going from me.

"She is your mother." The barriers were breaking, the darkness ready to spill out. "She is your mother. Nero, can't you see? It's incest."

Chapter Twelve

Faces moved in the darkness; voices murmured. I said: "Leave me alone."

Someone caught my arm; I looked and it was Otho. He was not laughing. He found life a game and thought it no crime to take an emperor's virginity; yet he was not laughing.

"Nero, listen to me," he said. He was earnest and serious, all the lightness of the dinner table gone. "You've got to stop. Rumours are already spreading in the city; they're even starting to make up songs about it. Do you realise what that means?"

I looked past him to Seneca who stood pale and agitated near the door. "It's true," he said. His voice was brittle. "Your mother doesn't deny it; in fact, she's proud of it." His voice shook; it was all distasteful to him, killing his dream of a Golden Age. "It is even whispered of in the Senate. My prince, I've told you so often..." He stepped forward desperately. "You can no more hide yourself than the sun. What a common person does is of no consequence; it remains behind locked doors. You cannot speak without the world hearing; you cannot kiss a woman without this city rocking on its hills."

I recognised the treatise on clemency; even in crisis he would go back to what he thought his best utterances. I stared at the ceiling and said nothing, gathering all my forces like a general near defeat.

"For the gods' sake Nero," said Otho violently. He shook me. "Don't you *see* what you've done? Romans will accept a lot of things but not this, *not this*. They know there are crimes at which even the gods hide their faces and they see family ties as sacred. Sweet Jove, not even Caligula—"

215

I said: "Stop it! For the gods' sake, stop it! "

"Otho, no." It was Acte, on the other side, still mild and compassionate. "Leave him; he is hurt enough."

"No; he's got to see. Nero, you've been living a fool's dream. Haven't you thought? She is not old; she could have a child."

The words struck me like lead; I looked to the shadows at the edge of the room and thought of Oedipus again. ... *that soil where I was sown and whence I reaped my harvest.* I had not visualised an Antigone.

I said loudly: "No; it's not possible."

My Antigone would not be loving, guiding her father to a last resting place. Her daughter would be a monster; *my* daughter—

I covered my ears and said: "Go away. I won't listen to you. Go away! "

"Tell your sin to go away," said Seneca.

I looked at him savagely. "Sin? You ask my mother where the sin is, Seneca. Three years she's been planning this like an animal which stalks and stalks before it springs. Oh gods above, I knew her power lust but I did not believe ... I was still her son; I thought she held some things sacred."

"Are you sure it was all ambition?" Otho asked quietly.

I looked bewildered. "She hardly sees you as a son," he went on. "Some women have strange desires."

I remembered my aunt's voice in the courtyard, under the fountain ... *has your mother impregnated you with her own monstrous appetites?* I buried my face in my hands. The dizziness had come back, the fatal sickness; I saw what I had done as though in a play acted behind my eyes. The triclinium with painted maidens, the wine, the couch, her face; then later, coming back for more, no longer ignorant. Oedipus was blind before he stabbed his eyes. I had turned sight to blindness through my own will, following where my blood led, treading fiercely on her scent like an animal. Twenty-one years ago she had given birth to me and there had been no oracle. I had found my own way into the shameful bed.

And she had known her power and known every minute what she was doing. All my life I had wanted her love; she knew that, too. The child in the stable prayed for warm arms and breast but she had come seventeen years too late. I could not give a child's love. I wept to think how I had despised Messalina; now I understood Britannicus' grief at her death; you weep to lose a mother's love. And all the time Oedipus' cries rang in my ears: *Hide me at once, for God's love, hide me away. Away! Kill me!*

Acte's hand was on my shoulder. "Nero," she whispered, "Oh Nero, my darling, don't cry."

The whirlwind drowned her voice, yet through it I heard Seneca. "My prince, the army will not support an emperor guilty of such a crime. It may be too late already. You must send her away."

I said: "No, I can't. Jove have mercy on me, I can't."

"You must." It was Otho now. "I told you once you must weaken her to survive. She is a fatal disease, Nero. Take the remedy before it is too late."

I said: "No, I should die. The medicine would be more fatal than the illness." The tears were coming fast. I believe I hated her but hatred is a spent arrow; it flies back in your face. "Oh gods, let me die, let me die now. I asked Xenophon at the begining but he refused. Think what we should have been saved." I looked at them squarely in the pale yellow lamplight, my tutor and the two people I had loved best in the world, and I said: "Kill me. How you like; I don't mind, only let it be quick."

They shrank; Acte started crying. "Don't be absurd," Otho began. They were cowards after all. But I still had a spark of Oedipus in me; I went to the door and said: "Guard, your sword." He handed it to me, puzzled. There was a lion head embossed on the handle; it flashed dull silver as I lifted it high and brought down the blade towards my eyes. Then strong hands caught my wrists. "Drop it, you fool!" Otho said. "Drop it!"

"Leave me alone," I said wildly. "If I must live let me be blind."

He twisted my wrist and the sword clattered down. I began to sob uncontrollably. The room swam into darkness and out

217

again as though I lay in a tunnel; the whirlwind wrapped me round.

Xenophon's voice said: "Lie him flat. Open the shutters and fetch some iced water." Faces flashed towards me and away; something cool and wet touched my forehead. Someone stood over me and I fancied it was Charon, come to row me over the Styx; they had been kind in the end and given me poison. I lay in a cold sweat and waited peacefully to die.

The gods are not so generous. I woke to another dawn and Acte's face leaning over me, swollen and pale.

"How do you feel?" she asked, trying to smile.

"My head is better," I said carefully.

I could see Xenophon at the door. I said: "Have I been ill?"

He nodded. "Several days, sire. A slight fever."

"But I didn't die," I said bitterly. "You're too good a doctor."

He got up, stretching, the job done. "You must rest, sire. You have suffered a bad shock."

I said: "Knowledge of oneself is always a shock. You told me you knew 'Oedipus Rex'."

He said firmly: "Sire, I'm a doctor, not a tragedian. And I have no poisons fit for emperors."

When he had gone Acte said: "What are you going to do?" Her voice was breaking with weariness.

"How long since you slept?" I asked, touching her hair.

"It doesn't matter." She was almost impatient. "Nero, what are you going to do?"

I said: "Exile my mother."

She was standing at one end of her reception room, part of the apartments I had given back to her in the palace.

I said: "I must ask you to leave." The words blurted out foolishly as though I spoke to a servant; I could not call her mother.

"Good heavens, Lucius," she said. "Why?"

It was a game again, a clever piece of acting. But her eyes gave her away.

I said: "You know very well why."

"Your moral friends have been at you," she said lightly. "An admirable decision, my darling, but are you capable of carrying it out?"

She moved nearer; her eyes were painted blue-grey and I could see the shape of her breasts under the tunic. A gold fibula shaped like an eagle clasped her dress at the neck and winked a ruby eye.

"Get out," I said between my teeth. "I don't want you near me."

"All men say that," she observed. Her breath was on my face; I could not see for her mouth. "I told you all men were weak." Her voice was soft. "Even noble Passienus. They all fall in the end. I know men better than I know myself, even you, my sweet."

A red light jumped at my eyes. I must have pushed her back for the next minute she was at a distance and looking startled like a beast ringed by hunters.

I said: "Oedipus' mother hanged herself."

"Oedipus did not know what he was doing," she returned.

"Neither did I." My hands trembled. "You planned it all like a conspiracy."

"Oh no." Her eyes went hard. "I forced the wine at your mouth the first time but after that you came back and pulled it from my hands. You were mad like a bacchante; don't you remember? You even threatened me with a knife."

The whirlwind was returning; I could hear its roar in my ears. Her figure was absurdly small, dancing about at the end of the room as if on a string. She was laughing. I started yelling. I think I called her every obscene name I knew but she still laughed like an adult at a child's futility. Then the whirlwind drowned me.

She was gasping and choking, her mouth open; her eyes looked wild into mine. I was saying something over and over, I forget what; then she dragged the fibula from her dress and lunged at my eyes.

I twisted away and the pin scored my arm. I let go of her and she stood panting, all dark and tumbled like a maenad ready to drink men's blood. It had left me weak. I stood looking stupid, my arm stinging and starting to bleed; then she reached forward, gentle again. "Poor Lucius," she said. "I didn't mean to hurt you."

She put her arms round me. I said: "No ..." and started to cry. She stroked my hair and said: "There, there, my poor darling. I'm not angry any more ..."

A voice in my ears said feebly: *My prince, the army will not support an emperor guilty of such a crime;* then it fell silent.

I had lost myself again. Somewhere in the middle of heated darkness she said: "How do you know there isn't a child?" but it made no sense. There were bruises on her neck again. I remember her hair as I left and her sleeping face on the pillow; it looked purified.

Xenophon put something on my arm to stop it poisoning. Like a good doctor he asked no questions but his face told me what he knew; and then I came to myself.

I went to Otho and said: "It's no good. I can't exile her."

I must have sounded fatalistic. He looked at me sharply and said: "That's no answer. What did she say?"

"She tried to blind me," I said wearily. "With her brooch. She knows Sophocles, too, and I always thought her illiterate."

"For Apollo's sake." He looked exasperated. "A personal attack on the emperor counts as treason and you say you can't exile her."

"Don't you know why?"

I tried to tell him with my eyes rather than speak what is forbidden. He groaned and looked despairing. "Oh Nero, what shall we do? Would you play helpless if a man came at you with a sword? It's the empire in the balance; only you can weight the scales one way or the other."

I said: "Let me think for a few days. It's the fever, Otho; I'm confused."

I saw he did not accept the lie. He made me sick and ashamed which brought anger, yet he and Acte and Seneca were fighting to save me from myself; they thought only of honour. Or did they? If I fell so did they, crushed in the collapse of the king oak. I saw now how she had soured me.

Within a few days the fever had returned, but not a fever Xenophon could cure. I lay weeping into the pillow and cursing her while my blood burned and my eyes saw nothing but her hair and eyes as though a universe could contain itself in a woman's face. Too late I realised that each indulgence had weakened my resistance. The germ had me now, body and soul, beyond medicine's help.

Acte brought me wine and food and bathed my face; she was so good and gentle, yet I tried to send her away. Any other woman would have scratched my face. I asked for a mirror; she brought one of her own, backed with silver and a relief of cupids. When I looked the face seemed reproachful, the cheekbones sharp with lack of food and the eyes hollow and red. Yet my grandfather was still there and something else as well; even in my reflection she mocked me.

I tried to make bargains. If she goes away I need never see her again; she can go to Corsica or Africa, somewhere far, or she could even stay in Rome. I argued like a crafty lawyer. If I send her away it will look strange, as though I hate her; Romans respect family ties. Then I thought: *How do you know there isn't a child?* It was another piece of blackmail like Caligula which could not be proved either way; only she knew. She had a hold on me all ways. Men say the Furies hunt a murderer down with his own conscience but I swear before Jove that they can destroy you through a madness of the blood.

There was no time to lose. Already I had missed two Senate assemblies and refused an embassy. Seneca had published bulletins on my poor health but I doubt if they were believed; *they're starting to make up songs* ... Even in my fever I saw all this. I sweated and wept and called her unspeakable names while Acte bathed my face and made me drink. Obscure figures waited in the shadows.

"If it goes on much longer," one said, "it will mean a military uprising."

At the end of a week Apollo the Healer cured my fever and left me clear. I knew what I must do.

"If you think it's the only way..." Otho said.

"I know it is," I said. "Exile is useless. She will still exist for me to recall when the torment becomes too bad. And it will. She has the power she wanted."

He watched me, sympathetic, but hiding his thoughts. We were in one of my private rooms; rain streamed outside the window and coldness rose from the marble floor. I sat huddled in a cloak, my hand struck through my hair in a tragic pose; only it was real.

I said vaguely: "I suppose I liked the sense of power, too. I had always feared her; now she was submissive to me as a slave might be. I knew that in this one thing all men and women come down to a level but with her it seemed impossible; she was my mother."

"Was?" Otho said.

"I cannot look upon her as anything," I said, lying. Oedipus' words drummed again in my head: *bride, wife and mother.* "She is an animal. There is no crime in killing an animal run mad."

But as I spoke the words turned to sickness on my tongue. He saw how it was and said quickly: "Come now, Nero, we must think. How is it to be done?"

"Her own way," I said. "The most potent poison I can get my hands on."

"Is that wise?" He was calm as he had been over Britannicus. How I had misjudged my laughing dinner companion; he had a strength and self-possession I could not summon. "Is a woman like that not likely to have antidotes?"

"Yes," I said, "you are right; in fact, I've seen them in her room."

I was shivering but he took no notice. "Besides," he went on, "it might point dangerously to you. Can't we do it respectably with the sword of justice?"

"Not without implicating her in a plot first. Oh, don't worry; ever since the Plautus business she has been extremely careful."

"Then I can't see," he said as if giving up.

I looked to the grey rain and said dismally: "Is she to defeat me even in this? Oh Otho, why did she have to give me life when she could have strangled me at birth?" then I remembered: *You were my key to open the door* ... "Do you know," I said, "I used to dream of playing Oedipus before an audience; Terpnus said you must *be* Oedipus. And I didn't ask for it; why me? Why was I born to suffer like this? Otho, do you know what it means to hate yourself so much that you want to—"

He said: "Stop it! You mustn't go back to that. My poor Nero, you have been a victim; no one blames you."

But I saw otherwise in his eyes; he knew.

"Listen," he said briskly. "A festival would give the cover necessary and preferably away from Rome."

"Quinquatria," I said.

He counted dates on his fingers. "It's nearly three weeks to the Ides," he said. "Four more days to the beginning of Quinquatria. Where do you usually spend it?"

"Rome. But last year I went to Baia. You were with me."

"Yes, of course. Then that's it, Nero. You invite her down to Baia like a loving—with all hospitality and when she is there we arrange something. Perfect! "

I said: "Is it really March already?"

"The first is tomorrow. The winter's nearly over, thank Jove."

"Two months," I said slowly, "since—it seems a week. Otho, I'm like a sick man waking up and not knowing where he is."

"I know," he said gently. "I've watched you. But it's over now."

"Three weeks," I said. "How can I live through three weeks and not go to her?"

In fact, she took a holiday. She was going to my father's villa at Antium where I had been born and wanted me to go, too; with a harsh effort I refused. I think I should have gone mad had I seen the room where she bore me.

Once she was gone a kind of madness did come. I was restless, depressed, unable to put myself to anything. I could not have Acte in my bed; one night I heard her crying and

223

felt like a murderer but it was useless; I wanted mature wine, not milk. Seneca was irritable and self-righteous, buzzing on my nerves till I wanted to scream. He had been badly frightened. A philosopher sees evil more than most men and he had written his own "Oedipus"; I had read it when it meant nothing, no more than a woman's kiss when you are small. I let out my inner turmoil in a stream of poems, all very bad but purging. They were ugly and passionate, a few completely impious. One, on her beauty, I named "Calpurnia" in case anyone should see; but I burnt them all after.

One night I went to the brothels, alone and in my wig. I don't know what I was looking for; I only knew I could not endure another night in my lonely bed. There was Acte but innocence should not be sullied. Prostitutes were my level.

And I found one who looked like her, even to the hair and eyes and shape of the mouth. Close up the illusion fled; she was ten years younger, yet commonplace like stone against diamonds, and when she opened her mouth the brothel came out. But she did not need to speak. I took her home and rolled her on the bed as the whore she was; a thirsty man will drink ditch water if there is nothing else. But lust not linked to love is a broken promise. Afterwards you are embittered. To this day I remember her face, thick with paint, and her large, graceless breasts; she exhausted me but gave no satisfaction. Next morning I sent her away with gold and waited in agony for Quinquatria. I did not think of freeing myself, only of seeing her again.

The grey, sick winter gave to spring; it comes early at Rome. The trees budded tiny green leaves, new and fragile, and the air lost its bite. We no longer needed braziers burning all day in the palace.

Two days before Quinquatria I travelled down to Baia. It takes a day even with a good horse and I had my retinue as well as donkeys loaded with clothes and the gold plate I dined off and took everywhere with me. Acte did not come; the crime must not touch her. We had sunshine all the way but the air was sweet and cool and the hills far and clear and green with winter rain; Southern Italy is high. The hills leap suddenly from a flat plain as though a god set them down without thought. We passed tiny villages high on their peaks and great rolling aqueducts, stone-arched, which carry water to Rome.

Baia climbs a hill facing a blue bay. As we toiled up towards it, the donkeys sweating and having to be whipped on, I could see the cool graceful villas, white against the dark points of cypresses and olive trees with the green hill behind and a washed blue sky trailing scraps of cloud. My villa was the biggest with fluted Corinthian columns and a garden in the middle where the fountain was a cross-legged Pan, his flute spouting water in six different places. The villas rise up the slope with stone terraces in between; these are pillared either side and lead to the edge of the cliff so that you can stand and watch nothing but the sea.

We were met by the Prefect of the fleet of Misenum, none other than my old Greek tutor Anicetus who, after his dismissal, entered the navy and having proved efficient earned promotion quickly. I was almost stupidly glad to see him. He brought back an innocent world of letters and numbers and beads on a frame, a time of happiness that I had not recognised because a child's mind is limited and cannot make comparisons. He had arranged an entertainment for us, a naumachy, naturally, after Augustus' style except that they used the bay and not an artificial lake. There was a naval battle first, fought harshly until the water was red and bobbed corpses, then a troop of nymphs swam on with flowers in their hair to make a pleasant change. Lastly, came a huge galley crammed with caged beasts, every kind you can think of. I counted a hundred lions and fifty tigers, even some elephants as well as those creatures with long thin necks which look as if they will break; also, crocodiles from the Nile and thick, ugly beasts with horns on their faces. It seemed a strange god must have spawned them. Anicetus said they came from the dark part of Africa where even the natives won't go.

You never heard such growling and screeching and bellowing; they battered their cages till I thought they must break even though the big creatures were hemmed in by iron. The ship sailed backwards and forwards a few times to let us have a good look, then split in half and spilled the lot in the water.

Some, like the elephants, went down at once, dragged by the weight; the lions tried to swim. The crocodiles seemed quite at home so some brave gladiator speared them from the deck of another ship; I should hate to think of them breeding round our coasts. When the last animal had vanished, gurgling, I said to Anicetus. "How is it done?"

"A device in the hold," he said, "which forces it open and splits the ship. Some system of weights, I think. You would need to ask one of my engineers."

The entertaining done, my mind slipped back like a loosened hound. I spent the eve of Quinquatria walking up and down the covered terraces and watching the waves bound against the quay. The hills above the bay were blue and mauve in the distance, green and wooded near at hand. It had become warm and the sun spilled clear yellow between the columns as I walked, turning it over and over in my head. It was there Otho caught me.

"When are you going to invite her here?" he said.

"I don't know." My stomach tightened at the thought. "Don't we need to think of something first?"

"I can think better in the sun," he said.

We walked along the grass terrace, planted with small vines and scarlet flowers, just blooming; you could see the bright blue sea between the leaves. There was a statue of Neptune holding a trident and a little stone wall with a fountain.

He said: "We've got five days to play with as it finishes on the twenty-fifth. You had better get her down here now rather than risk delay. Write one of your flourishing letters."

I leaned my hand on the warm wall and said: "And how do we—"

"I don't know. Let me think." He wandered up and down, staring at the ground like a philosopher. A tiny green lizard flicked near my feet and made me jump; my nerves were in pieces.

"Nero, of course!" He looked up and I knew he had it. His inventiveness was extraordinary. "The ship that split in half. Remember? All you have to do is fix the hold of one of your own ships the same way, then find some reason for getting her into it—I know. The evening she arrives I'll give a banquet in her honour at my villa and you place the ship at her disposal for the journey; it's about two and a half miles from here."

"Then we have to warn the crew," I said doubtfully.

"Oh yes, they will have to be part of it. You must pick trustworthy men."

I couldn't understand his calmness; you would have thought he was planning a game. But then it was to him: a game where you win or lose depending on your ability to cheat. He had never felt this cruel pricking which I had first known in the filthy stable, the pursuer on the heels of every misdeed.

"So many people involved," I said wearily. "Why can you never do wrong in isolation?"

He looked at me sharply and said: "Nero," in a warning voice; to him thought was the beginning of weakness.

"All right," I said. My body seemed to weigh like lead. "I'll tell Anicetus."

He proved eager and helpful. I had forgotten he would hate my mother; after all, she had dismissed him for no reason. He was a resolute man with a clear head, good for a crisis. His engineers went to work and the ship was ready next morning. He never asked the reason for planning such a crime but I don't doubt he knew; news goes fast, even in two months, if it is the emperor's name.

I wrote her a long, loving letter which drew the blood from my veins; despite the motive I meant it. I told the messenger to ride hard. He returned the same day and she came with him, thinking no formal acceptance necessary. I ran down to the quay like any love-sick fool, my heart leaping; I could see her unmistakable hair from a long way off. She turned and smiled, then I calmed myself and walked with dignity as an emperor should but when I kissed her it was Rome again and my two month sickness.

She had come by land with slaves and cartfuls of stuff. She could never move without her wardrobe. I escorted her to her villa which was near mine, aware of the admiring eyes either side, for her beauty and my filial attentiveness.

"How are you, Lucius?" she said.

227

She sounded formal and perhaps a little cold which un-nerved me. Had something leaked out?

I said: "Very well. I've been so lonely without you."

"I offered you my villa at Antium," she replied.

Had my refusal angered her? Yet here I was, declaring an affection which, heaven help me, was perfectly genuine. I shall never understand women.

I said: "I had pressing state duties. Don't be angry with me."

Then she melted and I left quickly; I trusted myself least of all.

Quinquatria is mainly Minerva's feast. Everyone under her patronage celebrates it, schoolteachers and pupils, spinners, weavers, and all artists, poets, actors and painters. Because of this I considered it my feast and prayed to the goddess for release from my horror; then I remembered that it is Minerva who carries the Gorgon's head on her shield. I did not believe any god had mercy enough to hear me.

In Rome the festival would begin with a state sacrifice at the Aventine temple; here, the people filled the streets cele-brating the birth of spring. For those not under Minerva's patronage it was the feast's main point. I could hear flutes and singing from the shore as I waited in Otho's villa for news. I had sent the galley round with a message that it was to bring her across the bay; the captain had orders to operate the device when they were in mid-water. The singing rose louder. There was no cares for them, my people. Not for them the whisper-ing shadows and stir of the Eumenides in the outer darkness; these things are reserved for kings.

I searched the sea for any sign of a wreck. Otho's villa was in a clear place, set high on the bluff of a hill, and I could see across to Baia and my villa. A red sunset splashed the water with blood. Then a litter arrived. The curtains parted and out she stepped, dressed for festivities in green and gold and spangled with emeralds. I stared, horror-struck, and yelled for Otho.

"She guessed," I said, my voice shaking. "Look!"

"Don't be ridiculous," he said. "How could she?"

"Someone must have heard; she has spies everywhere. Otho,

I'm done for. She'll rouse the army against me."

"Keep your head," he said severely. "It means she must go back in the boat, that's all. Get rid of any suspicions during the banquet; treat her with great affection."

"That won't be hard," I said.

He pretended not to hear. He indulged in all passions, yet kept a firm control upon them; games must never become a nuisance. I believe he despised me.

It was a rich, noisy feast like all Otho's functions. He had spared no expense. At the beginning he stood up and made a speech praising my mother, flattering her beauty and wisdom and saying how Rome owed the making of a just monarch to her. I wriggled in my seat while he spoke. She sat straight and smiling, apparently believing it; she had no reason to doubt my love. She sat in the place of honour and I sat on the steps of her couch, handing her wine as a slave might, offering her food, asking if her cushions were comfortable; was she too hot, too cold? I never left her alone. She looked slightly bewildered and treated me like a lover who had lost his head which embarrassed me before so many. I ran through a fantastic series of conversation topics, all innocuous, and allowing me to be at times gay and flippant and at others deeply serious. I exerted all the charm I had. I could see it working, softening her marvellous face and wiping out the suspicion.

The entertainments were respectable, very unlike Otho. He was tactful, knowing my mother must be entirely at ease. An actor gave us the story of Theseus and the Minotaur and a citharoedus sang Thyestes' speeches from Seneca's tragedy in order to sweeten the author who sat with us; he knew nothing of what I meant to do but I should need his good-will later. Anyway, Minerva's feast is a time for literary matters. I made sure my mother drank a lot; it was wine blended with pitch and resin and preserved in sealed amphorae, the most potent. Our drinking bowls were filled from a common dish into which the wine had been poured. It is considered debauched to drink it neat so I diluted mine well but I ordered the slave to add only a little water to hers. Wine dulls the sense of danger.

The time came. It was past midnight and she said she was

tired. As we stood up I remember the bright room with its door posts of yellow marble and Venus in a great pink sea shell on one wall, the heaped tables and crushed cushions, all caught in the glow of the lamps; but they were already burning down. Long shadows crept across the darkening floor. As we went I remembered a line from Seneca's "Oedipus": *With apprehensive feet / Let me go out upon my darkened way.*

It was a still, warm night. The stars were scattered brilliant over the hills like blossom spray and the sea heaved gently as if breathing. The moon divided the bay with silver. By the quay the galley rode at anchor, gay with pretty streamers and garlands. I had allowed her an exquisite coffin. The slaves stood back, waiting politely while we said goodbye.

Torches burned further along the shore where the celebrations were and snatches of song floated on the air. I could hear dancing feet and the sound of laughter. It was spring; there were no fears, no cares, my people sang; yet into such a night the Furies may come. Her emeralds glowed green fire. I could see the enchanting curve of her neck and breast and her hair which melted into the night; the paint on her face was fading with tiredness. My stomach turned to ice. I saw her at twenty-two in the pain and sweat of giving me birth, only to have a knife thrust into her back in the darkness; I saw her small, ravished by Uncle Caligula, then later married to a man who left her all bruises. But most of all I saw her face.

I said: "Mother! " and caught hold of her.

"Why Lucius," she said, "what is it? I'm not going away for good."

I said blindly: "For the gods' sake take care of yourself. I can't live without you. I only reign, I only live through you."

I meant it. The tears were filling my eyes yet I had to keep them back; she would wonder why. I held her tight for the last time and kissed her eyes and her hands; she said affectionately: "Lucius, dear..." then moved to go but I kept her back, burying my face in her breasts.

She said: "My darling, you feel hot. Have you a fever?"

"No, it's nothing." I drew back, trembling. "Take care, please take care."

230

I was almost pleading with her to make the plan a failure. She smiled again and in the darkness it seemed sad as if for a last farewell; just when I needed to believe her wicked and obscene she looked harmless, a goddess on earth, my dear, beautiful mother. She stroked my face, said: "Goodbye, dear. I shall see you tomorrow," and walked up the gangplank; the slaves pattered after, whispering. She never thought to ask for the litter. I had dazed her with wine and kisses.

The ship began to move; the streamers fluttered. She leaned on the side and waved, her face a pale smudge on the dark sea, flat as a painting. I stood shivering in the sudden cold, tears running down my cheeks. Many things went through my mind; the Circus with her sitting beside Messalina, the wedding feast when it was Uncle Claudius, her face white in torchlight on the night of my accession, and then two months ago, her laughing face in the triclinium. Something irrational battered on my memory; a bright fountain leaping to heaven and my hand reaching out towards it. This time I had not been pulled back. I had caught that fleeting brightness and possessed it, only to drown in its incalculable depths.

The ship was far out on the bay. Otho stood beside me, saying: "It's over now. Come inside." I said: "No," and still stood, watching. He saw the tears on my face and said: "She was a wicked woman, Nero."

"But still my mother," I said.

I could not go to bed. I sat up in the empty triclinium, staring at the cleared tables and the couch she had sat on. One lamp burned; I remembered that the Furies come quicker in darkness. She would not leave my mind. I thought of her life dedicated to power, the men whose hands she had passed through; by the time she came to me she had nothing more to learn. Yet she only gave herself for a reason, not merely for pleasure like Messalina. That was her fatal strength, the ability to rouse such passions in others but keep her own controlled.

I thought: perhaps it didn't work. Perhaps she escaped. But then there was a clatter of feet and Anicetus came in.

"It's done, sire," he said. "The boat collapsed somewhere near Baia."

I said: "Thank you."

The lamp fluttered and plunged shadows up the wall.

"Otho, the light!" I said in panic. "It's going out. Oh sweet gods, they're coming."

"They?" He was not very literary.

"Orestes," I said, flattening myself to the couch. "After Clytemnestra's death: *I know you do not see these beings; but I see them.*"

"Nonsense! You're dreaming." He was sharp again, holding me to reason. A kind of panic spun in my head; I said: "Don't leave me, Otho."

He tried to make me come to bed but I would not. Movement would leave me exposed, out in the dark passageways; here in the triclinium it was Venus on the wall, not a woman with snake hair.

An hour or so passed. I ordered more lamps and burnt them all round the room till it glared gold, yet the rim of darkness beyond them seemed to edge nearer. I turned my face to the cushion or pressed my fingers to my eyes but still I saw her, rising up like a sea-nymph, streaming water and crowned with seaweed. I could smell the salt in the room. A little later I imagined I saw puddles seeping across the floor and began to scream; he slapped my face. I hardly felt it.

There were voices again in the hall. Then Anicetus came in, pale and bothered.

"Sire," he said, "there has been some mistake. A messenger has just arrived from your mother, saying he is to reassure you that by the gods' grace she has miraculously escaped from a great danger."

232

Book Five

ORESTES

"To me these living horrors are not imaginary.
I know them—avenging hounds incensed by a mother's blood."
THE CHOEPHORI

Chapter Thirteen

The darkness beyond the lamps retreated; I stood up, shivering. I knew then that all the time I had wanted this.

I said: "She isn't meant to die. I'm the one doomed. How did it happen, Anicetus?"

"Some accident," he replied apologetically. "The device never worked. I'll have the engineer flogged. In addition a load of lead was to be tipped on top of the dais to make sure of her death or, at least, to ensure she would be too badly injured to swim. The roof dais broke the blow and only injured her slightly in the shoulder. Sire, your mother has considerable courage and self-possession; she at once made her slave pretend to be herself by calling out for help and as the sailors killed her she slipped into the water. It was the slave's corpse which suggested the operation's success."

"The gods are protecting her," I said wildly. "The Fates are against me; I'm doomed."

Yet as I spoke I thought of her lovely face still living, her breasts breathing. Otho looked at me, exasperated. "The Fates," he said, "act according to your disposition. Now keep your head; we must arrange something."

He called Seneca and Burrus and we held council in the triclinium. My head ached with reaction. I said weakly: "Did you know of this, Seneca?"

"I had guessed it, sire." He looked drawn; first Oedipus, now Orestes; he had thought only to teach an emperor.

I said: "Go on, attack me. I've broken all your rules."

"So did your mother," he replied. "Evil begets evil, my prince. A time has come to be merciless."

Perhaps it was genuine, more likely a clever compromise. My end meant his; and I could visualise my end very near. All the time we talked I saw her hurrying here with armed soldiers, seeking death for a would-be Orestes, or arriving in Rome to rouse the Guard and stir the people.

"Where is she now?" Otho asked.

"Her villa at Bauli," Anicetus said. "You know what a swimmer she is. She kept herself going till a boat picked her up and took her to Lucrinus Lake, the long way to avoid pursuers."

I said: "Can you defeat that kind of strength?" but they ignored me.

"The question is," Otho observed, "who is to do it? Burrus, what about the Guard?"

He shook his head. "They remember Germanicus. You must hire an assassin."

Then they just sat. I looked at them, my two official councillors, useless as a wheel when the lynch pin has gone. "For Jove's sake," I said, "someone do something. I shall be dead with fright if she doesn't get me first."

They looked sullen; Seneca seemed in a philosophic daze.

"Let Anicetus finish it," Burrus said. "He promised to. It's not my men's business."

"Very well," said my Greek tutor. "I'll take some men and go there now."

"There!" I said, turning to Burrus and Seneca. "I'm finally receiving the empire in my own right and it's a freedman who makes me a present of it."

Fear had made me angry. They remained silent, knowing conflict might finish us all. Then Otho, ever observant, said: "If she dies there must be a reason."

I said: "We have one; the very best."

"I don't mean that. Something respectable. A plot against your life would be best. I know."

He saved us again. That mind of his ran fast on its well-oiled wheels, no matter what. We called in her messenger and while he spoke to me I dropped a dagger down, called the guard and had him arrested. There was the proof. He meant to

236

stab me, the wretch. I acted my way through it blindly as though in a mask with no eye-holes; by the time I had any sense again Anicetus had gone.

I waited in the triclinium with Otho, the lamps replenished. Then hoofs sounded on the road and stopped, feet came, the door opened and there he was with two others; he said: "She is dead. There is no mistake this time."

I looked behind him to a naval centurion whose tunic was splashed with blood. I said: "How did she die?"

"Courageously." He was a truthful man. "We hacked the door down and found her lying on the bed; she was alone."

"What did she say?" I wanted the details like a man who hurts himself and thinks it virtuous.

"She said, sire: 'If you have come to find out how I am you can say I am well; if you have come to commit a crime I cannot believe my son capable of it. He has not ordered a parricide.' Then I struck her on the head with my club; she fell back. Obaritus, here, drew his sword and she dragged off her nightdress, crying: 'Strike me in the womb which bore such a son!' She was strong, sire. It took several strokes before she died."

He looked pale. Hatred or not, he was a teacher, not a murderer.

I said softly: "Did she suffer?"

"For a few moments, sire, though she made no sound. We burned her on a bonfire in the garden and someone rushed from the house as we lit it, a young man, sire. He stabbed himself, saying he couldn't live without her. We burned him, too."

"I knew there would be a lover," I said. "He was the sensible one. Otho—"

I would have fallen but he caught my arm and lowered me to the couch. I muttered: *"Strike me in the womb*—that's how she thought of me at the end. And if she told the truth and there was a child—"

They stood horror-struck but Otho shoved wine at my mouth; I was turning faint.

He said: "Come to bed for heaven's sake."

"If you stay with me." I had started to tremble. "And tell someone to bring a torch."

We passed through the atrium and up the passageway, the torch flaring above the slave's head. I remembered another corridor and torchlight on painted walls while a dog howled and feet hurried in the distance. It was my fate to meet crisis at night.

He lay down beside me, saying I was quite safe. I had more lamps brought with very long wicks to burn longer but the darkness would not go. The three Fates stood on the wall, painted naked but for flower garlands; I fancied they moved.

He touched the tears on my face and said: "Oh Nero, did you really love her so much?"

I turned from him and put my face in the pillow. My heart hammered against the mattress; I was Orestes, now, through to the bone, cursed of men and abandoned of gods, for no god had given me the order. *Like Gorgons with grey cloaks/ And snakes coiled swarming round their bodies.*

"Otho!"

"I'm here." He sounded sleepy; his hand touched mine in comfort.

I said: "Can you see them?"

"What?" His eyes were bright, near me. "Nero, stop that nonsense. There is nothing here."

"By the door." My voice cracked. "Oh sweet Apollo—I can see the snake heads; there in the shadows. And eyes—all round me. Otho, for pity's sake . . ." I caught hold of him. "Stop them; don't let them come near me. The lamps . . . stop the lamps going out."

I was shivering and crying; he gripped me and said: "Stop that. There is nothing."

"You can't see them; they only want me. Why won't the lamps shine properly? Oh gods, is it such an effort to keep the darkness back?"

Their hot breath touched my cheek; the claws reached out— I screamed and screamed and screamed.

"It's shock," a brisk voice said. "Men will see strange things then. He needs sleep."

I recognised Xenophon and said feebly: "Don't let them take me." He patted my cheek, saying: "Quiet, now. Drink this."

Otho said: "I'll stay with him."

I lay still; he pulled the cover over me, saying: "Try and sleep."

I said: "I'm frightened of the dawn."

"A moment ago it was the night," he remarked.

"But when dawn comes," I said drowsily, "I must look at my crime in the light and face other people. Otho, have they gone?"

"They were never here."

"Oh, they were. *Avenging hounds incensed by a mother's blood* . . ."

Next morning my Praetorian cohort presented themselves at the villa and assured me of their total loyalty and joy at my narrow escape; Burrus had been at work. Otho arranged for the local priest to offer sacrifices in thanksgiving.

As for me I looked at the dawn I had dreaded and saw my mother's face shine out of the sun. *Men will see strange things then.* Perhaps then we see reality. I could not stay in Baia. She was everywhere, peeping between the pillars, laughing in my room, walking along the grass terraces but vanishing when I tried to catch her. That night when I slept alone I saw her standing by my bed. Otho said it was imagination but I saw her clear as daylight, even to the glimmering emeralds. I did not cry out; I only said: "Mother," and tried to touch her but she vanished and then I wept. I threw my gold snake bangle away. When I looked at it I remembered her smooth hand holding the snake skin. Sometimes I glanced over my shoulder and just saw her disappear round a corner. Then I decided to leave.

I could not go to Rome. They might be in a fury at the death of Germanicus' daughter; besides I had sullied the city I loved and could not face the people yet. I sent a message to the Senate, composed by Seneca, explaining her plot, her dreams of ruling alone like Cleopatra; every scandal of

239

Claudius' reign was attributed to her. The gods had been good, removing such a woman. It made me cry to read it; she had been bad but Seneca had extended her badness to inhuman proportions. I had done enough harm; I did not want to see her memory spat upon. But the Senate named her birthday a day of ill omen and workmen began demolishing her statues.

I went to Naples, a few miles along the coast from Baia. It is an enchanting city, almost entirely Hellenistic in character with Greek buildings and general use of the Greek tongue. So far I had only seen Greece in books or travellers' tales. Now on either side I saw slender Ionic columns with curved capitals and people in light, drifting garments, quick and graceful, who spoke a soft, rhythmic language. They had an ease about them which suggested confidence in themselves. Because my own confidence was shattered this soothed me; somewhere, then, people existed who had not been caught up in my evil.

I visited their huge gymnasium where the young men wrestled, ran, and threw the javelin, then wandered under the cool colonnades of the palestra to talk art or philosophy. Their minds were keen and clear like polished crystal; you could not fool them. They sought truth. I should have liked to join them but felt unworthy. I also saw their theatres, one covered in and used for contests of singing and poetry, the other huge and open where plays were performed. They loved the arts and visited the theatre as Romans visit the Circus. In Rome they only cared for vulgar farces; here it was all Sophocles and Aeschylus or Aristophanes for lighter moments. I knew then that everything good in my empire had been learnt from Greece.

I stayed six months. Otho was with me and wanted to visit the brothels or spend all night drinking but I would not; instead I saw plays in the theatre and wrote poetry on Greek lines but it was soured and cruel, running on blood and thwarted passion. She was still in my bones. Seeing my frequent depressions he grew more affectionate and for a time he shared my bedroom again; but then I sent for Acte.

She came, pale and thinner, bringing my son. He was trying to talk. I explained what had happened and tried to soothe her for she seemed strange, more serious as though her thoughts were heavy. Then she started talking of some new cult she had become interested in which had begun in Syria and only recently come to Rome. I asked her about it. She said it concerned a young man who had claimed to be a god and died for it, then come alive again to show his divinity. I said: "It sounds like Uncle Caligula except for the last part. Which god did he think he was? Apollo?"

"No." She looked thoughtful. "He was the son of a god but not a god we know; the god whom the Jews see as their own. My mother said my father spoke of him but she thought it nonsense."

"Well," I said, "I expect he was mad like my uncle. And, anyway, there were lots of people who claimed to be gods' sons, Aeneas, for example; it's nothing much."

She insisted he was still a god and started talking about a crucifixion and sacrifice and a tomb found open one morning but it muddled me so I took her to bed to keep her quiet. I needed her love, not intellectual stimulation. But even there she had changed. While she lay in my arms there seemed a barrier as though our flesh would not meet; her eyes were no longer open to mine. I thought it my mother's death and tried desperately to distract her, giving her a wardrobe of Greek dresses and a beautiful vase painted in Hellene style, slender black figures on a red background. After all, she was half Hellene; I thought to wake some spark. But still she wandered alone or played with her child, deep in quietness. Then I began to see my mother again; Baia had followed me here.

I returned to Rome. As I drove down the Via Sacra in a triumphal chariot the crowds cheered and waved and threw flowers while the Senate and tribunes came to meet me in ceremonial dress. I saw children high on fathers' shoulders, crying: "Nero! Nero!" and blowing kisses. I was Orestes, not cleansed by god or man, yet here were my people in ecstasy, throwing up their love with August flowers; it turned my heart to water. I brought them only blood and the dark Furies.

I gave thanks on the Capitol, then went home to rule alone. She had given me the empire as a mother's present which she

241

had shares in; now it was all mine. Yet when I looked down the Palatine, bleached under the hot sun with only crickets chattering where she had walked, I felt a sick desolation. No one shared this high summit with me.

I flung myself into activity. Grief thrives in silence and I had no more room for it. I followed Seneca's policy and showed mercy to people my mother had wronged, recalling them from exile and allowing honours to ashes of the dead. They were acts of propitiation, offered to heaven like oxen or lambs.

I also began on an architectural project kept in mind since my accession. Imperial estates consisted of the palaces and gardens on the Palatine and various villas and grounds on the Esquiline; I wanted to connect the two. It meant building over the rough ground in between including a soft swamp-like depression right in the middle. At the foot of the Esquiline was the Carinae district, a slum area grey with dirt and disease. When I visited it with my architects I kept my nose to a scent bottle because of the stink. I said: "Sweet Apollo, I'd like to burn Rome down and start again."

"It might be an idea," replied one. "There is too much overcrowding; we need wider streets, broader houses."

Despite difficulties work began. It was not, of course, a palace in the true sense of the word, more a string of marble pavilions linked by long pillared colonnades. I intended to have fountains in each pavilion and keep the whole thing open to sun and air in the Greek style; I was so sick of suffocation. You would think Romans were descended from moles. The architect said the construction must have breaks in it for existing streets to pass through. I said was there no other way? He said not unless all the streets were demolished. The idea appealed to me but he hastily said it was impossible; I should need to rebuild Rome.

They began work on the Palatine with foundations on two different levels where the hollow between two hill peaks came; they joined them with marble staircases I personally supervised the building of the first pavilion on the lower level; its columns and pilasters were polychrome marble and water flowed down one wall between columns of green and red with bronze capitals. The small rooms leading off it had floors of blue, purple, and black marble and vaulted ceilings painted with incidents from Homer. Fountains sparkled everywhere. You could hear the water as you walked in the colonnades. Of course, this was only the beginning; they reckoned it would take four years or more to complete.

I was shaved for the first time, always an important occasion, and offered the hair to the only member of my family left, old aunt Domitia, my father's elder sister. She was ill when I went to see her; I hardly recognised her with the Ahenobarbus hair now grey and her face wrenched with sickness. She stroked my beard affectionately and said she would be ready to die when she had received it. Poor old woman, she tempted the gods. A few days after my shaving she died in her sleep. A nasty rumour went around that I had poisoned her for her money which I could not deny because emperors are not meant to hear gossip. Britannicus and my mother were coming home to roost. One morning Seneca told me that a baby had been exposed in the Forum with a notice round its neck, saying: "I am not going to rear you for fear that you kill your mother." I wouldn't talk to anyone that day.

I inaugurated a new feast to celebrate my shaving, dedicated to Juventas, the goddess of youth, which included all the usual games, races and spectacles in the arena; the latter I disliked. Having come from Naples where they regard the human body as sacred this prostitution of men to the blood lust of the mob seemed revolting. But the people rule. I could not stop it. I alleviated the brutality with concerts of poetry and music and performances of skill in the Circus; drivers leapt from horse to horse and picked up prizes from the ground in full gallop, gold, palms, or wreaths, then waved them high. Others raced lying flat to their horses' backs. I thought them superb. Here was excitement without blood, grace and skill combined. I swear the crowd never thought of that, only their bets and how much they might win.

The high point of the proceedings was my first public appearance as a singer. "My prince," Seneca said, "I strongly advise you not to do this. Painted actors may show themselves

243

indecently to the mob but not a descendant of Augustus."

"I'm not going to be indecent," I retorted, "and I shan't be painted. I shall merely sing one of my own compositions. Seneca, what is it; do you consider the arts immoral?"

"Frequently they are, sire. Acting may lead to licentiousness as it has in the Floralia where women dance naked; poets can always play at being Ovid. Where is the limit? Shall we see Sophocles or a performance of sodomy? No one knows where art stops and reality begins. Sire, I beg of you not to do this. The people will think you depraved, exhibitionist, they will imagine—"

"Oh Seneca, please, for heaven's sake..." I stemmed the flow of words. "The arts are perfectly respectable if interpreted well. Narrow-minded senators who find them debauched make me sick; I should like to stage an orgy and invite them all to show them that art isn't bound by their stuffy ethics. I should make them walk naked..."

"Nero!" He looked appalled. "Think of your position."

"Songs are sacred to Apollo," I plunged on, "and in statues he holds a lyre. Would you criticise such a great god? You don't. All right then, that's settled. I start rehearsing today."

However he managed to arrange that the performance be virtually private and the audience aristocratic, admitted by invitation. I was shaved first with great ceremony and the hair presented to me in a gold ball inlaid with pearl which I dedicated to Jupiter Capitolinus. I had a light beard and it hardly showed but now it was gone I looked a true Roman. It seemed symbolic. I had lost my mother and become a man, my youth locked in a golden ball as though precious.

I sang in Pompey's theatre. It was my own poem, a lyrical work on Attis and Cybele which I had composed in Naples; I accompanied myself on the cithara, wearing the conventional long robe with wide sleeves. It was white sewn with gold. First came the best Praetorians in parade uniform, scarlet plumes and masks of bronze fashioned to look severe and noble. Then the herald announced me and on I came to shouts and cheers, my knees weak and my heart beating in my throat; when I started my voice cracked. I wanted to die. Once I was into the melody I got better though I sounded husky which embarrassed me, remembering Terpnus. Burrus and Seneca stood either side, ready to prompt if my memory failed. I was infuriated to see that at the end of each couplet they waved the free ends of their togas as a signal for applause; I wanted spontaneous praise. In addition they had placed my Juventus Augustiana in the audience with orders to cheer. They were a corps of young men whom I had created on the lines of the athletes I saw in Naples, energetically devoted to sport and art. They would have important parts in artistic displays I wanted to give. I only meant them to cheer if the audience remained silent for my nerves were on edge and I had a morbid fear of rejection; but they started up as soon as I came on, shouting: "Hail Nero, a new Apollo," which terrified me. I expected the sun to plunge down in indignation.

I felt I had made a reasonable start for my age. Later, when I doubted the power of my voice I recalled the cheers and persuaded myself they had all been genuine. After the concert I gave a feast on the banks of Augustus' artificial lake which was situated on the northern bank of the Tiber, opposite the Aventine. It was six hundred yards long, smooth and blue in the summer heat; charming green glades rooted near the water with cypresses and flowering bushes. Shops were erected and money distributed as a free gift from me, food and drink set out on gilded boats on the lake or tables in the shrubbery. Amongst the buying and selling and general merriment there was a good deal of indecent carrying-on with disreputable dancing and prostitutes offering their services. I did not see it. I was in my own barge with Acte and ignoring the row from the banks. They were my people; I wanted them to be happy. Seneca grew reproachful, saying he had warned me of licence. "Some of it was too disgusting," he said, hot and self-righteous. "And I dare not describe what was sold in the shops." I nearly asked how he knew but thought it unwise. I said why shouldn't they enjoy themselves; it was my coming-of-age. "And," I added, "it will teach the reactionaries a thing or two. They need their eyes opened."

245

He thought I was becoming degenerate. In fact, since my return from Naples I had grown interested in things of the intellect and no longer went on midnight jaunts as Otho wanted. Instead I held select dinner parties where the entertainment was artistic singing, not dancing girls, and the talk on philosophy and art, not the brothel. My ideals were new and purified. My mother had dragged me down and down and now I felt released, capable of higher things. It was not easy to wash off the mud; the smell of a parricide sticks. But I persisted, gathering lively and intelligent people around me. One was Marcus Nerva, the young but already famous lawyer whose literary reputation had blossomed, another was Lucan, Seneca's nephew, a poet of some talent. I fancy his uncle had recalled him from Athens on purpose; he had been studying Greek literature there. Certainly he introduced him to me with great emphasis, commenting on his outstanding gift and how he had begun writing verses at sixteen which even then were brilliant. I was polite but restrained over this. Ecstatic praise helps no one. He was dark and sullen except when you admired him, then he broke into smiles and a pose which annoyed me. No one could deny his talent; it was his vanity I objected to. He recognised no one as equal to him, not even me, only a simpering friend named Persius who also managed to enter my circle, not with my approval.

After dinner we used to sit around and discuss poetry or have a philosophical argument. A Stoic thinker named Cornutus was much in evidence here, a brilliant man who practised the principles Seneca merely preached. I saw that my patronage of him did not please my tutor. These thinkers are like starved lions squabbling over meat, all snarls and unobtrusive bites. For fun I would pit differing philosophers against each other in argument and watch the sparks fly. But also I was searching; Seneca had never answered my questions satisfactorily and now I felt desperate need for reassurance. One evening they discussed Acte's new cult and mentioned odd things like ritual cleansing through human blood and a man who couldn't die; they grew quite heated.

"It's disgraceful," Lucan said, adopting his uncle's self-righteousness. "They strangle babies and drink the blood at their love-feasts."

"Is it proven?" Cornutus asked mildly.

"Near enough. One of my father's slaves got involved and used to disappear early every morning or evening and when my father asked about it he said he was attending the sacred meal. He didn't want to talk; it's supposed to be secret. But my father got out of him that they eat flesh and drink blood only not as we understand it; father said that was absurd—either you drink blood or you don't, after all—and forbade him to go again."

"And did he?" I asked.

"Oh yes. Father flogged him but he still goes. They're most fanatical over it."

"What makes them fanatical?" Otho said.

He sounded sceptical; I knew he disliked Lucan intensely for trying to oust him. Despite Athens and a philosopher uncle he was more interested in my bed than Socratic discussion; he knew the roads to power. Already I refused to sit near him at banquets.

"I'm sure *I* don't know," he retorted with an exaggerated shrug. "It's like Mithraism, I suppose, all blood and mysticism."

"I fancy it's their cult hero," Cornutus said. "He claimed personal divinity and used to cure people with a touch. I've heard some say he brought back corpses; of course, it was all a great wonder at the time and the Jews got very troublesome, thinking him a political saviour."

"And what happened?" I said. Despite Lucan I was interested.

"The governor had him crucified. It was an awkward business for him because a whole lot of local dignitaries swore they'd heard him claim to be a king of sorts which counted as treason, especially with Tiberius and his suspicions."

"And then," broke in Lucan, anxious for attention, "they found the tomb empty after a couple of days and his supporters said he was alive again, if you can imagine such nonsense. Of course, he looked very striking, golden hair and wonderful eyes with one of those commanding voices; all the women chased

247

him, even prostitutes. You'll hear some Romans say he was probably Apollo, especially as he had healing powers."

"In *Judea*!" I said. "He wouldn't bother."

"No one knows," Cornutus said, "how the gods work. Some philosophers will not agree that they even take human form at all."

Then they trailed off into religious argument which sent me to sleep after a time. But next day while signing papers I said: "Seneca, this sect—is it a public nuisance?"

"No, sire, not that I know of. In fact, the members are most law-abiding though they talk of equality in the eyes of their god and won't accept the gods of the Pantheon."

"They should be watched," I said. "We mustn't have trouble. By the way, do they call themselves anything?"

"Christians, sire," he said.

Most of my friends were my own age but I also sought the company of two older men, Calpernius Piso who was very rich and had a good singing voice, and Petronius who was a patron of all the arts. I did not want my people to think me young and silly. Besides, I could ask their advice and not feel guilty for ignoring it as I did with Seneca. Seneca was part of my childhood and my mother's domination; I mistrusted him.

Petronius was a fascinating person. Aged about forty he had a splendid bearing and a fine Roman head, dark and clean-cut with deep brown eyes which never showed his thoughts. I admired his elegance, his knowledge, his infinitely attractive manners. In some ways he was much like an older Otho but a refined Otho who thought deeply and did not live on the surface. He would never batter me with advice.

"Sire," he would say when I was considering a purchase, "I feel that this vase is by far the superior due to the exquisite workmanship and the rarity of good Augustan cameo engraving. However, I leave it to you," and, of course, I always followed him. I should have been a fool not to; he knew so much. He appeared to enjoy guiding my taste and answering my questions. At dinner he exercised his wit which was mature and thoughtful, often sardonic, not bright and clever like Otho's.

For a short time I quarrelled with Otho over him. "I can't see," he said, "why he is never wrong. Anyone would think he were the oracle at Delphi."

"He has great learning," I said, "and knows about important things."

"Doesn't he." He sounded spiteful. "Watch him the next time he looks at you. I should be careful; he is at a dangerous age."

I hit him then, a thing I had never done before and afterwards regretted. When I went back to apologise he was cold until dinner warmed him up but he looked poisonously at Petronius.

He was right about him. One night my Delphic oracle came to my bedroom and did not emerge until the morning. I was slightly drunk but I could have thrown him out; his charm stopped me, so did his obvious appreciation. I was like an Augustan cameo, worth having. In the middle of the night he said: "Who do you look like?" I said: "My grandfather," then shut up tight; he knew of my mother but said nothing. His tact was infinite, too.

He gave me an affection and security which I needed. I was adrift at the moment, my faithfulness to Acte or any woman finished by my mother. I was like Otho, taking to bed any girl I fancied. None of them satisfied me. Seeing that women were something of a failure it was wiser to have a Petronius who could keep me straight better than an Otho. Acte was slowly drawing away from me, anyway, preoccupied with her new religious leanings. She was still lovely, her hair pale gold and her body slim as a willow, but I saw now that it was her complete surrender I had loved, a giving of oneself with no reservations.

And then Otho married. I nearly spilled my wine when he told me. "Married! Good gods, Otho, you've become honest at last."

"Oh, she's a most exquisite creature," he said. "A Venus, a Psyche—such hair and eyes, such a complexion." I had never seen him so infatuated; girls were like racehorses to him, good for a run then turned free to graze. "And in bed . . ." he went on.

I could see erotic details coming and tried to turn him aside as Cornutus and Seneca were present; my dinner parties were respectable now.

"Anyway," he continued, taking the hint, "she is the best gift a god could give me so now I'll go if you don't mind and keep her happy."

Later, in private, I said: "Otho, is it genuine or are you at one of your tricks? Is she wealthy?"

"Reasonably so, but that's not it, my dear Nero. I mean it; I'm desperately in love—the game is over and I've embraced respectability."

"Impossible," I said.

"Nothing is impossible with this creature. She has the eyes of a goddess . . ."

"I know; you told me," I broke in. "Who is she?"

"Who? Oh, the granddaughter of Poppaeus Sabinus, that brilliant magistrate at Tiberius' time. She was married to Rufrius Crispinus who is an old fool and incapable of appreciating anything."

I said: "You've stolen someone's wife. How disreputable."

"Not at all." He smiled with disarming innocence. "I was doing her a service. She fell in love with me at once, of course, enchanted by my looks and the fact that you and I—" I looked at him sharply. "Not that I mentioned anything indiscreet but she knew I was your best friend. Women swoon at the thought of the Purple."

"When did you meet her?" I felt bewildered; it was all so quick.

"Before we went to Baia, while you— while your mind was on other things. I met her at a party first, then after that secretly under all sorts of pretences. She was so bored, poor child. They had married her young to Crispinius who is in retirement now ever since your mo— ever since he was dismissed as Praetorian prefect and replaced by Burrus. She left him, then the divorce was concluded in front of witnesses by mutual wish; he could not refuse. Nero, why are you staring?"

I said: "I want to meet her."

Her name was Poppaea. I should have known Otho would
not exaggerate. She was in the full flush of her twenty-three
years with hair the colour of amber, red in shadow and golden
in sunlight. It was richer than mine for I was bleached fair
by the sun. She looked at me with grey-green eyes, clear as
precious stones, and as she bowed I saw her upright breasts
plunge to a tiny waist and hands like a citharist's, delicate-
boned.

I said: "I'm very pleased to meet you."

She smiled; there was a look in her face I should have
recognised; that I did not showed how she had blinded me.

"As Otho's wife," I went on, "you are always welcome at
court."

I nearly added: I should like to know you better; but
thought it unwise; Otho stood behind her. An infatuated man
can be dangerous.

I invited them to dinner that evening. She wore a deep blue
palla with silver leaves on the hem and a white tunic edged with
a gold flounce, a badge of modesty. Her ears twinkled
amethysts and a huge ruby pendant winked fire on her breast;
the marks of wealth were restrained. Her hair towered like a
diadem with curls on the forehead and her paint was artful.
She did not need much.

I watched her all evening. She sat beside Otho, well-mannered
and submissive, yet lively in conversation and intelligent once
the arguments started. I was startled to hear her fight out a
point with Cornutus like any young blood in the palestra; one
expects women never to think beyond the kitchen. Acte had
been bright but not so assertive. This woman combined feminine
mildness with a thrusting intellect and when one was submerged
the other flourished.

When they were leaving I said: "Madam, may I congratulate
your thoughtfulness; we tend to think it a masculine prerogative."

She smiled graciously and said: "Sire, a woman has freedom
in her mind if nowhere else."

"Otho," I said, "how did you pick yourself such a witty wife?"

"You know me." He was laughing, pleased at her success. "I won't be bored."

As she bowed to me I caught the look again and this time the features struck a chord. She reminded me of someone. I retired to bed and thought, then I realised. The last time I saw that face was at Baia, leaning from a departing boat in moonlight. At first I thought it was me; I saw her everywhere and often in the strangest places; such was my mania, not yet cured. But I thought again and realised it was so; despite the different colouring the facial structure was similar, the stare of the eyes, the cool assurance. I thought: sweet Apollo, is she a monster in embryo? It made me cold. For I who loved beauty the hypocrisy of it seemed a backhanded blow of the gods, delivered when you are not looking.

I could not sleep for thinking. Her face was all round me, only sometimes the hair was black and the eyes blue; images shifted and interchanged. I thought; it's another fever on the way, and went to call Xenophon, but my pulse was steady; I had no sweat. I must have gone back to bed and slept for I thought I was holding her, my mouth buried in her hair. Then suddenly the hair was dark and the face not hers. I woke trembling. Too late I saw that the enemy had crept up quiet under guise of hospitality and intelligent interest. I was in love.

Chapter Fourteen

What happens when it is your best friend's wife? An upright spirit would disregard the idea and forgo pleasure but mine was flattened, beaten down by the passions of this last year. I felt myself a gods' outcast; like Oedipus I carried the mark, like Orestes I was pursued, but not externally. This hunger was a symptom of my disease and if denied it might destroy me.

I invited them to dinner again and again. I watched her, I talked to her; and then one day Otho astounded me by saying: "You fancy her, don't you?"

I said: "You have a perceptive eye. Why aren't you trying to poison me?"

"My dear Nero!" He slapped my back. "I'm not one of those mean possessive husbands. I like to share my precious belongings like that agate drinking cup you borrowed from me last month; why not? What's an exchange between friends?"

Still bewildered I said: "Who do you want? Acte?"

"Good heavens, no, I don't want anything. Take her for a night, Nero, and hand her back to me as you found her. I shall revel in my open-handedness."

I said: "Thank you."

So much for noble feelings. Though such odd generosity put her within my reach I felt he was being flippant; you would not throw precious crystal about and hope it wouldn't break.

She came, submissive again, in brilliant yellow which made her hair flare like a sunset; a square topaz held her dress. The pin pricked my finger as I undid it.

I said: "Are you doing this under sufferance?"

She turned, and with an extraordinary smile which sent my

heart to the ceiling, she said: "Find out."

She was all flame and storm, lightning from a clear sky, a wild horse feeling the whip; her burning hair lay scattered on the pillow and her eyes, when open, were a mountain cat's, feeding on the kill. It should have frightened me. A tigress ran in her blood and I had been bitten a year back; but I had no sense. Her breasts were ivory, rose-tipped. I raised myself from them and looked at her, saying: "This isn't just obedience. I'm not a fool." She laughed and turned her head, the damp hair sliding back.

"Neither am I," she said.

"What about your husband?" I asked.

"Oh, he's very attractive—but not like you. You are serious-minded and interested in art which he thinks is a waste of time apart from making your house look better than anyone else's."

I said: "I'm also emperor."

"Come now." She raised herself. "Do you think I'm an opportunist? Were you brainless I should leave this minute despite a husband's promise."

Her eyes provoked me again. I twined my hand in her hair and pulled her head from the pillow to kiss her but she fastened her hands across my back and pulled me down. She was no Acte. I had forgotten her two husbands.

By the morning I knew I could not let her go. I thought: you're a fool. The spider spins an attractive web to trap the fly. I looked at her sleeping face and wondered if she wanted me or the throne or both; last night had showed desire, not necessarily love. She was ambitious; it showed even in bed. She was also clever. I thought: what are you walking into?

Otho had to be got rid of. His generosity did not extend indefinitely and tomorrow he would expect his wife back. In fact, she did return; I had to think what to do. As she left she said: "Will I come back?" She was direct, no backways as with Acte. "Yes," I said. "To stay." It provoked another delightful smile, no more.

I was not cold-hearted over this. I had loved Otho, he had

been a faithful friend, but I could not let him stay in Rome with a hidden resentment which might fester into conspiracy. Or he might refuse to let me have her in a peaceable manner and cause a scandal. Though he appeared to be playing a game he was aware of personal rights. Naturally I never thought of murder. The province of Lusitania on the eastern side of Spain needed a new governor; after all, it was an honour to be granted such a post. It was remote and doubtless boring but still safe; a more callous man would have sent him to Britain or Armenia.

I summoned him and gave the news. He looked puzzled. "Nero, what are you up to? Is it a joke? Imagine me a sober governor." He started laughing.

"It isn't a joke," I said. "I'm appointing you; there is no one else I could trust so well."

"I don't understand." He was like a child, not seeing; it hurt me. Nothing in this world is gained without payment.

"You need some responsibility," I said, hedging. "How old are you, twenty-seven? Look at me, Caesar at seventeen."

"All right." He turned away. "You have the last word." He was calm; I had expected recriminations or anger, even an attempt at refusal. He had come to look upon me as an equal. "It means packing up everything," he said, half to himself. "Telling Poppaea . . ."

"Poppaea won't be going with you," I said.

He turned slowly back, understanding at last. His look cut me where I was sensitive with guilty regret.

"So *that's* it." The joke was over. "What a complete fool I've been. Well Imperator, I suppose you must get what you want."

He had a curious dignity; it made me feel worse. Crisis strips everyone bare and it had shown him to be silver, not tin as you might have thought.

"Otho, look—" I was making excuses. "You know how I am at the moment; I can't do without her. You can't think what it's like at night when I see—If she is with me I might feel safe again."

"But I have to be out of the way," he said bitterly.

"It will only hurt you to stay. And the post is a good one, well-paid."

"Yes. Thank you." He saluted ironically. "Hail Caesar."

At the door he turned back. "But remember, Nero, it's all too easy to blame something else. Will you always make your mother the excuse for getting what you want? How much was your fault, Caesar; how much?"

I never saw him again. He left without saying goodbye and his wife immediately came to live at the palace. One day she said: "You loved my husband. How very awkward."

She had a sly wit; I did not always like it but infatuation forgives everything. "I sent him away to get you," I said. "Does it make you feel more valuable, my darling?"

"A little." She sounded cynical. "I have seen my value in men's eyes since I was fourteen. But I don't wish to be an object of regret to you; one morning you will find me gone if that is so."

"No compromises," I said, smiling. "How honest you are."

"I must be yours body and soul," she said, "and you must be mine. No looking at other women behind my back or forgetting me when you are drunk with friends."

"My love, how could I even think of another woman? And nowadays I don't get drunk at night; I've other things to do. Tell me, how did you learn to be so calculating?"

"Through living." She was serious. "Men are basically faithless. If you don't state the terms at the beginning they will drift away, finding a legal loophole for neglect."

"Poppaea! " I had expected another Acte, sweet and yielding. Instead I heard my mother's voice. "Can you think of me like that?"

"I think of any man like that. You love me now because I am a new toy but when the novelty has gone you will look round for other amusement."

"Never! " I said.

She smiled; I saw now she had worked me round to this, astute as a politician. I caught hold of her, saying softly: "What man goes back to lead when he has possessed gold?"

She clung tight, laughing, and I left a love-bite on her smooth shoulder.

"Then," she said, "why don't you marry me?"

Octavia was still in isolation. In the past year, so concerned with other matters, I had honestly forgotten she existed. She did not even accompany me officially; the people seemed to have forgotten her, too.

"Do you love her?" Poppaea asked.

"No, I never have done. She is still a virgin."

"And Acte?"

How do women hear these things? I could have sworn I had said nothing. Despite her intellect she was a conventional woman in this.

"I loved Acte once," I said, committing myself to honesty. "But now I have a brother's affection for her."

"Yes?" She raised her eyebrows.

"Yes. Stop teasing me, Poppaea. I love you, I love you; I shall never love anyone else again. My darling, I have given you everything I can, sent away my best friend and prostrated myself at your feet. What more do you want?"

"The laurel wreath," she said. "Half of it."

I had recognised her ambition at the beginning but not this. Like a conceited idiot I had seen an emperor's love as her highest aim, forgetting that a legal wife is empress. I had an empress, soured and dull, locked away in private. I thought it over and over. Poppaea was a strange woman. She liked my adoration and I don't believe she doubted it but unlike Acte she was not content with a private status. She wanted public recognition. One could not blame her. She was a beautiful woman, born of patrician parents who would have instilled her with the idea of her own worth. To me that worth was infinite. I no longer lived through nights of terror, waking to see my mother bending over me or the glint of snake scales in the shadows. She lay beside me, a shield against the darkness. I believe love must be stronger than vengeance or the worst that men and gods can do.

In time I told her gently what I was guilty of. She listened calmly; patricians do not show shock. Perhaps she did not feel it, not like Acte, anyway, for innocence makes a person vulnerable; she was a woman of the world. But her mouth moved when I spoke of the murder.

I said: "Tell me truthfully, Poppaea, does this disgust or frighten you?"

"It frightens me a little." It was in her voice, not her face. "Can you not be purified?"

"No. I did it of my own free will, not under divine orders like Orestes, besides I was already guilty of—Poppaea, please believe me, she began it, not I, but diseases take a hold. I can't go back on it. I'm condemned, defiled; it's irrevocable."

"There were rumours at the time," she said. "Most people wouldn't believe it because they thought Agrippina perfect. I remember thinking that you looked too innocent..."

"And my mother's death?"

"Enemies made their own tale. Again opinion was in her favour. Oh Nero—"

She put her arms round my neck and spoke with her mouth near me. "Whatever you've done I still love you; I can't stop myself. If all the Furies came running, whips, snakes and all I could not go from you."

I said: "When you are with me the Furies do not exist."

Naturally I wanted to marry her. Such a woman deserved to share the throne even apart from the fact that I longed for a legitimate heir; officially Acte's son did not exist. She was obviously fertile, having borne a son to Crispinius but at the moment we took precautions. A child would give scandal. She was not like Acte, an unimportant slave in whom no one was interested. To please her I had sent Acte away, giving her a villa on the Aventine, though I still visited her sometimes to see my son. She showed no resentment, being caught up in her new religious beliefs.

Even in the middle of my enchantment I thought: will I find myself ruled? She had a strength of will backed by personal motives which you might have called selfishness except that she covered it in sweetness; but the bee makes sweetness and has a sting in its tail. She would argue with me even more

258

than Otho ever did and when our minds had battered each other in a love-hate struggle she collapsed laughing in my arms, always the victor. With anyone else I should have lost my temper. She knew my adoration and in private strutted like a peacock showing its feathers while remaining submissive in public: "Yes Nero, of course, Nero," with a feminine dignity which everyone applauded. To keep her happy I gave her everything I could think of, jewellery set with every stone from rubies to beryls, exquisite perfumes including the rare lotus oil, furniture of cedar and citrus wood for her apartment, ornaments of gold, ivory, bronze, shoes of pearl and mattresses stuffed with swan's down, even iridescent silks brought a year's journey by caravan from a land at the world's end where the people are said to be yellow. It impressed her that they should come so far just for her and insisted on knowing the route like a scholar, down from Asia and across the Persian Gulf. And then she said: "Doesn't it make you want to see these places thrown up by a god so far from us?"

"No." She bewildered me. "I like comfort, Poppaea, and to travel a year would be extremely *un*comfortable."

"I don't mind discomfort," she said, "if it brings me something worthwhile."

When she heard of a wingless dragon caught on an island in a far-off nameless ocean she insisted on seeing it so its keepers brought it to us on a chain. I nearly ran away. It was longer than a man with a flat, snake-like head and clawed feet, its eyes luminous as opals. I said: "What sort of god made that?" and stood safely behind a pillar while she went up close and touched its scaly back. I had never seen such courage in a woman except for one; Acte used to scream at spiders.

She still talked about marriage. "Ask Burrus," she said, "or Seneca. Someone who knows the legal aspect." Seneca was non-committal as always when faced with a question which demanded either unpleasant truth or skilful lies. I believe he disapproved of Poppaea. She was noble, not "a little nobody", and ambitious; she was also clever. I had seen her outmatch him in an argument.

"It is difficult to say, my prince," he observed. "To divorce

259

Octavia might be awkward; on the other hand the people like Poppaea. It is a matter open to question."

Then I asked Burrus. "If you divorce Octavia," he said, "you will have to give back her dowry: the empire."

I told Poppaea. She looked outraged, saying: "Do you mean to say you inherited the empire through a woman?"

"It was my mother's arrangement," I said. "She thought to strengthen my ties with Claudius, so legally speaking the empire was Octavia's dowry; I was his heir from that moment. The point is that if I divorce her she can take back her dowry if she feels like it and bestow it on a new husband."

She looked startled, then said: "So the only solution would be for Octavia to die."

My mother's voice spoke louder. "Poppaea! " I said. "Would you really consider..."

"I don't like to think of a silly, prim emperor's daughter keeping me from my rightful place beside you by clinging to aristocratic privileges," she said. "It's no marriage, Nero. Why should she hang on to her claim?"

I said: "She won't. I'll divorce her, don't worry, once I think of a good reason; with any luck she won't object very loudly. Ten years' isolation should have tamed her."

Then Burrus died. He developed some kind of abscess in his throat which baffled the doctors and even Xenophon, whom I sent specially, said it was with the gods. The infection spread so that he could not swallow and eventually it interfered with his breathing. I went to see him; he spoke coldly as though I had insulted him. When I said I regretted his illness he looked at me bitterly, saying: "Poppaea hated me. Is that why you did it?"

I thought he was delirious. Then he groaned and turned his face to the wall so I left. A few days later he was dead.

"Did you kill him?" Poppaea said.

"No, of course not." I was shocked. "Why should I kill an innocent old man who served me well?"

"I thought that," she said, "but there was a rumour."

I said: "I'm pursued by ghosts. No one will ever die now without it being me, not the gods. Did you hate him?"

260

"No, but I thought him a nuisance. His opposition to your divorce did not help matters."

I went back to the old custom and appointed two Praetorian prefects. It was my mother who had given power to one, thus ensuring a single loyalty. One was Faenius Rufus who had been involved in my mother's plot and, I suspect, her lover, but I had pardoned him and this seemed a good proof of my desire to forgive and forget. However, to make sure I gave him as colleague a man named Ofonius Tigellinus who was my man and trustworthy. He had been my mother's lover (was there any man in Rome who hadn't?) but I had met him in connection with horses; he trained them. He had done me good service, training a couple of mine. He became essentially the Prefect of the Watch and was responsible for commanding the city's fire-fighters and nightwatchmen besides chasing thieves.

He was forty, dark and lean, but going grey at the forehead. I did not like him as I liked Petronius, in fact, I always felt awkward in his company as he was so business-like and assured, a man of action. He feared nothing, he had no sensitivity and he thought Sophocles was a racehorse, but I trusted his judgement. Since my mother's death I had feared conspiracy far more; they had an argument to stand on now and even if your motives are not pure it sounds grand to oppose an incestuous matricide in the name of honour. It made me suspicious but it also made me generous. I gave lavish games to keep the public amused and assure them of my care; apparently it worked. They always cheered me with great conviction.

Despite this Tigellinus started ferreting out plots. I admired his observant eye and efficient handling of such matters but he disturbed my peace of mind. I no longer saw snake hair at night but the flash of knives and if I heard footsteps I did not think them the Eumenides. The details were sordid and I do not remember them, only names and a sense of dread which kept me sleepless. One involved Sulla, a descendant of the great dictator, and rumours of an armed revolt in Asia. Sulla's head was cut off and sent to me, shrivelled and white-haired. It made me feel ill. Tigellinus carried out some sort of purge with people's heads falling right and left; I grew alarmed. I summoned him and said: "Is all this really necessary? Too much violence isn't a good thing."

"No, sire." He was obsequious, yet something in his eyes said he thought me a fool. "But neither are underground conspiracies; they weaken a ruler's power even when they don't succeed, therefore it is better to catch them before they begin."

"But then you might kill innocent people," I objected.

"True, sire, but only one or two and what is that out of Rome's thousands? Besides, in my experience the more innocent a person may appear the more guilty they are in reality. Let me assure you, sire, that strong measures are the only way to keep your throne safe; be ruthless, cruel if need be. Let the people see you won't stand nonsense. You see, sire . . ." He coughed. "How can I put it? You have left yourself vulnerable in many ways. Enemies can fall back on your supposed 'crimes' and make deadly use of them; that is why you—or, at least, I, as your humble servant—must strike first."

His subtle nastiness annoyed me but I saw his point. I suppose I disliked him for telling the truth when I should have preferred rosy unreality.

"You sound convincing," I said, "but all the same I would rather you moderated your zeal. Tyranny can kill a ruler quicker than plots."

"True, sire." He smiled. "No one is more aware of the necessity for mercy than I am."

That was a subtle reference to his exile in my adoptive father's reign over some moral lapse; amusing when one considered his present attitude of self-conscious moralism.

Once the flurry of plotting was over I thought of Octavia again. As far as reasons for divorce went I could choose between sterility and adultery, the first being tempting but impractical as she would merely declare herself a virgin; the second was more dependable. I left it to Tigellinus who said it was a simple matter of providing the stimulus. He picked out a handsome Alexandrian slave musician from the imperial orchestra, black-haired and smouldering; before Poppaea appeared I had fancied him myself. He was literally thrown at Octavia; Tigellinus sent him first to entertain her, then to serve her at table with instructions to be charming and attentive. The rest was easy. Poor Octavia; ten years' frustration is a long time. They found him in her arms on a dining couch.

I was the outraged husband now. I did not find the part hard for she had annoyed me since our wedding day and I had no sympathy left. An enquiry was held and her maids gave evidence. They had all been instructed and gave good evidence as to her frequent immorality with the handsome Alexandrian; only one, her old nurse, denied the whole thing. Tigellinus had her tortured but she merely spat in his face, yelling: "My mistress is purer than your mouth!" It did not matter. My wife was found guilty and divorced; I sent her away from the palace, giving her Burrus' old house and some estates confiscated from a conspirator. Despite everything I did not want to harm her. My sense of guilt was still strong and functioned where affection did not.

Twelve days later I married Poppaea in the full sight of Rome with all official festivities, the sacrifice to Jupiter and great feast, the orange veil and myrtle wreath, the nuptial torch and giving of fire and water. When she subsided, laughing, beside me in the darkness, her nuptial girdle undone I said: "Well, now it's legal I suggest you have a child as soon as possible."

"I shall need some help from you," she said. I could smell her scented hair and taste the wine in her mouth.

"Falernian," I said. "You like the best."

"Always."

She smiled and slid her arms round my neck; as she drew me down to her warmth she murmured: "Two and a half years is a long time to wait for a wedding."

Whenever we appeared in public the people cheered and shouted her name; she got more admiration than I did. Sometimes, at the Circus or the temple or beside Augustus' lake I would look sideways and see why. It was not merely her looks; beauty without grace or spirit is a dull feeble thing. She had both, together with a natural charm and liveliness which showed whenever she smiled or waved or even moved; if a goddess ever lived she could not have bettered her. I loved her so much it was almost a pain.

We did not enjoy peace for long. Octavia had partisans in Rome all too willing to whip up feeling for her. They included friends of my mother and Britannicus, friends of various conspirators, friends of Burrus who thought I had killed him, in fact, anyone who imagined they had a grudge against me. Octavia was a rallying-point. Tigellinus told me they were gathering round her house and cheering, then as she appeared to greet them, shouted: "Long live the empress! Down with her husband!" I could imagine how she took it, a true aristocrat, so full of dignity and thoroughly obnoxious. With superhuman patience I removed her to a villa near Pompeii in Campania which, after all, was a most pleasant and fashionable spot especially now with spring here. I thought once she was gone her supporters would forget her. In fact, quite the reverse happened.

A slave came running one late afternoon, panting out that the crowd were attacking the statues of Poppaea recently set up in the Forum, throwing mud and trying to destroy them while chanting: "Down with the whore!"

I said: "How many?"

"It isn't certain, sire. Enough to cause confusion."

I looked at her. She was sitting straight and pale but unmoving.

"Why do they hate me?" she said.

"It's Octavia's mob," I said. "Damn them and damn her. Wait here; I'll try and find out what's happening."

In the corridor I met Tigellinus. "What is it?" I demanded. "What are they up to?"

"Destruction," he said. He looked thin-lipped. "Someone has incited mob feeling; it's mainly Octavia's partisans but others have joined in simply for the fun. Every city has its natural troublemakers."

I felt suddenly overwhelmed. I had grown used to their affection and no longer thought it wonderful, only the normal course of events. You can deal with a conspirator; what do you do with a city?

"I've sent a praetorian cohort," Tigellinus said. "They will deal with them."

"A little late, Tigellinus," said an ironic voice. I turned and saw Petronius; he looked perfectly composed. "Have you looked from the window?" he said.

Then I heard shouting; it came from the courtyard below. I ran to a window and looked down on a mass of upturned faces with torches blazing in raised hands; they were my people but not as I had ever seen them before. They had crowded up the Palatine and burst through the great gates, overcoming the few Guards. I could see a scarlet plume drag the dust. They were yelling.

"Give us the bitch, Nero, or we'll burn you down! "

"Take back Octavia! Give us our empress."

"Down with the whore! "

"Sire," said Petronius softly, "I warned you that all precious and beautiful things have to be paid for. Such is life."

I said: "You're not afraid. How do you manage it?"

He laughed. "I'm a Stoic," he said. His hand rested warm on my shoulder and brought memories of the bedroom, then I heard someone behind me and twisted away. She stood there, still calm, as though the shouts were cheers, not blood-lust. I said: "This is no place for you, Poppaea."

She managed a smile. "Where you are I am," she said. "Let me see." She stepped to the window; immediately the noise redoubled, striking the walls like hailstones. "There she is, the stinking bitch! Standing shameless where Claudius' daughter should be. Burn the palace! Kill her! Burn her! Bring torches! "

I pulled her back; she was shaking a little. "They hate me," she said. I saw that this was the unbearable thing, not the threat of death. She was in love with love. Her mirror showed beauty and people showed the effects of it. For her to do without either was death.

I said: "I *told* you not to look."

I was shaking, too, not able to bear her being hurt.

"I'm not afraid," she said. "They are like mad dogs. It would be a sordid death but at least I should die with courage as befits noble blood."

"For the gods' sake don't talk like that," I said. "Tigellinus, do something. We'll be in flames any moment."

"I'll order reinforcements," he said and left. Poppaea leaned against the wall and looked at Petronius; he was still smiling. I don't believe an earthquake would have shaken him. "My dear," he said, "let me say how much I admire you. Most women would be in hysterics by now."

"I'm not most women," she said.

A ghost had come back. But for the hair it might have been my mother. Down below they were beginning to set torches to the palace foundations and I could feel the heat carried on the breeze. I felt sick with fright. They were not crying for my blood but in this madness they would not differentiate; many an emperor had gone the same way.

Then a new sound broke. The praetorian reinforcements had reached the courtyard and were beating them back with swords and whips; I heard them crying in terror. Then someone screamed. I covered my ears, not wanting to hear slaughter; I had known it must come to this. The Guard pushed them back and back, then slammed the gates and leaned all their weight on them; the courtyard was a litter of the unlucky ones and the dust was marked red, the blood of my people on my own ground. I felt sorrowful, then angry, and my anger fixed on pale Octavia who never even knew it had happened.

That night I sat on the bed and thought while Poppaea's maids pulled out her pins and removed her jewels. Normally a man is not present at such things but this was not a normal time. The maids went and she came forward, her hair tumbling loose and her white nightgown gaping at the neck; without paint or jewels she was even lovelier, a flower not gilded. The lamplight caught her hair in points of fire.

"Dear gods," I said. "To think I nearly lost you."

"Nero, darling." She was in a persuasive mood. "I know it sounds terrible but can't you see there is nothing else to do except kill her?" I looked blank. Then she was down by my

266

knees, earnest and pleading. "Oh Nero, listen; it isn't just Octavia or even me. What about you? This could be the beginning of a revolution. There are people in Rome prepared to use the situation to gain power; all they have to do is find Octavia a husband and there you are. It will be your neck. Oh my darling, for heaven's sake take a stand. Have her killed and finish the danger."

She reached up and pulled my head down; her mouth was warm and living; you would not have thought it had spoken of death. I did not know whether she really thought of me or whether she merely wanted the end of a woman she hated. Women are jealous, cruel and merciless; I knew that well enough. In this one instance so might she be. But as she held me I felt a stirring warmth which was both the beginning of desire and the knowledge that she was right.

Adultery was not enough. To die Octavia must be proved criminally active against the state. Petronius produced a good idea; it had an artistry which one would expect from him.

I sent for Anicetus and said I needed his services a second time. It was not murder; he only needed to pretend he had been seduced by Octavia and become her lover. If he did I should exile him but only for appearances, and he would receive a large financial reward. If he did not he would die. That was Tigellinus, always an expert in persuasion. Of course, he agreed.

I held another enquiry (oh, I was growing so bored with them) and called him as a witness. Well, there it was. My sweet, virtuous ex-wife had seduced the admiral of the fleet at Misenum, hoping to gain the navy for her revolutionary purposes; in fact, she had been forced to have an abortion. Could anything be more disgusting? I was suitably outraged again and ordered her execution. The Senate and people accepted it all mildly; Octavia's partisans were quiet. I fancy Tigellinus had carried out another purge.

They removed her to the island of Pandeteria and imprisoned her in the cell where my maternal grandmother had died; a piece of artistic irony which pleased Petronius. But when I heard

267

how she went I could not eat for several days. I had given her orders to commit suicide and like her mother she had been unable to. It must be some fatal weakness which shows itself only at the very end when it is needed least; she had always seemed implacable. The soldiers had opened the veins in her arms and legs, then put her into a hot bath where the blood ran out freely; but she suffocated first.

They cut off her head and brought it to me. I was sitting with Poppaea at dinner and when the messenger entered with a leather bag I did not think what it might be. Then he opened it and out rolled a face I had last seen look arrogant at some feast.

I ran from the room, then yelled at the messenger: "Why did you bring it? I didn't want to see."

"I'm sorry, sire. I thought—"

The leather bag hung empty from his hands. I looked back cautiously and there was Poppaea holding it up by the hair and examining the face; she had never seen her rival. I turned away, trembling. This was her end, an emperor's daughter, as shabby and painful as any barbarian crucified on the highway; a long way from the nuptial bed and crushed orange blossom of ten years ago. How she must have dreamed and hoped and how the cruel inheritance had played itself out, her father and brother murdered, her place in my bed taken first by a slave and then a patrician, and now this: the pathetic little head on the marble floor. I was beginning to cry. She had revolted me, even frightened me, I thought I hated her—and yet I wept. The gods mock us every minute.

Britannicus had been a puppet, my mother a monster; but Octavia had been only in love. I knew how it was to have no love. That was the weakness which made me weep, recognition of my own disease in her; but now she was dead and beyond pain. I lived.

Chapter Fifteen

She was all mine now. It was the only thing which stopped me from brooding all day about Octavia and giving myself back to the Furies. If the darkness moved nearer she was always there; to look at her proved that beauty still lived and breathed in a world which had compromised itself into ugliness.

I had an idea that as emperor I should possess the power to bring back the rule of beauty. It is a thing of the senses but also of the mind; you perceive it through eyes, ears, nose, and mouth but you receive and accept it in your soul which must be willing otherwise there is rejection. Sometimes, looking at a vase or a painting or a rose or even Poppaea herself I felt that my perception was blurred; I did not see reality, only a faint shadow of it. Is it that we are half blind? Someone like Tigellinus is totally blind whereas such a person as Seneca looks in a distorting mirror. If I thought too long about this I grew depressed or frightened; there is a black pool which you will fall into if you stare too deep.

To mark my fifth year as emperor I had instituted Quinquennial games to be performed after the Greek style at Olympia. I called them the Neronia. The contest had three parts, chariot racing and gymnastics, singing and music, and poetry and oratory which meant all my great loves were gathered together in one splendid spectacle. I had a huge gymnasium built next to my new baths where athletes could train but the contest itself was held on the Campus Martius. I imported sand from the Nile to cover the ground.

To me there was nothing more graceful than young men improving their strength and skill, then wandering together to discuss art and philosophy; it was a little of Athens in Rome. But conservative old Romans of ancient family who thought they knew everything from divine wishes downwards objected loudly. First there was the nudity which was disgusting; then there was the practical uselessness—did all that ridiculous posturing and exhibitionism make good soldiers? Lastly there was the corruption; everyone knew Greece had fallen flat on her face due to idle luxuries of which the gymnasium life was one and led to perversion. "Young Rome," they said pompously, "is cultivating the body at the cost of the soul." Even Seneca mentioned the fat, lazy life of an athlete who sweats, drinks, and fornicates but never thinks at all. I said: "Don't be absurd. They train all the time; how could they afford that sort of life?"

"But the gymnastic life *is* that sort of life," he insisted. "A hiding away behind an empty Greek ideal."

"You can talk about hiding away behind empty ideals," I retorted, infuriated.

That angered him; more than once I had struck a vital spot. I was furious at such criticism; here I was trying to improve with a little grace and vitality a world they had made staid and ugly and all they could do was throw insults. "Romans all over," I said to Poppaea. "Why wasn't I born a Greek?"

"They are short-sighted," she said. "They don't see beyond their polite little villas and respectable dinner-parties. Don't try and make them, Nero. When a poor horse is forced it runs wild or drops dead."

"I *will* make them," I said. "If we abandon beauty and grace and all the values that come with it an earthquake might as well swallow us tomorrow."

I held my Neronia defiantly and it was successful. Out of sheer wickedness I made aristocrats join in various performances, including boxing and wrestling; their faces would have done for comedy masks. One well-known knight rode an elephant down a sloping tight-rope with great bravado and revelled in the cheers. He was not a reactionary. The poetry competitions were extremely satisfying. Lucan stood up and recited a dithyrambic eulogy of me, full of twirls and dramatic

270

flourishes and thoroughly unconvincing. All the same he expected to win. When the judges decided in favour of me as an honourable gesture (I had not even taken part in the thing) his face went dark as a storm cloud. Eulogy or not, he would have liked to kick my face in. I also won the citharists' contest (another tactful move) but when I received the crown I placed it at the foot of Augustus' statue; I had no wish to appear greedy.

I gave gladiatorial shows to suit the vulgar crowd, performed in a wooden theatre built specially near the Campus Martius. Again in defiance I would have no one killed, not even criminals; my Greek dream must not disappear in streams of blood. The fights were mere form like fencing matches and as yet another poke in reactionary sides I ordered four-hundred senators and six-hundred knights to perform. I must admit they put on a brave face although the sight of a noble grey-haired patrician tripped up and rolling in the dust was enough to shake the place with rude laughter. Just to scare them I included wild animal fights but they were well armed and assistance came quickly for the inept.

I also gave a naval spectacle on the artificial lake, drained and filled again with salt water, where sea monsters swam. Some were incredible—a vast grey thing with wicked eyes and dozens of tentacles like so many snakes only ten times longer, a fish as big as a house, and a monster eel which could snap off a man's leg in one bite. I could see the crowd wanted blood but all the same if men fell overboard during the battle I had them fished out again. One was unlucky; the eel got him. As I listened to the howls of delight I wondered what world my ancestors had made.

The climax of the Neronia was a performance of "The Fire" by Afranius which rested on its spectacular merits, nothing else. A house was actually set alight and the audience invited to keep anything they could rescue from the flames, precious furniture and ornaments, even a money chest. I had already been generous with gifts through the whole festival, giving out assorted birds including golden orioles and coloured humming birds, fat food parcels, vouchers for corn, clothes, gold,

271

precious stones, paintings, slaves and animals. Whatever the close-fisted patricians might say the plebs were happy. "The life-blood of a nation," Seneca had called them. What man bullies his body till the blood flows out?

Shortly before I married Poppaea there was a serious revolt in the far north of the empire, of all places tiny Britain with her barbarian hordes. It took me unprepared. The Iceni tribe under its new queen, Boadicea, had joined hands with the Trinovantes and risen up with all that savagery which barbarians can summon in a moment like animals. Colchester and London went under in flames with some seventy thousand Roman citizens butchered. When the news reached us people began thronging the Temple of Jupiter in a kind of panic; it sounded too much like a serious threat. There had already been omens; the grey sea between Gaul and Britain had run blood and nightwatchmen swore they heard wailings in an unknown tongue from the locked Senate house. When stories came of the screaming war bitch riding her chariot through fire and sword as though invulnerable it sounded like divine judgement.

"Judgement on *me*," I told Poppaea. "Must the empire go down as well?"

"Nonsense," she said. "A few savages rebel in an unimportant province and you talk like Priam seeing Troy burn." She was not illiterate; sometimes I thought her knowledge greater than mine. "Can't you forget," she said, "what has happened in the past and stop thinking of divine vengeance? Personally, I don't think the gods bother with revenge."

She calmed me as always and later came good news. Suetonius, the commander there and second to no one as a fighter except perhaps Corbulo, struck out the whole revolt with a pitched battle where eight thousand Britons died. "Roman strength tells," observed Poppaea and went back to her mirror. I ordered thanksgiving on the Capitol and thanked Jove that Boadicea had killed herself; description had made her sound like a barbarian Agrippina. No wonder the Furies are women.

Not long after my marriage Seneca slipped into virtual retirement. The reasons were complex and smelt of intrigue but

272

basically he was no more use to me, unless you count the pull of his name; he was still thought wise and virtuous by those who didn't know. I no longer cared for his advice which I thought pompous and unrealistic and I had a small army of secretaries capable of writing all the speeches I wanted. There had been some kind of feud with a senator named Sullius who attacked my dear tutor's fondness for affluence; heaven knows what he was worth. Apart from inheriting his father's fortune he had made a rich marriage and acquired various estates through his position as my chief adviser. In answer to Sullius he dug up some compromising details from that gentleman's life and I exiled him. I had to; it involved murder. My merciful tutor would have liked to attack the son as well but I stopped that. Enough is enough. Later came a tale that his demands for arrears in the payment of money lent to the Britons had sparked off the revolt. It couldn't be proved but his reputation suffered.

"I wonder you don't send him away," Poppaea said. "Is he any use to you?"

"What a utilitarian mind you have," I said, laughing.

"Perhaps I should have said is he any danger to you." She was thoughtful. "After all, if he thinks there is a possibility of successful conspiracies against you he may withdraw while still safe or even join the other side. Is he loyal?"

"Not when he can make a compromise," I said. "All the same . . ."

"Besides," she said, persuasive again, "you don't need him now. You're not a child any more."

"Poppaea, what is this?" I felt suspicious. "Of course, you don't like him, do you, and like all women you want to kick out where it hurts and when it isn't expected. You scheming little—"

I spoke affectionately and she began laughing. "He doesn't like me," she said.

As it happened he came to me first and asked if he could retire into private life as he wanted to devote his time to philosophy; he also offered me a large part of his fortune.

"Then," he said, "it can be administered by your stewards.

273

I'm growing old and incapable of bearing such responsibilities further."

It sounded suspicious. I thought rapidly. Tigellinus had been talking of plots stirring in Rome, mainly constructed by partisans of my three "victims" who were seen as pathetic sacrifices on an altar of power lust. No one saw that the victim was really me. But I had reigned eight years and there are always people prepared to think that too long. Taking this to be true Seneca was in an awkward position and evidently manoeuvring to get out of it. He had already been accused of pandering to my nasty habits such as singing and playing the lyre and should I fall I would drag him with me. By offering me his money and embracing obscurity he achieved a double purpose, gaining my gratitude and appearing a true Stoic which, in turn, suggested disapproval of me. All extremely clever; I don't think he had ever been so devious in his life. I looked at his earnest, submissive face with its carefully cultivated beard and philosopher's look and I said: "I wouldn't dream of it, Seneca."

His mouth opened; he looked like a man kicked in the stomach by a horse he thought docile.

"After all," I said, "I owe you so much. If you leave court, heaven knows where I'll be. You guided my first political steps and supported me in all my—ventures."

I emphasised the last word and he looked uneasy. I came forward and embraced him with all due courtesy, he stammered a bit, then looked resigned and left after giving thanks which must have stuck in his throat.

Thwarted in his grand gesture he instead reduced the splendour of his way of life, grew very quiet and learned, refused nearly all visitors and became a vegetarian. He made his point.

An unfortunate thing happened a month or so after I married. I received a summons from the chief Vestal virgin, asking that I go to their house as they had something of vital importance to tell me. I thought it odd. Normally the Vestals never interfere with imperial affairs; it isn't their concern. But then I thought: they care for the eternal flame, symbol of the sacred hearth and the family. What I have done is a violation of both. Poppaea said: "Don't be silly. How could they know?"

"The goddess told them," I said.

"Do you believe that?" She looked at me steadily. "Come now, Nero, it's a pretty custom to guard a sacred flame as though it mattered but does it mean anything more?"

"It meant something to our forefathers."

"Exactly. Now it's an empty oracle; it says nothing to anyone."

I had not realised her scepticism. She had been conventionally brought up and it seemed wrong, but then to me she was an ocean of unknown depth. I had vague fears of sinking.

"I can't believe," she had once said, "in statues and stories and gods who turn their backs on human misery. I would rather believe there are no gods at all."

I took a litter to the Vestal Virgins' house, passing their exquisite temple where the flame burned and going under the arch of Augustus built to commemorate his victory at Actium; to its left was the colossal temple of Castor and Pollux with their statues either side of the steps, gracefully leaning on the horses which had brought them to Rome that day, I looked and remembered my aunt's story; I could not believe it. The divinely blessed do not suffer.

I went alone into the vestibule of the house and waited; no man, not even a Caesar, may go further. Through the columns of the peristyle was a courtyard with flowers blooming in square beds and two water cisterns, green in the sun. Only the crickets moved. It was cool in the shadows, too cool; my neck prickled as though with danger but I knew there was no human danger here. If I felt anything it must be a god. I looked through the shade to the bright garden beyond and thought of Poppaea: *Do you believe that?*

"My lord?"

I turned and saw a woman standing at the end of the long gallery in the white, purple-bordered robe of a Vestal with ribbons hanging down from a tight band round her head; a white veil covered her hair.

I said: "Are you the chief Vestal?"

"No." She moved forward and blue shadows fled from her face. It was small with pretty dark eyes and a short nose, an innocent face. "My name is Rubria."

"The chief Vestal sent for me," I said. I began to feel uneasy. "Where is she?"

"She did not send for you. I did."

She was calm and smiling. My thoughts ran wild; could that chaste robe conceal a knife; suppose there were others—here, behind the pillars, in the garden?

"There is no one," she said, "but me. Come, let us walk."

I followed her up the gallery, perplexed; all along it stood statues of famous Vestals, facing the courtyard. At one end was a lararium with its family gods.

I said: "Why?"

"I want to talk to you. Is it not true you may have incurred some blood guilt?"

I stopped. "What do you mean?"

"The goddess tells us many things. And there is another matter; you are not merely defiled with blood."

I turned and said: "I'm going. I don't wish to hear any more," but she caught my wrist. "I have a price," she said. I stared. All the innocence had gone like a discarded mask. "My bedroom," she said, "leads off this gallery. It is easy to get at."

The shadows turned cold round me; I looked at her pretty, knowing face and said: "You are mad."

"Oh no, not mad. I know what I want. I have seen you too often not to." Her face was turned up to mine; the ribbons dangled like garlands on a sacrificial lamb. "Why that redhaired bitch?" she said softly. "Can she please you?"

My breath came thick. I tried to move but she clung tight round my neck and kissed me fiercely; I could feel her breasts under the Vestal robe. I pushed her off and she stood panting. Confused images swam on the summer air: Octavia in tumbled orange, my mother with a fibula raised to strike.

"You bitch," I said. "You shameless bitch. Here in your own house on ground sacred to the goddess."

276

She began to cry, falling on her knees to me. "Oh please, don't talk so. I love you and nothing else matters, not the goddess or the vows of chastity; I don't care. Please be kind to me, stop the fire before it eats me up."

I looked down in horror. Such is the tyranny of the blood; it knows no barriers, no sacredness; desire comes up more destructive than the lava fire of Vesuvius. And I had known it, too.

"Please," she murmured. "Please. Can it be so bad?" She looked up, a tear-streaked child. "What is a Vestal compared to a mother?"

I hit her across the face. She squealed and tumbled backwards, coming to rest against the pedestal of a statue where she crouched shivering. I said: "May the gods stop me from killing you."

I thought she would cry again, then suddenly her face changed; she began to scream. I watched, stupefied. She tore her dress to the waist so that her breasts showed and flung off the sacred veil, scratching her face till the blood ran; and all the time she screamed.

There was a scuffle of running feet and raised voices; at one end were more Vestals, at the other my litter bearers. She was wailing and beating her head on the pedestal. Some blood had dropped on to her dress.

"Sweet Vesta," said one of the virgins.

They were looking at me from either end; I stood, helpless, saying: "I haven't—"

There was silence, only her whimpering.

"Caesar or not," said the chief Vestal, "may the gods punish you."

The story was round Rome within hours. I could not deny it because no one would believe the alternative; the smell of crime sticks.

"Little whore," Poppaea said.

I said miserably: "I shall never till my death understand women. They cry out against rape, then pretend it to suit themselves, appear chaste at dinner and bacchantes in bed, produce children which they abandon and chase men they profess to hate."

"My darling, you are not meant to understand." She smiled and sat at my feet, one arm across my lap. "The day you do you won't want us any more."

I sat quiet for a moment, fingering her hair; then I said: "What sort of divinity allows such passion in her servants? To serve a god should bring true peace of mind."

"Yes." She frowned. "But only if the god exists."

Exactly nine months after our wedding my daughter was born. I called her Claudia. She was born at Antium like me in a marbled villa facing the bay, not my mother's villa; I could not set foot in there. She was a round, pretty child with her mother's hair, soft as swansdown.

Poppaea looked at me from her pillows and said: "It should have been a boy."

"I'm quite satisfied," I said. "The next one can be a boy."

She leaned back and laughed, saying: "Let me recover from this one, Nero. It isn't as easy as it looks."

She insisted on caring for it herself which I had not expected. Acte had looked a mother; Poppaea seemed too elegant to bother with baby milk. Yet I used to come in and find it at her breast or across her lap being anointed with wine, then maidenhair in rose oil to cure soreness.

We stayed in Antium till the spring; it was pleasant by the sea and quiet. You can pretend nothing matters in quietness. Then one evening the nurse came running to say the baby was sick; when we got there she was gasping and turning stiff and blue. Xenophon tried his best but even doctors cannot fight the Fates.

Poppaea wept till I grew frightened. "There will be others," I said gently. "And she died happy. She never had to know that life can be cruel." But when I looked back to the tiny corpse I felt tears in my own eyes; part of me had died. Had she lived I would have given her everything and proved that childhood can be happy.

Poppaea grew pale and would not eat. Her anguish increased

mine so that we were like two harsh stones rubbing against each other.

"She needs distraction," Xenophon said, "and so do you. Go away somewhere; travel is an excellent medicine."

We took his advice. I had already thought of going to Naples and then to Greece as a singer, performing where art was appreciated. I did not want to try my luck with narrow-minded Romans. Once I had proved my ability before people who recognised quality and would not bicker with jealousy or indignation I could go back to my own city, unashamed. We travelled south with a thousand carts between us, including my mules shod with silver and gold and her four hundred asses who supplied the milk for her bath; it was no secret where her dazzling white skin came from. When the sun was too hot she used a shade of peacock feathers with a gold handle.

We had a fine reception. An emperor had never given a singing tour before and to the common man it seemed an entertainment sent by gods, not to be missed. If I made a fool of myself they could laugh; if not, they could enjoy it. The streets of Naples were crammed; people had been sleeping out all night in the public squares, even on temple steps. It was warm and the marble burned white in sunlight; between the columns I could see the blue bay, bright as a sapphire, with little ships riding at anchor, empty. Everyone was here. As we drove down the main street in our gold-painted chariot they cheered and sang and threw flowers and at the forum a troop of girls came out, crowned with lilies and singing dithyrambs in praise of my majesty and musical and poetic genius. It softened my heart. For too long I had suffered the sharpness of inartistic Romans.

I should have sung in the closed-in theatre but the audience was too big and we had to use the huge open-air one instead. At first I was worried; one's voice must carry further outside and I wondered if mine were sufficient. I came out on the stage with a section of my Juventus Augustani, young boys with waved, scented hair grown long and rings on the left hand; they were my chorus. In Rome they had provoked bawdy comments. Here they were received with enthusiasm; Neapolitans love youthful grace but not as Romans do who think only in terms of bed.

I looked at the tiered seats full of eyes and realised too late that I had exchanged disapproval for critical perception. If I failed they would know. Suddenly I feared rejection, cruel laughter or, worse, an icy silence. My voice cracked again at the beginning. Sweet Apollo, I thought, if you exist, carry my voice on wings to the hilltops and make my music sweet as yours. Not until I was halfway through did I realise I had shared Poppaea's scepticism.

They clapped and cheered, perhaps because I was Caesar and they thought it tactful; my confidence was small. Yet they persisted so in applause and demands for an encore that I gave it to please them, thinking: perhaps they know better than you. I sang over several days, varying my repertoire. I had begun with my Attis piece because I knew it backwards and needed that confidence; I made a point of announcing I had written it in Naples, inspired by its beauty, which pleased them and started off more demands for encores. After that I did Orestes pursued by Furies and Oedipus blinded; it needed courage but once I began my own emotions took wing and I was back in the heated bedroom, the dark triclinium, waiting for news; I could obey Terpnus to the full. I thought they should never stop cheering. But as I bowed and looked into their faces I saw some darkened as though with nasty memories; then I knew what I had done was not art at all but emotionalism founded on experience.

On the last day there was an earth-tremor, only a slight one and I hardly noticed it till I saw the empty seats. Being deep in my performance I had gone on singing while the audience fled. I finished the song, not liking the vacuum of an unfinished melody, then came a sudden shock which threw me to my knees and tumbled down the top tiers. I thought: an omen; what is it now? Then I realised the Fates had been generous and taken no life; perhaps it meant nothing, after all. When I got home Poppaea said: "Dear gods, I thought you had been killed. Someone told me the theatre had fallen."

"No one died," I said. "Don't you think we should give thanksgiving?"

"To a blind movement of the earth?" she said.

I wrote out a hymn all the same, giving thanks to the gods, but it was more of an artistic exercise than genuine feeling. My work suffered from either too much or too little feeling. So often the words were unreliable, sliding here and there in a rush of emotion which harmed construction, or else coming out stiff and dull for lack of inspiration. I used to give my poems to Poppaea and ask for a judgement; she was too honest for flattery. Sometimes she would say: "Yes, very lyrical," and sometimes: "No; it hasn't worked," and then give reasons. She understood poetic theory so well I wonder she didn't write herself but she always said she had no talent. "One thing to theorise," she said, "but another to do it yourself."

After a month or so we set out for the Adriatic, intending to sail to Greece but then I received news which turned us back again. The old senator Torquatus Silanus, uncle to Octavia's first fiancé, had committed suicide having presumably been implicated in a plot by Tigellinus. The outward reason was the organisation of his household on imperial lines with superintendents of finance and so on, together with a generosity which rivalled even mine. He had been called for trial but forestalled justice. It struck me as ironic; had he only waited for my judgement he would still be alive. With the news came a message from Tigellinus. He respectfully suggested I return home as there was unrest in Rome due to lack of entertainment and a scarcity of grain distribution. He did not wish to worry me but he also thought he had found signs of a plot, if genuine a very serious one; I remembered the earthquake.

We left at once. I arrived nervously, expecting the place to be in a turmoil; instead, it was still as a summer day. I lost my temper at Tigellinus, saying would he kindly verify his facts in future rather than disturb my holiday. Then I summoned the officials in charge of entertainment and grain supplies and said what I thought of them; they retreated humbly, promising to reform. Tigellinus insisted that his spies had unearthed rumours of a plot; it was a question of proof. I said: "I'm not interested in vague theories. If you can't show me a conspiritor keep quiet."

I meant to go away again, principally to Alexandria which Poppaea wanted to see and perhaps to Greece later. The Alexandrians in Naples had been appreciative of me; I felt Egypt had much to offer especially with regard to her artists. But my family was too troublesome. When I announced my intention protests broke out and I judged it wiser to remain and keep them happy. The emperor is father, entertainer, and supplier of everything from Games to bread. That was how they saw me; that was how I must be.

About this time I noticed a change in Poppaea. She had grown quieter and spent time in thought or reading where before she would have sat in front of the mirror. I thought it reaction from the child's death. At times she looked very pale with marks like bruises under her eyes as though she had not slept; when I asked she said: "I'm all right. Just a little tired." My mind, sharpened by death, visualised the worst and I asked Xenophon to look at her; he only said: "There is nothing wrong. You worry too much."

I was too close to her; she could not alter for a moment without me knowing. Her grace and beauty was the same, so was her voice, her laugh, the way she looked at me. The change was inside. Her energetic enjoyment of life seemed tempered as though she had looked from a window and seen something more valuable in the distance. I knew her enquiring mind; she had always been restless even with everything I could give her. She was not like most women, satisfied with a dress or a necklace. Once she had said: "When you have everything you can possibly want what else is there?"

I said: "Nothing. You have it all. You're happy."

"No." She looked at me, serious. "It doesn't happen like that. Nero, are you completely happy?"

"When I'm with you." I had joked, trying to draw her out of it. She smiled faintly like a child when an adult tries to be amusing.

"I can't see why," she said, "when I have dresses and jewels and a lovely house, when I have you . . ."

I said, alarmed: "You're not happy. Why? Just tell me, my darling, and I'll give you whatever it is."

Then she withdrew. "I'm perfectly happy," she said.

Gods forgive me, I began to think she was unfaithful. She had started going out more than usual, often in the early morning; when I had breakfast there she was, smiling and fresh-faced as though she had run through the dew.

"Where have you been, Poppaea?"

"Oh, here and there."

Her hair was tossed; had a man's hand run it through? And why that bright, delighted look?

"What do you mean?" I was suddenly sharp.

"I went for a walk," she said, "in the gardens of Lucullus. They are so quiet and lovely. Did you know there was a peach tree there and crocuses, all mauve and white and golden?"

I said: "So early in the morning?"

"I couldn't sleep. And I could hear the birds singing."

I thought of having her followed. There were so many fascinating young men in Rome, all accessible; I felt Messalina's ghost at my elbow. I called for a mirror and looked. My face and neck had begun to thicken and I knew beyond doubt that I was growing fatter; I already had a paunch. It was all that rich food. But my nose was still straight, my eyes wide if a little bloodshot from lack of sleep, my hair still sleek and gold; the sun had brought out freckles but what was that? Then I thought: dear Jove, here I am at twenty-six, studying a mirror and wondering if I'm losing my lovely wife to a more attractive man. I put the mirror away and did nothing.

One evening she said: "Nero, do you think gods ever become men?"

"Seneca said they might. Why?"

"I was just thinking."

I said: "You've been thinking too much recently."

"Now, Nero." She pretended shock. "Didn't I always say that Otho's drawback was lack of serious thought. You never pretended to believe that I was empty-headed."

There was silence; I looked at her and wondered what went on deep in her beautiful head. Then she said slowly: "Nero, would you believe in something which washed away all the guilt of your incest and parricide without you doing anything?"

I said: "No." She spoke of horrors as if they were children's stories. "I'm condemned to the Furies. So far, only you have kept them back."

Then she smiled and grew affectionate, raising her face to kiss me; but when I looked into the grey-green eyes they seemed gazing far away from me.

As always I looked elsewhere for quick distraction. I took stock of various artistic works in temples and public buildings and where they were failing I supervised their restoration. Apelles' famous painting of Venus Anadyomene in the temple to Caesar was peeling from the wall; nothing could be done so I commissioned Dorotheus to paint another. I watched him at work and envied his ability to lose himself in creation, then stand back and see a part of him detached, there on the wall for all time. On such occasions men must feel as gods. I also had various statues restored and ordered a gold statue of Juno to be made for my child's temple; the Senate had decreed it for her together with divine honours.

Also, my grand construction between the Palatine and Esquiline was at last finished; I called it Domus Transitoria because it was a link, not a house in itself. It was like a jewel thread running through the ugliness. It took Poppaea and me half an hour to walk the length of it, not that we minded; I could have walked for ever. It gave me great satisfaction for though I had not built or even designed it the initial idea was mine. I had given a little beauty where it was needed.

Then there were feasts. Apart from giving my own I went to other people's, at one of which the host, knowing my love of roses, had spent four million sesterces on them; it was out of season. I said: "Congratulations. What is money for but spending?" which pleased him. I took to gambling and staked thousands of sesterces on the dice because I liked the excitement apart from the grandeur of throwing money around. What man can feel inferior with a fortune on the table? I even tried fishing in the Tiber or off a cliff in Antium when we were there; it was something new. I used nets of gold with meshes of purple and crimson silk which people said was extravagant but I found no beauty in the coarse stuff fishermen use. I was always at the races. I used to wear green and have the Circus floor scattered with green copper dust so that it glittered like emeralds in the sun. I got criticised for it but, after all, why should an emperor not show whom he supports?

In the August after Claudia's death Tigellinus gave a huge banquet for me which half Rome attended, a good sop for the bored citizens. He constructed an open-air banqueting hall on a great raft drawn by ships inlaid with gold and ivory and had it moored in the middle of Augustus' lake in the Campus Martius. Here were tables and couches covered in purple carpets and Babylonian rugs, with black-haired slave girls and pretty Greek boys to serve us, even an orchestra playing flutes and lyres at one end. I did not know this at the time but the boats' rowers were perverts picked out by Tigellinus from the city's brothels and arranged in the order of their special "talents"; he had that sort of mind. When someone told me I said: "Oh well, it will amuse the mob." The remark filtered back later to various respectable Romans who took it as final proof of my debauchery.

The food included octopus and a great capon, larks' tongues (a delicacy because of the sweet song), goose liver, a whole boar cooked and steaming and carried by four slaves, dormice rolled in poppy seed, mushrooms, truffles, and apples and peaches big as a man's fist. He and Petronius had put their heads together and been thoroughly ingenious; I could see who had thought of what. The donkey of Corinthian bronze with panniers holding black olives one side and white the other was Petronius. The Alexandrian boys, trained to spite the guests with cruel wit and thus amuse everyone else, were Tigellinus.

So were the brothels on the banks. They lined the lake on both sides, little arbours trailing flowers and thick curtains with their inmates in full view, most of them naked. Some were not prostitutes at all but young women of noble family, probably bored and thinking this the way to gain attention and excitement; inside all of us there is a monster demanding satisfaction. Perhaps a few had been forced; I knew Tigellinus. There were

285

attractive boys, too, for variety's sake. The proceedings began with water ballets performed by girl dancers in light, transparent garments which swirled like mist; it reminded me of Egypt. In fact the whole thing was a copy of spectacles the Pharaohs used to give. Perhaps that was Petronius again.

As night came down torches burned on the lakeside and made the water liquid fire. Activities livened up with the cover of darkness; I could hear singing and yelling with women's screams and trampling feet amongst the trees which leaned black against torchlight. I heard but did not look. Poppaea lay beside me on silken cushions, her hair spread wide like a fan; she wore all gold as my mother once had, the slits in her sleeves held together by tiny fibulas set with rubies. The air was warm and scented; I breathed its freshness and looked at the brilliant stars sailing over the lake and thought: this is a night to write poems on. I said: "Poppaea, are you happy?"

"I think so."

She hardly stirred; the night and the slight movement of the water had lulled her.

"You only think? Have mercy on me; can anything be more conducive to happiness than this?"

"I don't know. Where is all that noise coming from?"

"The bank," I said. "Don't think about it. We're an island unto ourselves out here. Everyone else is drunk or asleep and no one can hear us talk."

The water rippled with a shiver of moonlight. She said sharply: "Listen." A thin wild scream ran over the lake like lightning; it grew higher and repeated itself again and again, then died. "What is it?" She was white. "Oh Nero—"

"A girl being chased," I said, soothing her.

When I took her in my arms she felt cold; I kissed her but she was limp and unresponsive, a tamed tigress. It worried me.

Next day I heard people had died during the night. Men, fighting and pushing to reach the women, had caused a crush ending in panic where girls had been suffocated or torn to pieces; a couple had drowned. Remembering the screams I felt ill; I said to Tigellinus: "I don't consider that entertainment. How will it make me look?"

286

"A generous monarch, sire," he said, unperturbed. "After all, such disorders must be expected when men are maddened with wine and lust."

I thought of the Maenads; it made me tremble. Who can deny that Dionysus might not show himself in any one of us when the time comes? We do not know ourselves.

A few days later I made a fool of myself. High-class public opinion in Rome had been throwing self-righteous criticism at me, Poppaea was silent and strange and Tigellinus annoyed me; I needed distraction. I held a feast which started at midday and ended at midnight with entertainments at hourly intervals and all the food my cooks were capable of producing, arriving in long streams on gold, silver and bronze. By evening I was completely drunk yet still on my feet. Poppaea had left after two hours. I didn't know what I was doing and I didn't care; they had called me debauched and irresponsible, then let them see me so. Let them realise morality was nothing and art was all.

I forget details. I remember putting on a wedding veil and thinking it highly amusing, then someone brought in nuptial torches, Tigellinus handed over a mock-dowry with great solemnity and off we went to the marriage bed. I suppose if I thought at all I thought it a game in Otho's terms, a sick joke. My audience expected the joke to be carried to its conclusion.

Next morning I said: "Petronius, what did I do?" I didn't trust Tigellinus.

"Do you really want to know, sire?"

I said: "Yes," and covered my eyes; the light hurt them. My head felt sick and burning.

"You went through a wedding ceremony with a person named Pythagoras and retired to bed with him."

"In front of everyone?"

"Yes, sire."

I shuddered. "And who is Pythagoras?"

He coughed; I said: "Petronius, stop being so artistically sensitive. I want to know."

"Very well, sire." He paused. "He comes from a brothel near the Velabrum."

I stared. "Then how did he—"

"Tigellinus brought in a crowd of them because you asked for unconventional entertainment; they were at your water feast. If you'll excuse me saying so, sire, it is foolish to give Tigellinus so much freedom. He is irresponsible, a man without sensitivity who will exploit you if needs be; he has no artistry, no principles of any sort to hold him back."

I said: "This sounds personal, Petronius. What is it?"

He bowed and smiled; I felt the irony in the air. "Concern for your welfare, sire," he said.

Now it was done I felt ashamed and disgusted. I had imagined it would be grand to flout responsible ethics and show myself a true artist, oblivious of convention. Instead it was a sweet fruit bursting sour in the mouth. I crawled back to Poppaea with my head down like a whipped dog asking forgiveness. She said: "It doesn't matter. I know you were drunk."

I looked at her; she seemed to mean it. Any other woman would have thrown a vase at my head or refused to speak at all. I said: "Aren't you ashamed of me?"

"No; if you didn't mean it there is nothing wrong. And even if you did but are sorry it comes to the same thing."

Her tolerance frightened me. I said, trembling a little, "You're too good to me, Poppaea. It isn't natural."

She only smiled and stroked my hair. How strange that you can love someone so deeply and not know the roots of their being.

The following summer we were at Antium again. It had been a cold winter and Poppaea had drawn further from me, not physically for I found no difference in bed; something in her mind was a gate shut against me. I could not name it for she had not grown hostile or selfish. She was all sweetness and grace, a delight to anyone who looked on her.

I gave many feasts, long and extravagant, intended to keep me happy and show my people that I was a Princeps worth having. The Pharaohs did this and succeeded well. I did not like to count money; it struck me as mean and rather vulgar as though one's mental horizons were bounded with gold.

Naturally, my expenses were great and I liked to be flourishing over them even though people were critical. That was one small point in favour of Uncle Caligula; he had never been niggardly.

July was burning hot and I often swam or sat by the sea, composing poetry and singing to an invited audience. It was cool on the cliff tops. I had put on weight even more, due to continual feasting, and found the heat uncomfortable. Amongst other things I had an idea of writing a history of Rome in verse, a task not attempted even by Virgil. I thought that here I should prove myself a poet. It would be a tremendous work, of course. Already I visualised the rolling iambic hexameters, the complex similes, such a wide range of event and emotion; perhaps too wide. Cornutus estimated that it would fill four hundred books. "Too long," he said. "No one will bother to read it all." He upset me. "Are you sure?" I said plaintively. "But Chrysippus wrote far more on one subject."

"Ah, yes." He was ready for anything. "But what he wrote was of great value."

Perhaps he realised once it was said. I drew myself up and said coldly: "Thank you, Cornutus, You may leave me." He went, a little uneasy; you cannot insult Caesar and hope to get away with it. In fact, I was indulgent. I merely refused him admission to my house. Like my mother and Octavia, like so many people, he had hurt me in a vulnerable spot, a healed wound opened up again and again.

July the eighteenth was the hottest day so far. The sun drained the colour from everything and dried up the ground till dust stirred at every step, Poppaea sat gasping under the peristyle with slaves holding fans and sunshades while I drank iced water or went to the bath. That night I could not sleep. I had to call a slave to keep the flies away.

At half-past one I heard hooves clatter on the road outside, then feet came hurrying and a voice said: "I must see the emperor. It's urgent." I thought: dear gods, a conspiracy, an armed revolt. I sat up trembling, then in he burst, wild-faced and scattering dust from his sandals; a man who had ridden fast.

"Sire," he said, "I beg you to come at once. Rome is on fire!"

Book Six

PRIAM

"Quis cladem, illius noctis, quis funera fando,
Explicet aut possit lacrimis aequare labores.
Urbs antiqua ruit multos dominata per annos."
THE AENEID

Chapter Sixteen

To this day I remember the look on his face and the smell of his sweat on the hot night air; behind him the lamplight shuddered on the wall.

I said stupidly: "What do you mean?"

"It's burning, sire." He was distraught, no doubt thinking me callous. "A fire broke out somewhere near the Circus Maximus and spread within minutes; it has already reached the imperial palaces on the Palatine."

I said: "I'll come at once."

Poppaea had woken up and was saying sleepily: "What is it, darling?"

"A fire," I said. "It's nothing to worry about." The words tumbled out, unthinking; I was pulling on a cloak, calling the slave to saddle my horse. "You stay here. I must go now and see what is happening."

"Will you be all right?" Her eyes looked scared in the dark.

"Yes, of course. Go back to sleep; I'll send for you in the morning if necessary. Goodbye." I kissed her and went.

It takes three hours from Antium to Rome with a good horse. Mine was of Spanish blood, bred in Africa, the sort that make good race horses, and I drove him hard with no thought but to get there fast. My city was at stake. As the dark land flew past me with the shapes of trees and houses and an empty sky streaming above I thought of the Furies who wait in the night; can a nation suffer for its king? Had I bartered myself for my people? Only a fool thinks he can outmatch the snake-haired women. Then I remembered; it was the nineteenth of

July, four hundred and fifty years to the day since the Gauls sacked Rome.

You could see the blaze from far off on the Via Ostiensis; it was moving out from the Circus and leaping up the hillside in red streaks of flame; on the other side it had attacked the Aventine and reached for the Caelian mount. I thought of my mother's villa; if this were the gods then that was already doomed. As we galloped I saw the glow spread in the sky like blood in water. I said to my companion: "For the gods' sake, man, hurry! " The fire was raging over the Forum; any minute it would reach my precious Domus Transitoria. He said, breathless: "Sire, what can we do? The firefighters can't cope with this."

I said: "We can but try," though my heart seemed ice; I had seen snake heads in the flames.

Near the Circus fire and rubble had blocked the road; beyond came screams and the sound of feet and voices, buckets clanging and horses shrieking, a child yelling: "Mother! " and over it all the deadly hiss and crackle of flame. We could not force our horses through so I dismounted and went on foot, uncaring; it was my city and my people. They were everywhere, fleeing from the houses like ants from a tipped-up nest; they rushed past me and never even looked. When I went to help an old woman trying to carry out her few possessions she merely said: "The gods bless you, young man."

In the plebian settlement at the foot of the Aventine, houses were gutted and beginning to fall. Their blazing heads stood shuddering against the sky. I yelled to my companion: "Fetch help! Get Tigellinus and tell him to call out every man he's got."

The struts reinforcing weakened walls had burned through; some crashed down. I heard the screams of those who were not quick enough and would have liked to close my ears; it is a dreadful death to burn. But crisis lets no room for squeamishness. A child stood wailing in the blackened street walled in by flame; I caught her up. Seconds later a blazing beam fell where she had stood. I looked at the smudged, whimpering face; she did not know me, only that I had given protection in

294

the middle of a nightmare, and she wept against my neck for home and family and all she had lost. It was the face of my people.

I ran with her past the curve of the Circus, well ablaze, and tried to fight my way through the Forum Boarium which was safe as yet and crammed by people in panic, carts, loaded with stuff, horses, donkeys and barking dogs; they had sprawled up the steps of the temple to Fortuna and tried to climb on the roof. Others were streaming across the bridge over the river. Behind me came the roar of falling houses, the screams of the dying. Faces looked at me, red in firelight as though already marked for destruction, then away again; they saw no hope in me. I was not Caesar, not even Nero; only one of the nameless suffering.

My mind was working feverishly as though of itself. Where can I put them? They need shelter, food; if the Campus Martius is untouched I'll open it to them and get corn from Ostia—cheap, free if necessary. What about the injured? I'll send my own doctors. If only Tigellinus would come. We need water, gallons of it—the Baths, the Martian Aqueduct; I'll empty every fountain in Rome. My poor palace—the fire must be there now; all my statues and paintings, my clothes, my cithara ... The child trembled in my arms; I could feel her heart going like galloping hooves. We reached the other side of the river where the city stretched dark and flawless; I thought: fire can't cross water but there are the bridges.

I left her with a woman there, saying: "Keep her safe till I come back." She began to protest, then looked closer and gasped: "Yes, sire." One victim, at least, would have safety; my name had assured it. I went back across the bridge and through Velabrum which was already on fire; people rushed yelling from a brothel and a woman, half naked, screamed abuse for lack of payment. To the right was the Palatine, its crest burning red and gold and the black tips of buildings showing through the smoke. One side was dark with people. I imagined all those pompous senators and respectable matrons losing their dignity and flying for their lives; it should have pleased me. Instead, I saw snake heads again and my blood swam cold.

I ran, not knowing where. Perhaps to fetch help, to find Tigellinus. All was panic-terror and no one thought of stopping the danger at its source. As I neared the Forum I saw someone set a torch to the wooden struts of a house; I yelled: "Here, what do you think you're doing?" and he whirled round, flung the torch through the open doorway and made off. I caught him at the end of the road. He panted and struggled but I held him; fury had turned me wild. I said: "What are you, a bandit? Did you hope to spread the fire and loot?"

He was suddenly calm, standing quite still. "We're acting under orders," he said.

"Whose orders?" I felt uneasy.

He smiled. "You'll soon know."

A spark of the fire had reached my soul. I shook him savagely, shouting: "Do you know who I am?"

"No; it makes no difference. When he comes you will see him whoever you are."

"Him?" I fancied he was raving, then I thought: is this a planned coup after all? Tigellinus warned me. I struck him across the face and said: "How dare you! I'm the emperor." He blinked and straightened. "I'm not afraid," he said. "Your time has come. Evil perishes in the flames."

Outraged, I was ready to beat the life from him but then a burning wall crashed down, missing us by a handsbreadth; I felt sparks catch my hair. In the confusion I lost him.

The Forum was alive with people. Flames had poured down the Palatine and attacked the Via Sacra; shops to the south of it were ablaze from end to end with stocks of food, wine jars, flowers, perfumes, ivory, gold and jewellery and racks of clothes all burning up to the night sky; an empire's wealth vanishing in smoke. And no one did anything. Then I saw Praetorian plumes amongst the crowd; they were holding their ground even in that confusion, helping with salvage and human rescue, forming a line for water to be passed along in jars, buckets, bowls, anything that would hold it. In the middle was Tigellinus.

I ran up and said: "Thank the gods; I thought I should never find you." He turned round and said austerely: "Don't bother me, fellow. Can't you see how busy we are?"

I said: "Tigellinus!"

He stopped, examined me, then said: "I'm so sorry, sire; you are almost unrecognisable. It's the soot; your hair looks black. When did you get here?"

He had to shout above the noise. "Just now," I yelled. "How did it begin?"

He shrugged. "No one knows. It began about ten o'clock in the shops under the Circus; perhaps an oil lamp. But it's my belief, sire, that it's a plot of some sort; my men have picked up various people who were helping the fire along, saying they were under orders."

I said: "I know. I met one but he got away. Tigellinus, I'm afraid." He smiled; his total self-possession annoyed me. "Sire, I warned you. Rome smells of conspiracy; it always has done."

I said slowly: "How much damage, how many deaths?"

"We can't tell yet. When the fire is out we'll start counting."

"And my new palace?"

He smiled as if in pity. "Entirely destroyed, sire."

From the Esquiline you can see all the Forum, the Palatine, the Caelian mount and everything in between. I stood on a terrace of the Maecenas gardens amongst cool cypresses and fig trees; there was no stink of burning here, only blossom scent, no roar of flames, only the buzz of winged insects among the leaves. But below was desolation. I leaned on a stone balustrade and thought my heart would crack. Where my Domus Transitoria had stood in all its glory with shivering fountains and bright marble was now a smoking skeleton. The painted ceilings had crashed in and the pillars supporting them were charred bones; fire still flickered between them. Beyond was the Forum, blazing on one side, and flames leaping like a god's sword all along the Palatine, Mount Caelian and beyond again on the Aventine and by the river warehouses. The Tiber was a ribbon of fire crowded with boats; people thought to escape by water but there were too many and some capsized. I heard them cry out and thought: first Vulcan, now Neptune; they are all against us. Then I remembered the Aeneid: *it is the gods, the merciless gods who are throwing down the empire of Troy from its heights.*

I had wanted to play Priam, too. I stood in the scented darkness, watching the moon turn red in the glare, and with the roar of falling stone and wood and the screams of my people in my ears I thought of my favourite passage from Virgil. *It was like a fire catching a cornfield/The flames blown by the south wind/Or a mountain river running in flood...* The tears filled my eyes. I had loved Rome more than myself. I remembered standing on the blazing hill opposite and taking a vow to protect and serve her; it had been a mistake. All I loved came to destruction. *Who in telling of the tragedy of that night will tell of the deaths...* The words came easily on my tongue; I spoke them softly under the trees while Rome burned beneath; there seemed nothing more fitting. *The ancient city which ruled for century upon century has fallen to its ruin. Everywhere lie the corpses...* They were carrying them out from the houses, lying them in the street because there was nowhere else. Some still screamed, trapped in wreckage. *Look, there on top of the Citadel sits Pallas Athene with her shining garment of cloud and the fierce Gorgon's head.* It was my indictment; Medusa's eyes looked only for me but had found my city.

"Nero!" It was Petronius, anguished and soot-grimed, all elegance gone. "Nero, for the gods' sake what are you doing, reciting poetry while the place goes up in flames?"

I said quietly: *"Ruit alto a culmine Troia."*

"Nonsense." He was beyond artistic feeling. "Rome is very much still at her height. A fire can be put out."

"Not when the gods have sent it to destroy impiety."

He took me by the shoulders. "Stop thinking like that. Sweet Jove, I never imagined you were so fatalistic."

"There were people amongst the flames," I said vaguely, "keeping the fire going and saying they were under orders. They did not seem ... of this earth."

I forgot the human flesh I had gripped. He said: "Stop it!" It might have been Otho again in the dark bedroom at Baia. "I sometimes think you want to be mad. Stop brooding like a tragedian and come down where you can help. We've thrown open the Campus Martius as you wanted and started emergency feeding operations; the ships have already set out to Ostia. Tigellinus says with any luck they will have it under control in a few hours..."

It burned for six days. In the end I ordered teams of workmen to demolish all buildings around the Aventine and Circus and out even further at the foot of the Capitol and the edge of the Campus Martius. With nothing to feed on the fire starved.

It broke out again on Tigellinus' estate but only in a small way and never got far; I fancy it was someone with a grudge. His police activities didn't make him popular. I sheltered the homeless in the buildings on the Campus; they filled Pompey's theatre, the Baths of Agrippa, the Porticus of Pompey and my own baths; I even sheltered them in my Vatican gardens. It was summer and they needed no roof. Food came from the Ostian warehouses and up from Campania; Pompeii especially was generous, considering their earthquake not so very long ago. I cut the price of corn and opened my own treasuries for relief. It was propitiation again. They had burned on the sacrificial altar instead of me; it was my turn to pay back.

I found the child I had rescued and gave her to Acte that she might bring her up with my son who was now nine, bright and lively with Ahenobarbus hair and my mother's eyes. Some good had come from horror. Her parents had been slum dwellers; here she would live in comfort. Otherwise all seemed dark. The heart of Rome was burnt out: the Aventine was in ruins, so was the greater part of the Palatine; in the Forum the temple of Vesta with its precious shrine, the Regia where the Pontifex Maximus lived and the house of the Vestals were almost gone. One Vestal had died; Rubria. Someone in heaven had been careless, taking her and leaving me. The Capitol was practically untouched although the wooden eagles supporting the summit of Jupiter's temple were scorched. As for my beloved Circus, only the upper galleries which were wood and the wooden staircases leading to them were destroyed; some of the embankment had burnt away but not much else. My home on the Palatine was rubble. The ugly old Domus Tiberiana still stood and Apollo had protected his temple; I had been the target.

This was the price in stone and wood. In life it was as bad. I saw the black corpses laid out in the Campus waiting for funeral pyres to finish the job; Xenophon advised it to stop plague. For many of the living there was the pain of burns, sometimes all over. I sent my doctors with all available medicines. As for me I went to a couch hastily set up in my house in the Servilian gardens which was not ready for me; I did not sleep. As always in agony of mind I craved Poppaea but she was twenty-three miles away, safe in Antium. I would not want her to see this.

On the seventh day I looked at the wreckage with my architects who were already drawing up new plans and I thought: how did it happen?

"Christians," Tigellinus said.

I looked at him. "Are you sure? They're not a political sect, are they?"

"No, sire." He was confident, aware of the facts. "But they believe the Roman state to be evil and expect its imminent destruction. I imagine a few extremists got carried away and set the place alight."

"Have you any proof?"

"Prisoners, sire. About a dozen; half of which admit to helping the fire along because it was the will of their master. No one admitted to starting it."

I said: "That could have been an accident. They burn charcoal in those houses by the Circus and fire would spread quickly in such cramped conditions, especially with the oil the traders store."

"True, sire. But—"

As with Seneca there was always "but". It is an illness in these people that they can never agree.

He said: "There are rumours in the city. It is an unfortunate fact of history that nations blame misfortune on their rulers; Romans are no exception. They think you started the fire."

"What!" I thought he was joking till I realised that he never did. "Tigellinus, don't be foolish. Where would they get such an idea from?"

"First," he said as though counting off points against me, "first it has gone around that you would like to destroy Rome and build a new city to your own design."

"Partly true. But I wouldn't start a fire to do it."

"Then, they say, you wish to punish the people of Rome for the revolt in favour of Octavia. A third body of opinion says you are totally mad and madmen will do anything; there is a rumour that you watched the fire from the Esquiline, delighting in the flames and singing of the ruin of Troy."

I sat looking, wanting to see denials appear on the wall. By now I should be used to the inevitable decline of love but still it struck me hard, a sword in tender flesh.

I said: "Is it widely believed?"

"Widely enough. They are after revenge."

"But wait a minute." I began to see contradictions. "I've done all I can to help them. Is that a maniac's way, or a criminal's?"

"Some say Seneca instigated it; others that you are trying to direct suspicion away from yourself. I will admit, sire, that liars and scandal-mongers are at work but that does not lessen danger. They want blood. If you don't want your carcass to feed the lion you throw him someone else's."

I looked at him, nibbled my nail, and said unwillingly: "Christians?"

"It's a possibility, sire. After all, we have confessions. Begin with the few we have and move on to the rest after. It's reckoned there are nearly a thousand in the city; I'll hunt them out."

"I'm not sure I like your methods," I said. I leaned forward and stared into his eyes but you can look long at a person and not see motives. "Did they confess of their own accord or with help?"

"Of their own accord, sire. I tell you, they are fanatical, insulated against reason. They talked without being told, saying the time had come for all men to look up and see the coming

301

of Christ in wrath; evil had run its day, thrones would fall, the pagan would suffer and the faithful see God. Oh, they believed it, sire. Why do you think they helped keep the fire going?"

"Christ?" I said. "The faithful? You're talking in riddles, Tigellinus."

"Their riddles, sire, not mine. Christ is their cult hero, the faithful all who believe in him. In human terms he was Jesus Bar-Joseph, a Jewish carpenter, native of Nazareth, born Bethlehem, died Jerusalem, convicted under Roman law as traitor to his Imperial excellency Tiberius and condemned to crucifixion by Pontius Pilate, governor of Judea."

I said: "You are very informed."

Sarcasm was lost on him; he had a skin like a crocodile.

"Thank you, sire." He bowed. "I make it my business to know facts."

"So they believed a carpenter was divine," I said. "Well, it's no sillier than Jupiter being a bull."

"Silly but not harmless," said Tigellinus. I could see he was after heads. "They think in terms of overthrowing the established order and especially of dethroning you. My sources —which are reliable—say they see you as a devil incarnate."

He said it with relish like a man sampling wine. There are some men you cannot trust no matter how much they seem to prove loyalty.

"All right," I said. "You have my permission to continue investigations. But bring all findings to me."

When he had gone I felt absurd tears in my eyes. Nine years toil and only a slap in the face as thanks. A nation's people are like children, egoistical, cruel and demanding with no forgiveness for mistakes. My worst mistake had been to love them too well.

My Servilian villa had been cleaned and fitted out and was now ready to live in so I sent for Poppaea. While I waited for her I began planning my new home; your mind must not be still at times of grief or fear. Nothing was left. It meant a whole new start. I looked at the wide, burned distance between the Palatine and Esquiline and saw how it must be. I would cover

302

it all with one great palace and thus mock the gods. Ugliness is not absolute; you can always replace it with something better. Suddenly the fire seemed a gift, cleansing flame to renew, phoenix-like, the queen of cities. Then I realised, horrified, that unconsciously I was guilty of what they had accused me.

I had conferences with the architects and started drawing out plans.

"Here," I said, pointing with the stylus, "I want the actual palace which will be over two thousand yards long and a thousand at the widest part. Then, here, the gardens—"

I looked up and saw them staring. "Sire, it will be a complex business," one said. "Think of the clearance needed and then the ground covered once you start building."

"I *know* it will be complex." I returned. "But anything worth having is difficult to arrive at. Come, gentlemen, you are professional men; you know it is possible if you put your minds to it."

They agreed because they had to; no one flouts an emperor.

Next day Poppaea arrived. She stood in the atrium, bewildered, surrounded by chests of clothes and jewels and twittering slaves; outside, her asses were trampling the flowers.

"Oh, Nero," she said, "isn't it dreadful. I kept the litter curtains drawn back all the way up so that I could see. What happened?"

"No one knows," I said. "Yet."

I kissed her and took her to my own apartments where she sat sipping wine; she looked pale. Like me she was a Roman through and through.

I said: "It's not very grand here but it's comfortable. Poppaea, everything went—all our furniture and art treasures, all the clothes we had left behind. And my Domus Transitoria..."

"Oh my poor Nero. All your hard work." She touched my hand and I felt her comfort like water on a fevered face. "Have you found how it started?"

"Perhaps an accident. But Tigellinus thinks the Christians. Some were caught helping the fire to spread; they're mad enough for anything. Poppaea, what is it?"

303

She had put down the wine as though it sickened her. "Nothing," she said. "I'm tired. The journey..."

I called her maids and watched anxiously; she stumbled a little going into the bedroom.

Tigellinus had been busy. I often used to wonder how his network of secret police functioned; no one knew who they were, not even me. He assured me secrecy was vital. He was catching Christians like flies in a net and using his own ways of making them talk; some did, others were silent. One morning he put a long list of indictments on my desk and suggested I interview a suspect for myself.

He came in, a small, drab man with the look of a shopkeeper. I sat, startled. When you are used to terror or, at least, awe in the faces of those before you it comes as a shock to see such composure.

I said sharply: "Name?"

"Quintus Hostilius."

He stood straight; the words snapped out. I was not even going to receive respect. "When you speak to me," I said tightly, "you will use my title."

"Yes, sire."

"Now then—occupation?"

"Barber, sire."

"Your place of work?"

"Near the Circus Maximus, sire."

"Right." I banged my hand on the indictments. "Do you know what these are?" He looked blank. "They are a list of charges against members of your sect, many of them meriting the death penalty. Now, I want the right answers. Did you help start the fire?"

"No, sire."

"Did you help keep it going?"

"Yes, sire—at least, I threw one torch, nothing more."

"Why?"

"Because..." For a moment I imagined fear in his face; but it was gone. "Because, sire, this city is evil and must be destroyed in preparation for the coming of our master; no one started your fire, Caesar, not anyone you can get your hands

304

on. It is God's will, the beginning of a new age."

"New age?" Uneasiness stirred in my stomach. "Explain yourself."

"Our master is coming," he repeated. "Soon. Then you and all your kind will burn in the flames of his wrath."

I stood up, keeping control with difficulty, and yelled: "Guards!" They clanked in. "Take this man away," I said, "and flog him." He went without a murmur. I thought: calm yourself, Nero. What is he? An insignificant pleb. But something cold still moved along my stomach. That afternoon I said to Tigellinus: "Draw up an order for the execution of a dozen Christians. I'll make an example of them."

He smiled. "A wise decision, sire." The fish had got its worm.

"Why?" said Poppaea.

"Because they're dangerous," I said. "A nation can't afford to harbour rats nibbling at its foundations. They're well organised, they're fanatical, they're growing, and I fancy they have their eyes on political power. A dozen deaths might cool their ardour."

She said: "How will they die?"

Her voice sounded chilly and remote; since she arrived home I had wondered if she were weakening for an illness.

"The stake," I said. "They burned Rome so they can burn themselves."

"Then," she said, "you can burn me, too."

I looked, thinking I had misheard. She stared back, unsmiling, gazing over my shoulder as though at someone behind me. I said: "Oh, don't be silly, Poppaea. Could you start a fire from Antium?"

"It isn't that." Her face was set; it frightened me. "They are Christians."

I went cold. Only once before had I felt so and then there had been a couch and spilled wine and a woman tying the ribbons on her dress. I said: "What do you mean?"

"Oh, Nero." She spread her hands as if in propitiation, then let them drop. "Where did you think I went in the mornings and evenings, too, sometimes—when you were feasting?"

"I thought you might be unfaithful."

I threw it at her without care; fear brought brutality.

"Oh yes." She smiled bitterly. "I've been adulterous twice, haven't I? Crispinius for Otho, Otho for you—all unfair exchange. I suppose I've made another exchange, only this time it's ultimate. I can't go back, Nero. I am a Christian."

I sat down. She had gone very far from me, standing tiny near the window; dusk was coming. Its shadows spilled over her and crept against the wall.

I said: "Why?"

"Because I believe it."

The simplicity of it; a world rejected, status compromised, love thrown back in my face. *I believe it.*

"Oh no, Poppaea." My voice cracked on itself as though I were on stage and about to sing. "You don't mean it this time."

"I have never meant anything more."

The voice came from infinite distance. Grief closed round my heart like ice round a pool; my winter had come too early. Far, far away I heard the weeping of a child on dirty straw and a storm beating on a stable roof.

"Oh Nero, my dear, how can I make you understand?" She was beside me, kneeling, her face tilted and glaring white in the shadow. "If you think us evil you are terribly mistaken. He whom we follow taught love and mercy and tranquillity, not confusion and the seizing of political power. He was never a politician."

"Then what was he?"

She looked at me steadily; I knew her invincible honesty. "God," she said.

"Oh, come now, Poppaea." I got up, leaving her earnest, convinced face. "What deity allows himself to be killed?"

"A deity who saves."

"From what?"

"From ourselves." She still knelt by the chair, grasping the carved arm. "From everything we've done wrong. He offers forgiveness for all crimes through his blood."

"Even mine?" I said roughly.

"Even yours—if you are sorry."

"Poppaea—" I struck my forehead in despair, using her name as though it would break the hold this absurdity had on her. "For Jove's sake, what are you saying? A crucified god, forgiveness—even for what *I* did? Apollo himself shrinks before that. My darling, you're talking in delirium, it's a sickness; let Xenophon see you."

"I am not sick." Her voice was calm; I had forgotten her iron will. "I know what I believe and why?"

"Why, then? Why?"

"After the child died," she said slowly, "I felt lost and hopeless: nothing amused me any more. Then I heard one of my maids talking—she was silly; they are sworn to secrecy and even then it was a danger to confess yourself. I listened and it made sense so I found out more. I went to one of their meetings in someone's house; I won't tell you whose. There are names among them which you would know. I went again and again, morning or evening whichever was easiest, but I couldn't stay through all their ceremonies because I had not been initiated. Sometimes they met in underground burial chambers along the Via Appia; it was safer. Oh no, it's no use telling Tigellinus. Only they know the way. Anyone else would wander for miles and die. Besides, our dead were once buried there, remember, and the place is sacred."

I said sharply: "You're digressing. What else?"

"What do you do after looking a god in the face? After a time I was baptised—their form of initiation. You step into a pool, dressed in white and holding a candle and you swear belief in him; they pour water over your head to signify purification. Then it is done; you are committed. You attend the whole of their ceremony as a full member."

"And there is no way back?"

"I don't want the way back."

"Poppaea!" I dragged her up by the wrists and shook her as you might try to shake sense into a child. "Don't you see what you're doing? Don't you care about *me*?"

"I care about you very much." She was quiet in my grasp. "I care enough not to compromise myself for your sake because then you would never love me again." I let go of her. She said quietly: "We have waited for this since time began. All our other beliefs were like wrong turnings on a faulty map; can't you see? We've been wandering blind with no sense of direction, reaching for whatever seemed easiest because his face was still hidden. Can you honestly see any truth in the gods of the Pantheon?"

I said: "I see no truth in any god. At the worst times of my life they have withdrawn and I have looked into emptiness. Where was your god when my mother—"

"You did not know him then." I saw she was well rehearsed, every answer coming pat. "And even now he is there to forgive you."

I said no more. I went away from her like a blind man, seeing nothing but the darkness inside my own head. She had been mine; now she was his, committed to a superstition, a carpenter crucified in a far province I had never even thought of. It was ironic. I had thought death might take her or another man; I never imagine divine theft. Divine! A man dying on a cross. Who had said we want to be as the gods who can't be hurt? She was mad. Could it be the child's death? Such things affect women. Yet I had grieved as much and found no consolation in an eccentric cult. It seemed perversity, a defiant turning away from the world which gave her birth—my world.

You can do two things with a woman who has made up her mind to something: ignore her or fight her. I could not ignore Poppaea. Too late I realised the extent of the barrier I had sensed a year ago. Her physical love had not changed; it was her mind which contained the barrier, denying me the nearness of self I needed. I was an outcast, one on whom light had not shone. I imagined subtle contempt. She always insisted that those outside the cult were never hated or attacked, merely helped towards the truth. This was not an exclusive sect, far from it; slaves swelled its ranks side by side with patricians. She said: "He died for all men without exception and those who cannot see it must be dealt with gently until they do."

"Then," I said, "you pity me which is even worse."

308

She would not be drawn. This insane belief had rooted in her like wood in stone, immovable, and with it had come inexplicable quietness of mind. She was mild, loving, tolerant, kind and merciful with everyone from the lowest slave to the highest senator; and yet there was the barrier. In my worst moments I wondered if I had erected it myself. Had she offered me the way to truth and peace and had I rejected it? Then I thought: a god in a Jewish carpenter's shop. No.

I tried to find cracks in her defences. If I argued long enough and showed up the inconsistencies through logical argument as Seneca always said you should the whole thing would collapse. But it didn't; or, at least, she didn't.

"Poppaea," I said, "have you *seen* a man crucified?"

She shook her head. "I have," I went on. "Once in the arena; a robber. It's obscene. It isn't even fit for animals let alone a god, yet the glory of your god is that death. It's ridiculous. If he had died gracefully like Hyacinthus, sinking to the ground amongst flowers . . ."

"That's the point," she returned quickly. "You can't idealise it; you're not meant to. The agony of the death shows the extent of his love."

I said: "It's easy to talk when you haven't seen the horror of it. It's easy to talk of love and humility and justice when you haven't seen what can follow. I tried to be just and ended up killing. When I tried to keep my integrity my mother could do as she liked with me; once I murdered and showed my strength she grew tame. It's the world we live in, Poppaea; I know it, sweet gods, I know it only too well. The humble are humiliated, the just are swindled and those who love are rejected. Your way doesn't work."

"It does," she said. "Each day we strengthen and the world's evil slips back a little. It will never vanish completely because that is how we are but now there will always be a light in the darkness. Oh Nero, if only you could see—"

I said: "I don't want to see."

"I know you don't." I thought she sounded patronising. "I can't help you then, Nero, no one can; not till you come of yourself."

309

She made me furious, shut behind her walls like a town under siege. I thought: there must be a way; every rampart can be scaled if you have the right ladder. So I loaded her with presents and love, I was attentive and patient and never mentioned anything awkward. By the end of a fortnight the walls were still firm. In desperation I demanded explanations again as though something there might make it all reasonable; but she only talked of light and truth and endless water for the thirsty, then of dark, strange things which made the hair prickle on my neck as if the Furies had breathed upon me: night in daytime and a body gone from a tomb, a corpse sitting up on its bier, a Roman governor who thought he saw Apollo. Then I remembered Acte. I had heard some of this before and thought nothing of it; she had not possessed Poppaea's strength of purpose. Besides, my love for her had begun to fade; that was the fatal difference. Love is destructive; it leads to anger, hatred, grief, the murder of a mother and the impurity of a Vestal. Yet she saw it as a saving power. Love crucified. It made me laugh. Each moment of love is crucifixion and gods have nothing to do with it.

I even went to Seneca. There was no one else who could approach it intelligently; Petronius was disinterested and Tigellinus saw no further than the stake. He sat looking at me like a starved old owl, thin from vegetarianism and constant study; the politician had gone.

"My prince," he said, "this is a dangerous business. Your wife is a sensitive, intelligent woman and obviously dissatisfied with the gods of her ancestors. This new cult offers her consolation."

I said: "Could it be a passing phase?"

"I doubt it, sire." He had changed; there was no compromise. "If she is like the rest she will die for it."

I shivered; I had not thought of pushing her too far. I said: "No, not that. I would never demand that."

"Then what are you demanding, my prince?"

"Her love," I said. "Her total self. I won't share her, Seneca."

"You must, my prince." He looked at me pityingly. "Or else lose her. This is no brief superstition, you know."

"Of course it is." He annoyed me. "It's so eccentric it must be."

"Is it? Listen, sire, for centuries our civilisations have preserved the idea of a great god coming to birth. No one knew when; he would just come and all would know him. Some think him a Dionysus or an Osiris; your uncle Caligula thought it was himself. Astrologers marked this century as the time; others were more precise and fixed the date when your great-great grandfather held his world-wide census."

I said: "Seneca! You're wandering."

"Am I, sire? I knew the man who sentenced the carpenter to death. A more reliable, hard-headed Roman you could not hope to meet. Yet when this man came up before him he lost his nerve and tried to avoid a death sentence, even with the natives screaming for blood at his back door. Afterwards, when he had to give in, he wrote a most odd letter to Tiberius, rambling on about his wife's dreams and the sun blackening in mid-afternoon, and asking if he could be transferred. Tiberius recalled him and the next thing we heard of was his suicide."

I said: "He was ill. What is that?"

"Yes, sire." He smiled. "But it was strange about the daytime darkness. That day we had it in Rome, too."

The next morning I issued a proclamation to the Senate and the people. The commission of enquiry set up to investigate the causes of the fire had come to a unanimous conclusion: a perverted sect in our midst had tried to destroy us, being revolutionary and politically subversive, therefore it was an offence to be a member of it or to practise their degraded ritual. Any person so doing would receive the death penalty.

"Your orders, sire?" said Tigellinus.

"Extend your interrogations," I said, "and get every Christian you can. When you have we'll kill the lot."

Chapter Seventeen

It is easy to deceive yourself. When people asked I talked in terms of just punishment for Rome's incendiaries; to Tigellinus I said: "I have no choice, have I? It's them or me."

"Exactly, sire. Many dangerous emotions can be released harmlessly at the amphitheatre."

But he did not look at me straight; I fancied mockery there.

I began mildly, sending a few dozen to the arena to fight with gladiators but I soon had to stop it because they threw away their weapons and stood like lambs waiting to be slaughtered. It was no fun for the crowd. Some I had burned as an example; incendiaries to the flames. It seemed poetically correct. I did not go to the arena myself because I had always disliked it; in fact, I had tried to stop the slaughter there and replace it with harmless fencing bouts in which all social classes, even the highest, should take part. The Senate had blocked the move. To them it was unthinkable, a denial of ancient customs and humiliation of the upper classes. I believe they hated me for even trying.

Christian prisoners were streaming into my dungeons. Most of them had been named by those already in custody; even fanatics can stand only so much pain when it goes on and on with not even death to bring an end. The list of names was added to every day. Legally speaking one name should top the lot and by withholding it I was guilty in the face of my own law; but what could I do? I hoped to frighten her, I suppose. I should have known better.

She looked at me in bed one evening, saying: "What is it, Nero? Do you think I will weaken?"

I said: "I don't know. It's your own matter. But I'll push

them till they break, then perhaps you will see that their belief is empty."

"You will push for a long time," she said.

"Yes? Tigellinus has already forced confessions from many of them."

"Some are weak," she said. "We are all weak till he gives us strength. The fall of a few does not condemn the truth. And even those you imagine crushed will probably die bravely when the time comes. It's the denial of death which has broken them."

I could have struck her. I saw her fatal strength, something deep in the will which does not alter even in a storm. My mother had possessed it, too, but she I could manipulate through desire for power; my wife lacked even that. She was Agrippina purified. It was the irony of the gods that I should have loved her for that reason, only to fall again, deep into the same trap.

I said: "Your pure-minded friends tried to burn Rome. Does that fit with talk of love?"

"Perhaps one or two got carried away with the thought of his coming and helped the fire; they were mistaken. It's the enthusiasm he produces. Oh Nero, why don't you stop trying to argue it away? Whatever an individual Christian may be guilty of does not make the whole thing untrue. If you harness poor horses to a chariot they will lose the race; does that prove it can't be won?"

I said: "Now you're being rhetorical like Seneca. Don't try and fool me with words, Poppaea."

She shrugged and lay back on the pillows. In the lamplight her hair was copper; she looked all brightness as though burning from within. I wanted to make love to her but the barricades were up, stronger than ever, and I knew in bitterness that I had built them. I thought I hated her. I looked at her, so exquisite and complacent like agate polished to flawlessness, a prize beyond my purse; and I said: "I will show you, Poppaea; Jove help me, I will *make* you see sense."

I arranged it carefully. The arena was too conventional; I wanted something outlandish, horrifying. Tigellinus said: "Sire, permit me to make a suggestion."

I listened and it was good, what you would expect from him.

313

At any other time I would have flinched with the obscenity of it but some madness had got me; I had known it before. Dionysus owned large shares in me.

All was ready within a week. It had been advertised widely as a good audience always helps, as well as enhancing my prestige. The guest of honour was unaware; I intended to surprise her.

The day came. As twilight began I said to her: "I'm giving a public feast tonight in the Vatican gardens. We are expected to attend."

"Very well."

She was calm and remote. It made me angry and killed all traces of sympathy. We sat side by side in the litter and I could smell the rose oil on her skin and hair; gold leaves shivered in her ears, suspended on thin gold chains.

We crossed the Tiber; it was running low and stank. The air was heavy, even for evening, being the beginning of August; I saw her wrinkle her nose. Soon came the scent of lotus blossom and roses instead. We were near the gardens.

The stars were flecked silver above us. I helped her from the litter and she said: "What is that noise?"

"The crowd," I said.

"They sound—strange," she said. "Like the arena."

I said nothing but guided her firmly under the marble colonnades which marked the entrance. At the other end were expensive lotus trees imported from the east, dark laurels and spreading planes with beds of roses and flowering bushes; light shone spangled between the leaves. I could smell food and wine, perfume, flowers, oil and spices; but over it all was the stink of pitch.

There was an open place with colonnades either side and food set on tables down the middle where imperial slaves served the guests who did not sit but wandered as they pleased. I had given orders for them to start without me. Beyond the banquet area stretched my private circus with a waiting chariot and staked either side of both garden and circus were long, thick poles.

She said: "The torches aren't lit yet."

314

"No," I said, "but they will be soon."

"Strange," she remarked. "Are those bundles of clothes at the top?"

We were at a distance still; the voices drifted up like the murmurous hum of bees on a summer evening.

"In a way," I said. "They are covered in pitch or oil and wax to burn better."

Tigellinus was beside me, deferential and saying: "Sire, we are ready."

"Then," I said, "light the torches."

Slaves trooped along with blazing brands. Night was thick now and they dotted the darkness with eyes of fire. As we came to the head of the banquet tables they were setting light to the first stakes either side; then she realised. Her hand gripped my arm as though it would bite it off. "No," she said. "For God's sake, no."

The first torch had kindled in a rush of flame followed by an involuntary scream; I had expected it. It is a dreadful death to burn. The next went up and the next and the next, streaks of fire lighting the gardens and the tables and the staring faces. I looked at hers. In the flickering light it seemed a mask, pale and set as when the sculptor moulds it.

I said. "Come along. Eat."

To reach the food meant passing by the torches. I took her hand and pulled her with me; she had gone stiff yet trailed behind me, heavy and unaware like a sleepwalker.

A white-faced slave poured her wine. She took it and stood unseeing; torches were still being lit down the far end. The Vatican gardens are long. Screams came thin and irrepressible on the scented air, then faded and they called out his name instead as if it were a charm to cool the flames. There were men as well as women. If you listened hard enough you could tell the difference.

I had feared sickness in myself. This was all I hated, sordid ugliness, the pursuit of beasts, not men; and yet I felt nothing, only strong satisfaction. She was like a statue beside me, a marble Diana amongst green laurels. The torchlight made her hair burn.

I said: "Well, Poppaea?"

She put her goblet down hard so that it banged on the table. I waited for her to faint, to cry, to run away or call me a monster. She did nothing, only stood fixed. The crowd were yelling and cheering and someone shouted: "Filthy stinking Christians! Incendiaries! Cannibals!" Above the smell of Falernian wine and roast goose came the thick scent of burning pitch; and something else besides.

She turned slowly and looked straight at me, white and staring like the Sybil about to prophesy. I stepped back. "Nero Caesar," she said and the voice was not hers, "you think yourself all-powerful, a god among men. Let me tell you that four years will bring your end. You think you have stamped out truth and destroyed those who believe; but I say to you that where we now stand Christ will one day sit in triumph."

The blood stood still in my veins. Then a slave said: "More wine, madam?" and she snapped awake as if from a dream. I said: "Poppaea, what did you say?"

"Nothing." Her voice shook. "Nothing at all."

When I pressed her she looked blank and insisted she had not spoken.

Later I rode my chariot round the circus with a six-horse team but my judgement was poor; I almost tumbled out. Her words had put coldness in my hands and head. As I galloped round the course the still-burning torches flashed red either side, the colour of stale blood. I thought I saw faces in the shadows beyond. The crowd were not cheering as usual; they looked sleepy with wine and the warm air made warmer by torch-heat.

We left at one-o'clock. A moon had come up, hot and orange, and bats streaked black amongst the plane trees. She sat quiet in the litter, head on hand. Later in the bedroom she stood long with her back to me, pulling out pins from her hair; she had refused a maid. I saw her fingers tremble. I said: "Poppaea?" like a naughty child testing adult reaction.

"You hoped to frighten me." she said. "You did not. You only sickened me."

I said angrily: "I threatened to show you."

"Show me?" She turned round, her hair whipping out like a snake's tail. "Show me what? The fact that they can die like anyone else? You only showed their courage."

"Theirs, perhaps," I said. I felt at a loss, having expected a weakening. "We'll see how it affects the rest. Good wholesome propaganda, Poppaea darling."

She said slowly: "I never thought I would look upon you as my parents looked on Caligula and Tiberius. God forgive me; he said: love your enemies."

I said: "No, Poppaea; no."

My resistance had gone, not hers. I reached for her hand but she drew away and turned her back. I sank down on the pillows with the tears coming fast in my throat, saying: "I'm sorry, Poppaea, I'm sorry. Please don't hate me; I can't live if you do." Self-pity is so easy. It was soft linen against my face, not straw, but I thought I could hear a storm in the distance.

Then she said: "Oh Nero, why did you do it?" and came beside me, stroking my hair and kissing me. I clung to her warmth, shivering. She seemed responsive and compassionate yet when I put out the lamp and made love to her she was far from me again, a passive thing. Her hair smelt of burning. When she lay still, after, the sweat on her forehead looked like spots of blood.

Meanwhile Rome was being rebuilt. First the ground had to be cleared and I used the Ostian marshes as a dumping ground for rubble; ships coming up the Tiber from Ostia, loaded with grain, went back with a cargo of crumbled stone and burnt wood. Then there was money. Apart from my own and that sent by cities all over Italy I sold a valuable collection of statues, paintings and jewels in the Temple of Apollo near Octavia's Porticus.

I dreamed of a new Rome, graceful and spacious. Construction had begun to my orders, broad streets of regulated width, smaller buildings with open courtyards instead of the grey, unbroken face of tenement blocks. They had begun my Golden House, too. I called it that because I wanted many of the rooms plated in thin gold, Apollo's metal, and the design to allow

317

light in at every point; a palace of the sun. It was not that I believed in Apollo; I believed in beauty. I was influenced architecturally by Greco-Asian palaces and the marble heavens of the Persian kings; all light and colour with open courts and fountains. In this I had turned my back on everything Roman. The banqueting hall was to have a dome painted with the planets which would revolve with the movement of their counterparts in the sky, an idea copied from the Sassanid kings of Persia. I thought it exciting, novel and extremely artistic. Only when it was finished and I stood underneath looking up did I feel suddenly unbalanced like a man staring long into an endless whirlpool.

The vestibule of my new house was a colonnade with three rows of columns stretching from the mouth of the Forum to the Esquiline; just a mile. One party of workmen had begun building this; at the other end another were setting the foundations of the palace itself on Mount Oppius, one peak of the Esquiline. It was to be a square facing the four points of the compass. Xenodoros, one of our best sculptors, was casting a statue of me in bronze, a hundred feet high, to stand at the vestibule entrance. I was to be the Sun with a star-shaped crown, each point twenty feet long and my huge eyes set with gems to sparkle and intimidate. It was a piece of ridiculous vanity. All the same, I was in the throes of fighting a dangerous foreign god; it seemed politic to hint at my own power and glory, almost divine in itself, but ironic considering my inner sense of inadequacy. Supervising the planning and building and discussing with artists and sculptors took up much of my time and made me forget my difficulties with Poppaea. It was war again.

When she maddened me beyond endurance with her complacent conviction I turned on the captive Christians like an animal striking out at the nearest thing. The gods know how many died in her place. Tigellinus was still bringing them in and I had my pick. After one fight I covered the Caelian hill with a forest of crosses; you could hear their groans from the Esquiline. She stood looking on a garden terrace, not saying a word, but I saw her knuckles white and angry where they gripped the stone. From here the hill seemed to sprout rows

318

of burned trees; only the sour smell of death told you otherwise.

She turned and said: "Why not me? Leave the innocent alone."

"A cross would spoil your beauty," I returned. "Besides, they're guilty all right. Guilty of idiocy and subversion and obscene practices, not to mention blasphemy. I offered them the chance to incense our gods."

"You can't blaspheme against something which doesn't exist," she said.

"You can blaspheme against *me*," I snapped, "against the state and all Roman ideals. The incense is only a symbol of that; don't worry, I don't believe in Roman gods any more than you."

"Then why—" she began.

"Because I see no hope in such a philosophy, that's why; I've told you. Integrity doesn't work. Nor can I see a god rotting over there." I pointed to the hill. "Have you heard them crying out?"

"Haven't I been here since they were first put up?"

She was fighting again, pushing against me with all her weight.

"I shouldn't stay any longer," I retorted. "They won't die for three or four days and even the weaker could take a day." I was angry, then I made a mistake. "A fine death," I said, "for the worshippers of a crucified god. Don't you envy them?"

"In a way." Her face was sharp against the reddening sky; sunset was near. "They know true peace; even the pain won't take that away. Had I the choice I would take it."

I stood ice-cold. She stared me full-face and I saw too many things too late; her passion for mental satisfaction and willingness to suffer for the worthwhile, her ruthlessness after what she wanted. Once it had been me.

I said: "You would?"

"Yes. Even in the arena with all Rome looking."

I left her. I was caught, of course, a fish hooked on the tasty bait. It had seemed so easy to threaten agony. But it wasn't working, nothing was; I had thought to see them break one after the other, on the cross, under the flames, then to prove emptiness under fine words. It was a mockery. What I saw as

319

the ultimate threat they saw as the ultimate reward; an ironic trap. Petronius would have loved it. My mother had taught me the efficiency of murder as a weapon but she had never offered a substitute. I was powerless.

Near the end of December their leader was arrested. Tigellinus put the charge sheet on my desk and said: "Sire, I advise you to see him."

I said: "What is he like?"

He laughed. "A one-time fisherman, sire, with no breeding."

He came into the council hall, a dark-haired man going grey with the rough Jewish look, no refinement whatsoever. His robe was brown and belted with rope.

I said: "Do you know the charges against you?"

"I do."

His Latin was rough as well but he looked at me straight, as an eagle might in the net. I felt uneasy; lift the net a little and what happens?

I began the ritual. "Name?"

"I have two, sire. Which would you like?"

"Don't be insolent." My voice rose. "Name! "

"I was born Simon, sire, but my master named me Peter. Ingenious of him to make such a pun. He was to build his new world upon a rock and I was to be the pivot of it so here I am, Petros."

"I know Greek," I said irritably. "I'm not interested in your name, only the anti-social sect you govern. Have you anything to say in your defence?"

"Only, sire, that we are not guilty of what you accuse us. We keep the law, we do not plot against the state nor do we indulge in degraded ritual. We only wish to bring truth to everyone."

I said: "What *is* truth?"

He laughed. "Forgive me, sire, but you political men repeat yourselves. The Roman governor asked my master the same thing only he did not answer him; I will try to answer you."

I leaned forward and said: "Go on. I'm listening."

"Well, sire, it's like this. If you build a palace or a city you do it for a reason and according to a plan. Men are accustomed

320

to this idea. All through history they have been looking for their own reason and for the architect behind it. Some found him in Moloch like the Carthaginians, others in Ra or Zeus or Jupiter, my own race in Jehovah."

"But your god is the real one," I said dryly.

"My god," he said slowly, "is the one true God become man. He was born of a woman like you or me and lived to show us how we must live, died to cleanse our sins and came out of the tomb after three days to show us who he was. Believe me, sire, till then none of us knew. We thought ourselves deceived. It was a clear spring morning, I remember so well . . ." He looked over my head as though I did not matter. "We ran all the way because they said the tomb was empty and when we got there I could hardly stand. John wouldn't look; he was frightened. When I did I saw the burial clothes—not scattered as if from grave robbers but neat—as though they hadn't been moved. And I still didn't think. Not until later when I looked up in the dusk and saw him at my bedroom door . . ."

Cold fingers touched my neck. I said sharply: "Thank you for your reminiscences. I'm sure they are most interesting but I'm a busy man. Have you anything more to say?"

He smiled again. You might have thought me the child and he the indulgent parent. "Only sire, that if a building's foundations are not constructed to the architect's design it will collapse; I found my design in the empty tomb. The only thing is, sire, it's yours, too."

I said angrily: "Don't impose your superstition on me. I'm not an illiterate workman."

Any one else would have flushed or looked furious. He just shook his head and smiled again. I said: "You will be kept in custody until further notice. If you want the official charge it is subversion, obscenity, blasphemy, disloyalty to the throne and incendiarism. I emphasise the last one because it is proven. I met one of your men myself, setting fire to a house."

"A mistake, sire." He was unshaken. "Some are burning with a sense of outrage against immorality in the city and thought that the fire was God-sent, a preparation for his coming. We must be indulgent. I know that he will not come yet, not perhaps for a long, long time; but they are eager. Let me remind you, sire, that many around you have committed themselves. I believe that someone very dear to you . . ."

I said: "My private life is no concern of yours. Guard!"

Just before they marched him off he looked at me with curious penetration and said: "Sire, I can see in your face that your foundations are more insecure than most. The design is there. You can rebuild them."

I said: "Take him away."

Had he been rebellious or aggressive I should have thought no more. It was his rationality, his concern for me which itched in my mind; a fisherman and he had talked more sense in ten minutes than Seneca had in ten years. It was not that I fancied his superstition to be true. It was his straightness which impressed me, no compromises, no evasion. All my life I had suffered from deviousness. Then I thought: a fisherman and he tells *me* what to do? Rebuild my foundations! I'm past repair and even if I were not a fake god won't do anything for me. It was their complacency again, making me angry because I did not see where it came from. Something kept them going in the arena and on the cross. I felt like a man in a storm looking out through clouds and rain to a great calm on the horizon, unattainable.

Poppaea was still attending their meetings, sometimes every day. I begged her to be careful for if any one saw her I should either have to lose face or kill her publicly to prove my impartiality. She shrugged; I already knew this did not worry her and it terrified me. I was not capable of even imagining a life without her. I asked her what happened at the meetings but she would not say, only that to protect the secret they would die. My art was suffering. Any poetic talent I might have had was dwindling. I was tormented by the desire to express myself and the inability to do it so that when I sat down to compose it was a battle nobody won. Sometimes I threw the pen away and vowed to do no more but the artist is caught in a sweet trap. To break free denied my own nature; to remain tortured me with a sense of failure. In my early youth it had come easily with no thought and even a few years ago there were my poems "To Poppaea" which I set to music and sang for her. Now there was nothing. She had sucked me dry like my mother before her.

Then came the plot. Like all the others details have blurred; though I remember the number convicted I have forgotten many of the names. It was a nasty business, big and well-organised. When I think how close I came to emulating the divine Julius it turns my blood cold. It had first begun stirring in the year I married Poppaea and was a vulgar alliance made up of people who thought they had a grudge against me or were greedy for money and power. This is how dangerously an emperor sits. Give Tigellinus his due, he had suspected something of it when Poppaea and I were in Naples but I dismissed it through lack of proof. The first I knew of it was just before the Festival of Ceres in April which I intended to celebrate with games in the newly restored Circus. The day before, I visited the building site of my new palace where foundations were already growing. As I spoke to the workmen someone came out of the crowd, thrust something into my hand and muttered: "Please take this, Caesar. Keep it near you and it will protect you from all harm." Then he was gone, an obscure little man; I only saw his back. I looked down and saw what he had given me: a little bronze doll with bare breasts and two snakes coiling up her arms, not any god I knew. It looked very old. I did not believe in its luck for a moment but I put it beside my bed because there was nowhere else. Next morning they came and told me of the plot.

The informant was a man named Milichus, a servant of one of Petronius' friends, Scaevinus, who devoted himself to pleasure but apparently was sober enough to dream of a new Republican Rome instituted by himself. However, he was not the instigator; no one knew who that was. Calpurnius Piso was involved, a man who had been my friend and whom I had given much. Granted that recently I had been cold with him for his superior awareness of his artistic merits; he could sing better than me. The other names came out under threats or interrogation. I did this; when Tigellinus arrived it was torture.

The executioner came with assistants and a cart loaded with boards and rope and set up business at the far end of my gardens; I did not want to hear the screams. Scaevinus and Natalis were the first victims here. They stood and watched while instruments of torture were erected amongst the orange blossom and flowering cherry: the gibbet, the iron claws, the lead-tipped whips and red-hot metal plates. It was enough. Natalis broke down and named Piso and, gods have mercy, Seneca; this was a bad shock to me. All the same, I should have known that he would hate me for rejecting him and standing on my own feet. Scaevinus gave in next and named Quintianus, Senecio, Lucan and Lateranus. The second had been one of my good friends along with Otho; like Seneca his trouble was resentment for he had fallen when I abandoned night games for art. Lucan did not surprise me in the least. Quite recently he had written an insulting poem about me so I forbade him to recite in public. For Lucan it was a good enough reason. As for the last name I lost my temper entirely over it; this was Messalina's lover whom I had saved from my mother's knife and here he was aiming one at my back. I had him executed at once like a slave.

I held trial in the mild air of the garden with Nerva beside me to observe legal forms (not my strong point) and Tigellinus to interrogate where I failed. More names came out, even those of senators. One woman emerged, Epicharis, the mistress of Seneca's brother who had involved himself. Gods protect us from women. She was arrogant, obstinate and murderous, refused to speak before the tribunal and would not break even under extensive torture. They spent a day using the rack, the whip, and even the firey laminae applied to the tips of her breasts. The second day they had to carry her to the rack her limbs were so broken. On the way she strangled herself with her scarf.

Then Scaevinus revealed the involvement of the army. The other Praetorian prefect, Faenius Rufus, and Subruis Flavius, a military tribune, had worked up many of the officers against me. This really frightened me. If the army were on the move I was lost. I remembered the harsh, arrogant faces acknowledging my accession. When I demanded reasons Rufus accused me of neglecting the army in favour of my artistic Augustani; anyway, why should they put up with an absurd posturing emperor who thought he could sing? I had him beheaded at once. Then I purged the army, not an easy task, but I was half mad now with fear and anger; I managed it.

Many died. Lucan cut his veins and expired reciting his own verses on a soldier dying in agony; even in death he was true to himself. And then Seneca. I could have spared him; the evidence against him was slight, only amounting to a vague promise of co-operation with Piso. But he was dangerous; I saw that. He might not instigate the plot himself but should one arise he would give support and, being so well aware of my weaknesses, would know where to strike. A pupil is vulnerable to the teacher. I remembered his pomposity, his vacillation, his subservience to my mother when he might have helped me so much. I sent a suicide order to his house.

He died bravely. After a life-time of philosophy clashing with actions Socrates at last showed through. He told his friends that he left them the pattern of his life (not a very useful gift I should think) and told them to be brave. Someone later told me that he said: "Surely no one was unaware that Nero was cruel. After murdering his mother and brother there is only his tutor left." It was pomposity again, even at this stage. His young wife insisted on killing herself, too, though I had sent no order, and severed her veins at the same time as he did. My messenger hurried back and told me; I felt horrified. I would not see an innocent life lost. I sent instructions to the slaves that her arms be bandaged to stop the bleeding. For Seneca the bleeding was too slow; he was old and lean with little vitality. Frightened of being overcome by pain in his wife's presence he went into the bedroom and dictated a last speech to his secretaries as his life flowed away; I could see whose death he was following. Only the hemlock was missing. In the end they placed him in a warm bath; when this still didn't work he was carried to a vapour bath where he suffocated. Strange that so frail a life can take so long to flicker out. Perhaps he was hanging on tighter than anyone knew.

Afterwards I felt strangely lost. My childhood had died with him, a whole time of growth and learning; he had been some

325

sort of support. I remembered my first time as Praefectus Urbi, my accession, all the speeches he wrote for me; and there had been times, too, when he was the only one whom I could go to for advice. Now he was gone. He had once told me that the gods had been merciful in allowing suicide as a final escape route. It is not healthy to regret a death you ordered; it suggests you were in the wrong. Yet for several nights I saw him in dreams, white-haired and reproachful with his wrists and ankles streaming blood.

When it was all over we started counting. There were twenty-seven civilian conspirators and eleven military, of whom six were executed, eleven sent suicide orders, thirteen exiled and six (the military) officially degraded. Three were acquitted, three committed suicide voluntarily and one was pardoned. I did not have much scope for mercy, not that I really wanted it; I had been badly frightened. It turned out that they had planned to kill me on the last day of the festival when I presided at the Games. It was to be the knife. It seems the prerogative of kings to give up their blood. I spent hours imagining how it might have been: the cheers, the endless faces, warm sun on your own face, then the fatal shock, the pain, and while you are wondering why the world slips away. Then what? I did not like to think further; perhaps black Styx waters, the flutter of bat wings in the darkness, or even worse: the creep of the unknown.

It wounded me to know that I had roused hatred in so many. I cared for my people; I had done my best. I did not think that a man in power cannot help angering some and causing grudges in others; I saw only the colossal injustice. I saw, too, that I must be more careful in future; this thing had blossomed brazenly on my own doorstep amongst my own companions, yet it was a servant who saved me. I thought: less mercy from now on. Seneca said be clement but Seneca has gone. Mercy is for fools, for a man who thinks himself a god and dies crucified. If the lion is not whipped it will attack.

I spoke to the Senate, giving an account of the plot. There were only three hundred present and they sat nervously as though expecting denunciation from the skies. No man's name is pure in Rome. I noted the empty places and mentally listed the names; they must be watched. As I gave my speech I looked at their faces and recognised what I saw. They had long memories. They were thinking of a slender fair adolescent who stood between his tutor and the Praetorian prefect and quietly refused the high honours they had proposed for him. And now? I had looked in the mirror before I left. The slender boy had grown fat; his face was pouched and red from drink, his stomach bulged and his brows scowled through short sight. He wore his hair curled and long on the neck, raised up by a band; most disreputable and un-Roman. I got the idea from busts I had seen of Alexander, a style followed also by charioteers and musicians. After all, I was both.

The Senate applauded me with an effort. They assured me of their total devotion and proposed that the month of April be known as Neroneus. It was touchingly unconvincing. Then I went to the Capitol and stood before Jupiter with the knife Scaevinus would have struck me with; I had it engraved "Jovi Vindici"—to the Avenger. As I laid it on his altar I looked up at the great shadowed face and saw my own hypocrisy written there. He was part of my childhood, too, and had died along with the rest.

Book Seven

THE BEAST

"Who is a match for the Beast? they asked. Who is fit to make war on him? And he was given power of speech to boast and to blaspheme with, and freedom to work his will for a space of forty-two months."

THE BOOK OF REVELATION

Chapter Eighteen

I kept the little doll at my bedside. Poppaea said: "I didn't think you were so superstitious."

"It revealed the plot," I said. "I believe it can go on protecting me."

"Oh Nero." She looked despairing. "It's only a piece of metal; it can't do anything for you. How can you imagine—"

I said sharply: "It kept me safe which is more than Jupiter or Apollo have ever done. I used to think Apollo a gentleman but even he has gone now, taking my art with him."

She picked it up and said: "It looks like the Earth Mother Crispinius told me about after he had been to Greece, a very ancient cult but obscure. Even Greeks have forgotten what it means." I said: "Mother?"

She nodded. "Not very nice associations for you. I should throw it away."

"Oh no." I took it back from her. "I see what you're up to. It offends your new moral principles, doesn't it, for your silly husband to pin faith on an idol—'graven images' as the Jews would say. I got that from Acte; you're not the only knowledgeable one." I was in full flood now and immune to any sense of tact. "It's funny," I went on, "it's *very* funny for an adulteress to have such moral scruples."

Her mouth opened as if I had slapped her but her control was unbreakable. She turned her back. "And anyway," I added, unrepentant, "according to your fisherman friend your god had a mother so what's the difference?"

"We don't worship her," she said and disappeared into her own room. I slept alone that night. Next morning she was bright and affectionate which unnerved me; it was abnormal. I saw it was a lost hope, trying to provoke her into the hatred

331

which her god of love had preached against; yet the last thing I wanted was her hatred. It seemed I must be abnormal, too. Despite her good-will I could not be at ease with her, not after what I had said. It was unforgivable. From then on matters got worse and worse. She was always calm and sweet while I picked fault with her every minute, even accusing her of having lovers. After all, I had lost most of my attractiveness; all she wanted me for now was the throne. Why wouldn't she admit it? Why? I bullied and bullied, hurting myself as well as her; I tried to make her angry, to admit she was unfaithful but all she said was: "I still love you. I always have done." Instead of being grateful I should have liked to hit her; she showed how unreasonable I was. To make it worse I still wanted her. She was submissive and loving in bed but every time we made love I felt criminal as though it were rape. To attack her in the morning and possess her at night seemed an insult.

One evening at the end of April I followed her. She went on foot with her head muffled and plebian sandals on her feet like any serving woman. Little green clouds swam in the rose-glow of sunset as she came past the beginnings of my new palace, skirted the Circus and turned into the Via Appia. I came quietly at a good distance, wearing my wig. Most people were indoors; I could hear grasshoppers stir on the hillside but nothing else, only twilight stillness as I came past the funerary urns on their stone plinths. One contained Passienus' ashes; I saw his name engraved.

The walk was long. Wherever she was going must be far along the road. Tall cypresses stood still as lead near tombs and seated statues of the dead which watched me as if disapproving. She never looked round, only walked and walked and her shadow grew long behind her. Then she came to a dark hollow carved far back in the hill with steps leading down. I gave her a start. When I followed after a few minutes the sun shot its last fire over the horizon and going into the darkness almost blinded me.

The steps went down and down. I couldn't see where I was going. I put out my hands either side and touched cold rock; the air breathed dampness. Something brushed past my face.

I squealed like a child and jumped back, banging my head on the wall. My blood crawled. The priests say deep chasms lead to the dwelling-places of the dead; I thought of all the dead I did not want to meet and nearly turned back, then I saw her face with its complacent conviction and willingness to die for a secret. Would she defeat me here?

I went on. The steps ended and the ground levelled out still in darkness. I breathed in mustiness. Passages turned off at every corner; I had no idea which she had taken and cursed myself for delaying. These tunnels went for miles; it might be my death. Yet on I went, not commending myself to any god and not caring. I had known darkness before, worse than this; a twining labyrinth in the mind with snake heads at every turn. I would find her. If I walked till my death I would find her and face her out on her own ground. Perhaps I was just curious or even defiant, wanting to see what she hid so carefully; but I think not. Something drew me on into the night. I began to think it was my death.

The floor dipped sharply and I stumbled. My hand touched deep graven marks on the wall; someone had been scribbling. I traced out the shape of a fish, then a Greek word which made no sense. I went further; there were shelves carved into the walls with marble slabs shutting them off but some were open with something white and shapeless lying within. Reaching out I touched linen and withdrew, shuddering; one carried dark stains. I saw now where I was. High either side these rock shelves blazoned my indictment; the judge stood in the midst of his condemned. Some of the shelves were little with little burdens. I had forgotten the children.

I went on, cold inside my toga. The tunnels were twisting again, looping upon themselves, the passages narrow, the ceilings low. There were more steps. This must be the second level. I remembered our cemeteries were built on four or five levels. Of course, they would meet far down for safety. More tunnels, a floor full of bumps; more rock niches, names carved on the walls: sweet Julia in heaven, pray for us. More steps; the third level. My breath came harshly. The air seemed thick and I fancied the walls moved; sweet gods, they were collapsing—an

333

earthquake! No. I stood still, breathing heavily; no sound, only that; no movement. I was alone. Not quite alone; white shapes lay along the walls. That many? I had forgotten the number of execution orders signed.

I began to go faster. Where was I? I had seen this passage before; no, of course not, it was thé third level. How many feet down? How long before the air failed, unable to penetrate? *Where were they?* This passage, a sharp turning—there! No, nothing; I was confused. Everything looked the same. And the darkness—Then I thought: oh gods, I'm lost, which way forward, no way back; I don't remember. Darkness. White shapes. The dead on either side with their executioner trapped. It was funny, really, terribly funny. I began to laugh. I beat my hands on the wall; I choked. Coloured lights burned behind my eyes but no light to lead. "Light," I said feebly. "I need some light."

I began to run. My feet caught in the hollows, my hands scraped on the walls. I was cold and sweating, half weeping, and there were feet behind me; when I looked back I saw the glint of snake scales and the moving shadow of their robes; and then I screamed. Light, for the gods' sake, light! The triclinium with burning lamps, keeping back the night; they could only catch you in darkness. I heard the hiss of forked tongues, felt hot breath touch my neck—and then I heard voices, sweet voices singing.

Light glowed from a tunnel. I stopped, my heart slowed; I leaned thankfully against solid rock. I was a child again, lulled to sleep on the stable floor. They stood grouped in a little open place, men and women, even children, singing as though the world would hear them even through all this earth. Each held a candle. She was standing apart, head well bent. Sweet Jove, what would they do, knowing she stood with them and I stood watching? Kill me? Perhaps. They had tried to burn my city.

I remembered what Lucan had said about drinking blood and kept back behind the entrance. I did not want to see obscene ritual close to. They had stopped singing and were talking in chorus. The words did not reach me. I was weak from fear and running and took nothing in. Then a man in the centre, bearded and Jewish-looking, broke a flat cake of bread, saying: "Who the day before he suffered took bread into his holy hands and offered thanks, to thee God, his almighty Father . . ." I thought: it's gibberish. But if it's a libation of blood where is the sacrifice?

The voice said: "This is my body, take and eat—" and the bread was handed round. They took it reverently as though it were sacred and ate in the candlelight with shadows leaping from rock crevices behind. A wine goblet glimmered gold, lifted high; it looked expensive. "This is my blood, shed for you . . ." The voice was muttering again; I could make no sense of it. Where had the blood come from? All I could see was a stoppered wine bottle, probably Marseilles, the cheap kind. The cup was passed and they all drank. I watched her bend her head to it with a kind of awe as though it were nectar from Olympus.

They drew together again; the candles burned down, flinging out long shadows. The man said quietly: "My friends, we are gathered together in his name and in danger of our lives. I only ask that you take care when returning to the city and speak to no one; remember secrecy protects others than yourself. We live at a hard time. But remember, too, that he said: 'You will be hated by many.' We must bear what he did in order to share his glory."

No listener hears any good of himself. Seeing her there, so mild and quiet, seemed to prove her disloyalty. She was with them heart and soul; how could she come back to me tonight and pretend total love when she had heard this, an exhortation to courage in the face of my cruelty?

They sang again, their faces lifted and joyful in the dying light; then it was finished. As they began to come out I slipped back into the darkness of a passage and watched them go past, smiling and talking as though only sunlight waited outside, not the threat of death. The walls tossed back the echo of their voices. Then I saw that she was not with them. She still stood in the cave with the bearded man, her veil thrown back; I saw a pair of emerald earrings she had forgotten to take off. This was her loyalty. I had begged her to remain nameless.

The man said: "My child, what is it?" "I'm afraid," she said, "that my presence will endanger everyone else."

"In what way?"

335

"My husband." I pressed closer to the wall so that I no longer saw. But I heard. "He is—difficult. Every Christian in Rome could die through his possessiveness."

"My dear." The voice sounded gentle. "Have you suffered yourself?"

"Not physically; he would never harm me that way. It's his jealousy, his complete..." She was struggling for words. "... his complete inability to understand. Sometimes I think he would like to kill me; instead he kills the innocent. Don't you see? It's all an attempt to frighten me. He knows he can't do it but that only makes him try harder. When I think of all—"

"My child, calm yourself." I wondered if she were weeping. I had seen her cry only once and that was over the baby. "I know your position is more difficult than anyone else's but you are vitally important to us. Our master said the net must take in all fish, and we have them; conversions in the brothel and the palace. You are a hope of peace, of lighting the minds of those who govern us. Your husband—"

"He doesn't want to see," she said quickly. "I've tried. It's some block in his mind; it would make sense to him if he listened. It's what he needs. He's not wicked, you know, just frightened of losing what he values; his life hasn't been easy."

"It's hard for us," said the quiet voice, "not to see him as wicked; some have called him Satan trying to stop the spread of the kingdom. Yet if he wants peace of mind he need look no further than here."

"I know," she said. "I know. But he won't."

They came out, treading softly. I shrank into the shadows like a beggar or a criminal and watched the gold-stitched hem of her dress drag the dust. So this was how she saw me; an awkward bawling child. Oh the arrogance of it: ... *some block in his mind ... he's not wicked, you know* ... She might have been my nurse. I banged my hand on the cold rock and nearly wept to think of my wholehearted love. It was dashed back like spray in my face. She had merely patronised me; hadn't I possessed the sense to see it long ago when Otho lent her to me for a night? Then it had been patronage of my desire.

I followed them at a safe distance, in dread of losing myself

336

again. We came out into cool night air. She put up her veil and they walked back towards the city in deep conversation. I felt sharply jealous; they seemed so close. I wondered who he was, some idiotic friend of the fisherman, I suppose. It was chilly. Wind breathed through the cypresses like coldness from the Styx. There were not even any stars to light me home, only figures ahead slowly moving further and further from me.

We were due for Games. Ceres' festival had suffered because of the plot and the people were discontented. I intended to give them my Neronia again, earlier than scheduled, as a bribe, but I saw what I could give them before that.

A starving lion needs food. We had plenty of them, kept in cages under the ground of the amphitheatre for gladiators to fight; but I visualised different meat. In fact, the starving lion was within myself, roaring for blood, only I would not admit it. She still wore the calm mask, ignoring my gibes, playing the devoted wife when I tried to ridicule her. When she appeared loving I remembered how she had revealed me to an illiterate barbarian as though I were a difficult patient and he the doctor. And what was the point of it all? It made me uneasy; such simplicity must conceal a trap. It might have been so neat: *This is my body, this is my blood*. Condemned from their own mouths on a charge of cannibalism. But cannibals don't eat bread and, going by appearances, the cup had contained wine. Some form of witchcraft? A code such as commanders use in war? I thought and thought till I could have gone mad; not understanding, I feared, and, fearing, I hated.

It was a clear May morning. The crowds poured into my wooden amphitheatre on the Campus Martius as the stone one had burnt down in the fire. They cheered me when I entered. She sat beside me in blue and silver sewn with sapphires, and clusters of golden pearls in her ears; the canopy's shadow made her hair bronze. Then I saw the cheers were really for her. She looked at me sideways from under her painted lashes. I said: "You don't like the arena, Poppaea, do you?"

"Do you?" she said.

The gladiators marched on in salute, shouting: "Ave Imperator, morituri te salutant". I acknowledged their death-wish and fished out the emerald I used as an aid to my short-sight. In fact, it hindered more than helped, which I wanted. A front row seat gives too good a view. They were strong, coarse-looking men, no artistry about them at all. The whole thing depends on brute strength. Twenty-four Samnites with large square shields and embossed helmets faced twenty-four Thracians, light-built, fair men with little round shields, leaf-carved; their weapons and armour were set with amber. I had ordered it. "The colour of your hair, darling," I said to Poppaea.

She smiled. "Thank you," she said.

They fought well. It might seem unfair to pit heavily armed men against men whose chests are bare but Thracians are quick on their feet. It won them the battle. The place was littered with dark shapes of dead or dying; the crowd roared. Just below me the sand ran blood. Poppaea leaned back on her cushions, fanning herself.

"Hot, dear?" I said. "Extremely." Her voice was sharp. She was not used to public death.

In the interval Moorish slaves sprinkled fresh sand and attendants masked as Charon tapped the dead on the forehead to make sure they weren't shamming as an escape. As corpses were carried through the gate to the mortuary Poppaea said: "It's disgusting."

"I couldn't agree more," I said lightly, "but look at that blood-hungry mob out there. If it wasn't Samnites it would be us."

The heavy notes of tubas introduced the next act. This time it was tatooed Britons, armourless and carrying net, trident and dagger opposed with huge Gauls in visor and full armour, carrying sword and shield. They came out swaggering, playing to the audience for all they were worth. The Britons were watchful. For all their savagery they had some idea of battle technique. After half-an-hour only one pair were left and the crowd were going mad; large bets had been laid. I would have put my money on the Gaul because of his size but Poppaea said: "The savage will get it. He knows how to move."

I said: "Really? I didn't think you an expert."

338

"I'm not." She sounded strained. "But anyone with eyes can see."

Within five minutes the Gaul was flat on his back, helmet off. The mob howled: "Habet! Kill him!" and gave the thumbs down; I could see he was wounded. Only their pardon would save him. The Briton stepped forward and raised his knife to me in question. Poppaea said: "Spare him, Nero, please." The shouts came from all sides: "Iugula! Slay him!" and I saw a death sentence written on the pale paper of all those faces. I said: "I can't. They'll riot," and turned down my thumb. The cut was clean, the death brave. I put my emerald to my eye and looked through a comforting green blur.

There was more like this. Then came animal baiting with elephants, panthers, bulls, bears and leopards all fighting in a hideous scrimmage. Freed ostriches pattered across the sand, outlandish birds with necks like poles and fluffed up white feathers; for fun they had been tinged with vermilion. Men rode bridled stags, a pair of cranes pecked each other to death, a gorilla rode a chariot and mounted Praetorians fought four hundred bears and three hundred lions; the men won the day. At the end elephants danced to cymbals and one knelt before my box, tracing "Ave Nero" in the sand with his trunk. I thought it charming and clapped. Poppaea said: "Tell the slave to fetch me some water." "Why," I said, "I hope you're not going to leave early. The best is to come."

After the animals we had a rest. Sparkling fountains sprang from the floor and shot jets of water high as the top seats while perfume sprayed all round the arena; it was needed. The stink of blood made me feel sick.

"What next?" Poppaea asked.

"You'll see," I said.

The fountains stopped. The audience was hushed. Then the iron gates clanged open and out came a group of people, not gladiators or animal trainers, not even dancers. They wandered dreamily over the sand, holding hands and speaking quietly to one another like young thinkers in the palestra. The crowd muttered. In the centre of the arena they knelt, touching forehead, shoulders and breast in some odd, symbolic gesture.

339

I felt her stiffen beside me. When I looked she was white and staring, her paint standing out as if engraved. "Your friends," I said softly. She did not move.

"Why children?" she said. "You told me you loved them."

"My dear," I said, "children suffer for parents' sins as I well know."

The cage doors slid upwards either side. I heard the roar; they had been a week and more with no food. The crowd had woken up. "Death to atheists!" "Kill the incendiaries; let's drink the blood of traitors!" "Kill! Kill!" I thought she would not look; I still did not know her. While I raised the emerald she gazed without flinching. Some screamed, mostly the children. They could not see the reason. When I looked again a lion was trotting away beneath me, clutching something pale and torn-off in its mouth; blood spots marked its path.

Worse followed. I had not broken her; she did not sip water or fan herself, only sat as though already dead. Others crawled on hands and knees in animal skins with metal collars round their necks, trailing chains which the attendants held like keepers. The crowd howled laughter. Simple blood is never enough; you must give them humiliation, too. This time hunting dogs bounded from the cages, baying like wolves. They were slim and quick but savage. All they saw were the animal hides; they had the scent. The keepers dropped the chains and ran back, soon enough for some to stand on their feet and show themselves human had they thought; but the dogs were quicker. Besides, I think they were in love with death.

You couldn't hear the screams, not with that crowd. I never heard such noise. It had got beyond enthusiasm and become blood-lust which turned my stomach; this was the sordid little world I had tried so hard to beautify. But I sat and swallowed it because she was there. I would bear anything to see that flawless face crack. Below, amongst snapping jaws and the flurry of sand, I saw a girl's face look up straight at me, her hair dabbled with blood. It was a small, pretty face. I don't think she saw me; her eyes were already closing. She could not know that to me she was a memory come alive: Acte in my bedroom the day I took her from Octavia. It might be Acte herself had I not given orders for her to be untouched.

Poppaea said faintly: "Have you no pity?"

"No one ever had any pity on me," I said.

The noise was dying. The dogs were tired of the kill, moping in circles or worrying at what was left; one tossed a head. When an attendant approached it growled and ran to the side with it, standing guard. The sand was clotted with blood. Before the next part the Moorish slaves came out again and more perfume was sprayed into the arena. I had my own scent bottle.

Next came a novelty. Women were tied naked to stakes set at intervals round the arena and the gates opened this time to release bulls. They rushed out, heads down, mad from captivity. One, a black monster, pawed the ground and bellowed before charging; I remembered Hippolytus. The crowd screamed and groaned. Women in the arena always go down better; in this case there were plenty since the cult attracted them. Poppaea sat bolt upright, her fingers tight on the chair arms. Below was bedlam. The maddened bulls wheeled and charged, trying to break out through the iron bars protecting the audience; this was the idea. The stakes stood just inside them.

They did not scream. I saw their lips moving as if in prayer or pain and some called out: "Christus Rex," in loud voices; but no one screamed. It infuriated me to see such fatalistic courage. One girl sagged, gored in the stomach; another was pinned between the breasts. On one the ropes gave and the bull tossed her high again and again before trampling her underfoot. I felt warm blood spatter my face. That is how near the emperor sits. I wiped it away, then heard a clatter beside me; Poppaea had fainted. She lay in a huddle at my feet, her face turned upwards and looking at nothing; one of her earrings had flown off. I fancied it went in the arena.

There was confusion. I got down on my knees and lifted her head; I had waited all day for this, it was my victory. Yet I felt cold. In sudden panic I felt for her heart. It beat weakly against my fingers like a bird trying to escape, too weak perhaps. People came running. Someone brought a cup of water but I pushed it aside, saying: "Fetch a doctor and send for my litter." I wanted to say: "Stop the Games," but that was impossible; the people rule. She began to come round. I said: "Are you all right?" She seemed to look for a long time before saying: "I'm sorry. I've spoilt your show."

Next day Xenophon told me she was pregnant. I should have been overjoyed. Instead I was ungracious like someone feeling unworthy to take a gift. She said: "Isn't it what you wanted?" I said: "Of course."

She sighed and lay back on her cushions, saying: "I hope it's a son."

My other son was ten, a handsome Ahenobarbus with Julian eyes. I saw him often, feeling the pressure of parental responsibilities, and recently I had found that she was bringing him up in her own beliefs. Of course, I could not stop it. She had sole care of him and I could not authorise his education without revealing his parentage. It was ironic; my son a Christian. When I visited him he looked at me fearfully as though I might beat him; he must have heard talk. I asked Acte if she had put him against me. She assured me she hadn't. "But," she said, "the child knows what has happened to people who believe the same as him—through your order."

I went home with a new fear. For a couple of months it smouldered under the surface while I took comfort in other things, my Golden House which now had much of the building done and large areas cleared for parkland, my singing such as it was and a little painting; not poetry. I needed to be calm. Then there was something else to keep it from my mind, trouble at the prison where the fisherman was. Tigellinus came in one morning and said the Guards there appeared to be in revolt. "And another thing," he said. "The place is flooding water."

It sounded so odd I went and looked myself. The prison was tucked away behind the Senate House, a little dark building. The huge bolted door swung on to the guard room; steps went down from this to the cell. He was in isolation being an important prisoner. The guards jumped up as I entered, smart Praetorians. I said: "Who is the senior officer?" He stepped forward and saluted; I said: "I've had reports of disturbance here. Can you explain?" "Well, sire," he said, "perhaps they're referring to my baptism."

342

"Your *what?*"

I nearly fell backwards. He looked a sensible, clear-minded man; a typical soldier. "I'm a Christian, sire. The prisoner baptised me."

I turned and plunged down the stone steps, into the small cell; it reminded me of the catacombs, all dark and closed in but freezing cold. He sat in a corner chained to the wall. I could just see the blur of his face, pale as a corpse in the shadow. I said: "What have you been doing?"

"My appointed work," he said.

I moved nearer in anger, then felt wetness soak round my sandals; the floor streamed water. I said: "What is this?"

"The power of God, sire."

"Don't play games with me." My voice rose. "Is this a trick?"

"Come here, sire." His voice echoed in the small space. "Don't worry; it isn't a trap. Just put your hand down here, near my feet."

I thought: a knife? A poisonous snake? My thoughts were as wild as that. But I still obeyed him, fearing to make a fool of myself. My fingers touched dirty, uneven floor, then something ice-cold; it was water, bubbling out as if from green grass. I looked up. His eyes watched me, dark as stone but smiling.

"I prayed for it," he said. "Last night when I knew I might convince your guard. When it came he believed and I baptised him with it."

"Came?" I said. "Don't be absurd. Do you think I don't know an underground spring when I see it?"

"Here, sire? Are underground springs common in Rome?"

I got up and went to the door. He looked old and huddled in the darkness, harmless you would think. But I felt the water at my feet.

I said: "I warned you. People who are a nuisance to me don't live very long. I'll sign the crucifixion order today. The charge is subversive activities and influencing members of the emperor's Guard to rebel against him."

I came up the stairs into a sudden silence. They had been

343

talking and cut it off quickly. I said: "Have you been dealing with the mess down there?"

"As best we can, sire." It was the senior officer, polite and undisturbed. "It seems to be from a crevice in the ground. At first it was heavy and we had to bale it out but now it's only a trickle. It can be blocked off."

"Your friend has unblocked it," I said coldly. "He seems to think it something special. If he prefers to sit in the wet that's his business but if you've turned traitor it's mine. Do you know what it means?"

"Yes, sire."

"Do you retract it?"

"No, sire."

"Then you can go to the cross with him. Tomorrow."

"Sir!"

He snapped to attention as if I had decorated him for bravery. It is like a madness in them. Nothing is seen the right way round, no rules are followed; what you think a pain they find a pleasure.

He died next day, crucified upside down in the Vatican gardens. It was his own request; he said he was not worthy to die as his master had done. It meant a quicker death but more agonising. His convert died next to him, the right way up. I did not see it but apparently there was an appreciative audience. Within a few days another died, this time beheaded because though Jewish he was a Roman citizen. He had been sent to me a long while back by a provincial governor who had found him subversive but his papers were lost so I confined him and forgot about it. Then Tigellinus told me he was making conquests even from his cell and hinting at conversions in high places when he wrote to friends abroad. It was his death warrant. Poppaea's name must not come out. I had him for trial (a very brief one) and found him disturbing, an intellectual who reminded me of Seneca except that he spoke straight, not crooked. He was no barbarian. In fact, letters from him had been found amongst Seneca's papers. My tutor as well? Perhaps it explained the change in him. Or was it just intellectual to intellectual? Seneca had always fed on ideas like a leech on blood. He

344

died bravely, this one, no different from the rest, only with dignity and in private, a badge of citizenship.

July began in thunderous heat. I gave my Neronia again and sang to the audiences. One evening Poppaea came home from the theatre sick-looking with shadows ringing her eyes. I said: "Are you tired?"

"A little." She never admitted weakness.

She sat looking from the window on to the garden terrace where the flowers sank down for evening. Beyond was the Palatine, rimmed gold, and a sky of purple and flame. There was not much sign of the new life in her except for tiredness and a thickening at the waist.

I said: "What shall we call him if it's a boy?"

"You choose," she said.

And suddenly the fear I had been nursing jumped into view like an assassin, not prepared for. I said: "Will you let me choose how to train his mind?"

She looked at me, puzzled. "What do you mean?"

"Well, my dear, we differ sharply on many points. Whose road is he going to follow, yours or mine?"

Her brows drew together, then relaxed. "Oh," she said. "I see."

"Well?"

"Well." She was maddeningly non-committal. "A son must know his mother's views."

"But how well? I know how you think, Poppaea, how *all* of you think; everyone into the fold, no matter what. It's like political fanaticism, only worse. What are you after, world rule?"

"His rule," she said. "But not political power, only power over men's hearts."

"That *is* political power," I said. "Look at Alexander. Well, you're not doing it with my son. I've lost Germanicus but then he's not my heir; your son—" And suddenly I saw it in her eyes, my fear crystal sharp. I remembered the voice in the cave: *You are a hope of peace, of lighting the minds of those who govern us.* I said: "Sweet Jove, you would do it, wouldn't you? You'd cut him off from me entirely and train him as my mother trained me; power through a child. Oh, Poppaea—"

345

"Have I said that?"

Her voice was cool and brittle. The dying sun touched her face with pink and caught fire in her hair.

"No, but it's in your mind. I'm not a fool. I heard you talk in the catacombs that evening. You're a hope of peace, aren't you, despite your difficult husband?"

She sat unnaturally straight and I could see the slight thickness in her stomach; they say a son blossoms early.

"The emperor," I said. "That's all they want. With the apex of the pyramid turned the rest must follow. And you'll give them that emperor, won't you?"

"If I can."

She might have been discussing a dress instead of buying off my last hope of joy. I could not fight her on equal ground. The battle had been fought and lost in the darkness of her womb where I had no power.

I said wildly: "If you hate me why don't you say so instead of just attacking me in the dark? Even Scaevinus would have knifed me in daylight."

She said calmly: "Come, Nero, this isn't one of your tragedies."

I said: "Isn't it? *Isn't it?*" I was shouting but it seemed to pass her by. Where do you strike when your opponent is armoured from head to foot? "He's taken you. Must he take my son as well? What do you think I am, a blind fool to stand and do nothing while everything I love is thieved away?"

"No," She stood up and came towards me. "You have never been a fool. That's why I don't understand how you cannot see."

"Oh no," I said, mocking her, "not your difficult husband with a block in his mind; he isn't wicked but he's abominably awkward. Do they pity you in that place, tied to a monster who burns Christians, and do you play the long-suffering, virtuous wife who can show off her courage and be admired for it?"

"Nero—"

She looked appalled. It was too late; I had gone beyond myself. That was disgust in her face.

346

I said: "Go on! Say how you hate me. Tell me how I revolt you."

She shook her head. "You won't provoke me," she said. "It's what you want."

I forget what happened next. Night after night I have awoken almost remembering but I shut it away for there are some things we must not know. I only remember her retreating from me, her face washed blank as if with surprise. Far, far away she went, yet so slowly, her hands clutched wide over her stomach. Near the window she snatched at a chair and tried to hold herself up, yet her face never changed; only her mouth gaped, gulping air. It was like a dream. The chair slid, her hands loosened, flying out, and down she fell, into a pool of red sunlight.

I stood thinking: she will get up soon. The sun was lost behind the horizon but for a hot glow which lay like blood on her face. At last I went forward, saying: "Poppaea?" as if to a child playing a joke. I knelt beside her. It was no joke. The sun had vanished but her dress was spotted red.

One lamp burned. It showed yellow on Xenophon's face where he stood at the doorway. He had that doctor's look which tells you nothing.

I said: "Well?"

"She has lost the child, sire, in the flow of blood."

The lamp flickered. A world blown out, just like that, not only my hopes but hers, too: a world obedient to the carpenter. So much gone so quickly.

I said: "Why?"

"It could be many things, sire. Heat, exhaustion, too much movement; but from the strength of the haemorrhage I would say a blow in the stomach."

My heart turned over. You can see your guilt in another's face, even in lamplight; it is what the Furies show you. I said: "Nonsense, Xenophon. It isn't possible."

"I would say a very hard blow," he continued mercilessly. "A kick."

"And how," I said, "are you suggesting that happened?"

347

"I'm a doctor, sire, not a member of the police."

He had been like this before, a long time ago. In the middle of horror he retained diplomacy while his Greek eyes picked out truth.

I said: "How is she?"

He shrugged. "It is with the gods."

I thought of something long ago, Passienus inert under a red quilt and my mother kneeling beside him.

"What do you mean?" I said.

"Come and see for yourself. I cannot work miracles."

She was lying on heaped pillows with a gold-worked cover over the bed; her hands were limp on top. I saw the blue veins sharp in the wrists. Her face was drained clear like Phoenecian marble and looked at the opposite wall with infinite patience as though she could watch till it crumbled. The place streamed activity. Maids carried steaming bowls of water or vinegar and blackberry juice mixed with maidenhair which is supposed to stop bleeding; I saw it had not worked. They were taking out the stained bedclothes and a maid rinsed a cloth in scarlet water. Other doctors stood consulting. As I entered they coughed and drew apart, suddenly watchful.

By now I was past dreams or hopes. I wanted truth from them as I had from Anicetus in the dark triclinium. A time comes when you must commit yourself to the worst.

I said softly: "Will she live?"

No one spoke. They looked at each other, trying to pass the burden. Then Xenophon said: "I doubt it, sire. We cannot stop the haemorrhage."

I went to the bedside. As yet I felt nothing like a man in war who sees the spear go in but senses no pain. She smiled, a slow, gentle smile. "Don't look so sad," she said. "I'm not. I did not want to live and see myself grow ugly."

I said: "Are you in pain?"

"No. But I'm so tired. Oh Nero, our son—"

"There would have been—" I began, then went on: "There will be others."

I didn't know how much they had told her. She looked so peaceful. I had always found death ugly and cruel, a struggle.

348

She sighed, turning her head on the pillow as if ready to sleep, then she said: "He died in darkness, too. When the earth shook they said he was a god, then later, in the tomb, it shook again to free him." Her eyes wandered over my face. "Oh Nero, I loved you so. Give me your hand." When I did she grasped it tight and I wondered if she had lied over the pain.

I said bitterly: "If he healed the sick . . ."

"No." She shook her head. "There are no miracles for me, nor for those in the arena. We face it as he did. Miracles are for those brave enough to live longer."

"Oh Poppaea, has it been that bad?"

"Bad?" She seemed sleepy, yawning and looking past things instead of at them. "I don't know. We were happy once; oh yes, I've been so happy." She yawned again. "Nero, where are you? Don't go away. It's getting so dark I can't see."

I asked a slave to bring more lamps. In the end they were burning round her like a shrine, flaming gold on her hair and making a network of fire on the quilt. Venus could not have looked lovelier. The loss of blood made her skin translucent as though gleaming light from within.

I waited. Xenophon had given her an hour. I did not think in terms of time; a minute was a lifetime and every breath another hope. Incense burned before the Lar. It was a mockery for both of us, she who thought it an idol and I who believed in nothing.

She said: "I'm cold."

They brought more covers. Blood was soaking through but it was not worth disturbing her. The maids clustered weeping in a corner; the doctors stood impassive. I knelt with my hand in hers, a chill on every bone; I thought she must feel it.

I said: "I'm sorry, oh my darling, I'm so sorry."

"There is no need."

The light jumped and threw a shadow on her face. She coughed. I said: "Poppaea—" Her eyes rested on me for a moment, then her hand strained as if it would break free from mine.

"Christus," she said softly; and her head rolled down on the pillow. Xenophon's hour was up.

Chapter Nineteen

Since then I have lived but only as an animal does, existing from day to day. I walked from her room, past the failed doctors, past the slaves with their bowls and compresses, past the Pontifex Maximus come hastily from sacrifice and the senators waiting for news, past them all and into unreality.

I did not believe her dead. Soon I should go back and see her sitting up and smiling. But when I did they were clearing the room and laying her out for embalming.

I said: "What is this? Whose order are you carrying out?"

"Your own, sire," Xenophon said.

I said: "Nonsense, leave her alone. How can she sleep in the middle of this?"

He looked at me sharply. "Sire," he said, "she is dead."

"No." I heard my voice, strained and odd. "No, she isn't. Don't say such things."

He said: "Sire, you are not well."

"I'm perfectly well, well enough not to be deceived. Now leave her alone."

He went to the bedside, saying: "Put your hand on her heart." I thought him insolent but obeyed. Her breast was like stone; I looked at her mouth and saw it fixed as though in a gasp with the teeth showing.

He said gently: "She is gone. Now come to your room and rest."

He gave me something to drink. I lay with a woollen cover thrown over me, staring at the heavy ceiling till it faded into darkness.

*   *   *

She lay on a bier in the atrium, ready for the funeral. They had painted her face, styled her hair as if for a feast, and dressed her in cloth of gold with rubies twined in her hair and a great gold cluster on her breast, burning a single red stone. Her shoes were pearl-sewn, her earrings squares of gold with little hanging chains; a comb of mother-of-pearl set with silver in the shape of a fish held her hair parted. She had ordered it to be made specially and now I saw why. It was their sign.

She looked sleeping; I could have sworn she breathed. But when I touched her lips with mine they were cold. Her hands lay crossed on her breast and the ring I had given her on our marriage blinked in the sunlight from the roof opening. That was all done. No marriage survives the grave. Everything was done. She had gone beyond hope or despair, anger or fear, beyond desire and laughter and tears; nothing could touch her. Where was she now? Squeaking bat-like over the Styx or happy in the odd glory she had visualised, united with a man-god? Neither made sense. The only reality was this, the smoothed-out wax face and the scent of embalming spices; past that was darkness.

I stood for a long time. Memories pattered and echoed in the empty hall like leaves twirled on the wind. There was so much; bright hair on a crushed pillow, a mouth sweet with wine, tears for a dead child and courage at a window when the mob howled. But over it all was the voice in the catacomb, the shocked face retreating from my blow. She had died for him as surely as if I had sent her to the arena. It was my crime, her glory. When they heard, gathered in their dark caves or shuttered house, they would guess; then it would be her name on the catacomb wall. She had died saying his name, not mine.

It was cold. A slave came, saying: "Sire, do you want anything to eat? It's midday." I asked for wine. I drank it there, not one cup but several, then sat. As twilight streamed blue from the roof I ordered a bed to be made up beside the bier but I did not sleep. That night I saw my mother again.

I don't remember all the funeral, only the procession and

then leaving her in the Mausoleum of Augustus. She would probably have chosen to be buried in the catacombs, closed in darkness with my other victims, but I wanted her with my ancestors. I could not give her to the flames; instead she lay under the stone lid of her coffin as though in perpetual sleep. Somewhere I made a speech from the Rostra in her praise; that I forget. I saw people weep in the crowd. Despite Octavia they had loved and admired her for the things that I did. At the end they saw only her new sweetness, not the barrier which I had faced.

The cypresses stood sharp as spears on the roof of the great, round mausoleum with Augustus' statue raised above them, one arm in salute. Inside, the marble threw out coldness. Her coffin was white Phoenecian set with Arabian porphyry and carrying a relief of Venus and Flora twined in flowers. The piled gifts reached almost to its lid. The rich had given precious stones and ivory, the poor brought flower posies and bread soaked in wine. Someone had placed a bronze fish on the coffin; I knew where that had come from. I had provided enough perfume to fill the Campus Martius with scent and incense was heaped over the steps in silver jars. But you can give and give to the dead; it makes no difference. There was no propitiation I could make except with my own life and I was too cold to lift a sword. You need energy to hate yourself.

I went home to her empty room. The little make-up pots still stood on the table as if waiting to be used, the cover on her bed was fresh; I found some earrings on the floor. And then I wept. They came and led me out and Xenophon said: "Rest, sire, rest," but I had to be pushed on to the bed. I could not see, my breath choked me; I thought I was going to die.

But I woke up again. I woke every morning for the next three years.

You can live and not know it. You can go in search of violent sensation, yet feel nothing. My Golden House was finished and I retreated into it like a hunted animal to its lair. There I built my own world. It had no laws except for total subjection to art and beauty; it went nowhere. It existed for the moment, for the animal pleasure of existence *now;* I could not look ahead. There is nowhere to go in a desert.

My world glittered colour. Whole rooms were pearl-studded from ceiling to floor so that in lamplight they became luminous, others were walled in gold or mother-of-pearl. I had commissioned Fabullus, well known for his colour genius, to paint every nook and cranny, even passages where the light was too bad for designs to be seen. Nothing must be blank or bare. Emptiness filled me with horror like the sickness one gets on a great height or during thunderstorms.

He gave me winged goddesses and birds trailing a feather glory of red and gold, flowers and centaurs and monstrous creatures, half man, half snake. Borders were bright patterns, geometric, or flowers with vine leaves. Elsewhere there were scenes, landscapes seen small as if by a giant's eye or Jupiter in a vaulted ceiling with Nereids riding sea monsters, bordered by gold heightened with pink and blue like precious stones. He did not show me a real world. Reality is not bearable.

I gave feasts lasting all day in tricliniums where the ceilings were fretted ivory with panels which slid back to release a drift of flowers or perfume from hidden sprinklers. Guests would look alarmed, expecting knives or poison. They did not know that my world was inviolable; nothing ugly could touch it. Sea water and sulphur water ran into my bathrooms, plunging from gold into marble. No one knew how important the baths were; I was always in them. If you wash long enough you can imagine yourself clean.

When I walked in the gardens I looked on a world become little. Over the Caelian hill spreading clumps of bushes represented a forest where wild animals wandered; at night you heard them howling. I had imported lions, leopards, stags and even giraffes. Where the swamp had been I made a lake, big as a small sea with ploughed fields, vineyards, and pasture, feeding cows and sheep, on its banks. Fountains played in green shade; statues stood among leaves. Wherever you went there were flowers. She had loved flowers. I built a temple to Fortuna from Cappadocian stone, so transparent that the walls breathed light with the doors shut. I did not want darkness either. In darkness I heard snakes whisper and dead feet shuffle on the tiles.

I need never leave it and go into Rome. Everything was here, all that I wanted or needed; except for one. I had meant it as a shared home for us both; there were even rooms designed for her which I closed to everyone except myself. They were filled with statues and paintings of her, with her clothes and jewels and cosmetics and the covers on her bed as though any minute she might come through the door. Sometimes I stood there and thought I heard her light footfall.

But even an ideal world springs flaws. I needed distraction and I needed protection; Petronius provided me with the first, Tigellinus with the second. Both used me as my mother once had, a mindless puppet. Petronius kept going an endless stream of male and female prostitutes and expensive spectacles which were erotically artistic. Tigellinus ransacked Rome from end to end for traitors; his police had the city in a stranglehold. I lived in fear of conspiracy, of the knife in the back or poison in the drink; I knew many hated me. They saw my building operations as callousness, capitalising on their misery. Some had lost everything in the fire. They did not like my withdrawal either and spread tales of debauchery, the majority of which were true. I had ceased to care. Nothing outside my Golden House mattered; outside was reality and reality was a world bereft of her, personal guilt twined in the stone flowers on her coffin. They were openly calling me a matricide and incendiary, guilty of fratricide and incest and any other crime they could think of. The past had run quickly and caught me up at last.

The house was ringed with guards; they patrolled the grounds and each end of the entrance colonnade. They even stood in the room where I ate and by my bedroom door at night. When anyone asked for audience they were stripped and searched; all my food was tasted. But no guard could keep away the enemy who came in darkness, whispering above my pillow. Since Poppaea's death I had seen her often. She always wore the green and gold of that day and her emeralds glowed like witches' fire but her face was in the shadows; sometimes I thought it was Octavia. One night I thought the hair was amber, twined with rubies, and I woke reaching out. But she was gone. I asked Xenophon to give me the heaviest sleeping draughts he had; even so they often didn't work.

I knew people were dying. Tigellinus had a list and crossed off each name as he went. If there was no evidence he trumped up charges and ordered execution with no trial, often for nothing more than a careless remark. Some had been involved in Piso's big plot but were not convicted at the time. Others were probably guilty of nothing but owning a large fortune; I needed money. I had spent a great deal on Poppaea as well as Otho, Lucan and many others; then there were my building expenses. I found too late that the imperial treasury does have a limit. When the victims were dead Tigellinus seized their property and transferred it to me. I knew it was happening but I did nothing. He frightened me with stories of continual plotting which would end in my death if I didn't kill first.

"They hate you," he said bluntly. "No one is to be trusted."

I thought of the indiscriminate killing and turned sick; then I thought of my own death. That was the one thing which could end my world; final reality.

I lost myself in the distraction Petronius provided. Every day they came, the young and beautiful, with bodies to be abused and minds to be ignored. I knew what I was doing, this was the irony. Petronius and Tigellinus imagined they had me on a string, carefully guiding a degeneration of which I was ignorant. But I knew. I watched myself slide down and down in the dark well and every day I fell further. My only hope was to reach the bottom; then there is no more. But I already believed that the bottom did not exist.

I would watch their faces and see the murder of innocence; not all were prostitutes. Soon I no longer wanted brothel inmates at all but pure marble which had not been marked. Corruption is catching. I used them in any way I thought fit, boys and girls, and they would leave begging for the sword or the arena; afterwards they would find their own way: the escape route as Seneca had called it. But I who needed it most could not use it because I feared such cruel reality; and what might come after. When they had gone I saw what I had done and

355

became sickened but at the time I felt no conscience for it blocked off the emptiness, the dreams and fears and the snake heads. Anything which did that was permissible. After each bout Petronius would say: "Did they give satisfaction, sire?" and I would say yes or no, then he would note their names and make a list with the type of diversion each was skilled in. I knew this. He imagined I was ignorant again and laughed behind my back while marking down my degradation on papyrus. He enjoyed the power, yet he was infinitely refined over it. The whole thing was like a poetic exercise. I don't know whether he wanted the power of using me as a plaything or whether there was some more practical reason; preparation for a coup, perhaps. Once I had been foolish enough to trust him. I saw him now as an opportunist, all the more deadly because of his charm and subtlety. An inartistic man often fails in conspiracy.

He placed with me a woman named Silia Crispinilla who was to provide the boys and girls my delirium demanded. This appetite grows as you feed it; as time went on she had to increase her numbers. But this was not a comfortable delirium bringing senselessness; I knew the sickness. While the disease worsened my perceptions grew sharper. I fancy Silia was one of Petronius' mistresses, a slight, brown-haired woman, quick as a diving hawk, with something of his astuteness. She was always subservient to me but I knew she thought like the rest: pander to him until we can attack.

She tried to find me women who looked like Poppaea, thinking it would please me. I could have told her the impossibility of it. She did find one who had some similarity though it was rough and common like a bad sculpture of a beauty. I soon tired of her. Then one day she sent a girl into me wearing one of Poppaea's dresses and it might have been my darling standing there. Granted that if you looked close you could see flaws but with my short sight I could sustain the illusion. Then I found out "she" was a boy. Silia had put a dress and wig on him and left me to sort out the difference.

We are reluctant to lose our illusions. I ordered that the child be castrated and always wear woman's dress; he grew

356

his hair long, too, and used scent and make-up and sometimes I completely forgot that he had no right to do either. I saw the castration as a purification; sexuality leads us only to disaster. It had put the Furies on my trail and nearly cracked the Empire apart. Only when he was purified could I see him as my exquisite, gentle, perfect Poppaea, she who had been an ideal, yet died because I could not merely love her. I destroyed her, too. Perhaps destruction is ultimate possession though I think not. It had put her in peace and left me desolate.

Then Petronius died. He had become totally obnoxious, enjoying my humiliation, and I should probably have got rid of him even if Tigellinus had not denounced him as a traitor. They hated each other. When you have two people trying to control a dog's leash trouble naturally follows. Tigellinus pointed out that Petronius had not denounced Piso's conspiracy though he must have known of it through Scaevinus who was his dining companion. What more proof did I want? I was going to Baia and Petronius intended to join me at Cumae; instead I sent a message, saying I never wanted to see him again, and continued on my way. Petronius understood.

He returned to Rome and left this world as typically as he had lived in it, letting his blood ebb out during a lively, expensive feast with all the guests watching. While he waited for death he drew up a list of the prostitutes Silia had provided for me, inscribing "remarks" after the names. It was sealed and sent to me. His wit remained insulting to the end, so did his exhibitionism. I heard he shattered a valuable myrrhine drinking bowl in gold and blue which he knew I wanted. That was the sort of man he was, spiteful even on the death bed.

I did much to try and cling on to happiness. I visited Greece, the land I had always loved without seeing, to attend the Olympic Games and perform myself as an actor. That gave more scope for illusion. I rode a chariot at Olympia with ten white horses and felt like Apollo until I lost control and tumbled in the sand to the hysterical amusement of the crowd. I was not hurt; my stoutness protected me. Now I see that this was cruel for I might have died easily with a snapped neck; but no, a knife waited in darkness, marked with my name.

357

At Delphi I won singing contests, played my cithara and acted my favourite roles but I knew that success depended on my laurel wreath, not my ability. I was seeing now that my art had reached an end. Or perhaps I had never possessed any ability at all, allowing my vanity to persuade otherwise, and merely using the arts as a refuge, not a positive means of creation. I turned to more practical projects, namely, cutting a canal through the Isthmus of Corinth. I, at least, saw it begun in my lifetime. In the December I was thirty and accepted good wishes for a long life as though they meant something.

After a year in this earthly paradise I came back to Rome and my death. I suppose I had known that my time was nearly up but tried to ignore it by remaining absent; Greek tranquillity was deceptive. I had left as my deputy in Rome a freedman named Helius whom I trusted because he was clever and not to be deceived. He can't have managed very well. He came to Corinth to tell me of a proposal sent to him by Julius Vindex, governor of a province in Gaul who was supported by several other provincial governors. It entailed my death, "the liberation of Rome", as they called it. Helius begged me to go back at once. I said: "Don't fuss. I shall wait for good sailing weather." At this stage I did not believe it serious. Even if I had I would not have hurried for no one wants to meet their death before they need.

I returned in March and then I went to Naples, not Rome. They made a breach in the city walls to let me through in my chariot, the traditional entry of an Olympic victor. Looking at the smiling faces I felt no answering joy. My victory was an illusion like everything else and soon those voices would probably scream for my blood.

I had not miscalculated. On the anniversary of my mother's death I heard that Vindex had instigated revolt in Gaul. I did nothing. I spoke to no one, I gave no orders, I wrote no letters; there was no point in opposition. I saw my doom written on every wall I looked at. Did it matter? I had betrayed everything I thought good or beautiful. Some men commit one or two crimes in a lifetime; I was guilty of every human crime that exists and not only on my own account. I was dragging Rome down with me, in the hem of my toga. I remembered my childhood vow. How bright and near the horizon seems when you are too little to see black shadows beyond. At any other time I might have wept; now I was too dull. I had butchered my emotions until they no longer functioned. I should have liked to do nothing but sit by the sea and watch the waves rise and fall blue-green and feel the wind and sun, pretending I was no more than a seagull wheeling forever in freedom. Then I heard of the second revolt.

It was April now. This time Spain had rebelled under the leadership of Galba, their governor, who fancied himself as the next emperor, or perhaps other people did, Vindex for example. One piece of news reawakened the bitterness I thought dead. Otho had joined Galba. Of course, I should have expected it; Lusitania sits next door to Spain and I knew his resentment but I did not think it would live so long. I had loved him. I was too blind to remember that love and rejection walk hand in hand. When I heard I threw down the table I was dining from and watched the food and wine spatter the painted walls as though surprised. I had forgotten how anger felt.

I returned to Rome with a pretend triumph. It is always as well for the play to go on until the theatre doors shut. I rode to the Circus Maximus in Augustus' state chariot, dressed in a Greek chalmys sewn with gold stars which showed my standing as a citharist. I wore the Olympic crown. Behind came "applauders" shouting: "Hail, victor of Olympia! Hail, Augustus! Glory to Nero Apollo! " All most impressive. Attendants carried the crowns I had won and placards were attached to the guards' spears, marked with the place names of my victories. The Circus was crammed and an arcade had to be removed to let me through. Going back across Velabrum and into the Forum I saw animal sacrifices along the way and the appreciative crowd throwing ribbons and flowers, releasing bright birds to soar above my head. I thought for a moment it might be genuine. Then I remembered that the sacrificial victim is honoured before the knife descends.

There is only one thing worse than death and that is the false hope before death. It came even to me, resigned as I was. Merely as a gesture I ordered Rufus, the governor of Upper Germany, to attack Vindex which he did and defeated him; Vindex killed himself. It seemed a reprieve. Galba could do nothing without the military support of Gaul. I did not know that the traitor was already at my right hand, hearing my trusted confidences. His name was Nymphidius. I had dismissed Tigellinus because of his odd behaviour at the time of Vindex's revolt. He had told me nothing, yet he must have known; he could smell a dagger at fifty paces. His silence pointed to involvement. Apart from this he was an architect of my degradation and I hated him for he had traded on my weaknesses. Nymphidius took his place. Some people said he was Caligula's bastard; I certainly saw a likeness. If he really was of my blood then I could not blame him for what he did.

I did not see it at first. He kept telling me that Galba was not finished, despite Vindex; there was still Rufus. And what about Clodius Macer, the legate in Africa? There was a rumour that he had claimed the throne. I must admit that this was proved true. He suddenly cut off all our corn supplies from Africa and left me to feed a city on air. Nymphidius advised me to get out.

"Go to Alexandria, sire," he said. "Once the people begin to feel hungry they will want blood. You can stay safe in Egypt till the trouble is past. Why not send your German guard first? Then they can welcome you there and make a show of force to impress the Egyptians."

I still did not see. The idea seemed good and I carried it out, leaving only the Praetorian cohort to come with me. I was due to leave on June the ninth. I saw safety suddenly calling, an end of dread or hopeless apathy; instead, a time to recover and come back as the emperor I had always dreamed of being. In Egypt I would forget my horror, then I should let Rome take the place of Poppaea and devote myself to my first love. I had forgotten the Eumenides.

On the afternoon of the eighth I called my Guard and told them they would accompany me to Alexandria. They stood blankly. Then I looked closer and heard the first whisper of the Styx. They had been got at.

"Do you think it wise, sire," said one, "when the city is so disturbed?"

"Quite frankly, sire," said another, "I think you are misken," then an officer said: "Sire, may I say that I would rather not accompany you. Please excuse me."

That is how Praetorians are; they make the decisions, not the Emperor.

No one moved; then someone at the back muttered: *"Is it so great a misfortune to die?"*

He knew his Virgil. And I knew what was coming to me. I dismissed them and sent a messenger to Locusta, asking for an effective poison to be made up. The escape route might need forcing open but at least it would be there. I wanted to keep my dignity. It arrived in a small crystal phial which I put in a gold casket and placed in my bedroom. Then I went to bed. They might come in the night and finish it quickly or leave me free to try and abdicate in the morning. I started writing out a speech for this but grew tired and put it away in my desk. Did I want that chance? What is left for the man defiled before gods and men but an honourable death? I slept for a time. Then in my sleep I heard snakes hissing and when I woke they were standing by my bed. I screamed and lashed out, yelling: "Guard! " No one came. They vanished into the shadows and I sat up, shivering. I was alone.

No one guarded the door. No one stood in the corridor. The Guards' quarters were empty; so was the garden. I could hear night insects humming and a nightingale warble; nothing else. It was like the stillness before thunder. I grew scared. The clash of feet and weapons I could have stood, being recognisable, but I could not bear this silence. The daughters of night wait in silence.

I stood trembling, barefoot in the dew, and yelled for my servants. A few came, sleepy and apathetic. I said: "For the gods' sake find me some safe place to stay. At once! " They went off, mumbling; Phaon and Epaphroditus followed them, the only two I really trusted. Epaphroditus had been my secretary for several years. I could not stay in the garden where darkness might hide my death. I went back to my bedroom.

There I caught sight of myself in a long mirror on the wall and could have wept. It showed a fat, blubbering coward in a nightgown almost too small for such bulk, terror marked like a mask on his face. Since Poppaea's death I had cared nothing for how I looked. My hair hung loose and long, uncared for; it was beginning to come out. My straight Augustan nose had thickened and grown grotesque, my cheeks were hanging with fatness. Nothing was left of my beauty. It had gone, along with my ideals. I had not cared; now, in this new crisis, my perceptions were sharp and I saw it as the fatal ruin of all I had been.

I waited and waited. No one came. I saw too late that I had made it easy for them; they had saved their own skins. In panic I threw a cloak on my shoulders and ran to Nerva's house, near mine, meaning to beg for refuge. He had been my friend; I could trust him. I knocked for five minutes but there was no answer. As I walked away I saw a lamp burning in an upper window.

There was no one. All doors were shut, all routes of escape blocked; except one. I went back to my bedroom for the golden box. It had gone. So had my bedclothes, the rest of my wardrobe and a precious set of ivories on the table; I had forgotten the remaining servants. I was totally alone. Listening, I could hear the wind mutter in the leaves and the swish of a lizard tail on the terrace outside. The lamps were burning down; soon they would be out. I had nothing, not even my planned escape. Shadows curled dark on the walls and in them I saw snake hair.

I went running outside again in a sweat of fear. It had begun to rain; the drops pattered softly through the laurels like footsteps, then lightning came, flashing white in the dark trees and showing me the path I must tread; down to the Tiber. I had condemned my mother to drowning. It seemed fitting. I went quietly through my entrance colonnade with the thunder beating hollow on the marble and out near the Forum, then down beside the Circus to the wet bank. The water was high from recent storms. It ran thick and black like oil, not pretty, but it would carry me out to the sea and freedom; I remembered the

362

seagulls. The rain stung my eyes; I drew back for the leap—and could not do it. In this moment you must lose yourself entirely in a darkness of the will; I was still too aware. I did not want to die, not now in isolation which suggested safety. I slithered back up the bank, weeping with frustration. Even here I was failing.

I retraced my way to the Esquiline. There were voices in the garden; I thought of assassins and prepared to run again but then I recognised them. It was Phaon and Epaphroditus. I came wearily through the dampness, saying: "There is no hope. I'm deserted on all sides."

"Not necessarily, sire," Phaon said. "My country house, three miles or so from here, would be quite safe. I can take you."

I said: "Thank you."

It was a hope. Having tried death and failed the instinct to live was reasserting itself.

I dragged my fake Poppaea from his bed; I wanted to take along my illusions so that they could die with me. Apart from that I felt sorry for him. If the army arrived they would kill him on the spot.

We got horses from the stables, those which the servants hadn't taken. Before we left I took two daggers from the Guards' quarters, wishing to leave the last exit unblocked; I kept them clutched in my hand together with the reins. We took a roundabout route for safety though it was longer, following the city's outskirts instead of cutting straight through. The air streamed wetness; it soaked my flimsy nightgown and ran down my face. I had ridden hard before in darkness but then only to see my city in flames at the end. Now I did not know what the end would be.

The horses' manes stuck to their necks; the steam of their breath dissolved in the rain. The ground shook to their hooves or perhaps it was thunder. I was not hearing or seeing straight. I wondered what would happen if the others went too fast, leaving me behind, lost in the storm. We passed the Praetorian camp on the way. It was in uproar. When the lightning flashed I could see spears raised and sparkling and even through the thunder I heard them shouting: "Down with the tyrant!" Then came something else. I heard it fade in the distance as we rode on. "Long live Galba!"

I realised then who had done it. I had been blind once too often, not seeing Caligula's treachery in his small eyes when he spoke of escape. Oh, he had been genuine. There *was* an escape for me, but not to Alexandria. It waited somewhere in this drenched darkness along with the snake-haired women who had sought my blood for ten years. I felt the embossed dagger handles cut my hand.

The ride ended. While it continued I felt nothing, only the urgency of movement, the getting there. Now there was a villa, set back from the road, with a wall and plane trees and mulberries shivering in rain; beyond, safety. To reach it we followed a path trailing brambles which pricked my feet. I said: "I can't go on," and stopped. They looked despairing for a moment, then Epaphroditus laid his cloak down and I went on step by step like this. I no longer thought of speed. Either side I was trapped by the same thing except that going forward I could take my own way. With the villa so near I began to shrink.

Phaon said: "We can't go in by the gate; we'll rouse the servants. It means going over the wall."

It stood well above my head, rough and lichened. "No," I said. "I'm not climbing that. I'll stay here and die instead."

It sounded brave. In fact, I felt sick with the beating of my heart and the falling rain, the heat, the night; everything was a huge illness.

They pulled out loose bricks and hollowed a kind of tunnel which I could crawl through; it took time. I needed a large entrance. I struggled through into a dirty yard, smelling of pigs with straw underfoot and a cracked water jar in the corner. There was a part where the roof sloped over and here was a wooden pallet where the pig-herd slept. His charges were snuffling by the wall. I had always detested pigs. Epaphroditus put his cloak over the pallet and I lay down, breathing heavily. I was so tired. I could have slept but for the sickness at my heart.

There was the rain and the pigs; then only silence. I lay staring at the filthy straw and the water jar. I had been here before. The straw, the heat, the storm; guilt and bewilderment burning my head. The weeping child had come home. But for my cruel memory which held every detail clear nothing might have happened in between and I might have lain in that stable for a lifetime.

Suddenly Phaon said: "Sire, I advise you to take your own life and avoid the humiliation waiting for you."

I said: "Have you brought me here just to tell me that?"

"Is there any other way, my lord?" said Epaphroditus.

I said: "No."

There was silence. The boy crouched in a corner in his woman's robe, wet and shivering; he began to cry. He did not look like Poppaea now. My delusions were breaking up. Lightning split the place with silver and thunder came like a judgement. I thought of the camp a mile down the road; when they heard, as they soon must, it would be a matter of minutes. I raised myself and said: "Dig a grave for me."

Phaon fetched a spade. The earth under the straw was soft and as they began to dig I thought how easily life crumbles away, rotted leaves underfoot. I remembered my dreams; I meant to be another Virgil, an Augustus. I remembered my mother who had put me where I did not want to be, the cheers on my accession day; I fancied I heard them now but it was only the wind. The golden laurel wreath, the eagle sceptre; now the soft scrape of a spade and the stink of pigs. Perhaps everything is a delusion. Happiness holds grief at its core, power holds failure; nothing is what it seems. Perhaps the carpenter was right to claim himself a god for only gods are invulnerable but he spoilt it all by letting in pain.

I thought of the child outside Apollo's temple on the Palatine and I began to weep. It was so funny. I had seen myself with such hope, such assurance in my abilities; I had sung and acted and composed poetry and it had all been a fool's dream. "What an artist they are losing in me," I said and laughed. "Sweet gods, what an artist."

They looked up but said nothing and went back to their digging. Soon it would be deep enough. Then someone arrived behind the wall, saying: "Phaon, are you there? I have a message." He sounded genuine. Given the order he crawled through and handed a note to Phaon. I saw in his face what it said.

I said: "Who is it from?"

"It isn't signed, sire. It merely says that when they find you the punishment will be the traditional one."

"Which is?" I said.

"They flog you to death with sticks, sire."

He could not control his voice. I saw it then; the escape, the villa, the pretended help—it was all a trap. They knew now where to find me. He had pinpointed the spot. Had I stayed in the city or gone elsewhere they might have looked in all the wrong places.

I said: "One of you kill yourselves and give me a good example. As trusted servants you won't want to live when I am gone."

They looked horrified, saying: "Sire!" and Phaon said: "It is for you, sire, not us."

The daggers lay on the straw. I was blinded by tears, fear, self-pity; I don't know. I knew nothing but the shape of rejection and loneliness here, crushing me in the dirt of a pigsty. I was ending as I had begun. Yet I did not move; I thought to sit and pretend it was a dream. Then I heard the horses; they were galloping down the road we had taken, sharp, determined. Something blazed up in my mind from long ago, a line of Homer's: *The sound of the swift-footed chargers strikes my ears,* and with it I remembered the child in the stable, weeping over his powerlessness. I was not powerless now.

I can see the daggers lying near me. They run red amongst the straw. We used two for it seemed quicker and more sure. Epaphroditus helped me. Somewhere I felt pain. Now there is only a sense of something being sucked out as though of a cup emptied. When I move my fingers they touch wetness. It is all so ugly, so pitiful; I would weep but I have no more strength; now I can only look at the straw or the feet of those near me.

I tried to give them beauty. They rejected it and the world they grow will be ugly, a perversion from a twisted root. They hold power now. Soon it will be gone elsewhere, to Germany or Britain, perhaps, who have never been truly subservient, or to a country we know nothing of, somewhere over the seas of this sick world. Nothing is absolute, not here. They cannot see it. Galba will go, too, and the next and the next after him; perhaps Poppaea was right and the carpenter will sit in Rome, triumphant. She gave me four years and she was right over that.

I know my crimes. I have committed them knowingly and there is no way back; I have become my own tomb. In my childhood vow I promised to die for Rome if needs be. There could be no greater need. I have poisoned them along with myself and they must vomit me up. My adoptive father said to conquer oneself is to conquer the gods; how right he was. Somewhere there is a path to justice and purity; Poppaea found it but through means unacceptable to me so I killed her for it. I am of bad blood: that is my one excuse. That and the fact that it asks much of one man to play Oedipus, Orestes and Priam in one lifetime.

The feet shuffle. Someone clatters in with a military sound but I cannot see properly; it grows even darker. The lamp they had is burning out. The child weeps in a corner but not for me; he can never have loved me. There are others around me, among the soldiers coming in, and it is they I see clearest. The black hair, the amber hair, the small boy with Messalina's face; there near the pigs a philosopher's beard and by the water jar a pale creature with a dark line at her throat. An old man stands quiet in a corner with Claudian restraint, saying: "The gods tell us when our time is played out." I feel their tread in every beat of my pulse.

Something moves at my throat. It is an officer's cloak. He says: "Sire..." and tries to quench my death. I say: "So this is your loyalty. You are too late."

Perhaps the fisherman was right when he spoke of an architect's design and I have missed my chance. It is too late. The walls of the yard break down; the faces I know crowd nearer. My ears buzz, my heart strains, I no longer hear thunder or see the Praetorian face leaning above me. I can hear singing or laughter; I can see. I can see...

Epilogue

"How did he die?" asks the young woman with pale gold hair.

"Calmly in the end," says the young man.

He looks assured and responsible. Provincial governorship has changed his outlook. A child stands beside the woman, red-haired and wondering

"I will give him a good burial," she says, "as the father of my child and because I once loved him so much. I hope he did not suffer."

"Who can say?" The young man looks serious. "At least he didn't wait for military revenge. Can you hear the crowds?"

"Some are sad," she says. "I've seen them. They believed he cared for them despite what he did. He tried hard. His crimes were necessary, else how could he have protected himself and his throne? But had he listened to the right voices he would have found forgiveness."

"He did not believe in forgiveness. He believed only in success or failure."

In the distance voices are shouting: "The tyrant is gone! Long live freedom!"

"Freedom?" says the girl. "There is only one freedom and he slaughtered it in the arena."

"But he tried hard," says the young man. "He tried very hard."